"The Busiest Man in England"

"THE BUSIEST MAN IN ENGLAND"
GRANT ALLEN AND THE WRITING TRADE, 1875–1900

Peter Morton

"THE BUSIEST MAN IN ENGLAND"
© Peter Morton, 2005.

First published in 2005 by
PALGRAVE MACMILLAN™
175 Fifth Avenue, New York, N.Y. 10010 and
Houndmills, Basingstoke, Hampshire, England RG21 6XS
Companies and representatives throughout the world.

PALGRAVE MACMILLAN is the global academic imprint of the Palgrave Macmillan division of St. Martin's Press, LLC and of Palgrave Macmillan Ltd. Macmillan® is a registered trademark in the United States, United Kingdom and other countries. Palgrave is a registered trademark in the European Union and other countries.

ISBN 1–4039–6626–5

Library of Congress Cataloging-in-Publication Data

Morton, Peter, 1946 Apr. 10-
   The busiest man in England : Grant Allen and the writing trade,
1875–1900 / Peter Morton.
      p.cm.
   Includes bibliographical references (p.) and index.
   ISBN 1–4039–6626–5 (alk. paper)
      1. Allen, Grant, 1848–1899. 2. Allen, Grant, 1848–1899—Authorship.
   3. Authors, English—19th century—Biography. 4. England—Intellectual life—
   19th century. 5. Authorship—History—19th century. I. Title.

PR4004.A2Z78 2005
821'.914—dc22   2004050853

A catalogue record for this book is available from the British Library.

Design by Newgen Imaging Systems (P) Ltd., Chennai, India.

First edition: April 2005

10 9 8 7 6 5 4 3 2 1

Printed in the United States of America.

This book is for Heather

Now see how long a letter I have written unto you, going the Apostle one better, with my own left hand: only the busiest man in England could have found time to do it.

Grant Allen to "Fiona Macleod," 1894

Contents

LIST OF PLATES

PREFACE

"With coat-sleeve turned back, so as to give free play to his right hand and wrist, revealing meanwhile a flannel shirt of singular colour, and with his collar unbuttoned (he wore no tie) to leave his throat at ease as he bent myopically over the paper, he was writing at express speed, evidently in the full rush of the ardour of composition. The veins of his forehead were dilated, and his chin pushed forward in a way that made one think of a racing horse." Thus are we introduced to Sykes, one of the most desperate of the literary hacks for hire in George Gissing's *New Grub Street* (1891). We are left in no doubt that, down there in the Darwinian nether world of late-Victorian authorship, success is defined as the survival of the fastest.

No one knew better than Gissing that nearly all Victorian writers with no resources but their pen lived anxious and arduous lives. They walked a precarious path. With some talent and a modicum of luck, they could hope that their path lay upward—toward a bare living for most, cozy comfort for a small minority, luxurious affluence for a tiny few. Quite often, though, the path led downward—toward penury, the meager charitable pension, the workhouse, the gutter. The path could change direction with shocking abruptness, and how far writers advanced along it either way depended, externally, on one thing only: the readiness with which the public would lay down its money to read what they had written. Authors might hope, in the long run, to create and train an audience to appreciate them; but meanwhile they had to live. Many of them—a surprisingly high proportion of those in Grant Allen's generation who still have a reputation—were financially buffered in one way or another from the most brutal pressures of the market. But, for all the rest, whether you were George Eliot or an anonymous penny-a-lining drudge, the laws of supply and demand ruled, and, in the absence of any safety net of social security, fellowships, or sinecures, they ruled supreme. That was the regimen under which Grant Allen lived for the whole of his career.

This sounds too obvious to be worth stating, and so it would be if applied to a butcher, a baker, a candlestick maker. But in the case of the literary producers of the later nineteenth century, the economic facts of life rarely have been given their full weight. The spirit of our age is against it. In a climate which has celebrated the death of the author and the autonomy of the text, it can seem crass to find it interesting whether, a hundred years ago, any particular author died in a feather bed or on a workhouse pallet.

Such a dismissive attitude has been exacerbated by the ahistorical slant of much modern literary scholarship, but it is not, in fact, a new attitude. Even in the closing decades of the Victorian era some writers and critics thought it irrelevant and irreverent to display much interest in bank balances and the rewards of the "trade." It pained Henry James to hear his colleagues crying from the house tops their sense of solidarity with grocers and shoemakers. Edmund Gosse, critic and poet, protested against some of his fellows' unseemly interest in cash on the table, rates of production, deals with publishers, or what different periodicals paid per line. Yes, of course, Gosse conceded, business had to be done, contracts signed. But "there should be a little modesty, one feels, in this pursuit of the guineas. . . . These functions should be performed in private, not flaunted before the public. I no more desire to know what my neighbour the poet makes by his verses that I crave to see the account books for my other neighbor the lawyer."

Many did, in fact, desire to know. Gosse's attitude was not uncommon, but it existed in the late Victorian era alongside a hungry interest in writers' bank balances, houses, activities, and opinions on everything. We see the same paradox in our time: attempts to de-historicize literature somehow manage to coexist with an unassuagable appetite for big literary biographies that are more candid and inclusive than ever before. And, at the more scholarly level, studies in literary history have proven to be remarkably resilient over the last twenty years or so, especially in the area of the socioeconomics of Victorian writing and publishing. Peter Keating said rather gloomily in 1989 that the literary history, or more exactly the historical sociology of literature, which was then being written, was of an unadventurous and unenterprising kind. Keating's own *The Haunted Study* did much to counter that, and other studies of the caliber of those by Nigel Cross (1985), Michael Anesko (1986), Peter McDonald (1997), and Graham Law (2000) have continued the good work. One particularly welcome effect of this has been to direct attention to writers below the first or second rank, among whom the struggle for existence may be studied in its grimmest and most telling specificity.

This book had its origin in my earlier *The Vital Science: Biology and the Literary Imagination, 1860–1900*. That book is a study of the creative uses to which writers put the ambiguous data of biology in the immediate post-Darwinian years, and I grew interested in the way in which scientific popularizers interacted with their readers, and how some of them turned to fiction to dramatize their ideas. Grant Allen figured in a minor way in the earlier book, and I wished I had been able to explore his career further when I discovered how much he had written and how broad his interests were. But other projects drew me away, and there matters rested until 1999, the centenary of Allen's death, when a celebratory conference was planned at Bristol. Preparing the keynote address for that conference caused me to investigate his bibliography more thoroughly, and I grew astonished at the productivity and versatility of the man. He labeled himself proudly "the busiest man in England," and he seems to have been entitled to the label: given what he achieved in a career lasting hardly more than twenty years, it is rather alarming to consider what he might have done if he had had a career twice as long. I was particularly intrigued by his own vigorous, acerbic, and frequently witty examination of the professional freelance writer's lot, and this had a personal resonance too, for I had labored for a time in that same vineyard, just a century after Allen, and I found what he had to say about the trials and tribulations, and the rewards, of such a life was no less thought-provoking now than it was then.

The occupational disease of the biographer, said Macaulay, is the *lues Boswelliana*, the fever of admiring overstatement. I have been careful, I hope, not to catch that infection. Time has placed Grant Allen as an author of the third rank, and I expect him to remain there; it is not my task to reinstate him as an unjustly neglected writer or even to mount a case for bringing very much of his work back from obscurity. Much of his work—not quite all, to be sure—was done for the day and has vanished with the day. I hope to show, however, that his career gives us some insight into the opportunities and rewards available in late-Victorian England for the most industrious writers of the type to which Allen belonged—and that is not a type that has been closely investigated.

Readers may wonder why, in a book that deals so much with money, I have made so little attempt to indicate its modern purchasing power. Inflation tables readily show, for example, that the literary prize of £1,000 that Allen won in 1891 was equivalent to £64,341 in 2003 British pounds. But as a guide to what such a sum "meant" in terms of what it would buy, such a conversion is wholly misleading. It ignores on the one hand the multitude of goods not then available at any price (effective medicine and domestic technologies, for instance), and on the other the relative abundance of other goods and services 120 years ago (relatively cheap land and basic building materials; very cheap unskilled and semiskilled labor; readily accessible, untouched countryside). It ignores the effect of modern taxes, direct and indirect, which were low or nonexistent then. This is an omission so serious that it has been said that a Victorian income, after being adjusted for inflation, should then be *tripled* to give a real idea of its buying power at the time. I know of no reliable way of adjusting for these factors. As a substitute, I have occasionally indicated some specific late-Victorian goods and services that might have been bought with a particular sum that Grant Allen earned by his pen.

Adelaide
November 4

ACKNOWLEDGMENTS

The resources of the internet have transformed scholarly endeavor. Some of the primary research and virtually all of the exchange of ideas and information that stand behind this book have been handled via the web and email. No matter how recondite their interests, constant participation in worldwide discussion groups is available to all scholars now, and I have used these resources to the utmost.

Even the internet has its limits, however, and a good part of the primary research for this biography was carried out in the British Library and elsewhere in England in 2001 during an Outside Studies Program provided by Flinders University, Adelaide. Other grants from Flinders' Faculty Research Budget relieved me of some teaching duties, contributed to the cost of conferences, and supported several foraging expeditions into libraries in the United Kingdom, Canada, and the United States in 2002/2003.

Numerous institutions have allowed me to use their holdings: a complete list is provided in the Bibliography. Many people connected with these institutions, and others, have shared their knowledge with me, and although we shall probably never meet in person it is good to know that we have met, and will meet again, in cyberspace. Among them I wish to thank the following particularly: Victor Berch for many obscure leads on Allen's short fiction; Angela Kingston of Adelaide for several rare and important finds; Nicholas Ruddick for our extended and enjoyable discussions about various aspects of *The Woman Who Did*, of which he was preparing an edition; Alex Scala of Kingston, Ontario for much information about that city as Grant Allen knew it; and Sandra Stelts, the curator of the Special Collections Library, Pennsylvania State University, for generous and repeated help over a long period. My thanks also to the following people for their specialized help on other aspects of Allen's life and career: Mike Ashley and the Fictionmags forum; Pierre Coustillas, Sabine Ernst, Donald Forsdyke, William Greenslade, Richard Landon, Mark Lasner, Graham Law, Xavier Legrand-Ferronnière, Bernard Lightman, Barbara Arnett Melchiori, Christine Nelson, Patrick Parrinder, Lyssa Randolph, Terence Rodgers, Christopher Sanguinetti, Jay Shorten, John Owen Smith, Jonathan Smith, Jean Soudé, Phil Stephensen-Payne, Richard Sveum, Sue Templeman, Greta Turner, Rebecca Venable, and Chris Willis. And a final thanks to Tony Twohig for the use of his house in Blackheath at a critical juncture.

Grant Allen. This photograph was probably taken ca. 1890. Reproduced courtesy of Haslemere Educational Museum.

INTRODUCTION

"THE MOST HATEFUL OF
PROFESSIONS?"

A "SUPER-JOURNALIST" AT WORK

Forty years ago, in a ground-breaking article "The Sociology of Authorship," Richard Altick defined what he took to be "the essence of the literary situation" for professional writers in the last Victorian decades. By that time, said Altick, such writers were being forced to accommodate themselves to a new mass audience; an audience of "limited capacities and special expectations." Each of them, he continued, had to deal in one way or another with the following question: "To what extent was he obliged, as a member of his age's ruling class and supported, sometimes handsomely, by the pounds and shillings of his cultural inferiors, to debase his art, either for the sake of sheer intelligibility or for the more specific one of imparting desirable social, political, moral, and aesthetic attitudes?"[1]

"Debasement" is an ugly word, and it is unlikely that many late-Victorian writers saw their plight in quite that way. Still, Altick's question admits of many answers and permits many stances. Here is a voice answering Altick's question in a particularly stark, hard-headed way, a way that it is the aim of this book to define, illuminate, and contextualize. As it happens, it is a fictional voice:

> But just understand the difference between a man like Reardon and a man like me. He is the old type of unpractical artist; I am the literary man of 1882. He won't make concessions, or rather, he can't make them; he can't supply the market. I—well, you may say that at present I do nothing; but that's a great mistake, I am learning my business. Literature nowadays is a trade. Putting aside men of genius, who may succeed by mere cosmic force, your successful man of letters is your skilful tradesman. He thinks first and foremost of the markets; when one kind of goods begins to go off slackly, he is ready with something new and appetizing. He knows perfectly all the possible sources of income.[2]

This quotation is from a novel to which we shall have frequent reference: George Gissing's *New Grub Street* (1891), that indispensable *vade mecum* to the literary life of the 1880s. The speaker is Jasper Milvain, a brash young literary man on the make. Readers are not required to agree with the character's sentiments, for Milvain, as his first name hints, is the villain of the piece. Milvain seeks success, success measured in coin of the realm, and we see him trampling over everyone to get it. But he is a mightily attractive villain, especially when compared to the other writers whose careers Gissing charts with such loving despair. Indeed, it is exactly the tension caused by our awareness that the novel is of the devil's party without knowing it that engages us. It is propelled by a powerful if surreptitious envy and self-pity—emotions well to the fore in the sociology of literature in the years of Allen's career, and from which our subject himself was not free.

The action of *New Grub Street* is set back nearly a decade to 1882. In that year, in real life, Grant Allen, a Canadian resident in London, is in his mid-thirties. He has been rather a late starter, but his career as an author-journalist is now getting into its stride. He wants to be successful; or, more exactly, he wants to make money because he does not expect to live very long and has a family to support. Jasper Milvain's analysis is a fair account of the strategy that Allen really is pursuing at this point—not always willingly, it must be said, or without some poignant self-questioning, but to great effect.

Having returned to England some years earlier after a spell teaching abroad, with no job and few resources, and eager to make a reputation as a scientific writer, Allen starts with a couple of technical tomes on evolutionary biology. Quickly he discovers that this will not earn him a living on a par with that of a prosperous country solicitor or doctor, which is the level he believes is his due and is determined to secure. He moves into the best general monthly periodicals of the day, ignoring the unanimous opinion of editors and working journalists that it is virtually impossible to make a living in that way. But by dint of almost incredible labor, Allen forces this market to yield a living. Soon afterward, riding the boom of the New Journalism, he turns to writing miscellaneous essays for the weekly periodicals and newspapers as well. His favorite topics are those of popular science, especially botany, where his knowledge is prodigious, but he can and will turn his hand to anything.

Stumbling by accident into fiction, he finds that startling and sentimental short stories pay even better, so dozens of those too start to roll off his pen. He tries a serious novel of ideas to promote his political beliefs. He polishes it carefully but it makes very little critical impression. Instead of giving up, he responds by varying his output, going cold-bloodedly after different sectors of the fictional marketplace. Unremitting work produces several volumes of stories and some thirty-five novels, of which about six are valuable to cultural historians, if not literary critics, a century later.

Twice in his career Allen achieves great popular success. *What's Bred in the Bone* (1891) wins one of the largest literary prizes ever awarded in Britain: £1,000 from George Newnes, the publishers of the magazine *Tit-Bits*. It sells hugely in its first year, is adapted as a film in 1916, and is translated into several languages, including Icelandic. Nothing demonstrates better Allen's capacity for analyzing and meeting the popular taste.

Allen's other triumph, *The Woman Who Did* (1895), is a great and scandalous success. Written from the heart, this is the most ambitious result of Allen's long-standing interest in women's issues, especially the relationships between prostitution and marriage. About halfway through his career, we find him starting to articulate views on these subjects that border on the obsessive—views that, as later chapters will elucidate, were formed from painful personal experience. Both praised and reviled by critics right across the ideological spectrum from the radical feminists to the Social Purity league, this "sex problem" novel nevertheless sites itself at the head of its particular genre. Later on, some years after its author's death, it is made into a film. It goes in and out of print over the next century, but never vanishes entirely from sight or influence.

Somehow, on top of all this, Allen never loses sight of his "serious" interests, which are enormously wide-ranging. At Allen's memorial service the positivist Frederic Harrison enumerated them: "science, biology, physics, botany, mineralogy, metaphysics, history, paleontology, archaeology, theology, philosophy, sociology, ethics, art, criticism."[3] This may sound like the kindly exaggeration often thought appropriate at funerals, but it is not so. Indeed, Harrison could readily have added to his list: biography (Allen wrote three), classical studies, folklore, topography, geology, entomology, interior design, and travel. About half of his total output—that is, more than thirty books and many hundreds of articles—testifies to these varied interests, and Allen's power to synthesize, generalize, and find fruitful interconnections between them is remarkable. All his life he insists that his real work lies in science and philosophy, helping to extend the reach of Darwinian biology into sociology and ethics. Economic pressures, however, oblige him to write popular science, for which he has a rare skill. Some of his pieces, such as "The Bronze Axe" (1889) and "Mud" (1891), are fine products of the temporal and geological imagination. Almost none has ever been reprinted.[4]

It is tempting to emphasize Allen's sheer versatility as a writer, but that would be demeaning and misleading. It's inconceivable that any of the cast of *New Grub Street*—certainly not Jasper Milvain—would have spent ten years gathering the materials for a study in religious anthropology, well aware that the sales are going to be numbered in the hundreds. But Allen is not deterred, for he believes his book on religion, by exposing its folk-myth origins, will help to consign Christianity and all other revealed religions to the scrap heap. And for him that is a goal worth pursuing indeed.

This is what makes Allen an interesting study in the sociology of authorship. He straddles so many different areas in the literary culture of his day. He is the skilled marketer of popular fiction; the dedicated but unaffiliated scholar, reckless of his time and energy; the feuilletonist whose latest chatty "middle" for an evening paper is always mailed on time; the severely technical botanist with a thesis to expound on the evolution of flowering plants; the tosser-off of a long opinionated essay on London architecture or a profusion of other topics. And, most dramatic of all, the idealistic social reformer half-willing to immolate his own career for the sake of having his radical say.

Grant Allen suffers from ill health for all of his life. When he dies at the age of fifty-one, everything has been achieved in a career lasting two decades. His obituarists, glancing at a list of his books, exclaim in astonishment. The *Daily News'* opinion is that "if sometimes aggressive and irritating, Grant Allen was always suggestive and interesting. The amount of work which he turned out in his comparatively short life . . . was amazing, and there can be few contemporary writers who have alternately provoked and stimulated, alienated and attracted, so many readers."[5] Andrew Lang, man of letters and no slouch himself when it came to productivity, calls Allen "the most versatile, beyond comparison, of any man in our age."[6] But not one of them, not even his closest friends, could appreciate the full extent and quality of his labors.

An intriguing figure, then, Grant Allen: a fringe presence at many different sites of Victorian intellectual life. How did this prodigy strike his fellows? In character he was, all agree, a convivial man with a pleasantly enthusiastic, confiding manner. He was a superlative teacher. "A walk with him was an education," the editor Frank Harris recalled years after his death. "He had no whimsies or quirks; he was always reasonable, good-tempered, vivacious, bright, and interested in every human interest. To my astonishment he knew a good deal about painting and sculpture and architecture; he was certainly the best-informed all-round man I have ever had the good fortune to meet."[7] That is a memorable tribute from someone as egocentric as Frank Harris. Reviewers may have savaged his more controversial work, but he had few personal enemies. He was on good terms with most people in literary London— with some notable exceptions—and was no less welcome in scientific circles. He was no club man, but he was sociable. With his "silky silvery hair and beard, and the rather pronounced features so often associated with men of uncommon ability," a reporter scribbled on the occasion of some banquet, "Mr Grant Allen is the type of the contemplative man of science—the dreamer who is also an active thinker."[8] He was sweet-tempered, modest to a fault, and usually charitable toward his critics, even the most bigoted of clergymen.

Though he was far from being a typical Englishman, Allen did like to maintain the familiar English pose of the cultivated amateur. People commented how few books he ever seemed to buy or read. Yet his range of information was astonishing. In Italian art, English history and prehistory, geology, and especially in botany, he was all but omniscient. He claimed, quite without boasting, that he could identify forty thousand plants by eye alone. At one point he toyed with the idea of setting up in business as a sort of walking data bank, and his friends thought this was a reasonable ambition, for they used to chorus, when some questionable fact came up in conversation and no reference book was to hand, "Let's look it up in Grant!"

He always seemed to have plenty of free time. Anthony Trollope claimed that three hours a day will produce as much as a man ought to write. Allen got through his stint by working only in the mornings. They were long mornings, though, and he was capable of ferocious application at the typewriter, being one of first British writers to make full use of the machine. According to Frank Harris, that typewriter went in "one long even click," as the "super-journalist" turned out yet another "first-rate article on almost any subject from the growth of the idea of God to the habits of the caterpillar, at a moment's notice, and without perceptible exertion."[9] Richard Le Gallienne, perceptive critic, good friend, and neighbor, recalled how the typewriter started to click at nine o'clock and seldom paused until lunch time. Interruptions made no difference. Le Gallienne noticed how, when the gong announcing lunch sounded, Allen would stop typing in the middle of a sentence; then, finding the meal was not quite ready, would return to his typewriter and finish that sentence and start another.[10] Many modern writers might reflect, however, that the most significant detail in that story is the sound of the luncheon gong. Most intrusions were kept at bay by the several resident servants who looked after the family of three.

Of course there was a price to pay, and something of the personal toll this schedule imposed on him is suggested in a remark to Clodd in 1893 that the day's labor totally exhausted him.[11] On the other hand, this lament is addressed from an expensive hotel at Antibes, where his family enjoyed for years a winter suite. Allen made authorship pay well, though for him its rewards were painfully won.

Once the day's tasks were over, Allen liked to be out of doors. He talked best on his feet, during a country walk. "He loved nature as I have never seen it loved by any other man," wrote an editor friend. "He would dart towards some tiny flower by the hedgerow and talk of it with a quite beautiful sympathy; he would watch the movements of a bird or an insect with an observation that seemed extraordinary."[12] Allen was no nature worshipper, however. His observations were always scientific and the raw material of generalizations. The label he fixed on Herbert Spencer, "the prince of gener-alists," fits Allen just as well. Some hint of the mental universe he inhabited, a place where no fact, no statistic, no recollection, existed in isolation, can be caught from a stray comment he once made about a child's ideal education:

> A country walk will be richer in his eyes if he knows the birds and beasts, the flowers and insects. A Continental trip will be the richer in his eyes if he can delight his soul as much in a Mantegna or a Van der Weyden, in the spires of Cologne or the façade of the Certosa, as in the Boulevards and the Opera, the Rigi or the Matterhorn. Geology, history, poetry, make the world the fuller for him. Here rolled the Triassic sea: here brooded the ice plain: here Francesca paced the grey streets of Rimini. Every subject in which human thought can steep itself adds to the pleasure and the depth of life. That is why it were well to make the basis of our education as wide, as real, and as varied as possible. Let us ground our boys and girls in realities, not words: in knowledge of life and the world they live in, not in irregular verbs and rules of syntax.[13]

All very well, one might retort, if the teachers were all of the caliber of Grant Allen. Dr. George Bird told Clodd that, if he had had a son, he would gladly have paid Allen a thousand a year just to take the boy on a weekly rural walk. Another friend would have paid £2,000 a year if Allen had been available to her for a daily stroll. "He was so full of information," she said, "and had such a very lucid way of imparting it."[14]

From his essays and from all but his most pot-boiling novels, we can deduce a good deal about Grant Allen's temperament and attitudes. In social and political matters he sides with the underdog, the oppressed and the exploited, though surely for ideological rather than empathetic reasons. Nearly all his fiction has upper-class settings; his working-class figures are all stock characters. His views on racial differences are cringe-making, even offensive, today but unremarkable for his time and in some respects were in advance of it: even a severe critic might allow that his heart is usually in the right place. In his youth he described himself as a Communist, and perhaps always thought of himself as one in some idiosyncratic way, but if so he managed to reconcile this with a little personal speculation in building land, and he certainly did not approve of having the State spend his money for him. The Fabians' phrase "the inevitability of gradualness" sums up his political position well enough, although he took no interest at all in party politics. No little part of his charm comes from the occasional perversity, even the self-contradiction, of his views. He loved to tip a received opinion on its head and to assert a paradox; he was a contrarian by nature: he would have said it was the Irishman in him. In his first novel, *Philistia*, the young and poor Le Breton family wander the streets of Holloway looking for lodgings. Their landlady is a gaunt, hard-faced woman. We seem to be moving into the territory of *Jude the Obscure* and *The Nether World*, but Allen subverts our expectations by making her a domestic and maternal angel. She is, however, entirely unconvincing.

GRANT ALLEN AND THE "BOOKMEN"

Immediately after Allen's untimely death in October 1899 one of his oldest friends began to collect letters and reminiscences for a biography. It was published in the following year as *Grant Allen: A Memoir with a Bibliography*. The author was Edward Clodd (1840–1930) and he was well qualified for the task. The two men were similar in their interests, values, and temperament. Clodd was quite a prolific and popular writer, his main interests being the history of evolutionary theory, folklore, mythology, and the origins of Christianity. He was a rich man, a banker, and, in the nicest sense, a scalp-hunter of intellectuals, writers, and artists. Tolerant, sympathetic, unenvious, genial, and a generous host, his Whitsuntide parties at his home at Aldeburgh in Suffolk were an institution. Grant Allen had been a regular at these parties. In addition, the two men had been alone together every day for five weeks when they made a tour of Egypt in 1889.

Unfortunately Grant Allen was not served well by his biographer-friend. It has been said that biographies should never be written with one eye on the widow. The *Memoir* was practically a collaboration between Clodd and

Allen's widow and son, and nothing appeared in it that they did not wish to read. It is, for example, unhelpfully discreet about certain critical events in Allen's life, such as his first marriage and his spell in Jamaica. Nellie Allen was very satisfied with the result, saying how pleased she was with Clodd for giving "such a clear idea of my darling's beautiful personal character, and of the hard struggles that he had to bear."[15] George Gissing told Clodd that he was glad discretion had ruled.[16] But Gissing had his secrets, one of them not unlike one of Allen's, and he was surely voicing his own fears about posthumous biographical investigation.

No one else was as satisfied as Gissing. "It is to be regretted that Mr. Clodd has not produced a life of Mr. Grant Allen which would have been of more than ephemeral interest," said one.[17] Another lengthy review, in the *Academy*, was anonymous, but it was probably by James Sutherland Cotton, journalist and editor, and another friend of long standing. With his insider's information, Cotton could have done a better job than Clodd, and no doubt his awareness of this colored his review. He felt "utter disappointment" when he read it. Clodd, he complained, had reneged on the biographer's sacred duty to assist time in forming a correct assessment of his subject. He had made no attempt to set Allen into his social and intellectual context, or even to arrange his materials into a meaningful pattern.[18]

Even by the standard of the usual Victorian family-licensed stolid Life and Letters the *Memoir* is a failure. For reasons that are unclear, it was a rushed, sketchy, and occasionally inaccurate job. There are too many bland reminiscences, solicited from old friends and copied out verbatim. Clodd accepted uncritically the most complimentary remarks on Allen's scientific work, popular and technical, and never bothered to find out what his peers had really thought of it. He skated over Allen's radical and inflammatory views on social issues, and never traced out their origin in his early experiences, even though he must have known quite well that they had been formed there. Worst of all, despite the promise in the subtitle of his book, Clodd did not even try to discover the full extent and variety of Allen's writings, still less to evaluate them. Small wonder, then, that he was incapable of bringing into any kind of accord the two most disparate elements in Allen's career, which had put him under great nervous tension: the committed but unrewarded philosopher-scientist on the one hand, and the popular and affluent novelist-journalist on the other.

The most serious consequence of Clodd's rushing into print was that the *Memoir* was just about good enough to discourage anyone else from trying their hand at something better. Apart from another short overview a few years later,[19] the rest is (almost) silence. The lessons his career had to teach about the trade of writer in the late-Victorian era did not yet interest literary historians, and even if they had, many papers were still in private hands. Gradually his contemporaries and friends died off. Ironically, Clodd, who lived to be ninety, was probably the last survivor of Allen's friends who had observed his authorial career from start to finish.

In the interwar years there was a flicker of interest in Grant Allen as the spiritual grandfather of the new freedoms in the age of jazz and flappers.

There is an allusion to the title phrase *The Woman Who Did* in the "Cyclops" chapter of *Ulysses* (1922), as one of an absurd parade of pseudo-Celtic heroes and heroines. There were new editions of *The Woman Who Did* in America and England in 1926 and 1927. A silent film based on *The Scallywag* was released in 1921. A final attempt to evaluate Allen's career as a whole was made in 1928, in a long but flimsy essay by the American literary journalist William Chislett.[20] After that, there was little but an occasional academic paper, some expensive library facsimiles, a regular reprinting of a few stories in science fiction and other genre anthologies, and, in recent years, chapters discussing *The Woman Who Did* in works of feminist criticism and literary history.[21] No biographical sketch in modern reference books is entirely reliable.[22] The largest cache of Allen's papers, acquired by Pennsylvania State University from a private collector who had bought them from the family in the 1930s, were cataloged only recently and have never been properly investigated before.

Insofar as it is more than an account of an exceptionally busy and self-reflective life, this study aims to open up a portal on the socioeconomics of professional authorship, using Grant Allen's career to dig into the question of how his kind of writer went about extracting a living from the marketplace in the last two Victorian decades. How exactly, starting with no assets but a head stuffed with miscellaneous information and armed with a ready pen, did Allen rise to comparative affluence with the kind of wares he had to offer? How exceptional was his achievement? How much of it was due to his personal ability and how much to changing circumstances in the production and consumption of print? What kind of concessions to publisher and public was he forced to make *en route* to prosperity, and how did that affect what he wrote?

Certainly these questions interested Allen himself. The need to earn his daily bread was paramount—every penny he had came from his pen—and he had few illusions about what he needed to do to get it. The question of where he might have been, or should have been, as an author-tradesman was one he returned to many times. He gave his answers now this emphasis, now that; and he cast them in the forms of the polemical essay, the short story, the fable, and as episodes and authorial asides in his novels. Always they are tinged with an attractively grim humor. "Men are driven into literature, as they are driven into crime, by hunger alone," he asserted in gloomy tones, which (we must hope) contain a fair amount of self-mockery:

The most hateful of professions (as a profession, I mean), it becomes tolerable only from a sense of duty to wife and family, or the primary instinct of self-preservation. The wages are low; the prizes few and often fallacious; the work is so hard that it kills or disables most men who undertake it before they arrive at middle life. . . . We have to deal here with a crowded trade, in which competition is exceptionally and fatally severe—a trade which kills off its workmen faster than any sweating system ever designed by human ingenuity—a trade compared

with which (I speak seriously) match-making and silvering and house-painting
and coal-mining are healthy and congenial light occupations.[23]

Mirror-silvering sweatshop or cozy booklined study? Matchgirls' fatal "phossy
jaw" or merely an aching wrist? Which is nearer the truth about authorship?

Answering this question is the more difficult in that Allen's career falls into
a relatively unexplored stratum of late-Victorian literary activity. It is the
stratum first defined and inspected by John Gross in *The Rise and Fall of the
Man of Letters* (1969). In part of this lively, groundbreaking work, which
remains unique in its field, Gross analyzed the careers of what he called the
"bookmen"—the men and women who rose to prominence in the 1880s to
meet the voracious demand for material to fill the novels and the new periodicals. They were, Gross shows, a distinct new breed: not exactly journalists,
but freelancers who tried to make the bulk of their living from "miscellaneous
writing." Miscellaneous writing can be defined, in this context, as the production of popular fiction, semi-popular or specialized nonfiction, and activity in
what the French call high vulgarization—that is to say, the upper levels of
literary and scientific journalism. None of the bookmen was a creative genius.
But neither were they necessarily hacks. As a group they are distinguishable,
rather, for their ingenuity and shrewdness, and a determination to make the
most of their gifts by relentless hard work.

The stratum of the bookmen was a broad one, and it has several distinguishable layers. It is to one of the most prosperous of these layers that Grant
Allen's career belongs. It was a thin layer, because very few bookmen made
enough money from pen-labor alone to allow them to live out their lives in
solid, bourgeois comfort, at the same level, say, as that of the owner of a
flourishing family business, of a commissioned army officer of higher rank, of
a partner in a small but thriving legal firm. That was the level to which Allen
aspired and that he eventually achieved. For his self-definition as a "tradesman"
has to be understood in a particular sense. From his perspective, doctors or
lawyers or artists were tradesmen too, since they were all artisans who sold
their skills daily at the reigning price in a free market. What Allen wanted was
to become known and respected as a self-employed professional man. Certainly
he was no bohemian, not even in his earliest days, either in his personal tastes
or in his standard of living. From an early age he had commitments, which he
took very seriously, and he expected to live like a gentleman. Though he
wrote fast, and with a close eye on the market, his self-respect kept him to
a standard well apart from what Walter Besant called "the damnation of
the cheque."[24]

A salient feature of Allen's career is how much we know about his route to
prosperity. None of the bookmen, even those who rated a memoir or lengthy
obituary soon after their deaths, was ever subjected to any indelicate financial
probing. Edward Clodd permitted himself only the vaguest references to the
subject. Yet Allen had an almost neurotic interest in his earning capacity and
had no scruples about dilating upon it in private or in public. Then there is

the advantage that he dealt on intimately personal terms with three publishers and an agent (John Lane, Grant Richards, Andrew Chatto, and A.P. Watt), who were scrupulous about their correspondence and whose firms have well-preserved records of their dealings with him.[25] Then again, few of the bookmen had any scientific interests; yet for Allen the money he got from popular science was critically important, especially in his earlier years. The socioeconomics of popular scientific authorship in this period is another area only just starting to be explored.[26]

Finally, there is the factor of Grant Allen's own background. Nearly all of the successful bookmen were, as Gross says, preeminently Oxbridge men with smooth Oxbridge manners.[27] Allen was an Oxford man, and his connections secured him his first toe-hold in journalism. But he lost that footing quickly, due to illness; and afterward, as far as can be ascertained, he made his own way. In any case, he barely fits the specification drawn up by Gross (who does not mention him). He left Merton College with a mediocre degree in classics and regarded himself as being, in effect, self-educated. He was a Canadian who disliked Canada, and his international education deracinated him and gave him a flippantly sardonic outlook on English life. Apart from a few heroes including Meredith, Hardy, and possibly Conan Doyle, he had what Gissing called an "acrid" view of most of his fellow authors, and some of them returned the compliment. He was not one for coteries or committees or societies: "I dislike organization—I'm too individualistic to work together with them. . . . PS. I am an invalid and have enough to do to earn a livelihood for my wife and family."[28] He emerged from deepest Surrey only for business or social engagements—although these were frequent enough, for he was no hermit. But by background and inclination he was a colonial outsider, with an outsider's detachment, an outsider's idiosyncratic interests, and, potentially at least, an outsider's chip on his shoulder.

We may close with some statistics that help us take a first measure of our man. In his short life Allen produced seventy-seven volumes (counting each of his numerous three-decker novels as one volume). He therefore published an average of three and a half books in each one of the twenty-two years of his career, dating from his first book in 1877. Of this total, forty-five volumes were novels, collections of short fiction, and poetry. The rest were on an extraordinary variety of subjects. Some of them were assembled from periodical articles that had already seen print, but not all that many, for Allen did not reprint his own work very assiduously. For example, he contributed 102 long essays to the *Cornhill* right through his career, most of them very solid pieces indeed, closely argued and running to ten or more pages of fine print. This was well over a million words to that magazine alone. Yet he only ever reprinted twenty-six of these essays. Of the fifty-six articles of social criticism and commentary that he contributed to the *Westminster Gazette* in 1893/4, fewer than half were ever seen again. Finally, of the twenty-nine lengthy essays written for *Longman*'s, he collected only ten. Little of the residue is noticeably inferior to the items he did collect. Of his work in fiction, he left at least seventy (probably many more) of his short stories undisturbed in the magazines. Therefore his uncollected articles, fiction, prefaces, edited works, and other miscellaneous journalism together add many millions of words to the tally.

As a practitioner of the higher journalism, then—not to mention his three or four books a year—Allen was prodigious. He lived, of course, in an age of enormously productive penmen. In the preceding generation, the journalist G.A. Sala (1828–1895) was legendary for his output, and his breadth of interests came close to matching even Allen's. Sabine Baring-Gould (1834–1924), who shared some of Allen's interests in folklore and archeology, was said to have the longest title list under one author in the British Museum catalog of his day. His productivity was sometimes compared to Allen's, but Baring-Gould did not depend on his pen for a living, and his work was done over many decades.[29] The most comparable name that comes to mind at once is Allen's colleague and sparring partner Andrew Lang (1844–1912). But except for his anthropological speculations (which were considerable and influential), Lang's range was literary-historical and he could not begin to match Allen's versatility, a point that he readily conceded himself. In terms of quantity and rate of production, Allen's was a record that was not outstripped by many; and in terms of range was outstripped by very few, if any, during his heyday. Finally, when comparing his career with others', we should always bear in mind that Allen's *adult* life was nearly half over before he had produced a single publishable word.

CHAPTER 1

CANADA AND OXFORD (1848–1873)

A CANADIAN CHILDHOOD

As the great St. Lawrence river streams out of Lake Ontario, with Canada on its western bank and New York State on its eastern, its waters flow over a bed of limestone. But here and there, partly obstructing the river's passage, bosses of granite emerge from the water. They are the remnants of a band of tough Precambrian rock that is the geological underlay to the Thousand Islands. These shaggy, craggy islets, many more than a thousand in number, are thickly vegetated with pines and shrubs, and by the mid-nineteenth century they had become popular holiday havens. "Their beauty is so unlike anything that one may see anywhere else," wrote Grant Allen on his return to the region. "Tiny little islands, placed in tiny little rivers, crowned with tiny little chalets, and navigated by tiny little yachts; it all reminds one so thoroughly of one's childish dreamlands."[1] The dreamy memories were his own, for this curious riverine locality was the country of his birth.

Grant Allen's father, Joseph Antisell Allen (1814–1900), was an Irishman and Anglican clergyman, the son of a barrister. He attended Trinity College, Dublin, but left without a degree and spent some years hacking for a religious publisher in London. At some time between 1840 and 1842 (accounts differ) he emigrated to the New World along with tens of thousands of his compatriots, and presumably for the same reason: to try to better his condition. He must have succeeded far beyond his own expectations, because after being ordained at Montreal, and after occupying a couple of livings in Quebec, his fortunes improved dramatically. Somehow, around 1845, he met and married (Catharine) Charlotte Ann Grant, and Miss Grant was an heiress, the daughter of a Baron.

Charlotte Grant Allen (1817–1894), Grant Allen's mother, had a romantic family background in which were mingled aristocratic French-Canadian, English, and Scottish bloods. Her mother was a Coffin, from a Devonshire family of admirals and generals. Her father's family, the Grants, came originally from Blairfindy in Moray county, an area best known now for its picturesque

ruined castle and Glenlivet whisky. The Grants were Jacobites, and after
Culloden the four sons of the laird fled Scotland to save their necks. By the
end of the eighteenth century they had become a distinguished military family
in Canada. Charlotte's father, Charles William Grant, inherited the French
title of Fifth Baron of Longueuil through his mother's line, and the Grants
owned considerable property in and around Kingston, the town in Ontario
adjacent to the region of the Thousand Islands.

In 1833, because he needed to be in Kingston to pursue his political ambitions, the Baron built a large house just outside the town. "Alwington" stood
in spacious grounds reaching down to the water, and consisted of a central
rectangular block of two stories with a single-storey wing on each side, all in
the local limestone. After 1844 this house became the family headquarters.

Joseph Allen the clergyman could hardly have afforded by his own labors
to keep his wife in the style to which she was accustomed. That was not
required of him, however; instead, the couple lived with her family at
Alwington in leisured ease. Two children were born to them there before the
arrival of their third child and second son on February 24, 1848. He was
christened Charles Grant Blairfindie Allen.[2] The components of this name
reflect his mingled ancestry, and he was proud of his inheritance. It was an
inheritance not financial, for he never saw a cent of the family fortune, but
genetic. Allen liked to think of himself as a pure-bred, typical Celt, a race to
which he ascribed many virtues, especially in the arts. He claimed at various
times that such unlikely folk as Catullus and Dante Gabriel Rossetti were
"really" Celts. Without following Allen into one of his most enduring crochets,
we can surely concede that a blend of seigneurial French, witty Irish, sober
pragmatic Devonshire, and canny, brave Scottish bloods was likely to make
for a pretty effervescent mixture.

The town of Kingston that lay beyond the front gates of Alwington during
Allen's childhood was a small place whose chief distinction was some surprisingly grand public buildings. These were the relics of its brief glory as the
capital of the Canadas, a status it had lost just before Allen was born, and they
gave it a curious appearance. This was how it struck Allen in 1876, the first
time he saw it again after fifteen years in England and Jamaica. He had left as
a child; now he is seeing the town of his birth with thoroughly acclimatized
English eyes, as a mature man:

> a basking, blue stone-built town glowed in the foreground, its roofs all covered
> with tinned iron, and shining like gold in the morning sun. I could almost fancy
> myself in the East once more, looking out upon some domed and minaretted
> village of the Bosphorus. Building after building of a quaint debased American-
> Byzantine style, propped on pseudo-Doric pillars and surmounted by a false
> Italian dome (wood, tin-plated) stared upon us boldly, unabashed by its own
> pretentious absurdity. Incredibly monstrous they all are, if taken separately . . . yet
> looked on in the mass from the waterside, they really compose a pretty and har-
> monious picture. The effect is much heightened, too, by a few scattered
> martello towers, standing straight out of the shallow water, with red-rusted
> iron roofs, which contrast finely with the sun-gilded domes.[3]

The level and direction of the sarcasm here are difficult to determine. Is it aimed at the Canadians, or at the reader, or at the writer himself? How deliberate are those clichés and the dead similes? The jaundiced phrasing seems a bit too eager to mock, and so falls into uncertainty: pillars, even if made of concrete, are either of the Doric order or they are not: they cannot be "pseudo-Doric." A dome is still a dome, and not "false" even if it is made of wood and tin. But whatever the exact nature of his reaction at the time, we do know for sure that Allen soon steamed away down the St. Lawrence to Quebec and an Atlantic crossing, and found neither occasion nor necessity to visit the land of his birth for another decade.

Kingston was already home to what would become one of the great Canadian educational institutions, Queen's University. No doubt whatever intellectual stimulation Kingston offered at the time centered on that college, to which Joseph Allen was intermittently affiliated. But Kingston had another very different side to it. After 1847 the Orangemen were joined by tens of thousands of poverty-stricken Irish Catholic refugees fleeing the Potato Famine. Outbreaks of cholera and typhus in the slum quarters filled mass graves, which had to be dug along the waterfront, and violent feuds among the Irish immigrants, arising from distinctions of class and religion, marked the early years of Allen's childhood.

It is unlikely that these early events had much impact on the frail, bookish son of a rich, *rentier* clergyman. Grant Allen left Kingston when he was a teenager, and in any case he spent much of his childhood on Wolfe Island, five kilometers by ferry across a channel dividing it from the gardens of Alwington on the mainland. The largest of the Thousand Islands at about 34 km by 11 km, Wolfe Island has a different geology. It is of limestone and mostly flat. At the time of Allen's birth the Grants owned about a third of the island, or around 4,500 hectares, of which a small portion was cultivated.

Perhaps to give herself some space away from her son and his family, the Baroness preferred to live on Wolfe Island in another Grant mansion, Ardath House. This was a rambling property built in 1828 by the Baron in the French style with oak ornamentation. She had a small church built in the adjacent village of Marysville—was it perhaps to give her new son-in-law some pretence of an independent occupation?—and the Reverend Joseph Allen became the first vicar of the parish. It is unlikely that he found his duties onerous. Trinity Church—a small, plain box of a building with a stumpy tower—has the date of October 6, 1845 on its foundation stone, but for some reason the church was not finished until 1848 and probably saw little use for some years after that. By 1851 another clergyman had taken over the parish affairs on the island, and Joseph Allen continued to live as a gentleman of means with his mother-in-law, wife, and children at Ardath House. Grant Allen eventually had six siblings: five sisters, and an elder brother who predeceased him. But there was plenty of space for them all. Ardath House (called "the castle" locally) had twenty-five rooms, with a central manor hall heated by a gigantic fireplace.

Allen attended no school during his childhood. He passed a "rustic boyhood" under the benign tutelage of his father, wandering about on the island "with the raccoons and the sunfish."[4] He went skating and fishing and boating, and presumably laid the foundations for his later formidable knowledge of natural history in general, and for botany and entomology in particular. It is hardly likely, however, that this Huckleberry Finn-like existence filled very much of his time. For much of the year Wolfe Island was a taxing environment for a child with a weak chest. The channel between mainland and island was frozen solid from the end of December, with access only over the ice. And when the ice began to break up in the spring, the island might be cut off for weeks at a time. Later on, Grant Allen was fond of warning parents not to let their children's schooling get in the way of their education, but a warm study and a book-laden desk must have figured largely in his own childhood. His father reported fondly that he started the study of Greek well before his seventh birthday, and could read his Greek Testament by the time he reached it. He must have had four languages at his disposal before he was far into his teens.

The prevailing tone of the Allen family was humane, loving, and intensely intellectual. There was a constant procession of eminent visitors to Alwington. The naturalist Alfred Russel Wallace stayed with them in the summer of 1886 in their "roomy old-world mansion," noting that Joseph Allen spent his days cultivating a magnificent collection of gladioli and a small private vineyard.[5] Joseph and Charlotte must have had a strong influence on their precocious son's development, but since Allen rarely mentioned his parents in later years the exact nature of their influence remains shadowy. In his few surviving letters, Joseph Allen gives a slight impression of officiousness. For example, having persuaded his son to send on to Charles Darwin a copy of a paper that he, Joseph, had written on the evolution of morality, he then wrote to the great man directly from Canada, trying to secure an invitation for his son to visit Down House. No invitation was forthcoming.[6]

But a fairer reading, perhaps, might be that, unfulfilled himself, he found a vicarious solace in his son's expanding reputation. Many years later, when Herbert Spencer accused Grant Allen of "turning Socialist" he retorted that he could not turn because he had been born one. It is hard to credit that Allen would have heard much socialism preached at him from his tough, acquisitive Grant relations, but his father's politics may well have been fairly radical. He is said to have been an Irish nationalist, and his position in life, though externally enviable, may have chafed his sense of self-respect. "A private gentleman" was how Joseph Allen described himself in documents; a gentleman who dabbled in verse and politico-religious pamphlet writing. But the blunt truth was that he was living on his wife's unearned income; was a pensioner, one might say, of the Grant family, and yet at the same time he surely appeared to his social inferiors as someone who had craftily inveigled his way into the colonial landlord class. What the tenantry whose rents supplied those private means thought of their ex-pastor is unknown, except for one clue. In 1854, there was some fuss that the landlords of the island ought to be doing more for the spiritual welfare of their tenants.[7] Joseph Allen may have been the meat in the sandwich in such exchanges, and his perceptive son might well have pitied him for it.

Whether the son conformed to, or reacted against, his father's private philosophical and religious beliefs is also unclear. Joseph Allen resigned his ministry in mid-life over some theological dispute with his bishop, and it's conceivable that he had a scathing view of the clergy which he transmitted to his son, who, by his own account, was a militant atheist and Darwinian from childhood. The son's memorable birth year, 1848, the year of European revolutions, also saw the issue of Marx's *Communist Manifesto* in England; and the *Origin of Species* burst on the world when Grant was eleven. Joseph Allen ensured that their message was not lost on his son. He was himself the author of *Day Dreams of a Butterfly*, a prolix philosophical poem with an appendix of notes citing authorities from Kant to Carlyle. He certainly made his son read Herbert Spencer. Like several Victorian atheists, Grant Allen acquired knowledge of the Bible that would have shamed many a divine, and its rhythms and allusions are evident everywhere in his writings. On the other hand, he said once that he had no problem giving his villains an occupation, because he made them all clergymen. The converse is certainly true. He made most of the clerics in his fiction hypocrites, trimmers, time-servers, fanatics, arsonists, or murderous psychopaths. Presumably that emphasis came from the paternal views rather than the paternal practice.

When Allen was born the population of Wolfe Island was only about 1,300, nearly all of them tenant farmers, but in the years when he was growing up the community was expanding and prospering. By the time he left Canada, the population had almost tripled and a canal had been dug across the island to improve transport with the American side of the St. Lawrence. Even as a youngster he must have been aware that the transformation was enriching his family and was about to underwrite his family's long sojourn in the Old World. In his political articles, and in passages in his novels, the right of proprietors to sequester or "taboo" large areas of land is one of his most constant targets. Certainly he was good at expressing his naïve wonderment that, just because men like his grandfather had been able to acquire tracts of unowned Canadian wilderness, his family could, for ever afterwards, require the farmers who extracted their arduous living from Grant land to pay rent sufficient to keep the entire large brood of the Allens and the Grants in idleness. How odd, how primitive, how *laughable* our arrangements would seem to an anthropologist of the future! Perhaps the first seeds of Allen's anthropological satire *The British Barbarians* were sown on Wolfe Island.

When he was about thirteen,[8] part of the family began one of those leisurely tours of Europe, their duration measured in years rather than months, which were such an attractive feature of upper-class life of the time. The senior Allens returned to Canada eventually and took up residence at Alwington, where they lived for the rest of their lives with their unmarried daughter. But their son did not return. Grant Allen could never have made a living in Canada from his kind of superior scientific and polemical journalism

and novel-writing. He had to be at the heart of the literary-intellectual world
to sell the produce of his pen, and in the last decades of the century that
meant London. He went back to Alwington only three times. In many ways,
which we will be considering later, Allen was a renegade and an outsider, and
like many other expatriate writers was fiercely critical of British institutions,
which caused some animosity. For example, his views on sexual and marital
relations were partly formed, as he said himself, by the rather freer mores of
the New World. Some of his stories and essays turn on this point.

According to the shaky notes that the aged Joseph Allen made forty years
later just after his son's death, the furtherance of their children's, or at any
rate their boys', education was the purpose of this long tour. They lived first
in New Haven, Connecticut, from June 1861, and here Allen and his brother
acquired their "first rudiments of higher education beneath the shadow of
the elms at Yale College."[9] The peacefulness of Yale must have contrasted
strangely with the public events of that tumultuous year. The Civil War had
started in South Carolina a couple of months earlier, quickly followed by the
secession of the states of the Confederacy. The Allen family followed the war
closely and enthusiastically, seeing the struggle as an unambiguous fight for
human freedom. Early in the following spring, around the time of the slaugh-
terhouse that was the battle of Shiloh, they crossed the Atlantic to France.
They settled into the English colony at Dieppe, where Grant attended
the Collège Impérial, a stately establishment on the Quai Henri IV, which
catered particularly to foreign pupils. He stayed a year, presumably to perfect
his French, and he did become completely bilingual.[10] The family then
crossed the Channel and he entered King Edward's School, Birmingham
early in April 1864, when he was sixteen.[11] The surviving school records
show that he distinguished himself by winning a string of prizes in classics,
mathematics, and French—but not, apparently, in natural history, even though
science did appear on the curriculum. Since he had fixed his sights on Oxford,
perhaps he thought that the humanities offered more of a chance of gaining
a lucrative scholarship. If so, he was right, for only a tiny fraction of the
college scholarships available at Oxford at that time were for study in the
sciences.[12] So, when he left Birmingham in the summer of 1867 at the age of
nineteen, it was to take up a valuable postmastership in classics, which he had
won at Merton College. His life as an independent adult had begun.

A "Reading Man" at Oxford

In his old age the critic George Saintsbury wrote a memoir, "Oxford Sixty
Years Since," which captures a good deal of the atmosphere to which Allen
was exposed when he went up in the autumn of 1867.[13] Oxford in the 1860s
consisted almost entirely of the colleges and their supporting facilities. The
big, comfortable late-Victorian and Edwardian villas running out along the
main roads were not yet built, and few people above the lower middle class
lived in the town unless they were connected in some way with the university.
The monastic past still lay heavily on Oxford. There were some new buildings,

but also many crumbling ones, and the general atmosphere was one of gentle decay. The entire undergraduate body numbered only about 2,000—applicants were not plentiful, not even with the bait of scholarships—and, of course, none of them were dissenters, Roman Catholics, or women. No father who expected his son to follow a commercial, medical, or an engineering career considered Oxford; for all such youths, it was a waste of time. An eminent Scottish academic, himself an Oxford man, described the university in 1867 as a great expensive steam-hammer, used only for cracking walnuts.

When Allen went up in the autumn of 1867 things were tranquil enough. The religious turmoil of the Oxford Movement had long since subsided after Newman's conversion to Rome. In the previous decade Morris, Rossetti, Burne-Jones, and their friends had painted bright frescoes on the walls of the Union. It seemed appropriately symbolic that they had already faded into ghostly tatters, for Pre-Raphaelitism as a coherent artistic movement had come and gone. During Allen's time, what intellectual excitement was available was being supplied by theological debate and doubt—for this was the Oxford of the *Essays and Reviews*, of Swinburne's *Poems and Ballads*, of the Higher Criticism, of Darwinian controversy, of the conflict between religion and the growing authority of science as symbolized by the Huxley/Wilberforce confrontation. The effects were proving unsettling. Every second Oxford man, it was said, was a skeptic in religion.

Serious scholarship was at a low ebb, especially in the natural sciences. T.H. Huxley growled that a man could achieve the highest honors Oxford could bestow without knowing whether the sun went round the earth or vice-versa. Few people cared about the mathematical studies of a certain don at Christ Church, but he was famous everywhere for the fantasy he had woven for the small daughters of Dean Liddell. And that seemed appropriate too: some irreverent spirits thought the worlds of *Alice in Wonderland* and Oxford were not really very distinct.

Both Grant Allen and George Saintsbury attended Merton, a small, ancient college with about sixty undergraduates. Its academic reputation was slight. Most of the upper-class young men in residence were the very image of Byron's young barbarians, all at play. As there was no entrance examination they were free to treat Merton as a club or finishing school for gentlemen; a place where one might pass a few years in pleasant surroundings and congenial company, engaging in the acceptable amusements of cards, rowing, football, hunting, horse-racing, bump suppers and—if one were discreet—pursuing the less acceptable vices among the pubs and dubious lodging-houses of Jericho and St. Thomas's. Mandell Creighton, later Bishop of London, was an undergraduate at Merton in the mid-1860s. An earnest and arrogant cleric, Creighton was not inclined to facetiousness, but his opinion for posterity about his college fellows is memorable. "The majority were Eton men," his wife reported him as saying, "brought there through the influence of the Warden, Dr Marsham, men who loved hunting and other sports, had plenty of money to spend, and no particular intention of doing any work."[14] The "reading men," the postmasters, were tolerated but they hardly set the tone.

Even the dons thought it was rather vulgar for students to work for a degree as an aid to employment. Vulgar or not, it certainly was not a popular activity, since a full third of Oxonians left the University without bothering to take any degree at all.

"The Refuge of the Destitute":
at Brighton College

In April 1866, while his son was still at school in Birmingham, Joseph Allen was appointed lecturer in modern history at Queen's University in Kingston. The post was purely honorary, and for some reason he resigned it the following year, but it did have teaching duties.[15] We infer that by the time Grant Allen left Birmingham for Oxford his parents must have been back in Canada for some time. Whether the nineteen-year-old was left alone in England or was under the care of relatives is unclear, but there is no evidence that he felt any immediate impulse to take advantage of the lack of parental control. His first year at Merton passed uneventfully, for he definitely belonged in the camp of the reading men. He had rooms in Mob Quad, and he discovered in a windowpane some Latin lines scratched by a long-dead predecessor. They advised the reader, or possibly the inscriber himself, not to waste time while at Oxford but to be vigilant in studying day and night. It was not, initially, advice that Allen was likely to neglect. So far he had proved the very model of an industrious, intellectual youth from a loving family who was clearly destined for a career in one of the solid professions. He soon formed a small circle of studious friends: York Powell, later a lawyer and historian; Richard Pope, later a mathematics and divinity lecturer; Exley Percival of Brasenose, who had competed in the prize-lists with him at Birmingham; W.W. Fisher, a chemist. They found him very unlike the typical British undergraduate of the day. He showed no sign of rebelliousness, but he did have a reputation for "advanced" political opinions and for being a little doctrinaire and over-forceful in expressing them. He had the socially disconcerting habit of never allowing an interlocutor to think he agreed with him when he didn't. One did not need to be very radical or bluntly outspoken, in the tranquil Oxford of the 1860s, to acquire such a reputation.

The only surviving evidence of his youthful opinions, other than those recollected by college acquaintances decades later, is to be found in an evanescent magazine, the *Oxford University Magazine and Review*, which he founded and coedited with a friend. He contributed to it a few poems and a humorous tale mocking American pretensions. But his one article for the magazine reveals rather more. He gave it a challenging title, "The Positive Aspect of Communism," but its sentiments are hardly those of a political firebrand. In fact, it is not really about communism, or about politics at all. (Marx's *Kapital* appeared in German the year Allen went up to Oxford, but it is improbable that he had even heard of it.) What he really wants to talk about is "the present chaotic state of public morality" and the "laxity of morals" that are especially evident in France. He makes it quite clear what kind of morals are in question: "the licentiousness which we see in the reign of Napoleon III is complete and universal, and is infecting every relation of domestic life." Sexual vice is eating away at the fabric of French society. It is not pleasant to contemplate, but it has to be inspected by anyone who wants to "decypher the enigma of history." For the reaction is at hand; the cloud has a silver lining. Only "communism, or some form of government closely resembling it" will purge society of its decadence. That day, the writer hopes, is not far off.[16]

Such an eager anticipation of a regime of communistic puritanism might seem odd in almost any young man. It seems doubly so when we recall these are the opinions of a youth who one day was going to turn into a sexual renegade with a reputation as a neo-pagan apostle of free love. But there is no real incongruity. His views on French public life were founded on personal observation and in any case the essay had an immediate, if concealed, personal application. For by the time his essay appeared in the magazine at the end of 1869 Grant Allen had taken a very surprising step for an upper-class undergraduate of those days. It was a private matter, but it had serious public consequences. On the last day of September 1868, at Holy Trinity Church, Brompton, West London, he got married.

On that autumnal mid-week afternoon the little wedding party must have made a joyless and rather pathetic sight as it trooped up the long shady pathway leading from the busy Brompton Road to the church. The groom was twenty, and in a mood oscillating between defiance and despondency. His defiance is implied by his giving his occupation as "Gentleman" in the marriage register; his gloom by his awareness that he was in actuality just a first-year undergraduate whose valuable scholarship was being terminated even as he stood at the altar. His bride, Caroline Anne Bootheway, was a little older, minimally educated and probably a semi-invalid. Her face surely showed the alternate pallor and hectic flushes characteristic of the tuberculosis that was slowly killing her. Holy Trinity itself, a "Commissioners' Gothic" church of sooty yellow brick, was hardly the place for a fashionable wedding. Today it is hidden from the road by the swollen marble bulk of the Oratory, and its churchyard, now a little park, is a haven of quiet, but then it was simply the parish church of what was still a suburban and slightly raffish neighborhood. The young couple were already living together in rooms in a terrace off Thurloe Square, a short stroll away, probably because the area housed many students looking for tutors, and perhaps also because the Brompton Consumption Hospital was nearby. While the marriage was not exactly clandestine, it is doubtful whether the Allen family knew much about it, or, possibly, even that it was happening at all. One of the witnesses was Allen's college friend, Exley Percival, and it is unlikely that the other one belonged to either the bride's or the groom's family. The hard facts of this marriage are to be found in the public records alone, for later Allen and his friends would succeed in editing nearly every detail out of history. There is not a single direct mention of it anywhere in his writings, public or private.[17]

When Allen married his second year at Merton was about to start. The loss of his scholarship was a heavy blow, for it could be held for five years and he had drawn it for only one, and he had few other resources. The academic consequences were more serious still. If Allen harbored any ambition of gaining a fellowship at Merton his marriage put paid to it, for his studies suffered alarmingly in its wake. To his contemporaries at Oxford, Allen was "one of the most brilliant undergraduates of his time," as his friend Pope remembered years later.[18] But now he began to falter. He graduated in the summer of 1871, apparently having suspended his studies in the previous year. Obviously money had become a problem. The Merton archives show that the college offered him some relief by charitably paying his scholarship again "on the ground of poverty" for a single half-term, from Easter 1871, presumably so he could graduate, but there were also what Clodd calls vaguely "changes in family circumstances."[19] This was almost certainly the result of bank failures in Ontario and an economic decline on Wolfe Island. The farming population fell again, the canal was abandoned, the senior Allens' rent-roll diminished and perhaps they either could not, or would not, pay him an allowance any longer. Allen made ends meet by private tutoring work, which also cut into his study time, and almost at once he had an invalid wife to care for as well.

Certainly the strain was showing when, as a married man of a year's standing, he wrote twice to his friend Nicholson, a student of his own age at Trinity. The time was the closing days of 1869 and Allen was spending a miserable Christmas in lodgings on the Isle of Wight, trying to catch up on his reading. The tone of both letters is still half-disconsolate and half-defiant. He announces that he is pulling out of the coeditorship of their magazine; he is, he tells his friend, "much too poor a man to waste any more time on an unproductive place like Oxford. . . . All I want is a degree. I go in for no fellowship." He wanted only "the two letters, and as good a class as I can manage," after which he intended to "get an easy mastership, where there is lots of work and very poor pay, and subside into obscurity."

The recipient of this confidence, Edward Nicholson (1849–1912), was to become Bodley's Librarian, and he and Allen shared several interests, including numismatics and folklore. At this time they must have been quite close, for one of the letters is signed, fantastically and presumably jestingly, "Yours Davidically, Jonathically and Pythia-damonically." But Caroline's name is never mentioned. Perhaps her presence was understood. He does say that he is "troubled about many things, very troubled indeed, and by no means up to writing," and he seems to expect Nicholson to understand that he has good reason to be in semi-hiding on the island: "When I leave Ventnor, I shall probably not have spoken to a soul (except tradespeople) outside this house. Young Williams of Merton is at Sandown, and I have seen him once, but shall try to prevent a recurrence of the circumstance."[20] "Young" Williams was Gerard Williams, also a postmaster at Merton and just the same age as Allen; he became a vicar.

The class of the two letters turned out to be a not especially creditable Second at Greats. A few years before, and despite working very hard, George Saintsbury had got only a Second also. It rankled for the whole of his life.

"The sting of a Second is almost incurable," he said, admitting to having recurrent dreams about it for years afterwards.[21] It is most unlikely that Allen felt anything like the same pain. He did rail a little against the unfairness of his fate at the time. Fifty years later, a fellow-student who lodged in the same house recalled that Allen turned up in his rooms on the day the results were posted, saying that Oxford's inability to rate him properly would make it look downright silly one day.[22] Whether or not he was joking, his attitude soon hardened into a lifelong distaste for the education he had received there. His course in the Final Schools, *Literae Humaniores*, was based exclusively on the Greek and Roman classics and amounted to an unrelieved diet of their literature, history, and philosophy. But, multilingual himself, Allen thought little of the acquisition of languages. Anyone can pick up a new tongue. Who learn languages most easily? "Children, negroes, servants, the uneducated." And are the classics so supremely important as to merit three or four years of a young man's education? He seriously doubted it. Oxford had not developed his faculties in any useful way at all. Only travel and observation, especially travel in Italy, had taught him anything worth knowing.[23] His comments make a piquant contrast with Saintsbury's essay, which despite that incurable sting of the Second is soaked in dreamy nostalgia in the *Brideshead Revisited* mode.

So, after graduating BA, Allen did as he had gloomily forecast he would do; did what many men with modest degrees and no prospects have done before and since. He turned schoolmaster, that "refuge of the destitute," as he called it.[24] He got a post down on the south coast teaching Greek and Latin at Brighton College, which was one of the new private school foundations run on strictly business lines. Before the term started, he almost certainly spent some of that summer in the Commune in Paris. He must have missed the street-fighting of *La semaine sanglante* in May when perhaps 20,000 died, but he was there in time to examine the aftermath of the insurrection: the dismantled barricades, the shell craters and pock-marks of bullets in the Père-Lachaise cemetery where the firing-squads had been at work, the burnt-out hulk of the Tuileries, the mass trials of August. Three of his poems, including the powerful "À Bas La Bourgeoisie: A Psalm of the Commune" read as though they are based on personal observation. All his sympathies, naturally, were with the doomed communards, during those brief months when it seemed as though a true proletarian revolution was at hand; Allen, perhaps with his working-class wife at his side, must have been in his element. On top of these excitements, Darwin's eagerly awaited *Descent of Man, and Selection in Relation to Sex* had appeared that February, and Allen swallowed its epoch-making if predictable message at a single gulp.

Teaching at Brighton must have seemed tame by comparison. His brief time there has left few records except for a note in the school magazine bewailing his loss to the Reading Club, which prepared boys to deliver public recitals. However, a photograph of the little group of masters at the school, taken in the porch of the headmaster's house, furnishes the earliest known image of Grant Allen, at the age of twenty-three. A pale, spare figure under his mortar-board, he stands slightly apart at the rear of the group, perhaps to gain height from the extra step. His mouth is turned down and he grips his coat with a self-protective air. Even allowing for the conventions accepted by photographic subjects at the time, he looks distinctly unhappy and out of place among the other beefy pedagogues. Since Allen had been careful to keep Caroline out of the way of his Oxford acquaintances, one wonders what impression she made at Brighton, particularly on the teachers' wives. In the introverted atmosphere of a small private school, how could there not have been gossip about whether her past bore inspection? In *Philistia*, Ernest Le Breton has to reckon with the enmity of the headmaster's wife, who accuses him of getting his job under false pretences when she discovers his wife is "positively a grocer's daughter from a small country town."[25] But at least Ernest's wife Edie is indisputably a lady. In real life the young couple may well have had to endure harder brickbats than that from the worthy matrons of Brighton College. Not that the Allens were at the school for long. They stayed only for a term. The egregious Frank Harris, man about town and, as the editor of the *Fortnightly Review*, one of Allen's many paymasters, claimed later that it was he who replaced Allen as a teacher at the school. This is about as true as most of Harris's assertions.[26]

Perhaps Allen took the Brighton post hoping that the sea air would do Caroline good. The same motive may have governed their shift that Christmas to Cheltenham, a spa town and a well-known resort of consumptives, where Allen took a new post as a tutor. It was at Cheltenham that Caroline Bootheway Allen died of tuberculosis on March 23, 1872. She was twenty-six. So ended the first excursion into matrimony for the man who, twenty years later, would be demonized in many quarters as the foe of that institution and the frankest, most uncompromising spokesman for free unions of his day.

A New Beginning

When his wife died Grant Allen had just turned twenty-four. The tragedy that had overtaken the pair was of course a commonplace one. Tuberculosis was the familiar, implacable killer of 60,000 people a year in Victorian England, most of them young adults, and an unpublished poem, existing only as an autograph copy in the hand of Edward Nicholson, implies that the couple knew within a year of marriage that her death was inevitable:

> We stood upon the Westward-fronting cliff,
> And gazed athwart the calm. The red sun dipped,
> Purpling the blue. Between him and our eyes
> Drave a black hull, black-sailed, that stood, and loomed
> Huge, on the water's edge. The red sun sank,
> And all was dark, save where one silent light
> Bore slowly westward: and we watched its course
> Awhile in silence: then we turned and went.
> And all the cliff was dark, and all the fields.[27]

The death-ship is a rather too obvious and not very appropriate allusion to Tennyson's Arthurian barge, "black as a funeral scarf from stem to stern" carrying the immortal hero to the island of Avalon, but there is no denying the sinister and ominous tone of this poem: the single light being borne westward after the sunset; the couple watching it silently and then moving away into the darkness. The poem's title is "1869."

But, then, young men in their early twenties are resilient and Allen quickly married again, this time forming an eminently successful union that lasted the rest of his life. Really, he could not have been thought heartless if the whole episode had left little behind it except some fading sorrows and gentle regrets. Yet, as we shall see, this is not what happened. His wife's life and death played some central, if not perfectly comprehensible, role many years later in giving a decisive form to Allen's views on social questions; those highly controversial views that would animate and outrage the emerging feminism of 1890s England. Why was this so? That is a question for a later chapter.

After Caroline's death Allen went back to Oxford, where he worked as a private tutor and tried unsuccessfully for a university fellowship. He then took a last brief teaching post at Reading Grammar School. This rapid turnover of schools suggests Allen found it hard to settle to school-teaching. Perhaps his politics got him into trouble, as they do Ernest Le Breton in *Philistia*, who indignantly declines to adopt the "quiet and gentlemanly, but unswerving Conservatism," recommended by his headmaster, and continues to consort with Socialists. Very soon he is sacked.[28]

While at Oxford Allen met the woman who became his second wife, Ellen (Nellie) Jerrard, the youngest of the five children of Thomas and Patience Jerrard of Lyme Regis in Dorset. At only twenty, Nellie Jerrard was very much the baby of the family, for her siblings were all ten years older or more. Her elder sister Ethel was married to Franklin Richards, an Oxford don and a close friend of Allen's. One of their children, Grant Richards, Allen's nephew by marriage, was treated later on almost as a son by his uncle and aunt, and became in due course the publisher of most of his last books.

Although she shared most of Grant Allen's adult life, Nellie Jerrard Allen remains an indistinct figure. Nothing is known of her influence on her husband's views, or of his on hers. His only public reference to her is found in *The Woman Who Did*, a novel which, despite inveighing against marriage, is dedicated to "my dear wife, to whom I have dedicated my twenty happiest years," a sentiment which some thought undercut the message of the book right at the start. Their marriage really was to all appearances idyllically happy, a circumstance that, given his acerbic view of that institution, badly disconcerted his opponents. An anecdote implies as much. Just after *The Woman Who Did* appeared, Allen gave an interview to air his views further. Impressed by his sincerity, the journalist closed his story with the defiant sentence: "He is happily married." The compositor who set up this text was incredulous that this assertion could be true of a notorious pornographer like Grant Allen. He introduced a couple of commas, so that the printed sentence read: "He is, happily, married."[29] In her middle years Nellie Allen was in poor health, like her husband, and was prone to those mysterious Victorian "breakdowns" and general debility, which demanded frequent rest cures in private hotels at home and abroad. When they married, she was the same age that Allen had been at his first marriage. No wonder that was the age he later pronounced was the right one at which young couples ought to be pairing off, though without benefit of clergy.

Nellie Jerrard had no money of her own, and Allen, now drifting between Reading, Oxford, and Lyme Regis, needed a more stable and rewarding post before they could marry. When one turned up it involved a drastic change of scene. Early in 1873 Allen was offered a position that sounded much grander than school teaching. It was an academic post with the title of "Professor of Mental and Moral Philosophy." The snag was that the post was in the West Indies, at a new government college on the island of Jamaica. Allen may have got the job through family influence, since the governor there, Sir John Peter Grant, was probably a maternal relation who was then in his last year of what had been a very successful posting. There was nothing better on offer, and it would at least be an adventure; so, stifling their doubts about such an alarming step into the unknown, Grant Allen and Nellie Jerrard got married that spring on the strength of the appointment. This time the wedding was a thoroughly decorous affair in the parish church at Lyme, with due observance paid to all the provincial niceties. Yet once again Grant Allen had, by Victorian standards, married beneath him. Thomas Jerrard is described variously as a butcher and, in the census of 1881 when he was seventy, as a "retired purveyor." We guess, though, that he was in a prosperous line of business and could afford to raise his daughters as ladies, since two of them were found acceptable in Oxford's academic society. Certainly the family home in Broad Street, in the center of the town, must have been congenial enough for the Oxonian brothers-in-law, because both the Allen and Richards families spent a good deal of time there. Allen loved the Lyme area and wrote a good deal about its topography and unusual geology.

After hosting a farewell oyster-lunch at the Mitre in Oxford for all their friends and acquaintances, the young couple took ship for Jamaica in good time for the first term, which was due to start late in September. They traveled out on the Royal Mail Steam Packet Company's *Don*, probably in the company of William Chadwick, who had been appointed Principal. He too was in his early twenties, and had also been a postmaster at Merton. He was currently a Fellow of Corpus Christi, Oxford, where he taught mathematics. He and Allen were to be the only academic staff at the new Queen's College; one other man was appointed as steward and secretary.

CHAPTER 2

JAMAICA (1873–1876)

TO THE WEST INDIES

The passage to the West Indies in the 1870s took about twenty days. In a typical voyage, after boarding at Southampton, one left behind the Wolf Rock lighthouse on the Scillies—the last sight of Britain and, indeed, of any land worth mentioning. Then one spent the next four miserable days tossing on the Bay of Biscay and another two weeks or so crossing the Atlantic deeps in the company of a cow, some sheep, and a small poultry-yard; a menagerie whose initial racket diminished steadily as the voyage went on. There was plenty to eat, hot water to wash with, but only cold seawater baths. Unless marred by a hurricane, the trip was safe, comfortable, and monotonous, the featureless days broken only by meals, watching petrels and flying fish, and the sweepstake on the ship's daily run.

Like everyone else on board the *Don*, the Allens were heartily glad to make a first landfall at St. Thomas, an island that was then a Danish colony. From a distance the view was picturesque enough. Before them lay a wide, calm bay with the white houses rising beyond with their green shutters and red shingled roofs. But as they drew into the harbor with the bum-boats crowding eagerly around, this, their first glimpse of the West Indies, was far less prepossessing. Allen had seen something of the tropics already, having traveled in the southern United States as a teenager before leaving for Europe, so he was fairly prepared for the reality of Caribbean life, but it was still a shock. There was the ferocious heat, for a start, "like a Dutch oven." He liked the look of the people: he described them as "Anglicized negroes, with a touch of American smartness" very unlike the Jamaicans as he was to know them later with their "listless *laisser-aller*" style; and different too from the "sauntering Spanish nigger of Cuba, or the independent and relapsing African of Haiti." Their town, though, was alarming. St. Thomas was a bustling trading port, but that was about all one could say for it. The Allens surveyed the houses ("mean and shabby-looking"), winced at the assault on the senses, and they did not like it. ("The smells are terrific, the dirt undisguised, and the heat past human endurance. A broiling sun pours down upon the whole festering mass of unwashed humanity, crowded negro huts, narrow lanes, decaying rubbish, and dry dust.") Everywhere they heard the opinion that "nobody ever dreams of living at St Thomas unless he has business in the town; and then his one object is to save up money and go away again." It was not reassuring to the ears of two young people who had just let themselves in for a working life of indeterminate length in the Caribbean.

When the Allens finally anchored in Kingston harbor a few days later on June 20, 1873, it was St. Thomas all over again, only worse. In the foreground was a long low sandy beach, from which palms rose at all angles with their foliage covered in an inch of grey dust. Beyond, the town appeared as "a ruinous mass of flat wooden shops and houses, in every stage of decay" running back from the sea on a low, sweltering, swampy plain. In the background were the Blue Mountains—not blue at all, but a dark mass silhouetted against the whitish-grey horizon. Over everything lay a blanket of damp heat, while a pitiless flood of light revealed every sordid detail.[1]

That Allen's first impression was no exaggeration is well attested to by other visitors at about this time. One of them described Kingston as "a town which has lost its self-respect. Like a man who has seen better days, it has given up attending even to its personal appearance."[2] Fourteen years earlier, that inveterate and generous-minded traveler Anthony Trollope had been blunter still: "of all towns that I ever saw, Kingston is perhaps, on the whole, the least alluring, and is the more absolutely without any point of attraction for the stranger than any other."[3] Ruined, even burnt-out, buildings were everywhere. The houses, flimsy constructions, consisted of low brick walls and posts supporting the roof, with the space in between filled with jalousies like Venetian blinds, mostly faded to a dusky olive green. In the unvarying seasons nothing more was necessary and the frequent hurricanes and fires did not invite any more solid construction. Since these blinds were normally kept closed against the heat, the houses looked permanently vacant. None of the streets, not even Harbour Street, the main thoroughfare, was hard-surfaced and every visitor commented on their state: "as dingy, dirty, gloomy ones as I ever encountered," said one.[4] The streets had no sidewalks and were quite unlit at night. There were few facilities to welcome the visitor: no hotels or boarding houses of quality, just a couple of not very inviting "halls" or inns. The main public buildings were a prison, an old barracks then being converted into a court-house, a little theater, a lunatic asylum, a hospital and a circular building of corrugated iron which was the central market. All were exceptionally ugly. There were few organized decent amusements, either public or private. The main leisure activity was strolling the streets or driving about in the cool of the evening. The population of Kingston was about 35,000, and of the whole island, about half a million. Four-fifths of them were illiterate.

Ninety percent of Jamaicans were Negroes, the descendants of West African slaves imported to grow sugar. In Kingston itself, however, Negroes formed rather less than half the population. The balance was made up of racially mixed people whose genes had been variously contributed by East Indians (a few hundred brought in as indentured laborers to replace the slaves), a scattering of Chinese, and other assorted Europeans. All these races and the Africans had interbred with greater or lesser freedom.

The whites were a mixed bag, the main constituents being the British, some Jews from Portugal and Spain, and French refugees. None of them lived in Kingston if they could help it; everyone of any means occupied the villas, some of them quite grand, which were spotted around on the surrounding hillsides. The local aristocracy was the British planter class, spread across the island on their estates and now mostly living in reduced circumstances. The pride and arrogance of some, and their obsession with racial purity (for in truth most had their admixture of African blood) provide the mainspring for one of Allen's best novels, *In All Shades* (1886).

The woebegone appearance of Kingston accurately reflected the current economic and political reality. King Sugar was down, if not quite out. The palatial sugar and coffee estates, like Rose Hall or Morgan's, whose slaves had made fortunes for their British absentee landlords, were now struggling to survive or had fallen into ruin. Few of them had recovered from the effects of emancipation forty years earlier. It was now said that one could not travel for more than five miles without coming across an abandoned plantation, and Allen himself recorded that he was eighteen months in Jamaica before he saw his first sugarcane. On the other hand, small sugar-mills operated by the new free peasant class had sprung up, and more of the island's rich soil was still under sugar than any other crop. But prices were dismally low. Jamaica could barely compete with other slave-owning producers of sugar elsewhere in the Caribbean.

The island of Jamaica has a long and blood-stained history, and plenty of blood had been spilt during the Morant Bay rebellion as recently as 1865. The island was peaceful throughout the Allens' years there, but the threat of another uprising could never have been far from people's minds. Certainly this became a plot-device in most of the stories set in Jamaica, which Allen wrote years later in England.

By the mid-1870s, when the Allens arrived, most Jamaicans were just as poor as they had ever been, but they had been placated by the cautious but reformist management of Sir John Peter Grant. "Papa Grant" was by far the most popular, energetic, and effective governor that Jamaica had ever enjoyed. He had overhauled the civil service, the courts and the police force, and he thought he had remedies for the economic situation. Why was Jamaica so poor? Because of a lack of external investment. Why were investors lacking? Because the workforce was unskilled and unproductive and labor relations were terrible. It was a long story of strikes and riots, long-standing sullen resentments and intransigence on both sides, gingered up by religious revivals based on a syncretic blend of Christianity and African cults.

Grant's solution was a very Victorian one: self-help. He wanted to produce a race of enterprising smallholders by settling them on cheap government land and encouraging them to produce more rewarding cash crops for the American market—bananas, pimento, coffee, and tobacco. In the city he wanted to expand the educated middle class, and the key to that, he thought, was higher education. What Jamaica needed was a local tertiary-level institution. Grant promoted this idea to his political masters in London, and they eventually agreed to finance one. The first such college anywhere in the Caribbean, it was to be nonsectarian and, in theory, open to anyone—any male, that is—and not just Afro-Jamaican boys. But it was unlikely that the British planter class, or the prosperous tradesmen, or the higher officialdom, were ever going to use it, and in fact they never did. They routinely sent their sons to Britain to be educated, as did the tiny affluent minority of the other racial groups. The few students who ever enrolled at the college were all of mixed race.

So, after some years of planning and the spending of much public money to convert existing buildings, here was the spanking-new Queen's College; empty at this moment, the end of June 1873, but all ready to take its first batch of students. Curiously, the college had been located not in Kingston, which was by far the largest town, but in the much smaller Spanish Town, which had been the capital of the island until the removal of the government to Kingston the year before.[5] This had caused much resentment among the locals, and no doubt the college had been put there as a sop to their pride.

LIFE AT SPANISH TOWN, JAMAICA

After a short spell in Kingston getting their bearings, the Allens moved west to their new home. The distance was less than 20 km, but in Jamaica no conveyance was speedy. One could chose between the road and a very slow train. Either way there was little to see. The road ran through dead flat country between hedges of thorny dildoes, varied with bushes of prickly pear, other cacti, and lignum vitae trees. About half-way one traversed a large swamp, from which dank vapors and swarms of pestilential mosquitoes arose at night— this was where the notorious "yards" were to develop late in the next century. So "along the dusty high road, and between the malarious swamps, and through the grey streets of dismantled Spanish Town," as he remembered that first journey long afterwards,[6] Grant and Nellie Allen came to their home for the next three years.

If Kingston had little visual appeal, at least it had some life and color— paradoxically, as Allen noted, because the streets were full of loungers with nothing much to do. Spanish Town was merely a decayed shanty town. It had the dismal look of a place that had been running down for years and whose reason for existence had now vanished altogether. It dated back to the sixteenth-century Spanish conquests, but little remained of its colorful past. Some of the fine, highly ornamented mansions where these people had lived were still standing, but all were let off as rooms and were crumbling away. It was rare to hear a wheel in the streets, whereas the sight of pigs rootling amid the garbage was commonplace. Again, Trollope's description is vivid:

> It is like the city of the dead. There are long streets there in which no human inhabitant is ever seen. . . .
>
> But the place is not wholly deserted. There is there the most frightfully hideous race of pigs that ever made a man ashamed to own himself a bacon-eating biped. . . . These brutes prowl about in the sun, and glare at the infrequent strangers with their starved eyes, as though doubting themselves whether, by some little exertion, they might not become beasts of prey.[7]

There are several more pages in similar vein. Trollope's travel book, *The West Indies and the Spanish Main*, appeared in 1859. One wonders if Grant Allen had read these words before accepting his post.

The only public place worth a second glance in Spanish Town was Parade square, consisting of a central garden surrounded by buildings in neoclassical style, in yellowish limestone. One of these was the old House of Assembly; another the court-house. To the west was the former governor's residence, Old King's House, with its Ionic portico, and other government buildings, which had now been taken over and adapted for the use of the College. King's House was more impressive inside than it looked outside. It had spacious rooms with faded gilt paneling, ornate furniture, wide passages, polished mahogany floors, and a grand ballroom to hold five hundred, rarely used and infested with bats. In King's House were the teachers' apartments, the Allens on the ground floor and Chadwick on the first. The Allens had a huge sitting room and bedroom, the latter so sparsely furnished that there was, Allen told his mother in a letter a few weeks after they arrived, "space enough in the middle for five sets of lancers to dance easily." Another building across the square had been turned into dormitories and lecture rooms with scientific instruments. There was plenty of room for several hundred students. Chadwick and Allen planned for an initial enrolment of about thirty.

In reporting conditions to his mother, Allen tries to put the best gloss on things, but it is clear enough that he had become disillusioned quickly enough. "We are getting accustomed to being a little tumble-down," he says ruefully, "and have this comfort, that we are much less tumble-down than anybody else. . . . We are getting quite accustomed now to find civilized and fairly educated people living in moderate comfort in the broken and shabby cottages of Spanish town."[8]

Still, like it or not there was work to be done and a salary to be earned, and the two teachers got down to the job of publishing the curriculum and advertising for students, ready to start the first term on September 22. The college had been established as an institute of higher education, which would award its own degrees, so it had to have a complete sequence of courses. The entire curriculum was to be taught entirely by the two young men. The full program for a degree was to be nine terms spread over three years, and for an Honors degree, five years. Tuition was not free, but the fees were heavily subsidized, and modest compared to those charged by private secondary schools in Kingston.

To enter Queen's College, boys had to be at least fifteen years old and able to pass an entry test. The results of this test quickly exposed the dismal standards prevailing at the Kingston schools. These schools boasted that they turned out students capable of meeting the entry requirements of Edinburgh, Oxford, Cambridge, and London universities. This claim had rarely been tested and was quickly revealed to be hollow when six youths presented themselves for the entrance examination. Only two reached an acceptable standard. It was reported that one of the other four expressed the belief, in the geography test, that Jamaica is located in the Mediterranean. There was hostile publicity. Some newspapers blamed the "cruel and misdirected flattery of the schoolmasters" who had beguiled well-to-do parents for the sake of the fees.[9] Others, like the *Colonial Standard*, took up the cause of the schools and the clergy, and engaged in a vituperative campaign against Chadwick, trying to pressure him to lower the bar. But all Chadwick would say was that he had not come to Jamaica to turn schoolmaster.

Despite this bold front, both men realized very quickly—within a few months of opening—that Queen's College was not going to work. The public arrived at the same conclusion just as quickly, thanks to the newspapers. One of those predicted that what it called the "grand fiasco" would not survive past June 1874, the end of the first teaching year.[10] But it did struggle on into its second year, still with only three students. Allen and Chadwick tried to integrate the College into the community more, by a program of public lectures. Allen advertised one on "The Philosophy of History" in Kingston as they were finishing their first year's work, but one wonders how well he competed against the delights of the Victoria Circus, newly arrived in town, with Mademoiselle Paulino Lee, the dashing equestrienne, and Andrew Lehman, "the Side-splitting Clown and jester of all jesters."[11]

Sadly, William Chadwick had little time left to do any more for the Queen's College. He fell ill with yellow fever over the Christmas holiday of 1874, when he was staying at Kingston with E.A.C. Schalch, the Attorney-General, and his sister. They nursed him devotedly, spooning arrowroot and brandy down his throat every half hour day and night, which was the only recommended treatment. Eventually the crisis passed and Chadwick recovered, but both the Schalchs caught the infection from him and died within an hour of each other on the last day of January 1875. Chadwick went back shakily to work, only to succumb to an attack of typhoid fever later that year. He was twenty-eight, and had not survived even two full academic years in Jamaica. Allen took over the title of Acting Principal and went on alone. Presumably it was some time after this that he wrote up an account of his day in an ingenious rhyming letter to his brother-in-law Franklin Richards, for he refers to the "one-man-power college." The letter gives a vivid picture of life in a tropical backwater at the time:

> Here I am, my dear Franklin, in Spanish Town still,
> as usual, grinding away at my mill.
> On Logic and Ethics, on Latin and Greek
> I have been talking for hours till I scarcely can speak.

> Then I have come back from College and muddled my brain
> with getting up lectures on Spencer and Bain,
> so I think that by way of a respite I had better
> sit down and reply to your last welcome letter.

The pace of life was slow, even soporific. First came the awakening at seven, after ten hours of slumber always rendered fitful by prickly heat and mosquitoes. Then a bowl of sago gruel in bed, brought by the housemaid, followed at eight by the single unalloyed pleasure of the day: a cold bath. A slow and deliberate toilet—even at that early hour, the slightest exertion made one's collar unpleasantly damp—was followed by an unappetizing breakfast of curry and bacon, and then came the daily round:

> At ten I depart for the College to lecture
> on every subject of human conjecture,
> from the weight of the sun and the path of the planets,
> the earthquake that shakes and the breezes that fan it,
> to the freedom of will and the nature of feeling,
> on the relative wrongness of fibbing and stealing.
> For, this being but a one-man-power College
> I alone must explore the whole circle of knowledge,
> appraise all our poets from Chaucer to Tennyson,
> prove Hamilton wrong and give Bentham my benison,
> show how the comitia used to assemble
> and crib Anglo-Saxon from Palgrave and Kemble.
>
> Meanwhile, in the household department dear Nelly
> inspects the production of pudding or jelly,
> and, in short, overlooks the entire commissariat —
> no easy affair in the town that we tarry at,
> where we count ourselves lucky if five days a week
> we can get us some jam and a morsel of steak.

After lunch, more teaching till three, then idling and a visitor or two filled up the time until a stroll in the short tropical dusk; dinner at seven, card games or reading till nine, and a thankful retreat to bed, only "to repeat the whole programme *da capo* next day." The poem closes on a bravura note:

> And here this epistle at length must be ended.
> It's double as long as I ever intended;
> but, having begun, I ran on by the gallon.
> Believe me, as ever, Yours truly, Grant Allen.
> P. S.— I subscribe myself "truly" instead of "sincerely,"
> because it agrees with the metre more nearly.[12]

But the jaunty tone should not mislead us. Chadwick's death had been a shocking blow. It brought home the uncertainty of life in Jamaica; the ever-present risk of contracting an incurable infectious disease like typhoid or yellow fever or, worst of all, smallpox, a virulent strain of which was endemic to the island. These diseases were no respecters of class. Death could visit anyone, at a moment's notice. A judge in Spanish Town living near the Allens caught yellow fever that October, and though he could afford the best medical care his doctors threw up their hands in despair once he had progressed to the final stage, known gruesomely as the Black Vomit. The annual mortality rate in the island was supposed to be about forty per thousand, more than double the rate in England, but as there was no compulsory registration of deaths nobody knew for sure. This may be the reason why Nellie Allen was back in England by February 1875, less than halfway through their second year. The rhyming letter, in mentioning her domestic activities, implies that she returned later that year, but that may be poetic license. It is possible that she never returned to Jamaica at all before her husband's final departure in the summer of the following year.[13] Another unpublished poem of Allen's makes it clear that he was desperately lonely and homesick, and perhaps even socially ostracized, for most of his later time there. Thirty years later, gossip had it that one Harrington, a reputed son of Grant Allen's "by a black woman" was still living in Kingston.[14]

Allen quickly decided that he hated Spanish Town and did not trouble to conceal his feelings. He told visitors there was nothing whatever to see, and that even the cathedral nearby—the ugliest brick cathedral in all Christendom, he thought—wasn't worth inspecting except for a glance at the monuments inside.[15] The local people resented their town's loss of its capital status, and objected to the closure of the roads around the square to make a quadrangle for the students. The college, or rather its representatives, took the blame for these things. By the time Allen reached the end of his second academic year, in July 1875, the protests had redoubled and his position was being undermined. There were public meetings in Kingston, led by a cabal of nonconformist clergymen who took their concerns to the governor. They were demanding that that the college be reestablished as "an institution of popular benefit," with a new intake of thirteen-year-old boys in junior classes. And there are signs of a move against Allen personally, for another demand was that "no chair of the College would ever become a medium for disseminating views antagonistic to the religious sentiments of the community."[16] Allen's free-thinking views, and possibly his behavior, had not gone unnoticed.

Nothing much came of these protests. Grey, the governor, did nothing. Allen labored on by himself through his third and final year, but as no one else enrolled his duties were light. The *Handbook of Jamaica* noted sadly after Queen's College closed that "its ultimate failure to carry out the work which it was intended to accomplish" was because

> too great a distance intervened between the common schools of the country and the Queen's College, and to bridge over this interval good grammar schools are needed, and as these are for the most part wanting it must take some years of educational progress before such an establishment as an island college can hope for success.[17]

This is so obviously true that it is hard to understand why it did not occur to anyone at the planning stage.

Allen stuck it out until his three students graduated in the summer of 1876; then the college closed down and his job vanished. He returned to England via North America, where he gathered some meteorological statistics for a learned society, visited his parents at Kingston, and filled his notebook with material for several future articles.

Little remains of Allen's Jamaica. Soon after he left, the King's House was converted into a teacher-training college, but the building was almost derelict when Edward Clodd inspected it in 1905. He found little inside but cases filled with insect-eaten mortar-boards and gowns.[18] King's House burnt down in 1925 leaving only a façade standing, and the court-house on the Parade also went up in flames in 1986. In Kingston, a severe hurricane in 1880, a fire in 1882, and finally a devastating earthquake and fire in 1907 obliterated the commercial center and indeed most of the town as Allen had known it. A memorial to Chadwick in St. Jago de la Vega cathedral and a plaque outside are the only visible remnants of the whole educational episode.

SEX AND RACE IN JAMAICA

What did Allen make of his three years in Jamaica? How did the experience shape him, at that plastic stage in his life? Certainly he was quick to record his loathing of most aspects of his life there. He hated the enervating, muggy heat of the lowlands, and the ramshackle settlements ("the whole town has an air of neglected decay, which seems ten times more evident through the blinking, staring sunlight that falls in full force on every squalid detail"). Surprisingly, for such an enthusiastic naturalist, he took no pleasure in the countryside. He could see nothing but rank, dispiriting vegetation and "squalor, dust, sunlight in abundance." He stands in marked contrast to Philip Henry Gosse, who had visited Jamaica in 1844/5 and was entranced by the island's bird life. Being intensely religious, Gosse found in the splendid variety of birds and their behavior the most wonderful evidences of God's benevolence and ingenious handiwork. Allen, the evolutionist, would have thought the latter sentiment ridiculous because it was anti-Darwinian, but he had nothing good to say about the flora and fauna anyway. There were "no trees, no birds, no flowers, no scenery" he recorded flatly; by which he meant that there were none worth looking at with eyes attuned to damp, temperate, misty English landscapes.

What Allen missed most in Jamaica were the civilized resources essential to a man of his temperament. Perhaps he would have agreed with Dr. Johnson's growl, when he heard that a rich West Indian planter had died, that the deceased would not be noticing much change in either the climate or the company. He suffered badly from an "utter famine of books, pictures, music, theatres, society, science, thought, all the pursuits that make life worth living to a civilized and rational being," as he put it dolefully.[19] At some point he took a holiday trip from Kingston up to the Port Royal Hills, staying at Mango Top with a "little colony of officials." Although he grudgingly admitted that here at least it was cool and the scenery and the trees and flowering plants in this area were beautiful, he was determined not to be mollified. "Though we idle away our time pleasantly enough, I cannot for a moment pretend that life among the Jamaican hills is really enjoyable. . . . In short, let alone heat, negroes, and atrocious cookery, the mosquito is by himself enough to poison life in the West Indies."[20] Allen was not much interested in food, but he made a wonderfully despairing catalogue of the shortcomings of Jamaican cookery in an article with the ironic title of "The Epicure in Jamaica." The natives, we hear, live on boiled yam and salt-fish all the year round. For the newly arrived Englishmen the first impression is that there is nothing to eat but "ground beetles and baked boots." Chicken, flabby beef, and some scrawny mutton provide the only meat, and that has to be killed and eaten within twelve hours. To get fish of any kind requires serious long-term planning. All the tropical fruits are useless, except the ones everyone eats in Europe anyway. One fruit is "sickly," another "pappy and nauseous," a third tastes like "brown sugar and water," a fourth like an overripe gooseberry. Tins from England and America, the products of "Messrs. Crosse and Blackwell or the Portland Tinned Meat Company" are a too-frequent resort. How one longed to say "farewell to the gritty and fly-bespangled loaves, to the suspicious foreign bodies in the soup, to the flying ants which obstinately immolated themselves in the sherry, to the queer interest surrounding the dubious mammalian bones in the curried chicken"![21]

All in all, Allen felt that his time on the island was "just so much dead loss of time cut away from one's allotted span," or, at best, rather like reading Herodotus: something one is glad to have got done in one's youth, but that one would never do again for any money.[22] It should be borne in mind, though, that most of these jaundiced views were recorded in 1878/9, soon after he had returned to England and was struggling hard to make his way as a writer. Perhaps the assessment was true, in terms of the advancement of his career; in that sense, Jamaica had been marking time. But certainly he had not been idle. That quick, observant eye had been storing away impressions that would be surfacing in print for years to come.

He had complicated feelings about the Jamaicans themselves. His contempt for the economic mismanagement of the island, and his own difficulties at the college, and the general narrowness of the life there, darkened his views. He despaired over the Jamaicans' propensity for idling, which he put down not to any racial trait but to the "fatally fertile" soil. "A negro earns nine shillings a week by labor which even as a Communist I consider easy; of this he spends two, and saves seven. After a few weeks of work he has done enough for the quarter, and lies by in absolute idleness." Higher education, he thought, had no utility in Jamaica: "the people don't want education, and won't take it even if it is literally given away to them." On the other hand he had only con-tempt for the planter class, which he thought formed the drowsiest, most mindless version of the national John Bull type, and the planters' treatment of the blacks appalled and disgusted him. "I have no exaggerated sympathy with blacks, yet I must say the way they are regarded by the whites is simply shameful," he told his parents-in-law.[23] His observations reinforced his radical social and political views, and he mined his experiences several times in his fiction, most effectively in *In All Shades*, which is set in what is supposed to be Trinidad but is plainly Jamaica. (One guesses that he moved islands to evade any risk of libel.) *In All Shades* presents a young lawyer, Edward Hawthorne, who marries in England and returns to his parents in the West Indies, having secured a judgeship there. The young couple are completely ostracized by the planters, who have discovered the Hawthorne family has a trace of African blood in its family tree. Edward Hawthorne becomes the sworn enemy of a leading arrogant planter family, the Dupuys, when he favors a black laborer in a court case. Later Hawthorne is joined by an aristocratic and rather autocratic friend, Harry Noel, who is the heir to a Lincolnshire estate. He is made to suffer as much, if not more, when it becomes known that he too has black relatives in Barbados. All these events are treated from a liberal perspective, and the novel does offer some penetrating and unusual insights into Victorian race issues from several different points of view.

Allen was, however, far from being immune to the racial stereotyping common at the time, and he expounded it as lucidly as he did everything else. His early years were a time when new sciences of life were emerging: paleontology, comparative anatomy, and physiology. As far as the concept of race was concerned, all these sciences seemed to point in one direction. Racial characteristics are not the product of local culture, climate, and geographical conditions, but of biological heterogeneity due to natural selection. They cannot be altered easily. Like the vast majority of his contemporaries, and his fellow-scientists, Allen at this point in his life took it for granted that humankind falls into a hierarchy of races, that some of these are markedly inferior to others, and that the Negro is near the bottom of the scale in intelligence and moral fiber. One of the earliest racial theorists, Edward Long, had specifically relied on his own observations in Jamaica to promote the notion that Negroes are not part of the genus *Homo* but belong to a distinct species. In the 1860s scientific racism had become thoroughly entrenched, particularly in the leaders of opinion who were associated with the Anthropological Society. Though their views did not go unchallenged, there was broad agreement about the notion of a hierarchy of races, which cut across all socio-political divisions. Herbert Spencer asserted that Europeans are higher on the mammalian ladder than any other race. Francis Galton thought the adjectives that best defined the African nature were lazy, stupid, and perversely cruel. Darwin argued only that all mankind is biologically one species; he still believed that the races are distinguishable in all sorts of ways, and that intellectual activity varies innately across them. John Tyndall, physicist, opined that Negroes were peculiarly indolent and savage. T.H. Huxley took it for granted that his dusky cousins, with their larger jaws and their smaller brains, would never reach the highest places in civilization. Even A.R. Wallace, strong liberal and socialist, thought the only question at issue was exactly how far the degree of intellectual inferiority of the lower races extended.

The only point on which Allen had slightly unorthodox views was over the question of people of mixed blood. He thought that the best hope for the tropics was to increase the population of people of mixed European and African ancestry. W.G. Palgrave, reporting on the conditions in Jamaica at the time when Allen was there, agreed: "the coloured man, thanks to the tropical admixture in his blood, endures in-doors manual labour to a degree impossible for the pure-blooded European, while the intelligence and perseverance that he derives from his white parentage supplies a fortunate corrective to the irreflective carelessness and habitual negligence of his light-hearted, but often light-headed, nigritian ancestors. . . . Superior in neatness of hand to his European half-brother, the coloured man is not rarely his equal in intelligence."[24] Though this too is a tissue of absurdities, it was contrary to the prevailing view, which saw people of mixed-race as inferior to the "pure-bred" of any race. They were assumed to lack breeding (in all senses) and were probably infertile and highly sexed simultaneously. (Bertha Rochester in *Jane Eyre*, a Jamaican Creole, is the epitome of the type, though it's unclear whether she is presented as a white woman who has "gone native" or a degenerate mulatta.)

Allen probably would have agreed with Palgrave, but in his fiction, particularly in the subgenre that he called "the romance of the clash of races," he plays with the notion of the hierarchy of races, and the quality of mixed races, from several different positions. *In All Shades* introduces us to just such a man, Dr. W. Clarkson Whitaker, a mulatto returning to practice medicine in the island after training at Edinburgh. He is also a brilliant composer, violinist, and botanist. Even though he is presented very sympathetically as a victim of deracination and racism—in some ugly scenes he is virtually hounded to death after he arrives home—we also hear that "[he] talked on to them hour after hour, doing the lion's share of the conversation, and delighting them with his transparent easy talk and open-hearted simplicity. He was frankly egotistical of course—all persons of African blood always are—but his egotism, such as it was, took the pleasing form of an enthusiasm about his own pet ideas and pursuits."[25] We may wonder if this is being offered seriously— sometimes the suspicion arises that the apparently ingenuous narrative voice is surreptitiously mocking some of the assumed prejudices of his readers— but in this case it surely is. Allen's essays of the same period not infrequently touch on racial issues and offer sentiments that are conventional enough but disconcerting for the modern reader. On his way home from Jamaica via Canada he noted how pleasant it was to see black waiters on the trains. They make the best servants, as they never resent being treated as an underclass.[26] Another early article, "The Human Face Divine," defines the hierarchy of races in terms of physiognomy: the "most human" face is that of the "civilized Aryan; the most simian is that of the African Bushman." Those of negroes, Andaman islanders, and Indian hill-tribesmen are "more brutish" and "to put it in the truest way, more ape-like." At first sight, Orientals pose a problem: they are prognathous and noseless, which are clear signs of primitivism, yet somehow they have managed to become quite civilized. How to explain this? Because they only *seem* civilized; actually they show "every mark of arrested development." The Chinese language is monosyllabic, like baby talk; their writing never discovered the alphabet; their mental powers are mostly imitative.[27] Several of Allen's essays on this theme are perfect reminders that, just as the old prejudices based on caste and religion were beginning to lose their force, a cruel twist to the ideology of racial differences was given when a quasi-Darwinian anthropology, ethnology, and sociology allowed a whole new set of prejudices to arise and flourish.

Jamaica worked on Allen's radical sympathies in another way. His views on sexual morality and behavior, which had been thrown into a turmoil already by his first marriage, now came up for examination again. The sexual life of the West Indies was a matter for scandalized observation by every Victorian visitor to the islands. "Devoted to sensual pleasure," they noted breathlessly, "the negro has little respect for the marriage tie. Concubinage is a universal institution, and bears with it no disgrace."[28] From the moment his steamer arrived at Kingston harbor, Allen must have noticed that gender roles in Jamaica were a little bit different to those prevailing in Victorian Oxford. When the ship docked, the arduous process of coaling began. It was handled by casual wharf laborers of both sexes. It was mostly men who filled the baskets; the heavier job of heaving and tipping was handled by muscular young women; bold, quarrelsome viragoes. The following scene met the startled eyes of a British visitor less than a year before Allen arrived:

> We had the fortune to witness a fight between two of these interesting maidens. Catching her opponent by the neck, vixen No. 1 commenced the attack by delivering a vigorous "buck" with her head right in front of her antagonist—a compliment which was instantly returned. Now both were wrestling on the ground, legs twined with legs, and arms with arms, and the blood flowing pretty freely on either side. How long this might have lasted we cannot say, for nobody seemed to think it his duty to interfere. But just at this juncture a constable was seen approaching, and the two termagants bleeding, wounded, almost naked, hurling abuse at each other all the time, with many tears and objurgations, were incontinently marched off to "the cage."[29]

Such a fight was, of course, no rarity in Whitechapel or the Seven Dials either, but Jamaica differed from London's East End in the strongly matriarchal cast of its social organization. Women were cheaper to hire and, being more willing than men to take on the hardest physical work, enjoyed economic independence. So a pattern was set, which continued well into the next century: "the idle boys and men of Kingston were supported by their mothers, aunts or grannies, who worked as servants or in other domestic and feminine occupations, or by their women who worked on the wharfs, in coaling, or in loading bananas."[30] In such a matriarchy, with a measure of economic power, and careless of exhortations from missionaries whose doctrines took on strangely mutated forms in the eclectic religion of the island, women took the sexual initiative. They chose their partners, and the fathers of their children, at will. About three-quarters of births were illegitimate. Families were, in the jargon, "matrilocal." Men were a floating presence in many households, for it was traditional for the children, "bye-children," or "out-children," or "love-children," to be raised by the mother and her family.

Allen wrote nothing about this directly, although his own experiences must, in part, stand behind his polemical novels *The Woman Who Did* and *The British Barbarians* (both 1895) and behind many of his later essays promoting extreme solutions to the problems of marriage, divorce, women's roles, and prostitution. The closest he came to a direct account of what must have been for him a matter of daily observation was in an article, "Tropical Education," and in one of his best stories, "Ivan Greet's Masterpiece." Both were written many years later when he was planning his onslaught on Philistia, which was his name for censorious, bourgeois England. In the article, he used his Jamaican experiences as a stick with which to beat Mrs. Grundy. Those people who get to know the tropics in their formative years are like a higher brotherhood; they have taken the "Tropical Tripos." In particular, the tropics can give you a liberal education on sexual matters; they can disconcert your prejudices, get you away from the "reduced gentlewoman's outlook" on life, and send you back home with shattered faiths and broken gods. "How can Mrs. Grundy thrive," he asks rhetorically, "where every woman may rear her own ten children on her ten-rood plot without aid or assistance from their indeterminate fathers?"[31] With some suitable modifications, this is not far from what Allen was recommending for his utopian version of England in the 1890s.

In the story, an idealistic young English poet, Ivan Greet, moves to Jamaica, where he hopes to live as a child of nature while he ruminates his epic poem. He quickly acquires a brown-skinned mistress, Clemmy, and Allen's observations about the sexual life of the island, now lent enchantment by time and distance, are couched in soft, romantic terms:

> To Ivan it was an Eden of the Caribbean Seas; he loved it for its simplicity, its naturalness, its utter absence of guile or wile or self-consciousness. 'Twas a land indeed where the Queen's writ ran not; where the moral law bore but feeble sway; where men and women, as free as the wind, lived and loved in their own capricious, ancestral fashion. Its ethics were certainly not the ethics of that hateful Mayfair from which he fled in search of freedom.[32]

But it would be a long while yet before Allen would prescribe a dose of Jamaican morals, of men and women living "free as the wind," to cure the sins of philistine England. What Jamaica gave him most of, in the mid-1870s, was free time. It was a period of great intellectual growth. He got through an immense amount of self-directed reading in literature, philosophy, natural history, and psychology. He read Merivale, Caesar, Tacitus, Gibbon, Comte, and Schopenhauer. His talent for explication and synthesis were expanded by his teaching duties, where perforce he had to be a universalist. And this developed his air of authority, clear-cut opinions and capacity for swift, colorful generalizations, which served him so well later on. He looked closely into Jamaican folk practices, especially the fear of "duppies," (ghosts) and the ways of placating them by placing a saucer of sprouting cereal on the corpse, and the belief that the duppy was less dangerous once the grass had grown green on the grave. These observations helped to elucidate his theory of the origin of religion in ghost worship.[33] He even dissected a couple of bodies. His friend Dr. Stamers, the government medical officer in the town, got hold of the corpse of a murderer, Daniel Madden, warm from the gallows, and decapitated it so that Allen could dissect the brain with his students. Dr. Stamers had stored the body in his coach house and it caused great excitement, almost a riot, when someone stole the detached head, probably for purposes of witchcraft, and then thought better of it and threw it away in a back yard.[34] The dissection in that climate was filthy work, with no refrigeration or even effective preservatives, and he could not face his dinner for several days afterward.

MEETING "THE MAXIMUM BRAIN ON EARTH": HERBERT SPENCER

In the foreground of Allen's mind throughout these three years was the name and works of Herbert Spencer (1820–1903), the last of the great philosophical system-builders of the nineteenth century. He had known Spencer's work since childhood, as his father was an admirer, and he had talked of Spencer enthusiastically to his friends at Merton. The philosopher was in his fifties by the time Allen was reading him closely in Jamaica. He had published many of the key volumes of his Synthetic Philosophy in their original form, although he continued to tinker with them and expand them for the rest of his life. Allen had access to *First Principles, Social Statics, The Principles of Psychology, The Principles of Biology and The Study of Sociology* when he started to compose essays of his own, and as he read and reread these volumes in Jamaica they struck him as being work of consummate genius. He thought out an evolutionary theory of aesthetics on Spencerian principles, which eventually became his first book, and he got published in a Canadian general magazine a paper on physics, trying to correct some details of Spencer's account of some of the central concepts of thermodynamics. The fact that Spencer had misunderstood them in the first place, and Allen's paper only garbled them further, attracted no attention at the time, though it would do later.[35]

By the time his second teaching year began Allen was suffering badly from intellectual isolation. The only connection with the wider world was the fortnightly mail boat. Spanish Town continued to offer nothing to stimulate the mind. The resources of the twenty or so white families living there were soon exhausted unless you wanted to talk about rum, sugar, horseflesh or outdoor sports, and this, for a lively sociable being like Allen, who rejoiced in free-flowing, speculative conversation, was purgatory. So he was all the more inclined to express something of his admiration for his far-off hero in a fulsome poetic eulogy. It starts:

> Deepest and mightiest of our later seers,
> Spencer, whose piercing glance descried afar
> Down fathomless rifts of dead unnumbered years
> The effulgent waste drift into sun or star,
> And through vast wilds of elemental strife
> Tracked out the first faint steps of yet unconscious life . . .[36]

This he posted off to the sage with a letter; the letter of a typical young intellectual just finding his way, half-admiring and half-arrogant.

It is safe to say that no one had dared to address a poem to the crabby Herbert Spencer before. The philosopher was too independent a man to welcome flowery praise from a would-be disciple, and he was notorious for his rough handling of people who tried to scrape acquaintance with him. Still, even Spencer was human, and no doubt it is hard to resist the attractions of a poem which speaks of you as one who has "scanned the glittering fields of space" and "gazed through the eons on the fiery sea" of Creation itself. So this time he broke his usual habit and dispatched a dignified and modest reply to the West Indies.

Allen's own letter had been a little disingenuous. He professed to be amazed when Spencer answered, but he had surely anticipated a reply because his next move was to solicit Spencer's help in placing a manuscript in one of the big British reviews. Spencer tried for him, but failed; still, a rapport had been established. The moment he returned to England in the autumn of 1876 he sought out Spencer at his London boarding-house. It was a dramatic moment. As it happened, Allen had forgotten the house number, and was astonished to find on inquiry along the street, that none of the locals had even heard of his hero.

> Great Heavens, I thought, could this happen anywhere else in the world but in England? The greatest philosopher that ever drew breath, the maximum brain on earth, is living in this squareand not a soul in the place has ever heard of him. It was clear that the name awakened no echo in these dense British heads; to ask for Herbert Spencer in his own street was like asking for Jones, Brown, or Robinson. And, indeed, to the last, it was difficult for me to understand the relatively small place in men's minds which was apparently filled by the greatest thinker of this or any other epoch.
>
> At last I found the house; but Spencer was away. I left a card, and wrote a little later, requesting the favor of an interview. I got a gracious reply; would I come and lunch with him? I accepted, of course, all agog at the privilege. On the day appointed I called at the house in Queen's Gardens . . .[37]

And there they met at last. At their first meeting, as Spencer rose from his anatomically designed armchair (his own patent), Allen confessed to being a little disappointed. For a "maximum brain" Spencer was so very *ordinary*. With his smooth, untroubled features, he looked like a confidential clerk.

Allen was always confident of his ability to read the mind's construction in the face, and he thought the forehead was noble but the chin and mouth were weak. Right from the start he was very well aware of Spencer's shortcomings as a man and, indeed, alludes to his "serious moral defects of character," though he does not tell us what they were.

So began an odd relationship which had its ups and downs but somehow held together to the day of Allen's death. Very soon they were on good terms, and met frequently during the short period when Allen was living in London. They would stroll across the park to the Athenaeum club, where Spencer played billiards most afternoons. If Allen is to be believed, he was even given the password permitting entry to the bare room over the Bayswater milk shop that Spencer rented as a study and to which virtually nobody ever went. Spencer's influence on Allen's scientific and philosophical thinking continued unabated to the end. His initial sense that Spencer was blessed with enormous and unique powers grew ever more extravagant as Spencer's star waned quickly toward the end of the century. But one way in which he differed from Spencer was in his manner of life. The philosopher's proud independence and readiness to sacrifice everything to his self-assigned task greatly impressed Allen. Yet though he admired it intensely, no such course was open to him. He had given his hostages to fortune. He had a living to earn.

Chapter 3

Setting out the Stall (1876–1880)

The "Ten Years' Hard Struggle for Bread": Allen as Freelance

Back in England in the cheerless autumn of 1876, Allen must surely have wondered where his life was going. He was jobless, poor, married with a dependent wife, and his thirtieth birthday was on the horizon. He did continue, on and off, with private coaching work at Oxford for four more years. But the job of dinning the same foolish round of Horace and Livy and Latin elegiacs in the heads of useless, eat-all, do-nothing young fellows (as he put it)— fellows who should have been apprenticed to a useful trade years earlier— appealed no longer.

Trying to write for a living appealed a lot more. In his luggage from Jamaica were some draft chapters of a book, but they were part of a treatise on sensory psychology and not at all the kind of thing which a professional author would have thought of tackling. He put that aside for the moment, and started to scribble in earnest while living in digs at Oxford or down at Lyme with his in-laws. He said later that he submitted "a hundred or more magazine articles" on various scientific subjects to editors, only to have every single one of them rejected with thanks.[1] If this is taken literally, he must have submitted most of that hundred in the single year after his return, because his first article was accepted by the *Cornhill* in the following autumn. Could he really have been writing and having rejected two fresh articles every week? Perhaps he meant that he suffered one hundred rejections from various editors.

But even if the number is exaggerated, it does indicate his determination to make his way into the higher journalism. Yet he had no special reason to be optimistic. He had shown no particular aptitude for writing for a semi-popular audience, for money, and against the clock. His only publications had been nothing remarkable for a man who was pushing thirty. They amounted to a handful of poems, stories, and articles, and most of those had appeared nowhere more profitable than a university magazine. And he had just spent the invaluable years of his mid-twenties, when a man secures his first footing, far from the seat of literary power and patronage.

Financial need, poor health, and a distaste for teaching boys, we can guess, were the motives driving him into the toughest sector of late-Victorian authorship: that of the freelance writer, journalist, and literary jack-of-all-trades. In due course Allen would shed any romantic illusions about the fraternity he had joined. "The profession is recruited almost entirely, I believe, from the actual or potential failures of other callings," he would write.

> The man who has knocked in vain at all other doors, or the man who has not capital enough even to approach any other door with the silver key which alone admits to the outer vestibule, takes as a last resource to literature. Some of us are schoolmasters or college tutors; some of us are doctors who failed to draw patients; some of us are "stickit ministers" or disfrocked parsons; a vast proportion are briefless barristers. When a man who knows how to put an English sentence grammatically together has no other resource left in life, he sells himself, body and soul, in the last resort to the public press, and produces the fabric they call literature.[2]

But that outburst came after ten years at the mill, when he had not only grown adept at selling himself "body and soul," but had also been able to mark out a small private zone of activity where he was not for hire. By that time he could afford, emotionally, to entertain a certain flamboyant cynicism about his calling. But in the beginning he was much more naïve that that—naïve enough, indeed, to hope to make a career out of scholarly scientific authorship. Certainly his first book was not written with any eye to the marketplace. He finished it over the winter of 1876/7 at Oxford, and gave it a title—*Physiological Aesthetics*—that he guessed would be quite enough for most people. Even he expected nothing from it but the beginnings of a reputation.

Actually, though, the contents are much less intimidating than the title. What it tries to do is to explain aesthetic judgment in terms of the physiology of the senses. Obviously Allen, no more than anyone else then or now, did not have a truly reductive explanation of aesthetics in terms of neurophysiology. Most of the book simply collates and categorizes a mass of information about how the senses function, and then describes which kinds of stimulation of them we find pleasurable and which disagreeable. Apart from a few vague remarks about nerve pathways in the brain, that is as far as the book goes in meeting the first term of its title. Allen, in this respect, does no better and no worse than Spencer or Darwin, both of whom had been over this ground in the 1850s and 1860s. And Allen's book does have the virtue of being more lively than either.

As might be expected, in attempting to tie down the principles of taste to the physiology of the sense organs—thereby fixing them, implicitly, as objective and immutable—Allen is merely betraying his own cultural and personal prejudices. And as we will see in the case of his travel guides and art criticism written at the far end of his career, Allen did have an endearing certainty about the universality and objectivity of his own tastes. So, for example, in *Physiological Aesthetics* we are told that "sexual feeling . . . defies introduction into Poetry, because the feelings aroused, though they may be pleasurable, obviously fall short of aesthetic disinterestedness. It can only be introduced under a veil of mysterious reverence." Presumably, therefore, if we take pleasure in Rochester or Byron, Donne or Chaucer, despite their signal lack of "mysterious reverence" about sexual feeling, this merely proves that our sensory physiology is out of kilter. Again, asks Allen, what does our physiology make us admire most in architecture? It is "perfect examples of any particular style, age or nation" that give the fullest pleasure: the Parthenon, Diocletian's Palace, and Cologne Cathedral. On the other hand, we feel a "conscious critical disgust" when we contemplate the Brighton Pavilion, the Capitol at Washington or the Albert Memorial. Our senses, or Allen's anyway, are repelled by the "mongrel and meaningless fabric" of such edifices. But if we insist that, in fact, the Brighton Pavilion pleases us because we find it a "perfect example" of the Regency, then Allen can only condole with us over the deficiencies of our sensory apparatus, and move on.[3]

The good points of *Physiological Aesthetics* are ones which would be standing its author in good stead later. Already very evident are the tools essential to a worker in the craft of high vulgarization: a plain, smooth unassertive style, an effortless command of detail, and a gift for striking metaphor, memorable analogy, and concrete illustration. Its weakness is that to which all of Allen's original scientific work is prone: that is, it is wholly Spencerian in its approach. Allen thought of his first book as a contribution to psychology—he calls himself a "psychologist" in it—whereas it is really a compendium of assertions and value judgments under grand but arbitrary headings, with almost nothing in the way of testable hypotheses. There is no doubt that the result is interesting and informative. But there is little meat in it; it goes nowhere. The trouble is that, like Spencer, Allen never seemed to pause to ask whether this kind of activity is, in any useful sense, *doing science*. It was a problem that would recur.

H.S. King, a reputable scientific publisher, took *Physiological Aesthetics*, but Allen had to pay £120 for what was, in effect, a vanity-publishing deal to get it into print. The money came from his Jamaican compensation payment. It was an expensive gamble, for the book sold fewer than 300 copies. But it was not a bad investment. He ended up only about £30 in the red. Reviews were few, but they were respectful. Allen was no longer completely unknown. He had at least the makings of a reputation in scientifically influential circles and, as an expert networker, he made sure his name at least became known to as many members of the intellectual aristocracy as possible.

Emboldened now, he fashioned an article condensing the central thesis of the book and gave it a mildly intriguing title, "Carving a Cocoa-nut." He shows how the impulse to make decorative art can be traced back beyond the origins of humanity into the animal and even the insect worlds. He dispatched this to Leslie Stephen, the gaunt, erudite editor of the *Cornhill*. This time not a rejection slip but a check came back, and the piece appeared in the October 1877 issue. Allen was jubilant. "That was the very first money I earned in literature," he recalled. "I had been out of work for months, the abolition of my post in Jamaica having thrown me on my beam-ends, and I was overjoyed at so much wealth poured suddenly in upon me."[4]

He was being sarcastic, of course, but the *Cornhill* did pay him twelve guineas, calculated at its generous standard rate of a pound a page. Could one make a living by churning out articles for pay like this? It depended how you looked at it. Entire Victorian families, many thousands of them, and (a trustworthy observer noted) "clean, well-fed, well-clothed, and well-mannered" families at that, were well used to living for *two months* on the sum Allen received for that single article. Harold Biffen, the young Realist novelist in *New Grub Street*, could have sustained his monkish existence in a garret for twenty weeks on such an inordinate sum.[5]

But Allen was no monk, and no bohemian either. He was not thinking of taking a pair of back rooms in Islington, and ensuring a regular flow of those twelve-guinea checks was no easy thing. The *Cornhill* had high standards but a sliding circulation. The number of periodicals willing to take articles on the origins of art was, to put it mildly, limited. Still, Allen worked the same vein with several more pieces for the *Cornhill* on related themes. They were close-knit, lucid and packed with lively notions, although they are much stiffer in style than the mature one which Allen eventually devised for himself.

The trouble was that these pieces were all offshoots of *Physiological Aesthetics* and its successor scientific book, the one which Allen was now researching in great detail. This was living on one's fat. What he needed was an outlet for more varied wares. He found it in the *Belgravia*, a middle-brow monthly designed to appeal particularly to the genteel female reader. He started to appear there from April 1878, continuing right through the next decade. For the first time he adopted a pseudonym, "J. Arbuthnot Wilson." The name was a private joke: it formed the acronym "jaw," a slang term of the time for gossipy talk. The *Cornhill* pieces had been unsigned, or appeared over initials only, although of course everyone, or everyone who counted, knew who had written them. But now Allen not only used a pseudonym but devised a semifictive voice to speak for him. When writing on the Thousand Islands region of his birth, for instance, this persona claims that he has never been there before; and in another he asserts that he has lived in Jamaica for years longer than Allen actually did.

The pseudonym was taken to separate his identities as a serious essayist/scientist and as a more frivolous journalist and story-writer. But the use of a fictive narrator hints at darker psychological waters. It is as though Allen wants to half disown what he is doing. It is the first sign of the bifurcation that became the dominant, troubling note of his career. But for the present the attempt was only half-hearted. He retained the "Wilson" identity for a while for fiction, but soon abandoned it for his nonfiction, which he now began to turn out in quantity. For the *Belgravia* in these early years he wrote on almost anything: closely observed travel articles; the merits of American food; the undeserved "romance" of tropical scenery and so on. In the *Belgravia* appeared Allen's first short stories also. He stumbled into fiction by accident, having no idea that it might be more profitable than miscellaneous articles.

Andrew Chatto printed his first effort in July 1878, and encouraged Allen in this new venture. He produced three more over the next eighteen months: a slow start.

Placing articles in the monthlies was not a living, even if one could do it every month (and Allen soon got close to that, even though most editors said it was impossible). He needed more regular hack work. Late in 1877 he joined a group of editors working on an *Imperial Gazetteer of India* under Sir William Hunter. He had to move to Edinburgh to work on this, and stayed there for some months. Eventually the work stretched out to three years of part-time labor spent in the "dreary Indian Statistical Department," and the *Gazetteer* did not appear until 1881. In the documents he worked with, Allen, the colonial, found plenty to reinforce his views about British imperialism. He also took a jaundiced view of Hunter himself, who was nothing better, he thought, than a "literary whitewasher of the Indian Government." This experience bore fictional fruit later.[6]

Once he was back in London he got work for a few evenings a week on a Liberal morning newspaper, the *Daily News*. It was all anonymous and is now lost forever amid the *News*' acres of close-packed, smudgy print, but it included social leaders on questions of the day, natural-history articles, and book reviews. It must have developed further the lightning productivity and versatility which marked him later. Other young men were going through the same apprenticeship there: Richard Whiteing, William Black, and Robert Louis Stevenson among them. But the two who most put him on his mettle were Andrew Lang and George Saintsbury.

Allen, Lang, and Saintsbury had all been students at Merton College, but although the years that the trio had spent there had overlapped a little, none of them had known each other. Andrew Lang, the oldest, born in 1844, had won a Merton fellowship, but he surrendered it in 1875 in favor of marriage and journalism in London. He was the first to settle at the *Daily News*, and very soon his fanciful literary leaders were attracting attention: "fairy tales written by an erudite Puck," was one slightly barbed description.[7]

George Saintsbury, born in 1845, had arrived with a postmastership at Merton four years before Allen. But he had failed to get a fellowship. He left Oxford early in 1868, in Allen's first year, and went school-mastering. He shifted into journalism in 1876, when Lang got him on to the *Daily News*, and started to build a formidable reputation as a critic. In an active career lasting sixty years, he wrote nearly fifty books and hundreds of articles, and edited some 450 editions and selections. (The exact number is unknown.) Saintsbury was never entirely self-employed, as Lang and Allen were. Between 1880 and 1892 he was a subeditor and leading light of the aggressive *Saturday Review*. Allen's novels suffered regularly from the attentions of the "Saturday Reviler." By 1883 Saintsbury's editorship plus his own work and a small private income was bringing in about £1,400 in some years: a splendid sum by any standard, especially for a writer who had no recourse to fiction.

Grant Allen could not possibly have taken much genuine pleasure in the company of a pair of romantic-Tory dreamers and dyed in the wool *littérateurs* like Lang and Saintsbury. For one thing, both of them were a little older than he—in their early thirties. Saintsbury was a perfect example of the "young fogy" who even at Oxford had been ribbed for sounding like a reactionary clubman. He had the highest High Church leanings, and enjoyed getting a little group together to read St. Augustine's *Confessions* out loud.[8] He was a wine and food bore, whereas Allen cared little about either. He was so little the gourmet that in later life he lived on an almost unrelieved diet of oysters and Benger's Food, an invalids' pap.

And then there was the question of their literary manners. Grant Allen's style evolved quite markedly as he matured, but his conscious goal from the start, in nonfiction anyway, was a relatively undecorated, conversational, even breezy style. Saintsbury, like Lang to a lesser degree, cultivated a maddeningly mandarin style larded with quotations and allusions in half a dozen languages. His later work reads more like the clue-list of a difficult crossword puzzle than English prose. Both men were masters of the put-down: flippantly dismissive in Lang's case; saltily contemptuous in Saintsbury's, and neither found much talent to praise in their own age. Such attitudes were far from the generous, even effusive tributes which Allen liked to heap on new writers, including some who manifestly did not deserve it. "They say that I discover a new poet once a fortnight," he said once, with self-mocking exaggeration.[9] His colleagues' shallow disparagement of everything modish and challenging could not possibly have been to his taste. Even more damning— surely the ultimate condemnation from Allen's point of view—was the fact that both men looked on science with blank distaste. "He took to *popular science*," Lang wrote of Allen after his death, with an almost visible shudder, "by which a tiny income may be made by an extremely clever man in this educated age . . . the public does not care whether 'petals are in all cases transformed stamens' or not, and I confess to sharing this *hideous* indifference." Well, of course. It was Lang who summed up Allen's practical scientific enquiries in one expressive noun: "stinks."[10]

Though Saintsbury must have struck Allen as merely preposterous, Andrew Lang was harder to ignore. Though Lang posed as a dilettante he had, after all, freely abandoned academia for journalism. For most of his career he lived on his wits with no salaried post as a safety net. Yet he made the handsome living that Allen felt forever eluded him, simply by becoming a titan of productivity in his chosen areas. And Lang was ubiquitous. Every time Allen appeared in *Longman's Magazine*—and thirty-seven items appeared there—right next to his piece was Lang's regular causerie, "At the Sign of the Ship," which appeared in every single monthly issue for the rest of Allen's life.

Lang's capacity for work was legendary. No doubt Allen heard all the stories: how he could turn out a leading article in a stray half-hour before the dinner bell, or a longish essay during a single ride in a hansom cab. Then there were all those books, nearly eighty of them, eventually. Saintsbury once said that, if collected, Lang's work might have filled nearer 200 than 100 volumes; possibly not a great exaggeration.[11] It's true that Lang's achievement is, on closer inspection, not *quite* as overwhelming as it seems. For one thing, his writing career lasted more than thirty-five years. And although he did work of more lasting value than Allen in folklore and anthropology, his range of interests was narrow and sometimes superficial. Many readers noticed how careless he could be about factual matters, and indeed his reminiscences of Grant Allen are evidence of that. They are surprisingly inaccurate considering they had known each other for so many years. In an obituary he gave the wrong years for Allen's second marriage, his stay in Jamaica and for the date of his first ghost story in *Belgravia*.

Still, the fact is that for his entire career Allen had the provoking Lang right alongside him. It wasn't even as though Lang had to compromise much with the marketplace: he wrote just what he wanted to write, and found it was just what the public wanted to read. And, in the few scholarly interests which they shared, in anthropology and folklore, Lang was taken more seriously than Allen ever was. When Allen's labor of love on the anthropology of religion, *The Evolution of the Idea of God*, appeared in 1897, Lang reviewed it thoroughly. It was a learned, polite, and fair review. It was also destructive. But what he said turned out to be the common judgment on the book.[12]

Although their relations remained fairly good, good enough for Allen to ask Lang to puff at least one of his novels, Lang's self-possessed manner and bantering style of conversation irritated many. An anecdote does suggest something of the tensions between the two men. Just after Allen's death, Lang wrote an obituary for the *Daily News* and related this incident in his typically feline fashion:

> As an instance of his kind temper, I remember that he showed me proof-sheets of a novel in which I appeared as the Villain. The personal portrait (apart from my series of heartless crimes) was flattering, but recognizable; and, at my request (for it could only cause gossip), the villain was altered out of all possibility of recognition.

Unrecognizable? Hardly. The character is very obviously Hugh Massinger of *This Mortal Coil*: a minor poet with a line in cynical, fantastical, and rather tiresome talk. It was an exercise in veiled creative hostility, and it seems that Lang detected this at the time and did not like it at all.[13] But most of the time they preserved a chaffing, joking relationship. They bickered endlessly over Darwinism and psychical research, but they kept away from personalities in their reviews of each other's work. Literary London, or at least their sector of it, was not so large a place, and each man was influential enough to cause the other serious damage; it suited both to be tactful and supportive as far as they could. During the episode of the *Athenaeum* letter in 1892 discussed later, when Allen's mental equilibrium seemed to be teetering for a while, Lang was careful to show him a segment about the matter due to go in his *Longman's* column, offering to pull it out if he found it offensive.

Apart from his work on the *News*, Allen, like the other two, had several more irons in the fire. He joined them, and Robert Louis Stevenson as well, in contributing pieces to *London*, a short-lived Conservative weekly erratically edited by the boisterous, red-bearded, truculent W.E. Henley. Nothing was signed in *London*, which was just as well when some issues were cobbled together entirely by Henley and Stevenson with the printer's devil at the door. Only a little of Allen's work can be identified now. The pieces most obviously from his hand are three vividly unpleasant papers about animal experiments, which appeared in November 1878, giving Allen the chance to deploy his capacity for really ferocious sarcasm.[14] But *London* offered few such opportunities, and Allen could hardly have enjoyed writing for such a stodgy journal. Apart from its Tory politics, the tone of *London* was curiously peevish considering that all the copy came from bright young men. Many a column was filled with "why-oh-why?" laments about prisoners being molly-coddled with mattresses in their cells, barbers who gossip too much, and over-crowded first-class train carriages. Very occasionally there is a more subversive, sly touch. *London's* reviews went in for some really shameles log-rolling, trading on the anonymity of its contributors. It invariably rec-ommended Allen's own articles in the *Cornhill* as earnest and intelligent, and when his second book appeared it was greeted with an outrageous piece of puffery. "We do not know one so audacious, so grave, and so completely competent as the writer of the book before us," it begins, making the work sound like the *Principia* and the *Origin of Species* rolled into one.[15]

Foolery of this kind was rare in the pages of *London*. But still, it was all experience; amusing, no doubt, and quite invaluable for a man entering the cut-throat world of higher journalism. But it was daunting, too. When he sat in the sparsely-furnished *London* office in the Strand, watching Saintsbury, Lang, Henley, and Stevenson vying with each other and limbering up to become the most athletic pens of the day, Allen must have realized just how competitive was that circle which he was trying to enter.

Certainly he fully intended to be in the race. He was working hard and, for the moment, making good money. He could afford to take a house in Ladbroke Grove at 22 Bonchurch Road. The Allens did it out in a light, bright, functional Arts and Crafts style, about which he would soon be writing enthusiastically in the *Cornhill*.[16] Allen was interested in interior design, and in clothes. Some of his wife's dresses were made up from his own designs. His own tastes ran to the quaint, the hand-finished, the quasi-medieval and (later) the Moorish, more or less along the lines set down by Clarence Cook in *The House Beautiful* (1878) and other such guides to the aesthetic home for the perplexed householder eager to be in the swim.

At Bonchurch Road the Allens' child, Jerrard Grant, was born in July 1878, five years after their marriage. This was unusual for the time—about 80 percent of Victorian wives produced a child within a year of marriage—and there were to be no others. Were the Allens early adopters of family limitation? If so, they were part of what was becoming, in their class, a very discreet majority; a major-ity to which Allen would be addressing some acerbic comments in due course.

We may calculate that Allen's annual income from all sources was very briefly £650–700. This was the income of an up-and-coming professional man.

On it, he could run to a terrace in, say, Kensington, with four bedrooms; a cook, a nurse, a parlor-maid; he could afford a month at the sea-side in the summer, and six long weekends in the country.[17] Life looked more promising. But then a familiar Victorian catastrophe loomed. He fell seriously ill.

ILLNESS AND RECUPERATION

Of all the calamities that might crush the professional writer, incapacitating illness was one of the most dreadful. The career of Richard Jefferies, a naturalist, novelist, and countryman who was born the same year as Allen, is a reminder of this. Jefferies had an even shorter life, but while it lasted the two men's careers marched alongside each other. Jefferies contributed nature essays to the *Pall Mall Gazette* in 1877–1880, the same slot that Allen took over when Jefferies vacated it. Had he lived a normal span, Jefferies might have made a decent living from higher journalism padded out with some reasonably marketable novels. But tuberculosis put paid to that, and he and his family were charity cases before the end. All that lay in the future when Allen fell so ill for the first time, but he could very easily have ended the same way, and he needed no precognitive powers to know it.

Allen always had to reckon with his health. He had been a sickly child, and by early manhood was already afflicted with the "lung" that would plague his whole life. He had other worries too. *London* was drifting on to the rocks early in 1879 and folded on April 5. Well before then he was casting about him for work: any literary work at all. In a pathetic letter to Nicholson, now working as a librarian, he begs his friend to help him to find something. "I cannot make money enough to keep us afloat. It strikes me that you may possibly know of some literary hackwork—index making, cataloguing, compiling, or anything of that sort. . . . I am ready to turn my hand to anything."[18] Things must have reached a fairly alarming state to make him swallow his pride and write in such terms as those. George Gissing knew all about literary penury. (He could, indeed, have been visited at that moment in his garret off the Tottenham Court Road, where he was struggling with his first novel and living on lentils). He defined well the fate that, potentially, awaited Allen. A failing writer's wife questions him anxiously:

> "Was there ever a man who did as much as you have done in literature and then sank into hopeless poverty?"
>
> "Oh, many!"
>
> "But at your age, I mean. Surely not at your age?"
>
> "I'm afraid there have been many such poor fellows. Think how often one hears of hopeful beginnings, new reputations, and then—you hear no more. Of course it generally means that the man has gone into a different career; but sometimes, sometimes-"
>
> "What?"
>
> "The abyss." He pointed downward. "Penury and despair and a miserable death."[19]

The abyss beckoned, but Allen was no Edwin Reardon. He knew how to struggle. The scientific and other quality journalism, which he turned out in 1878/9, is already redoubtable in its range. He wrote on psychology for *Mind*; he wrote solid essays on the origins of civilization and on national characteristics for the *Gentleman*'s; on the physiology of nutrition and digestion for the *Belgravia*; he appeared for the first time in the *Fortnightly Review* writing on the puzzle posed for Darwinists by the loss of body hair in humans.

The last was something of a coup for a man of Allen's beliefs. The *Fortnightly* was the prime organ of rational agnosticism, and Allen found John Morley, its editor up to 1882, a congenial spirit. Morley put some book-reviewing Allen's way, trying him out with Stevenson's *Travels with a Donkey in the Cevennes*. Allen hated cruelty to animals and, perhaps because he thought it would go down well with the *Fortnightly*'s liberal readers, referred disgustedly to Stevenson's use on his donkey of a "wooden goad, with its eighth of an inch of pin."[20] Stevenson was becoming a desirable property for editors, and no more general reviews were required after that. Still, he did contribute twenty-nine lengthy articles and review-articles to the *Fortnightly* right through his career, including several of his most incendiary pieces, which probably no one would have taken except Morley's replacement Frank Harris (editor 1886–1894). But then, Allen wrote as well for that pillar of Christian orthodoxy, the *Contemporary Review*, and even for the Society for Promoting Christian Knowledge. In truth, he cared little at this stage whom he wrote for, as long as they printed all his words and paid him promptly.

In addition to all this, and on top of the work for Hunter, he had been slogging away right through 1878 on his second scientific monograph, which was published at the start of the new year as *The Colour-sense*. More than half of this is about the evolution of color vision, but the genesis of the book was a debate of the day about whether humans' color vision has evolved in historical times. The case for this was first put by the classical scholar and prime minister, William Gladstone, in a paper in the *Nineteenth Century* in 1877. Gladstone claimed, by examining color words in classical literature, that the people of 3,000 years ago could distinguish red and yellow, but not blue and green. His subtext here was, of course, that the Darwinian account of human evolution must be wrong, since 3,000 years, or three million for that matter, could never have produced such a complex mechanism as color vision by natural selection alone.

The Colour-sense is a more effective book than Allen's first, because it allowed him to exercise one of his most powerful talents: the mustering and arrangement of a vast array of dry data into a logical, readable, lively narrative. It demolishes Gladstone's theory easily enough, and offers a convincing and testable one of its own: namely, that the lack of highly discriminative color terms arises from the small number of dyes or artificial pigments available in primitive cultures. One wonders, though, if devoting 280 pages to the job was not overkill in the circumstances. After all, the original speculation was a silly one which, as he himself says at one point, a few visits to museums ought to have knocked on the head quickly enough. But it did give him an excuse to bustle about getting in touch with the leading names in biology and anthropology. He and Darwin exchanged several letters about it in April and May 1879 and it is clear that, in the wealthy and influential circle centered on the great naturalist, Allen was becoming a young man to watch. But when the book appeared Allen was shocked to discover that it earned him a miserable £30. "As it took me only eighteen months to write," he reflected sardonically, "and involved little more than five or six thousand references, this result may be regarded as very fair pay for an educated man's time and labour."[21]

It is unlikely that he took such a detached view at the time. He was risking literally killing himself with work. His illness, which was probably bronchitis exacerbated by a tubercular lesion on a lung, grew steadily worse as 1879 wore on. Victorian medicine had nothing to offer except a warmer winter climate. But the order South was one thing; funds were another. Allen replayed the predicament, with some satirical inventions no doubt, in *Philistia*, five years later. Edie Le Breton, wife of the consumptive hero, scrapes together three guineas to get an opinion from the most expensive specialist:

> "Take him south at once [the great man tells Edie], in a coupé-lit of course, and break the journey once or twice at Lyons and Marseilles. Next, as to diet, he must live generously—very generously. Don't let him drink claret; claret's poor sour stuff; a pint of good champagne daily, or a good, full-bodied, genial vintage Burgundy would be far better and more digestible for him. Oysters, game, sweetbreads, red mullet, any little delicacy of that sort as much as possible. Don't let him walk; let him have carriage exercise daily; you can hire carriages for a mere trifle monthly at Cannes and Mentone. Above all things, give him perfect freedom from anxiety." . . . So that was the end of weeping little Edie's poor hardly-spared three guineas.[22]

Fortunately, Allen, unlike Ernest Le Breton, had affluent friends to rally round in this emergency. One of Allen's well-wishers was the young biologist George John Romanes (1848–1894). Romanes and Allen had every reason to take an interest in each other's careers. Not only were they of an age, but also both had been born at Kingston. Romanes's father had been an academic in Canada, but when he inherited a fortune, soon after George's birth, he moved the family to England. The young Romanes went to Cambridge in the same year that Allen went to Oxford. An accomplished student in physiology with ample private means and a ready entry into the best circles which they permitted, Romanes pursued a course very similar to the one that Allen might well have followed given the same advantages.

Romanes's health was never good either, so he could easily sympathize with Allen's plight. Now he joined forces with the philosopher George Croom Robertson, the editor of *Mind*, and the two men raised £202 from fifteen well-wishers, including Lang, Leslie Stephen, and Darwin.[23] The money was enough to send the family off to the Riviera for the entire winter of 1879–1880. That October, the Allens with their baby and a nursemaid took the notorious ambulance train, which trundled south from Paris each day with its cargo of sick and dying patients swaddled in blankets. The trip was horrible. The train had no sleeping cars, dining car nor, probably, any lavatories. They had to overnight at Lyons in a filthy hotel.[24] After another night at Marseilles they finally reached the small town of Hyères, near Nice, one of the oldest of the sanatorium resorts. Living in southern France was cheap then for Britons and getting cheaper. You could hire a cook for £2 a month, and a mid-range furnished apartment cost £64 for the whole winter season. A pair of rooms at the Hotel des Hesperides, *en pension* with everything found, cost even less than that. The hotel was cozy rather than glamorous, but it had splendid views of the mountains and of the glittering sea, some five kilometers away across an intensively cultivated plain. Hyères was rather a backwater at this time because the railway had bypassed it, but there were still fifteen hundred resident British in every stage of decrepitude and recovery.

Sitting on his balcony in the mild, soothing sun, Allen had never felt lazier in his life. "The ordinary course of existence for the invalid world—and we are all invalids—is remarkably unruffled and serene," he reported. "At the hotels, people get up, take their roll and coffee, stroll about till twelve, then have a *table d'hote dejeuner*, and devote the afternoon to a long walk or drive. Dinner at six makes the great event of the day, and a rubber in the public salon occupies them till nine, when they generally melt away to their private rooms."[25] After a few days of this vegetable existence he even dared to weigh himself.

The Allens stayed at Hyères until May 1880, and despite his protestations of laziness he must have put in several hours a day at his desk. Allen was one of those writers whose pens travel daily across the page by reflex action, whatever else is happening in their lives. He wrote a story for the *Belgravia*'s Christmas annual, four substantial articles for the *Cornhill*, fifteen pages of technical evolutionary speculation on "Pain and Death" for Robertson's *Mind*, and a couple of lesser articles for the *Gentleman's Magazine*.

It was hardly a rest cure, to be sure, but rather surprisingly as the winter passed his tubercular symptoms abated and his health was almost fully restored. He was able to resume a titanic working schedule, and remained in good enough shape to sail through the next appalling winter, the worst of the century, without leaving England.[26] Believing that his months in Hyères had saved his life, he wrote much about the charms of the Riviera, including one article that gave some man-of-the-world advice on how to avoid making a fool of yourself at Monte Carlo. A passage from this reveals Allen's new pliancy of style when he was left to his own devices, characterized by a nice balance between easy colloquialism and richer sentences filled with rolling subordinate clauses:

> You have had enough of it, have you? That is well. Let us come away, and go out into the fresh open air. The heat in these rooms is stifling. I am tired of these fat German princesses, these sleek Parisian elegants, these stolid American gamblers. We swing the great door open upon its hinges, and go out into the

corridor, bowed from the room with great dignity by a well liveried attendant. There is plenty of obsequiousness at Monte Carlo for everybody, even if he has lost his last louis.

We emerge once more upon the beautiful terrace, the glorious view, the waving, penciled palm-trees. All around us, the Italian sun is lighting up the lovely coast with brilliant splendour. Bay and rock and mountain look all the more exquisite after that hot and crowded gaming-room. And there, high up on the shoulders of the Turbia, the great Roman tower looks down majestically with a kind of mute contempt on the throng of busy idlers who pour in and out all day through the marble portals of the Casino. It is well to have seen Monte Carlo for once, but one feels it would be a healthier excursion to climb up those grand old ledges and visit the silent monument which still gazes down with such calm serenity upon the motley throng who come so rudely to disturb its peace to-day after twenty centuries of unbroken solitude.[27]

Allen preserves this tone of sardonic detachment throughout the piece, but perhaps his article had some effect because the very next year a society was formed in London to lobby for the closure of Monaco's gambling hell.

THE STRUGGLE RESUMES

Allen's illness was another turning point in his career. He had had to give up the *Daily News* work. (Though he salted down his experiences as a working journalist for fictional retrieval later.) While at Hyères he had celebrated his thirty-second birthday. It was now a question of seeing what his wits could do for him. He was fairly healthy again, but he had had his warning. Was he likely to see old age? It was unlikely. And if he died young, where would his wife and son be? His first priority was family. "I never cared for the chance of literary reputation except as a means of making a livelihood for Nellie and the boy," he wrote later from a more secure vantage point. "I can now make a livelihood easily: and I ought to turn to whatever will make it best."[28] At this early stage his ambition was to make a lot of money quickly. Possibly he weighed his opportunities, assessed his powers and recognized his physical limitations, and decided that the life of a freelance author-journalist offered him the best chance, tenuous and unstable though it was. Even if his planning was not quite as deliberate as that, once he was back in London Allen redoubled his efforts in this dangerous arena.

Superficially, the signs were better now. He had brains, diligence, and the regard of some editors. He had proved that he could write quickly and well about many different things. But could he really make a living with the products he had to offer? And what would the personal cost be? Certainly the first few years of that period marked him for life. The work was fearsomely hard and the pressure to produce relentless. Later, in more prosperous times, he reflected: "I had a ten years' hard struggle for bread, into the details of which I don't care to enter. It left me broken in health and spirit, with all the vitality and vivacity crushed out of me. . . . I would say earnestly to the ingenuous and aspiring—'Brain for brain, in no market can you sell your abilities to such poor advantage. Don't take to literature if you've capital enough in hand to buy a good broom, and energy enough to annex a vacant crossing.' "[29] If the "ten years" is to be taken literally, then it must refer to the period up to about 1887 or 1888, when he was forty. It will help, then, if we pause to examine the competitive but potentially rewarding world that Allen was entering.

Writers' Rewards at the Close of the Century

> *"But, sire, I must live."*
> *(L'Abbé Guyot, excusing himself for having written a libelous pamphlet.)*
> *"I don't see the necessity."*
> *(Le Comte d'Argenson's response).*
>
>   *—Quoted by Voltaire*

Even from the perspective of a century or more, the socioeconomic position of the professional author in late-Victorian England is still a contentious matter. By selecting the evidence it is equally possible to argue that writers had never had it so good either in terms of income or status; or, alternatively, that authorship had become a trade whose rewards were ridiculously low and declining by the year. Indeed, both of these cases were made at the time, and both could sound convincing. Where, then, does the truth lie? Were authors right in feeling exploited, marginalized and underpaid? Or was it, rather, that their expectations of their own worth has risen recently—to unrealistic heights, perhaps? What, in any case, was the rank and role in society that writers "deserved" to occupy? What rewards "ought" to be due to them?

These were difficult questions, not very amenable to reasoned analysis. But authors being an opinionated and articulate breed, the questions were thoroughly aired anyway throughout the twenty years of Allen's active literary life. The period is neatly bracketed by the appearance of Trollope's *Autobiography* (1883) at one end and Arnold Bennett's *The Truth about an Author* (1903) at the other: those two study-confidentials that shocked and titillated readers with their meticulous and unromantic accounts of their authors' working habits and rewards. Over the period between, dozens of articles and guidebooks investigated why writers wrote, how much they were paid for doing it, and where the best rewards were to be had. One locus of discussion was the Society of Authors, founded by Walter Besant in 1883/4, especially after its monthly mouthpiece *The Author* started to appear from May 1890. A great talking-point was the publication of *New Grub Street* in the following year, as it supplied a fine occasion for the stoics to pit themselves against the breast-beaters in the *Author*'s columns. According to the stoics, everybody knows that authorship is the only profession where even the genuinely talented often cannot make a living; so why the fuss? In fact, doesn't the new notion of treating writing as a trade, implying that a living wage can be had from it, itself encourage false expectations? Andrew Lang, that happy man, thought Gissing had over-supplied his novel with wretched cases.

This drew indignant rebuttals claiming that the Olympian Lang knew nothing of the habits of the "unattached journalist." (An unfair charge in Lang's case; Lang was attached to no one.) "What of the horror of a slack season, when nothing is going on except the unhappy journalist's appetite?" wailed one correspondent. "What of the unexpected collapse of the 'column' which brings in the modest sum of one guinea weekly?"[30]

What indeed? What answer could there be, except that the world owes no one a living, not even the author? Such, more or less, was the position Allen himself took up. Whatever reservations he may have had about his master Herbert Spencer's *laisser-faire* economics in other contexts, he seemed prepared to accept its iron edicts for his own trade. He did not rebel against the economic plight of the writer, nor did he expect it to be ameliorated; his view was that either one accepted it or got out. Geniuses might chart their own course, but even they had either to sell or be subsidized one way or the other. Allen's kind of author had to supply the market just as the baker or grocer does. One cannot dictate to it, any more than the baker can elevate the taste of the back streets by having croissants in his basket instead of the homely quartern loaf. He took a similar Spencerian line on publishers, whom he regarded as humane businessmen who usually did what they could for their authors—when they could afford it. His sheer delight in paradox, always a strong element in his nature, infuriated his fellow-authors with its talk of "the harmless, necessary publisher, that most indispensable of go-betweens, that most justifiable of middlemen" who is made "the innocent scapegoat of literary economics."[31]

The often acrimonious debate about sweating publishers ebbed and flowed in the general press as well as the literary organs, because many people were interested in hearing about it. For, well paid or not, authors were important people. Throughout Allen's career, writers of all stripes filled a peculiar social role in the society of English-speaking countries; one which they had never held before and have never regained since. In the period bounded roughly by Forster's Education Act of 1870 at one end, and the first challenge to the world of print by the cinema at the other, writers, even quite minor writers, were celebrities. Their slightest doings and most trivial opinions were publicized, not only in the newspapers but in what were effectively fan magazines.

Robertson Nicoll's *Bookman* (1891), for instance, is often described as a trade journal for booksellers. But it was more than that. Month after month, on large, richly illustrated, coarse pages like blotting-paper, this was a magazine that ministered to a broad range of quasi-literary appetites. It chronicled the small beer of writers' private lives: we hear, for example, that Lady Somebody is "recruiting" at Bournemouth before starting her new serial for the *Belgravia*. It also supplied ticker-tape information about the literary stock market (Kipling is steady; Hardy climbing; demand for biographies is tapering off). Then, at a rather more elevated level than the *Bookman*, stood the weekly *Athenaeum* and the *Academy*. Both were grab-bags of information about the printed word and its producers. Apart from reviewing almost everything worth noticing, they offered erudite articles whose very titles sound like parodies ("The Etymology of 'Elope'") and a superior class of gossip ("Dr Buelbring has gone to Dublin to collate the Trinity College MSS of an early Psalter").

If literature was being commodified and repackaged for the mass market, so were the authors themselves. And not only in their own eyes, but in the eyes of their readers. Furthermore, the working space of these tradesmen was usually a room in a private house. The sites of work and of domesticity were blurred in their case, and it is not surprising that the house or living-space became metonymic of authors themselves. The *Bookman* offered portraits, and line-cuts of authors' country houses. The general picture magazines invited their readers into the holy of holies, the Study itself—the writing chair, the desk and its accoutrements, the prints on the walls—as though these objects had soaked up the *mana* of the author. At a higher level, it's notable just how minutely attentive *New Grub Street* is to interiors. We move from Biffen's garret with its scrap of weedy carpet, the three inches of head-room, the chair-bedstead and fireless grate; to Reardon's flat with its eight flights of stairs, the stove behind a screen, the cheap engravings near the writing-table; and finally to Milvain's select dinner-party for six in Bayswater, with a table of silver and crystal presided over by his "matchless" wife.

In real life, authors who knew what they were about actively conspired with their readers to make this metonymic transference. Allen himself did it once, in "My Lares and Penates"—we note the high-flown title for what is, in fact, a tour of his Dorking house. He concludes with an elaborate appeal for tolerance:

> Accept it, I beg of you, not in any carping or unfriendly spirit, but as the confidential afternoon small-talk of a humble English journeyman journalist, anxious to exhibit to you something of his own life, as an illustrative specimen of the life of the class in which he is included. Literature in England (save for a few great names) is a hard trade, but it has, by the way, its incidental consolations. I have tried here to put a few of them before you. Do not think too harshly of me for my garrulous confidences . . .[32]

A more discreet way of backing into the limelight it would be hard to imagine.

This piece was written for Americans, but the demands of British readers were not greatly different. Their pattern of consumption varied, but the most important thing was that they were all avid consumers of text, and that there were more and more of them. Text was the supreme conduit of culture at a time when some of the traditional sites of oral culture—the sermon, the public meeting, the salon, the reception, the soiree—were either losing their appeal or had never been accessible to people who were now eager and sufficiently educated to be informed and entertained. An array of new technologies were able to put more printed words in front of more people more frequently and more cheaply than ever before, and in ever more attractive formats. From the lowest class to the highest, every literate Victorian read something, and by the century's end nearly everyone was literate to some degree. And these readers had more to spend on their solace and instruction. Books and the more serious periodicals were bought or borrowed mostly by people in the income band between £150–400 a year, and the number of people in that band had tripled by the time Allen died. As the ever-cheerful Walter Besant put it, "reading, which has always been the amusement of the cultivated class, has now become the principal amusement of every class." And that, he thought, was a good thing, as it kept people from more vicious pleasures.[33]

The sheer size of the reading market in the English-speaking world guaranteed that some authors would grow very rich. The burrowings of several generations of biographers have revealed in fine detail the finances of the literary giants—or, at any rate, the big-selling names—of the Victorian age. If we want to know how Dickens or George Eliot or Thomas Hardy or Mrs. Humphry Ward made their fortunes from the pen, it is easy enough to satisfy our curiosity. Some of the figures are extraordinary. John Ruskin managed to get through an enormous inheritance—he gave a lot of it away—but his books were still bringing in £4,000 a year at the time of his death in 1900. Tennyson received 300 guineas for a single ballad in the *Nineteenth Century*, a startling earning capacity for a poet and one that allowed him to shrug off as simply too tiresome an American lecture tour, which had promised to net him £20,000.

It was the small body of best-selling novelists who built up the most impressive bank balances. We gasp at the stupendous £10,000 that Longman paid Disraeli for *Endymion* in 1880. George Eliot had an income of about £5,000 a year in 1873—more than the top echelon of barristers could command, or a society physician. Earnings rose steadily up to the end of the century and beyond. The British and American serial rights alone of Kipling's *Captains Courageous* went for £5,500 in 1896, which was then the highest price ever paid by a magazine for fiction. These were the literary millionaires of the day, but even at a lower level novel-writing could pay very well. The forgotten James Payn, a sub-Dickensian talent of huge energy, and very popular, is said to have earned a steady £1,500 by his pen year in and year out. This was a very fine income indeed when a family could live in solid upper-middle-class comfort on half that.

The prospect of ending dismally as a drudge may have dissuaded some people from taking up the literary trade, but the chance of making at least a competence by sitting at one's own desk for a few hours a day spurred others on. At the census of 1881, when Grant Allen's career was gathering steam, six thousand people in England and Wales defined themselves as "authors, editors, journalists, reporters." By 1891, when he was pulling hard at full throttle, the number had grown to about eight thousand people. Just after his death, in 1901, it was eleven thousand. So, speaking very roughly, the number of people who were trying to make a living from the printed word doubled during the active phase of his career, and this may be a considerable understatement. Another estimate claimed 14,000 men and women in London "lived" by writing in 1888.[34] It is very unlikely that many of these really lived exclusively by the pen. Anthony Trollope's optimistic assertion, in his *Autobiography*, that, if a man can equip himself with a table, a chair, pen, ink, and paper, he can start his trade without a moment's delay, must have sent hundreds off to the literary diggings. Not many paused to notice that, at the particular point in his career to which he is referring, Trollope was a salaried official in the post office. He was fifty-two before he felt confident enough about his authorial powers to resign. And that was characteristic of the generation preceding Allen's. Few people had expected to make a living out of authorship. In Isaac D'Israeli's *Calamities of Literature*, a splendid compendium of disaster published in 1812, not the least "calamity" he considers is that of having to write expressly for money at all.[35] Traditionally, writing had been a side-line. The truth of Walter Scott's maxim had seemed self-evident: literature is a good stick but a bad crutch. Only three groups of people who lived entirely by the pen were exempted from this principle in the mid-nineteenth century, and they were all small: first, journalists who were more or less permanently on the staff of magazines and newspapers, like G.A. Sala; second, the penny-a-liners who supplied much of their copy and felt lucky if they escaped destitution for another week; and third, the household names at the top: Scott (who was the exception to his own rule), Byron, Collins, Dickens, Disraeli, Eliot, Ruskin, and so on.

Even in the last part of the century unassisted professional authorship rarely paid a living wage, except for a talented and popular few. Taking a sample of Grant Allen's close contemporaries, it is surprising to discover just how rarely it did so. (We may define as "close contemporaries" those who were born around mid-century and reached or began to climb to the apogee of their reputations near the end of it.) Financially speaking, nearly all of them fit well enough into four categories. First, there were those who came from moneyed families: W.H. Mallock (b.1849), R.L. Stevenson (b.1850), George Moore (b.1852) and Oscar Wilde (b.1854) all belong to this group. Henry James (b.1843) does not precisely fit into this category, but he has affinities with it. Thanks to Michael Anesko, we know a great deal about James's literary earnings. Though he came from a wealthy family, James was dependent on his pen until the age of fifty, and Anesko's figures permit the calculation that he earned an average of £869 a year during the period of Grant Allen's active writing career; certainly more, but probably not greatly more, than Allen's own average over those years.[36] In other words, his rewards were considerable but hardly princely, especially considering his productivity coupled with the total dedication he had for his art. But James was in a very privileged position. As an American national resident in England he enjoyed copyright protection in both countries, and thanks to his transatlantic connections he earned much of his income from serialization in the most lucrative portions of the American periodical market, like the *Atlantic* and *Harper*'s. In addition, from 1893 until his death in 1916 James had quite a large private income. Had he lacked this, and if he had suffered from the attentions of marauding U.S. publishers and editors who expropriated his work for nothing—as Grant Allen, a Canadian in England, did for most of his career—then the figures tell their story: the older James would have lived and died a relatively poor man.

Second, there were those who married money as youngish men, so that they were free to expand their literary gifts in ways that would otherwise have been difficult: Wilde, Meredith and Rider Haggard (b.1856) are examples. Further down the social scale, W.H. Hudson (b.1841), the natural-history essayist and novelist, was largely supported by his wife's boarding house and, eventually, a Civil List pension. Almost all, if not quite all, Victorian women writers were in this class, too: they had at least a roof over their head and clothes on their back supplied by a husband or father, even in the few cases, like Mrs. Humphry Ward or Mrs. Oliphant, where they were more than able to supply their own.

Third, there were those whose literary endeavors were cushioned by other earnings. Walter Besant (b.1836) was a secretary; Edmund Gosse (b.1849) was for years a civil servant at the Board of Trade; W.E. Henley (b.1849) held a series of paid editorial chairs heavily subsidized by rich backers; Hall Caine (b.1853) started as a secretary and journalist; Conan Doyle (b.1859) had a doctor's modest earnings.

Surprisingly, for the exceptional person who could secure an endless flow of work, a semi-permanent berth as a straightforward book reviewer could provide the foundation of a decent living. George Saintsbury reviewed in his "spare" time and boasted that he could produce a lively review of a book on any subject whatsoever, averaging £3.10s for an evening's reading and a morning's writing.[37] This was about the weekly wage of a capable bank official and more than double a skilled workman's wages. Here was the basis of a good annual income, if one could keep up the murderous pace and if one were prepared to tolerate the draining effect on one's creativity. Grant Allen added that particular string to his bow at an early date. For most of his first decade of labor he wrote a book review first thing in the morning on every single day of the year. It must have supplemented his income considerably, but as nearly all of it is untraceable now, it is hard to say by how much.

All this serves to reinforce the closing assessment of J.W. Saunders in his socioeconomic study, *The Profession of English Letters*: "It was an age when the possession of private means, apart from professional earnings, was an almost indispensable asset in the preservation of integrity."[38] Integrity was not always the key issue, in fact. Saunders' last phrase might well be qualified to read: "the preservation of integrity *or of a gentlemanly way of life*." Those who were determined to retain a foothold in the middle classes at any cost soon discovered that selling out was no easy thing. The case of Joseph Conrad is particularly instructive. Peter McDonald's striking term for Conrad's stance in the opening phase of his career is "principled aloofness." Conrad refused to publish in the down-market *Pearson's Magazine* when invited to do so, on the grounds that his story "was much too good to be thrown away where the right people won't see it." He was able to take this stand because he had received two separate inheritances, so that in 1895 he was a comfortably affluent bachelor who could write as he wished. But things deteriorated quickly after that. He lost most of his capital in 1896, and he got married. He was forced to compromise. As McDonald says, "he had always held that 'shallowness, imbecility, hypocrisy', not 'pure art', succeeded. The only difference now was that he was prepared to enter the game." Conrad explained his new strategy to his friends in insouciant terms. He had started, he said, to write stories with "lots of second-hand Conradese" in them, and "henceforth my concern shall be to discover and steadfastly pursue a dishonest and profitable course." Conrad makes it sound like child's play, but he soon discovered that it wasn't. Humiliatingly, his total earnings up to 1897 averaged out to less than the thirty shillings a week of the skilled workman. He received a Royal Literary Fund grant in 1902. If that was shallowness, imbecility, hypocrisy, and dishonesty at work, then Conrad could not make them pay any better than he could his principled aloofness. Conrad was pleased to call Grant Allen "a man of inferior intelligence" whose work was "not art in any sense."[39] Perhaps, after he was forced to rely for a while on charity, he changed his mind about Grant Allen's intelligence. Writing for the crowd is not as easy as it may seem.

There was one other recourse for any writer who wanted to maintain the balancing-act somewhere between purist and profiteer. It could pay well, and so, in theory anyway, it could free up time for less profitable labor. But it had to be exploited to the full, and it demanded skills that Conrad, Gissing, and many other accomplished novelists lacked. That recourse was producing miscellaneous periodical journalism on a freelance basis.

Writing for the Monthlies

Perhaps only those who have tried it know what a serious tale of scattered articles at five and ten, and even twenty guineas each it takes to build up a respectable income.[40]

Grant Allen knew it well; knew it with bitter intimacy. For he belonged to the fourth and last group we need to consider, and that was the hardest-driven of all. It comprises those who had to live by the unsubsidized labors of the pen, and were prepared to write anything, including fiction, when it suited them; but whose natural bent and interests lay in criticism, philosophical speculation, political theory, science writing, or belles-lettres. In effect, that meant working for the weekly or monthly magazines. The rate of payment for top-quality pieces was not ungenerous—by present standards it was very generous—but to make a good living in this fashion demanded the skill and energy to produce with untiring regularity. Very few writers hauled themselves up from nowhere into the comfortable realms of the late-Victorian solid middle class by unsubsidized labor of this kind. Fewer still stuck the course from first to last as fully self-employed workers who were never on anybody's payroll as an employee. Many aspired to it, but never made it because they lacked the stamina, or they were not sufficiently astute in handling their affairs, or they were not prepared, or not able, to supply the market in ways that might have paid them more.

That such people existed at all in any number was a new and distinctive phenomenon. For the first time in literary history it became a reachable goal for people of middling talents and ambition to make a respectable living by this sort of pen-labor alone. A fictional specimen of this new species is Alfred Yule, a character in *New Grub Street*. He is about fifty and lives in a terrace house in Camden Town. His household consists of his wife, a daughter, and a servant. His income "has never exceeded two hundred and fifty pounds, and often—I mean even in latter years—has been much less."[41] The Yules are neither poor nor rich, but penury always beckons. Yule commutes regularly to the British Museum library. His life, effectively, is that of a suburban clerk. He is a lettered Mr. Pooter. There is nothing to distinguish him from the other occupants of his street, except for one peculiar thing. His household is sustained by the sale of articles on subjects like the minor French dramatists, or contemporary English writing styles, or James Harrington, the seventeenth-century author of *Oceana*. Never before, we may safely say, had anyone made a living entirely by such means. Yule is an historical curiosity, made possible by socioeconomic changes in the production and consumption of printed matter. When he had started his career, presumably in the later 1850s, the market was already becoming so fragmented and specialized that even such limited wares as his could supply a hard-working pen-driver with a living wage.

Yule writes books as well—though not fiction—but the mainstay of his career has been the periodicals. It is true that his is a fading career, for by the early 1880s the particular vein he has worked for thirty years is almost exhausted. Tastes are shifting and Yule cannot meet them; he is doomed to extinction. But other pens had done a great deal better than Yule over the same years. In the *Belgravia* of January 1881 there appeared an insouciant article entitled "Does Writing Pay? The Confessions of an Author." In remarkably swaggering style, the anonymous writer reports on a literary career, which is, we gather, coming to an end at about the same time as Alfred Yule's. This man, too, describes himself as a *littérateur*, as Yule would have done, but his range has been infinitely greater and the rewards he assesses, in a studied understatement, to have been "a fair return for the off-hand, rattling, and somewhat careless attention bestowed." And it has not been a full-time attention either: "Anon" is a barrister. He has produced biographies, novels, tales, essays, criticism, and plays. He has written advertising copy and been a roving reporter on the Continent. Our barrister concludes that no intelligent person needs to suffer want with their pen at the ready:

> As for my essays, sketches, descriptions, they are simply innumerable. It is agreeable work, and so lightly done. You covet something, or are extravagant to the tune of five pounds. You sit down for a morning (having found a subject in your last walk), and the debt is paid. . . . Adding all up, I should fix my total earnings at about fourteen thousand pounds, of which I retain, alas! but fifteen hundred duly and securely invested.[42]

How delightful it sounds! And though "Anon" was retiring from the scene, the game was not over. The periodical market was still there, still offering, at least to the naïve eye, glittering opportunities for the tyro. It was still natural for new authors to turn first to the generously paying monthly periodicals, as Allen did at the outset.

Allen had started with the two most necessary skills: speed and versatility. The second was essential, for, as Margaret Beetham has reminded us, the "text" of a Victorian periodical is not, properly considered, the individual numbers but the whole run. To stay in business the editors' objective had to be not so much to satisfy consumers with their single purchase but to stimulate them sufficiently to buy the next issue. The periodical was the first consumer item with a distinct "use-by" date built into it.[43] That is why even the staider monthlies offered their readers a dizzying miscellany of topics in each issue. For example, in the course of a single six-month period in 1885 the reader who had the stomach for it could read Matthew Arnold's "Comments on Christmas," or follow Andrew Lang making an erudite comparative study of ghost stories, or tackle something very solid on "The Hittites." Then there was someone anonymous on "The Decay of Irish Humour," a potted biography, "Samuel Johnson," by Edmund Gosse; someone else on "The Future of Electricity and Gas." The reader could watch the Catholic anti-Darwinian biologist Mivart tying himself into knots trying to reconcile his religion and science under the title of "Organic Nature's Riddle," or swallow "Some Turkish Proverbs." After a dose like that, Percy Greg's advice on one's best choice of drug in "Stimulants and Narcotics" may well have gone down well. This is only a tiny fraction of what was on offer in half of a single Victorian year. The Niagara of print grew so overwhelming that those shrewd men W.T. Stead and George Newnes realized that there was a readership prepared to pay for someone to undertake a preliminary stage of mastication. Their *Review of Reviews* (1890) boiled the mental foodstuff down a stage further, for those who could not even find enough time to take the serial diet straight.

The digestive metaphors are appropriate. There was plenty of hostility directed at the desultory reading habits that this seemed to encourage, and epithets were hurled against the sort of reader who was force-feeding himself on such a diet: it resulted, it was said, in a stuffed "sausage of a man" who is likely to suffer, mentally, from a "desolating dyspepsia."[44]

Such opinions ran right across the cultural spectrum. At a more elevated level of cultural commentary, Matthew Arnold would not have used the metaphor of mental indigestion, but his concerns were similar. In a well-known passage, Arnold, who was ambivalent anyway about the new democratic forces unleashed by Reform, spoke of the New Journalism—which he took to be the most characteristic product of recent political developments—as so corrupting the public that it was becoming feather-brained and incapable of any serious thought at all. It is not always noticed that Arnold's scornful phrases themselves appeared in an article in the *Nineteenth Century*, and that denouncing the popular taste earned him fifteen guineas or so.

Arnold's comments appeared in 1887 when the boom in the periodical market seemed unstoppable, and it's unlikely that the nimble young men (and a few women) who were jostling for a position in it knew or cared about his anxieties. Such people were more streamlined versions of Alfred Yule.

They aspired to Kensington and Bayswater rather than Camden Town, and their gossip was more fashionable, but they were in the same line of descent. They were still bowing to the twin deities of Bread and Cheese, but now they were doing it more deliberately, with a more acute sense of business to be done; in short, as a trade. As the boundaries between the novel, the short story, belles-lettres, the causerie, the interview, the leader, the "middle" and the outright gossip column blurred and merged, there was good money to be made, providing writers were flexible enough to produce distinctive, varied, sellable work in the new shadowy borderlands where committed artists and down-at-heel ex-scholars rubbed shoulders with slick young graduates and shameless hacks. In her novel *A Writer of Books* (1898) Emily Morse Symonds ("George Paston") presents a hard-boiled woman journalist, Miss Nevill, who is one of this new breed. Each of her articles is the product of four days' work or so, and if imagination flags she is not above "faking up" something by lifting the raw materials from old magazines. Then she offers it to descending levels of the market until it sells: first to one of the illustrated monthlies, then, if it bounces back from there, to one of the weeklies, and finally, as a last resort, she chops it into "pars" not exceeding one inch of print for one of the scrappy papers like *Tit-Bits*. Such a piece might earn anything from five guineas down to five shillings, depending on its final resting-place. Such are "the secrets of the prison-house," according to Miss Nevill.

Nor was her type rare in real life. An excellent example is afforded by the career of Arthur St. John Adcock (1864–1930). Adcock actually belonged to the next generation, but his career is otherwise strikingly similar to Allen's. If there was ever a literary all-rounder, Adcock must surely take the palm. In describing how he reached prosperity, in an essay titled "The Literary Life," written in his fifties just before the war, he starts by quoting no less a person than Grant Allen himself. "It did not encourage me," he says, "when, at a very early stage of my career, I read an article by Grant Allen in which he had roundly asserted that a man had better sweep a crossing than take to literature."[45]

Allen made that discomfiting proposition in an article in the *Idler* at a point where he himself is glancing back at his early years. When it appeared, in 1892, Arthur Adcock was twenty-eight years old and just about to abandon a minor but secure clerkship for the freelance life. His is one of the most impressive cases on record of the writer who started with literally nothing; no supportive family, no university friends, no private means, no semi-sinecure in government employ. His only concession to security was to take a part-time post working for two days a week as an assistant editor for an obscure trade journal. For the rest, he trusted to a moderate talent and a heroic persistence. He had two rules. The first was never to have fewer than twenty manuscripts going the rounds of editors simultaneously. The second was never to let a rejected piece lie on his table overnight. He claimed that he had placed *five thousand* articles and stories—all but five or six items of everything he had written—in this fashion. Adcock was no genius, and he never enjoyed any sudden breakthrough into prosperity. He simply went on screwing a living out of the market by putting out two books a year come what may, and laboring at literally any pen-task that he could get hold of. It is pleasant to record that Adcock found a haven in the last few years of his life as the editor of the *Bookman*. It was a job that must have suited him perfectly. Such a career shows that a little talent coupled with extraordinary diligence could raise the miscellaneous author into prosperity under those peculiar end-of-century publishing conditions.

It was inevitable under such brutally demanding conditions that social envy and naked ambition should become the driving force, not perhaps of genuine creativity, but certainly of productivity. "Let me give you a useful hint," says Jasper Milvain—a smoother and nastier Arthur Adcock—to Marian Yule in *New Grub Street*. "If ever I seem to you to flag, just remind me of the difference between these lodgings and a richly furnished house. Just hint to me that so-and-so, the journalist, goes about in his carriage, and can give his wife a box at the theatre. Just ask me, casually, how I should like to run over to the Riviera when London fogs are thickest. You understand? That's the way to keep me at it like a steam-engine."[46] The house, the carriage, the theater box, and the excursion abroad: for the new tradesman, these trappings were the golden markers on the upward path.

Fragmentation in the Periodicals Market Place

But for many, no matter how hard they tried, the path never led upward at all. It is easy enough to paint a much more dismal picture of what probably awaited the young aspirant. We know something about "the wrecks," as Walter Besant called them with fine scorn: the ones "who now live sordid lives, doing the lowest drudgery of literary work for the pay that is tossed to a drudge."[47]

There was, for example, the reality of how all those periodicals were filled. Even the quality ones had a tiny editorial staff and few salaried writers. Most of the great effusion of print was being poured out by literary soldiers of fortune like Grant Allen. The relation between them and their employer the editor was entirely one-sided. Although the demand for good material was insatiable, the supply far outstripped it. Some editors had around 3,000 unsolicited manuscripts a year to choose from, and a surprising number of periodicals never paid their contributors anything at all, subsisting entirely on the labors of writers who worked for glory more than gain. Such Incursions of the Amateur was one of the two main causes that drove down authorial wages, according to Allen's own analysis in a brilliant essay, which might well have been written a century later. "If a great doctor, a well-known soldier, a popular painter, a familiar singer or actor or beauty writes a book, it sells, not only as well as the average book of the professional author, but a great deal better," Allen commented bitterly.[48] The net effect was that literary products of every quality fetched a very cheap price. The only remedy, the only hope, was unremitting hard work.

But in an environment as competitive as this, even hard work could not buffer one against the psychological punishment. One manual by a working journalist, who sounds as though he has been through the mill himself, warned that the tyro "must be prepared for some of the most bitter and possibly the most humiliating disappointments that it is possible for the lot of humanity to come in contact with."[49] Most writers of spirit rebelled against such requirements as these sooner or later. Arnold Bennett, who endured it for some years, finally got his own back in a torrent of self-loathing:

> The freelance is a tramp touting for odd jobs, a pedlar crying stuff which is bought usually in default of better. . . . His attitude is in essence a fawning attitude; it must be so; he is the poor relation, the doff-hat, the ready-for-anything. He picks up crumbs that fall from the table of the "staff" . . . and the shame of the free-lance is none the less real because he alone witnesses it—he and the postman, that postman with elongated missive, that herald of ignominy.[50]

A fawner careless of kicks so long as pence follows, a doff-hat waiting for a long envelope containing the editor's regrets: the picture is not appealing. Few people could submit themselves to this doleful regime with the resignation of St. John Adcock. It took a special type of temper to boast, as Adcock did with a kind of proud masochism, that "until the last six or seven years practically all [my] work has been sent in uninvited, with stamped envelopes enclosed for its return if it were found unsuitable."[51] And that was when Adcock was in his forties and a veteran with fifteen books under his belt!

For their part, editors, not surprisingly, downplayed the amount of damage they inflicted on their contributors' egos and concentrated on the economics of the business. They sounded the same pessimistic note, however. All experienced editors said that trying to make even a bare living by writing for the monthly periodicals was more than difficult; it was next to impossible. No one had a grasp of the marketplace better than the editor W.T. Stead. By 1892 he had an unrivalled knowledge of the economics of the trade, and he claimed that he could count on the fingers of one hand the number of contributors who made even £200 a year from the magazines. A fellow editor spelt out the facts of the freelancing life in this fashion:

> Do the monthly magazines offer better rewards? If in one or other of them a single writer made one monthly appearance (and what a brilliant writer he would be!), the result would certainly be less than £150 per annum; yet the amateur, seeing that writer's name in the *Cornhill* one month, in *Macmillan's* the next, in *The Contemporary* the month after, would, perhaps, imagine him to be rolling in wealth.[52]

Presumably the calculation was based on a hypothetical twelve contributions at about £12 at time. Obviously an income of under £150 a year was intolerable for anyone who had the brains and resourcefulness in the first place to make that "one monthly appearance" as regularly as clockwork. Even Walter Besant's sunny optimism deserted him when he estimated the opportunities in the monthlies market: "let them be a help, but not a means of livelihood, if you value your reputation, your independence, and your self-respect."[53]

He particularly warned against supplying papers of literary history and criticism, which he regarded as a sinking market. In 1892 Besant went to the trouble of sampling 800 articles published over a three-year period in some of the leading magazines. He found they were produced by about seventy different writers, who averaged no more than four papers a year each. Like Stead, he drew the obvious conclusion. "One cannot, therefore, live by writing for the monthlies."[54]

But why should one have to? retorted the optimists in turn. The traditional monthlies were no longer the only outlet for one's wares. And they surely had a point, when one contemplates the general buoyancy and fragmentation of the market. Much earlier in the century it had been enough for those heavy-weights, the *Edinburgh* and the *Quarterly*, to slug it out just four times a year for the Whig and the Tory interest. It was in the second half of the century that the new quality monthlies had supplanted them, and, having inherited the solid reputation of their predecessors, they were still going strong. But now new weekly and daily contenders, quicker and lighter on their feet, were bouncing one after the other into the ring. By the 1890s the rush of journals of all descriptions had become a torrent, a fantastic profusion. They catered for the broadest range of interests and levels of sophistication, to a degree that social historians are even now only beginning to appreciate. Simple statistics capture the essence of the situation. In 1870, just 626 magazines appeared regularly on the news stands of Britain; by 1900, after thirty years of relentless growth, the reader had the choice of 2,446 monthlies and weeklies. London alone supported more than a dozen daily newspapers in 1890, and there were 150 more in the provinces. Collectively they consumed vast quantities of non-news material, and new kinds of middlemen had sprung up to service them: agents like A.P. Watt, wholesalers like Tillotson's Fiction Bureau, the National Press Agency and the Northern Newspaper Syndicate. They were increasingly the prime movers in a commodity market where manuscripts were bought and sold like pork bellies in Chicago, and with the same dispassionate efficiency.

Walter Besant may have been gloomy about the monthlies, but he saw plenty of openings elsewhere in the New Journalism. The number of papers "is simply enormous; there seems no end to them," he crowed. Some of the weekly penny papers had circulations in the millions, and all were vying to get the best fiction, the most striking articles. "They offer," said Besant

> a means of subsistence—not a mere pittance, but a handsome income—to hundreds of writers. Out of one office alone there is poured every week a mass of fiction representing as much bulk as an ordinary three-volume novel. The daily papers with their leading articles; the high-class weeklies, such as the *Saturday Review*, the *Spectator*, the *Athenaeum*, the *Guardian*, the *Speaker*, and a few others, with their leaders political and social and their reviews, give occupation to a large number of the best literary men and women, and the popular weeklies employ a much larger number of the rank and file.[55]

It was a seductive picture. Even the hardened professionals were half in love with the fable themselves, or at least were willing to countenance it.

Grant Allen could hardly have been more skeptical about the likely rewards of literary activity, but even he permits several of his heroes, when poverty looms, to rescue themselves by going out and buying pen, ink, and paper. Toward the end of his career he wrote colorfully about this avalanche of print as he had seen it gathering speed and bulk in his own lifetime. In his boyhood, he recalled, "the Christmas number of the *Illustrated London News*, with a coloured plate of bluff King Hal, after Sir John Gilbert, sufficed for some thirty millions of Britons at home and in the Colonies." Now, forty years later:

> Now that there are sixty millions we might reasonably expect to find the *Illustrated* supplemented by one rival—the *Graphic*. But how about this pink and blue invasion of Christmas numbers innumerable—the *Gentlewoman*, the *Lady, Black and White, St Paul's, Truth*, the *Penny Illustrated*—a round dozen of imitators? And then the magazines! the double Christmas numbers! The *Gentleman's Annual, Phil May, Good Cheer*, the unco'guid, the world, the flesh, and the devil! Every variety of creed or taste is represented; every form of chromo-lithography is pressed into the service. You can be domestic or wicked or intermediate as you will.[56]

Allen titled this article "Depression," and his chief subject is the severe economic downturn of the mid-1890s. Allen's title cannot avoid having, in his personal context, a mildly smug connotation. His main point is the same paradoxical one George Orwell would be making about another Depression in a later decade: that, when hard times come, people turn to cheap luxuries; and for the Victorians the bright, cheerful comforts of undemanding text were among the cheapest and most satisfying. Allen's own career had shown by this time that the literary tradesman with the right kind of goods on sale was in an occupation that was practically recession-proof; and not only that, he himself was about to put before the public an item that would jump him up several rungs on the ladder of affluence. For "Depression" appeared in the *Westminster Gazette* when all literary London was buzzing with the news of the imminent arrival of *The Woman Who Did*.

Fifteen years earlier, though, it had been a different story. Then, he had had a much more tentative hold on the market and was still feeling his way into the most profitable areas of enterprise. He knew quite well that what he had to do was look beyond—and, if one cared to look at it that way, well below—the *Cornhill* and the *Fortnightly*. He needed a foothold in the weeklies and dailies. Only these, interspersed with a regular output of fiction or other saleable volumes, offered the freelancer any chance of climbing into real prosperity. Such a foothold was what Allen sought when he plunged back into the fray after returning from France in the spring of 1880. And despite all the handicaps and gloomy predictions, for him it worked wonderfully well.

CHAPTER 4

"A Pedlar Crying Stuff": Selling
the Wares (1880–1889)

"Tootling" for a Living

Allen got back from Hyères in May 1880. As we have seen, he had not idled his way through the months of recuperation. Indeed, in the month after his return there appeared in *Fraser's Magazine* an article, "Geology and History," which is a very typical and fine example of his early work. It explains how the agriculture, the manufactures, the arts, and even the religion of a society stands, quite literally and well as metaphorically, on its geology. Britain's recent history was founded on coal; just as Egypt's civilization was based on granite and Nile mud; Greece's, on marble; China's, on kaolin clay; Assyria and upper India's, on sun-dried brick. He points out that the delicate tracery of English cathedrals would never have existed if the only building material had been ragstone or basalt. Fortunately, there was the limestone of Caen, Bath, and Portland to hand. For twelve pages Allen expands this notion with the most fluent and confident generalizations and a wealth of illustration.[1] Still, he must have been only too aware by this time how hard it was to make a living wage by doing this kind of thing for the monthlies, and he must have been uncomfortable with the thought that he had no book on the stocks for 1880. But a big breakthrough, and something of a change of direction, came almost as soon as he was back. It was another opportunity with a newspaper, but work of a much more appealing kind than scribbling leaders or reviews for the *Daily News*.

Up to that time, the late-afternoon slot in the London newspaper market had been filled by the *Pall Mall Gazette*. The *Pall Mall* was a quality paper, as its appearance proclaimed. Though indescribably drab to modern eyes, it was a format to which readers were accustomed: two solid columns of print to a page without many cross-headings. There were, of course, no photographs; nothing but an occasional map or chart, and few enough of those. It had a readership of about 8,000, most of them well-educated commuters who wanted to read, in the train or at their club, a detailed summary of the day's events plus a few solid leading articles interpreting those events from a congenially Conservative stance. At the end of the paper they wanted business news. And in between they were accustomed to find a few "middles," short, opinionated, lively, and perceptive essays on almost any subject. They were supplied anonymously by various people, but men of the caliber of Trollope, Froude, Arnold, Lewes, Kingsley, and Wilde were happy to write for the *Pall Mall*. This was not tabloid journalism.

A new proprietor had recently acquired the *Pall Mall* with the intention of turning it into an organ of the Liberal Party. This transfer of allegiances produced a considerable upheaval. The editor, Frederick Greenwood, and some of the staff left and set up a new Conservative paper, the *St. James's Gazette*, in competition. The *St. James's* layout imitated the *Pall Mall's* closely, and it needed fresh blood for its middles. One of the first things Greenwood did was to hire Allen to write a natural-history column for the paper on an irregular but frequent basis. He contributed his first piece, "A Sprig of Crowfoot," about the peculiar leaves of that semi-aquatic plant, on June 23, just a few weeks after the first issue. He went on to contribute another 136 articles before the last one, "Our Winter Visitors," appeared rather more than two years later, on October 28, 1882. Almost certainly he contributed many other unidentifiable reviews—more properly, review-essays—as well. Another lengthy series was made up of local historical and topographical pieces on all the counties and most of the noteworthy towns of England. He maintained an extraordinary rate of production for these essays. In August 1880, for instance, they were appearing once every three days, on average.

What makes this performance even more remarkable is that after his first six months on the *St. James's* Allen was simultaneously writing another set of middles. Presumably impressed by what Allen was doing for the competition, John Morley took him on at the start of 1881 to do the same kind of sprightly article for the *Pall Mall Gazette*. His first piece, one of eleven essays on the topography of the country around Lyme Regis, appeared on January 31, 1881. This was where his in-laws lived, and he playfully disguised all the names of "[this] sunny corner of a southern shire whose exact position its present historian has no intention whatsoever of disclosing, seeing that he himself has taken up his abode there."[2] These too appeared irregularly, but rarely more than seven or eight days apart.

By the time the *St. James's* series finished in 1882, he had already contributed at least forty-five articles to the *Pall Mall*, and probably many more. Morley put him on a loose rein, permitting him to write on almost anything he liked, from trends in Canadian tourism to the ancestry of the donkey; from the folklore attached to Welsh cromlechs, to the wood-spurge as a botanical survivor in the micro-climate around Bath. Some of these he collected as a book, *Vignettes from Nature* (1881), his second collection of that year. Allen's topics may seem outside the likely interests of a tired, homeward-bound newspaper reader, but his lightness of touch and his ability, while seeming to know everything, never to patronize his audience, let him engage almost anyone's attention. In fact, if Allen is to be believed, the two *Gazettes* gained some unexpected readers from his activities. He once saw a workman in muddy clothes sitting in a third-class carriage reading one of these papers, and when he was asked why, received the answer, "Because I always read the articles about so-and-so," these being Allen's own. He had the gift of being able to come up with a wholly unexpected angle on a subject. What, for instance, could be more hackneyed a topic than spring? Yet Allen finds something new to say, by exploring the fact that when the poets of Queen Anne's day wrote of spring their portrayal was constructed from a classical stock of images in absolute defiance of reality; and, moreover, this has infected our stock phrases, so that we speak of a perfect climate as being a "perpetual spring," which is certainly not what we mean:

> The common expression is correct enough in the mouth of a South European, for whom spring is the delightful middle breathing space between the draughty chilliness of open winter and the sweltering aridity of high August noontide; but it is simply ridiculous on the alien lips of the remote Hyperborean Briton. Nobody who took his language and his ideas direct from nature could ever dream of holding up as the model of a delicious climate that alternation of swirling, dusty nor'-easters and boisterous, drenching sou'-westers which we in England recognize as spring. The *ver perpetuum* of the Roman poet meant something very different indeed from that. . . . That is one of the greatest delights of the otherwise rather arid and often disappointing Southern scenery; the familiar images and descriptions of classical poetry begin for the first time to live before one, to assume a concrete and natural reality in one's mind. The arbutus ceases to be an abstraction and becomes a visible shrub: the cicada no longer bears company with the wyvern or the hippogriff, but chirps most audibly and undeniably in the neighbouring thicket. There you have the true enchantment of it.

But, after all, this is only newspaper chat, not a tract on intertextuality *avant la lettre*, and in closing he lightens the tone with a humorous example of literature molding life:

> "What! pork pies!" exclaimed an enthusiastic American tourist in the railway refreshment room at Liverpool. "How delightful! By all means let us have a pork pie. Why, you know, one reads about them in Dickens!" We sober English, to the manner born, laugh quietly, of course, at the association; but, after all, there is really something enviable in the conditions which permit one to invest even the staple product of Melton Mowbray with a genuine and picturesque literary interest.[3]

John Morley gradually moved Allen forward in the paper until he was writing "turnovers," a turnover being the article following the leader on the front page, which ran on to page two and had to be written in a style bright enough to encourage the reader to turn over. A typical piece was titled "The Composition of a Very Mixed People," and discussed, skeptically and humorously, the cranium-measuring activities of the Anthropometric Committee of the British Association. This piece is also notable for being signed. All of his previous work for the *Pall Mall* had been anonymous. He claimed later, not quite accurately, that this was only the second signed article ever to appear in a London daily paper.[4] He continued to contribute to the *Pall Mall* at erratic intervals long after W.T. Stead became editor in 1883 and repositioned the paper far down-market.

Even the tally above by no means exhausts Allen's journalism of the early 1880s. At the end of 1881, while he was appearing simultaneously in the *Pall Mall* and the *St. James's*, he started contributing to *Knowledge: An Illustrated Magazine of Science*, edited by his friend Richard Proctor. He jumped aboard this new popular weekly right from the start, with a lively essay "What is a Grape?" and throughout 1882, 1883, and 1884 he contributed more than sixty articles to it, most but by no means all of them on botanical topics. One was a palaeoanthropological series "Our Ancestors," and another ran through the round of the seasons under the title "A Naturalist's Year" at the rate of two essays a month; yet another dealt with "The Evolution of Flowers" at the same rate. Proctor gave him pride of place on the first page of *Knowledge* for some of these.

It remains something of a mystery how and when Allen had managed to acquire such an extensive knowledge of his chief subjects, especially botany. Of course, he was well grounded in evolutionary theory, but many of the essays he now began to write display, among other things, the minute observation of a trained field naturalist. It is not very apparent when Allen had had time to learn so much, particularly about the British flora. Presumably he had started as a youthful collector. A letter of his in *Nature* mentions discovering a rare snail "when I was a schoolboy" at Kinver, near Stourbridge. This village is not far from Birmingham, so this must have been during a school excursion when Allen was a teenager. It implies that he was already a fairly experienced naturalist.[5] But that is the only hint, and if these amateur enthusiasms continued during his Oxford years, or when he returned to England from Jamaica, they have left no record.

Still, he had got the knowledge somehow, and no one was more adept at putting it to use. With this semipopular journalism Allen quite suddenly moved into a new and higher gear. As his powers expanded he found he could produce these essay-articles effortlessly, or at least give the impression of doing so. For each of the years 1880–1883 he produced around a hundred articles, reviews, and stories, and it seemed immaterial whether the topic of the moment was scientific, philosophical, social, or critical, or what length was required for any particular job of work. In a hilarious scene in *Philistia*, his hero agonizes for a whole morning about how to stretch a social leader on Italian barrel organs out to the requisite fifteen hundred words. He only manages it with desperate divagations into the natural history of guinea pigs and the scenery of the Apennines. This is one of the many ways in which Allen asserts his superiority over his poor fool of a hero, for he was never troubled in that way; or if he was, it does not show. He could turn out a solid 1,500-word leader in half an hour and, if more were needed, could expand his scope of treatment almost indefinitely without any obvious padding.

One piece, "The Philosophy of a Visiting Card," is noteworthy in that it revels overtly in its own ingenuity. Starting in autobiographical vein, Allen tells how he found himself bookless at the start of a five-hour train journey from London to Dartmoor. He has just "one solitary piece of literature" for company. It is nothing but a visiting card engraved with the name "Edgar B. Chadwick." He resolves to convert that scrap of pasteboard into a philological article:

> This is how the thing is managed. I pull the elements of Mr. Chadwick's name to pieces; I jot down the analogies and illustrations that strike me on the back of the card; and when I get to-night to my lodgings on Dartmoor, I shall take pen in hand and write the notes out in full. . . . Think it all out between stations; scribble down the key-words whenever we stop at Swindon or Chippenham; and there you are—the article is practically written.

"Practically written," that is, if you can move effortlessly through the etymology of personal nomenclature. Starting with the family name, with digressions on how names can be fossil remnants of places that no longer exist, he traces out all the implications of the root *wic*, a village, and its many cognate forms. Then he traces out the varying fortunes of "Edgar," passing finally to reflections about the recency of middle names in England and why the feminine forms of surnames—Baxter, Brewster, Webster—rather than the masculine have so often survived. He closes with a flourish:

> as I write the last note "Baxter, Brewster, Anson, Nelson," the train is just steaming into Newton Abbott station. I have no time for more, as I have to look after my luggage in the scrimmage. But is it not a wonderful thought that every one of us thus carries about with him every day a perfect philological fossil in the way of a personal name. . . . Is it not a wonderful thought—label for Moreton Hampstead, if you please, and just two minutes to catch the five-forty down train.[6]

Expanded, the result of this self-referential exercise filled seventeen packed pages in the *Cornhill* for September 1882. Allen was capable of producing an article like this at a single sitting. The resulting payment could have bought him a train ticket to Rome, not Dartmoor.

For these early labors Allen chose subjects so various that it is impossible to find any unifying themes in them. But when he collected some of them his strategy is obvious. He picked out those pieces which assert most lucidly and unmistakably the truths of Darwinian evolution. The title of his third collection, *Colin Clout's Calendar* (1882) was a particularly good one, for as well as being a generic name for a countryman, "Colin Clout" was the persona assumed by the poet John Skelton in 1552 for his satirical attack on the powerful prelate Cardinal Wolsey. As we have seen, Allen took a dim view of clerics in general, and one of the things he liked to do whenever he could was to discomfit them by tugging away the last shreds of the theological argument by design. Not that his approach is aggressive; he believed, as he put it, more in permeation than confrontation. What they do is merely to reiterate, over and over again, that descent with modification, acted upon by natural selection, can explain the present form of the organism under inspection—whether it be the structure of goose-grass or the habits of the squirrel—more profoundly and more economically than any other conceivable explanation. No one could manage this job for a wider spectrum of readers than Grant Allen. He was disappointed that all this work for the two *Gazettes* and *Knowledge* did not lead to the offer of a science editorship on one of the big dailies. The *Standard*, for instance, had such an editor. It is possible that no such offer ever came because of his notoriety in some quarters as a doctrinaire atheist and Darwinian. Darwinism was still a bitter pill for many to swallow in the 1880s, and he may have paid the price for his advocacy.

Still, it was all good, profitable fun, and he was pleased to be making headway at last. It was only gradually that a certain disenchantment set in. Was this to be his life, then? When was he to find the time for those deeper philosophical and scientific speculations that he believed were the real business of his life? Was he not pouring out his very life-blood on to the thirsty sand of daily journalism? Was he to be a circus performer, capable of mental dexterity and agile contortions, but essentially a pen for hire, a well-informed gossip, a mere "tootler"?

> Sometimes the tootle takes the form of a third leader—that wonderful social leader in all the daily papers, which begins with a fresh squabble in the St Pancras Vestry, goes on to consider the history of vestries in general from the days of the Stone Age onward, alludes playfully to our Aryan ancestors, digresses into the constitution of the Athenian demes, discourses casually of Roman municipia, is learned on the subject of early French communes, and ends abruptly with an amusing anecdote of Gustave Courbet. Sometimes the tootle becomes a middle in a weekly paper, sometimes it assumes the guise of an amusing review, sometimes it presents itself to the candid reader as the present article.[7]

But even at the time it must have struck some readers of this self-lacerating description that such tootles do at least presuppose a newspaper audience, which knows what the *municipia* were; which could take on board a reference to the communes of France; which has heard of the painter Courbet. Thirty years later, the journalist-novelist Arthur Machen would be sighing nostalgically over the lost *St James's Gazette* of his youth. He remembered it as a quality newspaper produced by and for educated gentlemen, contrasting it with its degenerate successors like his own paper, the *Evening News*, written, as he jeered, not even for the cab-men, but for the cab-men's wives.[8]

In addition, this kind of journalism was much better paid than anything else Allen had done. According to John Dawson, a veteran journalist, the pay was three guineas an article in the *St. James's* and four or five guineas in the *Pall Mall*.[9] Writing two or three such pieces a week was very much easier work than one densely constructed article for the *Cornhill*, which even he could not put together without a modicum of background reading. Not that he gave up the latter. He continued to do both for the rest of his life, averaging an article or story in every other issue of the *Cornhill* alone, and he almost always had a couple of book manuscripts on the stocks as well. Leslie Stephen was no mean pen-man himself, capable of writing a six-thousand word article at a sitting. He wrote sixty articles for his own magazine. But Allen wrote a lot more in a shorter space of time than that, and Stephen expressed wonderment at the younger man's facility. He found it unbelievable that—as Allen had complained to him—he could not place all that he wrote. But perhaps that is not surprising for a man who, in May 1882, was capable of putting fourteen separate pieces of original work into print in a single month: a story in the *Belgravia*, seven articles for the *St James's*, two each for the *Pall Mall* and the *Cornhill*, and one each for the *Academy* and the *Magazine of Art*, on subjects ranging from the lost polychrome coloring of Greek statues to the invasive properties of yellow-rattle in cornfields.

A LOVE AFFAIR WITH RURAL ENGLAND

These labors had a benefit other than the strictly financial. Though the life of the freelance was hardly enviable in most ways, it did have a few valuable compensations. The best one was that the freelance could live anywhere that he could do his work. Allen made it clear that he had not only done for ever with the tropics, but he had done with the New World as a place to live as well. Some of his earliest journalism is scathing, sarcastic denunciations of North American rural life, especially on the farms of New England. These articles perhaps indicate some of the stress Allen was under as he strove to make his way, or they may have served the psychological purpose of cutting himself free of his New World origins. In sentiment, and even in phrasing, they are very similar to the notorious comments, phrased as a string of negatives, about the American cultural landscape that Henry James had just made in his *Hawthorne* (1879). Allen stressed the dreariness of the physical setting of these farms, set as they are in a countryside devoid of any human interest: "no scenery, no history, no antiquities, no associations, no architecture, no beauty of any kind—nothing to tempt any human being out of his road."[10] What he particularly disliked, in Canada especially, was the spurious imitation of English life which had surrounded him as a youth; but whose culture (he now perceived) was wafer-thin. Certainly he was quick to dismiss the Canadian farmer, in particular, as "that mild modern Vandal with a tinge of Methodism" who has produced a "Philistine paradise" without bothering his head over the aesthetics of landscape.[11]

But it was more than just the landscape. Several features of raw American life—the pseudo-universities; the small-town Puritanism; the quack doctors—attracted his satire. Allen foresaw and feared the Americanization of the West, a prognosis which he made in surrealistic detail fifty years before *Brave New World*:

> a world all made up of infinite turkey and illimitable pumpkin-pie; a world full of circular saw-mills, and Pullman palace cars, and mammoth hotels, and light blue satin, and white-and-gold drawing-rooms; a world wholly given over to

raising corn, and sticking pigs, and distilling old Bourbon whisky, and making vulgar love through the nose to vulgar, overdressed, underbred young women. Its one literature would be the editorial screamer; its one excitement, an annual boom, and a quadrennial orgy of presidential elections. Picture to yourself such a society, without any painters, without any thinkers, without any musicians, without any of those rare souls, poets.'[12]

By contrast, this is the essence of the image of England that Allen was in love with:

We have in every part of England a varied national life, close communication with real centres of thought and culture, infinite interweaving of classes and interests. The squire goes for half the year to London, and fills the hall for the other half with guests from distant shires. The parson has taken his degree at Oxford or Cambridge, and diffuses among his people a constant civilizing influence. The farmer himself generally knows London and the seaside towns, goes on Sundays to a church adorned with mediaeval art, and catches frequent glimpses of a life and a society far more elevated than his own.[13]

Despite the opening clause, one notices that, by implication, Manchester or Sheffield or Birmingham or even London do not figure in this encomium. Allen's "England" is a fairly circumscribed place. It is, essentially, the market towns south and west of the Wash, and (with some exceptions) his topographical, natural history, and geological studies reflect that. He saw English life through literary spectacles too, in his early days: Litchfield meant Dr. Johnson; Nuneaton, George Eliot; Crewe, Colonel Newcome; Blisworth, Dick Swiveller.

But, much as he hated rural America, he hated London, that "beflagged and macadamized man-made solitude," even more.[14] One of his best essays is "Beautiful London," a little masterpiece of impassioned irony, which caused quite a stir. In it, he first imagines a naïve traveler arriving by sea at Venice, a small mercantile town whose population at its zenith was not much larger than Brighton's. He imagines this innocent traveler, after surveying the splendors of Venice, whose overseas possessions even at its height amounted only to Cyprus and the Morea, saying to himself then: "What may I not expect from the land which owns India and Australia, Jamaica and Canada, Hong-Kong and Singapore, New Zealand and Cape Town?" and, full of anticipation, sailing up the Thames to the headquarters of Empire:

How every true Englishman's heart would swell with the pride of world-wide empire as he contrasts in memory the way up from Greenwich to the Tower with the way up from the Lido to the Doges' palace! What luxury of ornament! What excess of splendour! The exquisite front of the Victualling Yard at Deptford, the storied beauties of Bugsby's Reach, the charming facades of the Isle of Dogs, the noble and sweet-scented tanneries of Bermondsey! At each bend of the river new and beautiful groups of buildings rise gradually into view . . . till he comes to anchor at last by the British Molo, at the song-inspiring steps of magnificent Wapping.

Well, all right, he imagines his critics saying, perhaps the Pool of London is not that appealing, but there is the South Bank of the Thames: that at least is picturesque. Allen pretends he hears this plea in Florence, that "second-rate and obsolete Italian town," and he has to close his eyes to picture the scene from Lambeth Bridge:

Yes, yes; I could picture it in all its glory—the six exquisitely varied blocks of St Thomas's Hospital, standing side by side like the ribs of St Lawrence's gridiron; the charming sky-signs of somebody or other's soap and the patent pain-killer; the mud that gleams brown by the yellow Thames; the palatial row of warehouses that occupy the background. With a penitent sigh I admitted my error, and dismissed the Arno. I allowed the superior beauty of the silvery stream that glides by lovely Lambeth. I remembered Cleopatra's Needle and its well-chosen situation, when compared with the Luxor Column in the Place de la Concorde, the great obelisk between Bernini's Colonnades at St. Peter's, and the towering monolith in the Piazza del Popolo. I thought of a thousand such points of superiority in our own beloved London, and thanked heaven under my breath that I was born an Englishman, and not a Papist Italian.

By the time this withering exercise was written Allen's touchstone of scenic and architectural excellence had become Italy. But his love affair with rural England came first; and now, as his freelancing life got under way, he had the chance to consummate it. In 1881 the family shifted to the small market town of Dorking, in Surrey. Dorking today is a nondescript commuter town, but in Allen's time it had the advantage of being utterly rural—it consisted of just one long, old-fashioned main street with its antique coaching inn, the White Horse, halfway along it—while still being on the direct line to Victoria. This was the perfect combination for the not-yet-prosperous writer, and this part of Surrey had long been popular with authors. During the summer busy journalists like Eliza Lynn Linton took cottages for rest and recreation.

The Allens took a house on the south side of the town, just off the Horsham Road, and christened it "The Nook." It was a square-built, double-fronted villa in a vaguely Queen Anne style. This was their home for the next twelve years. Here, for the rest of the 1880s, the first full decade of his career, he worked himself half to death as he polished his skills, studied his markets, met its needs, and eventually raised himself to the point where he could say convincingly that his family would never want, come what may.

Living was cheap in Dorking. By the end of the year he was in a position to repay the "loan" raised by Robertson and Romanes for the recuperative trip to the Riviera two years earlier. His letter is revealing about a characteristic but shadowy Victorian institution: that informal network of charity by which the professional classes—or the public school and Oxbridge fragment of them—supported and assisted each other at critical junctures:

I never felt more relieved or more grateful in my life than on the night when you and Mrs. Robertson came and first proposed your kind and thoughtful plan to us: it was a lifebuoy to a drowning man, and without it I don't know where we should all have been by this time. But now, we hope and believe, the danger is over, and there are many reasons why we ought to repay it. Some of the subscribers are themselves literary working men, and they know that I am now making a good income. It would naturally seem strange to them that we should go on keeping money which was advanced under such different circumstances. There are some of them, no doubt, who have no need of any such return, and to whom I should not feel it so necessary; but I agree with you that whatever is done should be done towards all alike.[15]

As this painfully scrupulous letter attests, Allen hated debts and obligations, even though repaying the money must have been a sore burden at that stage of his career. Romanes did his best to talk him out of it, but Allen was obdurate, and so was his wife. The contributors acted on Darwin's suggestion that the money could be returned in a different form, and eventually they presented Allen with an expensive microscope, which became his most treasured possession. In his personal letter of thanks to Darwin—who died the next month, in April 1882—he said, rather optimistically, that he did not need to do quite as much hack-work as formerly, and hoped to have time to use it to do some real science in future.[16] Perhaps so, but his thoughts were turning more and more to fiction, and substantial fiction at that.

THE TRIUMPH OF THE
UNCIRCUMCISED: *PHILISTIA*

By 1883, buoyed up by his success with short stories, of which he now had nearly enough for a first collection, *Strange Stories*, Allen felt ready to try a full-length novel. He embarked on an ambitious sociopolitical novel of ideas, which he hoped would forge his reputation as a serious novelist. This was *Philistia* (1884) and into it he poured his social idealism, albeit satirically treated. He said later that it "embodies to a great extent my own ideals of life and conduct. . . . I regard it to a great extent as a religious work. At any rate, I tried to put my religion into it."[17] As originally conceived, and as the working title, *Born Out of Due Time*, suggests, it was to have been a deeply pessimistic work, too, dramatizing the fate of high literary principles in the workaday world.

Allen's religion was, of course, a purely secular faith. *Philistia* is much concerned with high-minded, nonrevolutionary socialism of the permeative kind. In this, as in so many things, Allen was in the vanguard, for his novel was one of the very first overtly socialist fictions, along with Shaw's *An Unsocial Socialist*. The time was ripe politically, too, for both the moderate Socialist Democratic Federation and the high-minded Fabian Society were formed in the year that *Philistia* appeared.

Precisely what influences had shaped Allen's socialism it is hard to say. If he had links with people in any branch of the movement they remain invisible. Certainly he was never a political activist nor a member of any party except, briefly, the Fabians; nor is it apparent that he so much as dropped in on any socialist meetings. Allen's was always a party of one, and his angle of vision on all practical political issues was sardonic. Still, like most of the political Left of his day, he recognized that socialism had to shake off its millenarian and utopian origins to become an effective force. It has been claimed that *Philistia* is a mock-epic with an internal network of religious allusion, but that is going too far—Allen had nowhere near enough literary sophistication for that.[18] But his chapter titles with their references to the Biblical conflicts between the Israelites (here, the chosen race of the socialists) and the Philistines (the occupants of the mundane, materialistic world) are humorously astringent: titles like "Askelon Villa, Gath" (the names of two of the Philistines's chief cities), "The Mountains of Gilboa" (where Saul lost to the Philistines), "The Streets of Askelon," "The Daughters of Canaan," and so on. The central action concerns the adventures of the three young Le Breton brothers from an aristocratic Anglo-Indian family as they move out into London life, the latter-day Philistia of the title. They are Ernest, the high-minded political idealist and teacher/journalist; Herbert, foppish Oxford man, cynic and cad; and the saintly unworldly Ronald, a member of an Apostolic Christian Missioners sect. Other characters include Lady Hilda Tregellis, a bold and bored young aristocrat eager to marry someone "different," and Arthur Berkeley, a composer of comic operas and the first in the long line of Allen's self-sacrificing heroes who decorously love another man's wife from afar.

"Tell it not in Gath," thunders the Hebrew prophet, "publish it not in the streets of Askelon; lest the daughters of the Philistines rejoice, lest the daughters of the uncircumcised triumph." In *Philistia* the uncircumcised are seen triumphing in no uncertain manner, and they would have done so even more if Allen had been allowed to retain his original ending. He planned to have all the idealistic characters dying in misery, destroyed by their elevated ideals. But *Philistia* never saw print in that form. Neither the *Belgravia* nor the *Cornhill*, Allen's usual short-fiction outlets, would take it as a serial, allegedly because it dealt with socialism, but more probably because of the rather jejune views put into the mouths of some characters. So Allen sought an inclusive serial and book deal from Andrew Chatto, who agreed to take it for his firm's *Gentleman's Magazine*. However, he insisted on a happy ending. Given that Ernest Le Breton's pathetic death after his tribulations have crushed him is foreshadowed from the start, and was intended to be the moral lesson of the book, this amounted to a demand for a different product. Allen protested, quite mildly in the circumstances, that "if one made him recover or get on well in the world then there would be no *dénouement*, and, as a matter of character, I doubt whether such a person ever *would* get on well."

But it was no good. Chatto wanted Ernest alive. He used the thinnest of arguments ("you may want him again—you know how Anthony Trollope regretted killing Mrs Proudie on the impulse of the moment after overhearing the talk of two club loungers") but really he wanted a morally improving lesson showing that even a radical might come to his senses one day and then " 'get on' by steady perseverance in principles which at first may appear opposed to his own immediate interests."[19] Chatto's ultimate argument, of course, was that he held the purse-strings, and there is no sign that he saw the weird irony of pushing Allen into exactly the same corner as his hero. It was the first time Allen had felt explicit pressure to conform to what he called sarcastically the "imperative" demands of the public.[20] But, unlike Ernest Le Breton, whose obduracy nearly destroys him and his family, Allen knew how to kiss the rod. One can easily imagine his frame of mind as he grafted in a new chapter, "Out of the Hand of the Philistines," which restores Ernest to perfect health and puts him into the editorial chair of a richly subsidized Radical journal. He must have found it the very height of absurdity to rewrite the close in a way that both undermined and exemplified the lesson the book teaches from its first page. But if Allen resented what Andrew Chatto had made him do he disguised it well. His relations with the house of Chatto & Windus continued to be excellent, and much of his work appeared under their imprint. Andrew Chatto was no prude and sometimes took work that others refused; but what he would or would not do for Allen certainly affected the latter's career path as a controversialist. Publishing in the streets of Askelon turned out to be simultaneously lucrative and expensive in terms of one's integrity.

Once he had earned Chatto's benignant smile, he secured £250 for the entire copyright, including the serial rights, payable in twelve equal monthly installments. It was a puzzlingly large sum, far above the going rate for a first novel. A more typical price would have been £75–100, and it is virtually certain that some other unknown factors were in play. After all, *Philistia* was a three-decker for the conservative readers of the circulating libraries, and a publisher so perspicacious as Chatto could not have expected large sales there for a "talky" novel espousing socialism. It is true that Allen was not an entirely unknown quantity: Chatto liked both his natural-history essays and his short stories. On the other hand, he could not trade on Allen's modest journalistic reputation because the latter insisted on using a pseudonym again to make sure of getting an objective critical opinion. But this time it was not to be "J. Arbuthnot Wilson." That name was good enough for hack articles and fiction, but this new work demanded something different. Chatto managed to talk him out of his ridiculous first choice, "Gertrude Beresford O'Sullivan," by saying tactfully that it smacked too much of a "somewhat shabby aristocratic amateur author" and that they preferred short *noms de plume*.[21] They agreed eventually on "Cecil Power."

Allen took *Philistia* very seriously, and expected great things to follow. He told his friend Croom Robertson afterward that he had put his whole soul into it. "When it was finished, I felt I had done my utmost . . . I didn't write hastily; I satisfied utterly my own critical faculty: and I can't do any better. Indeed, I can never again do so well."[22] And, in a way, that is a true judgment. *Philistia* is much more densely written than any of its successors and is worth engaging with on several levels. The scenes set in Herr Schurz's salon, to which the émigré socialists, "all that was best and truest in the socially rebellious classes,"[23] make their way each Sunday evening to hear the master dilate upon the path to revolution, can usefully be set against the handling of similar material by Shaw, James, Conrad, and Gissing.

And as an autobiographical document it is psychologically intriguing. Of the string of novels which Allen turned out in the 1880s, it is the only one where we sense a real personal engagement, and where we feel that he really had, imaginatively speaking, bitten off more than he could chew. *Philistia* was planned from the start as a study of idealism under stress, and it had plenty of personal reverberations. It was designed to illustrate his perception that, ultimately, in the present state of affairs, you can be either a martyr to your principles or an uncomplaining cog in the social machine; and that no one will care very much, probably, if you choose the first role. It is, in psychological terms, an elaborate attempt at self-reconstruction; a novel where maladroitness, estrangement, and self-division loom large, as Allen looks back on his younger self trying to pull all the parts of his nature into some kind of harmony. Ernest is not as deracinated as Allen was himself, but he does cut himself adrift from his aristocratic mother's world, just as Allen had cut free from his maternal family of the Canadian Grants.

Allen put something of himself into each of the three Le Breton brothers. Ernest is partly a Candide figure, partly a Holy Fool and partly a Samson as he grinds away at the mill of journalism to support his family, and in turn is ground into powder by the predatory world in which he has to make a living. The narration distances itself markedly from Ernest and gives regular ironical commentaries on his intransigence. By the time he came to *Philistia* Allen was a seasoned journalist of thirty-four, and he had learned several hard lessons about accommodating one's ideals to the demands of the marketplace. A character remarks that living with Ernest Le Breton "would be like living with an abstraction," and a woman "might just as well marry Spinoza's Ethics or the Ten Commandments." The reader is likely to agree. But the painfully scrupulous young Ernest has potential; the potential to become his creator. As Herr Max lectures his daughter:

> The best socialists never come from the bourgeoisie, nor even from the proletariate; they come from among the voluntarily déclassés aristocrats. . . . The aristocrat who descends is always thinking, "Why shouldn't these other people have as many rights and privileges as I have?" . . . [It] begets a certain gentle spirit of self-effacement. You don't often find men of the aristocratic class with any ethical elements in them—their hereditary antecedents, their breeding, their environment, are all hostile to it; but when you do find them, mark my words, Uta, they make the truest and most earnest friends of the popular cause of any. Their sympathy and interest in it are all unselfish.

Voluntarily unclassed, self-effacing, a stalwart man of the people: Ernest as we have him is a prig and a young idiot, but it is easy to see how he might yet become a version of Grant Allen as he liked to think of himself in his early thirties.

Philistia is most autobiographical in its handling of another of its central themes, exogamy. All three Le Breton brothers acquire working-class lovers or wives. Ernest's wife Edie is a grocer's daughter. His odious brother Herbert has seduced a rural greengrocer's daughter, Selah Briggs. Though their relationship is presented as decorously as the *Gentleman's Magazine* required, its nature is plain enough. This couple play out a version of Allen's relations with Caroline Bootheway, seen through a distorting mirror; it is as though he is trying out, imaginatively, brutalized versions of his own behavior fifteen years earlier. A certain amount of self-laceration may be detected, too: "Selah turned her great eyes admiringly upon him once more. 'Oh, Herbert,' she said, looking at him with a clever uneducated girl's unfeigned and undisguised admiration for any cultivated gentleman who takes the trouble to draw out her higher self." That sounds like a touch from life, softened in recollection. Herbert persuades her that they cannot marry, because that would mean surrendering his fellowship. Selah says eagerly that "a very small income would do for me, with you, Herbert," but his frigid line is "Pardon me, but I could not. I've been accustomed to a certain amount of comfort, not to say luxury, which I couldn't readily do without." When alone he meditates a theme whose personal resonance is transparent: " 'It's an awkward sort of muddle to have got oneself into,' he thought to himself as he walked along the asphalte pavement in front of the sea-wall: 'a most confoundedly awkward fix to have got oneself into with a pretty girl of the lower classes.' " He resolves to take a break in Switzerland, and reject her by letter. Eventually, in a spirit of self-mortification, Allen's third fragment of himself, the saintly Ronald, picks up the betrayed and cast-off Selah on the Embankment, just in time to save her from the streets or worse.

There are some further striking autobiographical elements drawn from Allen's more recent life, especially in the scenes where Ernest Le Breton, dreadfully poor and burdened with a family, works for the *Morning Intelligence* while trying to keep his soul undefiled. Allen claimed that the model for the editor was Frank Harris, who, when he received an article in manuscript, thought nothing of adding or deleting a "not" in a sentence to make it accord better with editorial policy.[24] Allen could not have suffered from this treatment from Harris himself, but he uses it to mordant effect in *Philistia*. Presumably he is glancing back at his own experiences working for Hunter as well as on the *Daily News* in a scene where Ernest, desperate for money, writes a supportive leader about an Indian hill-tribe, which has cast off British rule. It is distorted into its opposite meaning by the editorial pen. " 'The insult to British prestige in the East,' ran that terrible opening paragraph, 'implied in the brief telegram which we publish this morning from our own Correspondent at Simla, calls for a speedy and a severe retribution. It must be washed out in blood.' Blood, blood, blood! The letters swam before his eyes." The following confrontation with a subeditor almost bears comparison with Evelyn Waugh's *Scoop*.

When *Philistia* appeared it failed to arouse any special interest. "Clever" was the term most of the reviewers used. In truth, *Philistia* has several failings typical of a first novel, especially of a novel of ideas, that notoriously tricky form. The tone is uncertain, wobbling uneasily between documentary realism, comic satire, and tragic melodrama. The essayist and leader-writer peeps out at every point, particularly during the mannered and implausible dialogue, where the characters lecture each other for whole paragraphs at a time. The sickly sentimentality of the love relationships also has to be reckoned with. Most of Allen's novelistic skills, especially his plotting and dialogue, improved quickly, but sentimentality was to be a recurrent feature. Virtually all his love relationships are childish. Its presence at the start, in the serious *Philistia*, proves that this style of love interest was native to him; he did not introduce it to improve his commercial prospects.

Still, *Philistia* was a start. As he told Croom Robertson confidently, "I shall doubtless write lots more novels, many of which will hit the public taste better than *Philistia*, for I am learning to do the sensational things that please the editors. I am trying with each new novel to go a step lower to catch the market. . . . I have very little doubt that by carefully following the rules given me by Payn and others, and by feeling the public pulse, I shall in time succeed in being a fairly well-read average novelist."[25] And he was right. Soon his work was paying the bills comfortably; indeed, as the decade moved on, a lot more than the bills. More attractive commissioned work began to come his way. One was to write an introductory chapter to a book of original drawings by W.L. Wyllie. The drawings were views of the Thames, as seen from a yawl, *Puffin*, as they sailed upriver one glorious day from the estuary mouth to London Bridge. Allen supplied a narrative of the trip, done in some of his most relaxed and fluently descriptive prose. He sets out to please, and one would never guess, from his easy-going, urbane commentary, just how much he loathed London architecture and London squalor.[26]

THE REWARDS OF DRUDGERY

By the mid-1880s the Allens could afford much more adventurous travel than sailing up the Thames. They had had at least one spring tour in northern Italy by 1883 and a little later, with their son away at Charterhouse school, they started to winter abroad in rather fine style. For the rest of the decade they evaded the worst months every year. Usually it was the Riviera. The Riviera Allen knew was a region still so primitive that it tests the imagination to reconstruct it. Along the entire coast from Marseilles to Menton, only one town, Nice, had the look of a substantial, modern resort. Antibes had hardly changed since medieval times. Allen mentions Juan-les-Pins as a place almost unknown even to Frenchmen; a fishing village where within a few kilometers of the town "you can lose yourself in trackless forests."[27] Other small towns of the hinterland were picturesque but appallingly primitive. Bornes, he reported, had no lodgings whatever where an Englishman could stay, and no food to be had but black bread, olive oil and abominable *vin du pays*.

Allen's great discovery was the Cap d'Antibes, then a wild promontory almost in a state of nature. A dull olive-grey spit of land, it was covered in wild myrtle and mesembryanthemum which from a distance gave it an uninviting look. But the view from the point, looking back to the coast from La Garoupe lighthouse, was spectacular, as it still is: on one side is the Bay of Cannes, the Croisette and the little islands of Sainte Marguerite and Saint Honorat, with the hills of the Esterels behind; on the other side lie Villefranche and Monte Carlo, and, as a backdrop to the whole, visible from this vantage as they are not on the coast itself, the gleaming summits of the Alpes Maritimes, covered in winter snow. Allen loved this spot and did not fear that publicity might spoil it. "There isn't the very slightest danger that the wrong sort of people will ever go to ruralise on the end of the point," he wrote boldly. "It's nonsense to talk about all the nice places getting over-run."[28] Within a mere twenty years of his death, the Cap was well on the way to becoming home to some of the most expensive real estate in the world.

Even in Allen's day the Cap had a good hotel, which had started life in the 1860s as the Villa Soleil, a private chateau owned by a consortium of Russian aristocrats. Then, in October 1887, at about the time Allen started to patronize it, it had come into the hands of a skilled Italian hotel-keeper, Antonio Sella. A century later it had metamorphosed into the Eden-Roc, a hotel-resort of almost fabulous exclusivity, where, it is rumored, all bills are settled in cash; but when the Allens stayed there each winter it was small, comfortable yet quite luxurious. The daily life and pleasures of the English people who wintered there were simple enough. According to Alice Bird, reminiscing about some four winters she spent there with her brother George in the company of the Allen family, almost every day there was a picnic:

> each person carrying his own simple lunch. Grant Allen never started with us—the morning was the time he gave to work. We named a favourite spot, and when his task was over he and his wife (and his son when there for the holidays) used to join us. The myrtle bushes abounding at the Cap supplied us with perfumed springy couches. It was a favourite trick to walk slowly backwards into these compact wind-cropped masses; and as we crushed our way leisurely down, the air became charged with delicious resinous exhalations.

There were lively discussions in the evenings at the hotel, in which, according to Miss Bird, Allen alternately charmed and scandalized the guests:

> The commonplace and the conventional seemed to vanish in his company, and we loved to follow him into an ideal land where he vividly pictured things not as they are but as he hoped they might become. At the Antibes hotel it was natural that the majority he met differed from him, but to dissentients he was invariably gentle and forbearing. And it not infrequently happened that a sharp opponent, if not converted, would be turned into a respectful listener. . . . He never deviated from the one great object of his life—"to make the world accept as a truism in the next generation what it rejected as a paradox in the present generation."[29]

Alice Bird was a good friend and a great admirer, of course; doubtless the "dissentients" she mentions would have had a different view. Indeed, a sourer note is struck by Edith Nesbit, the novelist. A member of Nesbit's party later reported that when Allen came over from his luxurious hotel to dine with them in their much humbler surroundings, he made a great fuss about whether he might catch typhoid, and later he held forth about the inferiority of women, "a thing which may seem curious to those who recollect that a couple of years later his novel, *The Woman Who Did*, was looked upon as a feminist tract."[30] Curious, perhaps, but not too surprising to the informed reader.

Still, a Riviera winter was hardly a matter of *dolce far niente* for Allen. Despite these evidences of greater prosperity, his financial position was still insecure. He was living well, but constant bouts of illness supplied regular warnings that he might break down altogether; and then . . . The main problem was that he was accumulating no capital, no reserves. His books, fiction and nonfiction alike, sold tolerably well at their first appearance, but they had little staying-power. Even the ones on which he had retained the copyright brought in little enough. If one of Andrew Chatto's accounts can be believed, the first half of 1886 generated only £55 in continuing royalties on four books. "I am greatly disappointed that it is not for a larger amount," said Chatto, no less aware than the author himself that the bread-winner could not afford to slacken pace for an instant.[31] He was so ill over the winter of 1885/6, another winter of terrible cold, that Nellie Allen was writing almost despairingly to their friends. That January, Clodd made a special memorandum to himself about a request his friend had made: "should he not survive, I am to get Romanes, Lang, Cotter Morison and Croom Robertson to apply for Civil List pension for Mrs. A."[32] Such pensions were hard to get and notoriously stingy, and the prospect of his wife and young son being obliged to live on £100 a year must have driven him to even greater exertions in uncongenial fields. No doubt the fact that in the preceding months he had written two long three-deckers and a pot-boiler full of occult and mystical ingredients (*Kalee's Shrine*) on top of all the journalism, had something to do with his collapse.

By the spring he had recovered sufficiently to take his family on a much longer trip: to the States and Canada for a visit lasting some months, to see American friends and the family at Kingston. Allen had not seen his relatives for ten years, since his visit on the way back from Jamaica, and they had not seen their grandson and nephew at all. They were in Concord, Massachusetts, in June, where they stayed with Lothrop, the publisher, and finally sailed back from Quebec at the end of August. On his return to England Stead interviewed him for the *Pall Mall Gazette*, first asking him, predictably, what new impressions he had gained of North America. Allen replied that one unexpected thing in particular about the eastern United States had struck him *very forcibly*. One can imagine Stead leaning forward eagerly at this, expecting to be regaled with some witty observation on the mores of the New World. Yes; the fact was, Allen continued disconcertingly, that he had previously quite underestimated just how fiercely the glaciers of the Ice Age had scoured the landscape of the eastern seaboard, compared to their action in Europe. (Typically, he expanded this perception to fifteen pages for the *Fortnightly*, later in the year.) No doubt Stead leaned back again at that. Allen went on to make it plain that his attitude to American rural life had not softened. When asked what he had written while away, he said cheerfully that he had written nothing at all; he had spent the whole time lazing and recouping his energies. He modestly refrained from mentioning that three more of his novels had come out during his absence, or that he had somehow written *en route* and then published the twenty-eight short essays making up his collection *Common Sense Science*. And there were the *Cornhill* articles, still appearing almost monthly as regular as clockwork: five of them while he was in America, on subjects ranging from sea-serpents to the origins of the decimal system.

The following winter, from November to March, 1887/8, he was away again; this time to Algiers, where there was another health resort for the English at Mustapha Supérieur, in the hills above the capital. This visit was arranged at the last minute, when he suffered such a serious bout of bronchitis again that he dare not stay in England. From the Villa du Palmier he wrote rather pathetically to his ten-year-old son: "Mummy went out with [an invalid girl staying at the villa] to pick violets, but Daddy was too ill and stopped at home in bed. Today I'm better and able to be up. . . . Now good bye, my birdie. I hope you'll be able to read this, for my hand shakes rather."[33] At least all these travel experiences could be used as grist for the fictional mill. The Algerian visit, for instance, produced *The Tents of Shem* (1889), which, considered as a piece of journalism rather than fiction, is most perceptive in capturing the French colonial atmosphere and sentiments of the time, which would lead to the ferocious war against the *colons* decades later—and, indeed, to the country's present miseries.

Back in Dorking in the spring of the new year of 1888, quite a different experience loomed. Herbert Spencer came to stay. The aging philosopher had been suffering from one of his vague and interminable illnesses, and he proposed that the Allens should take him in as a boarder for the whole summer. It says much for their kindness and hospitality that they agreed to this. "Dear Allen, *You* must be very well if you can stand H.S. when he isn't!" wrote Andrew Lang in mock consternation.[34] The weather was bad, and after a few months Spencer persuaded them that he was too ill to return to London and had to stay longer. In the end they left (or fled, according to one account) Dorking for their winter on the Riviera, leaving him behind as tenant of their house. He was not particularly grateful. His own account conveys well his self-absorption and expectation that his state of health ought to interest everyone else too:

> The end of June found me at Dorking, where I took up my abode with my friend Mr. Grant Allen for the summer months. . . . Improvements and relapses filled the time till the middle of October, when Mr. Allen was obliged to go, as he habitually did, to a warmer climate; and I, unable to move, took his house for the winter. The five months passed in it, more monotonous even than the

fifteen months passed at Brighton, were made more bearable in the one place as in the other by various friends, who came to spend sometimes a few days, sometimes three weeks, with me; and especially were they relieved by two children of my friend Mrs. Cripps.[35]

The children were "borrowed" because Spencer liked to have children about him to fuss over. It is a commentary on the times that a mother was prepared to send two young girls to stay by themselves with an elderly and odd bachelor for weeks on end, in a house that was empty but for the servants. Spencer beguiled the time by firing off missives to the Riviera complaining about the laundry arrangements. Allen seems to have regarded these quirks as nothing worse that the pardonable eccentricities of genius.

That summer visit of 1888 did give Allen the chance to observe Spencer at close quarters and for several months on end. Ever since he first met him twelve years earlier the man Spencer seems to have intrigued Allen as much as, or perhaps more than, the thinker; and the reason for this bias is not hard to discern. Part of his hero-worship was based on aspects of Spencer's personal history with which Allen readily identified, especially Spencer's early adoption of his vocation and his monkish devotion to it, which had carried him over emotional and financial hurdles that would have crippled anyone lacking his iron will. Allen, too, saw his own natural bent as lying in unremunerative philosophy and speculative science; but he had in early life given hostages to fortune that Spencer—had he ever felt the temptation—would have evaded without hesitation. Most of all, the whole tendency of Spencer's thought fed, reinforced, and legitimized Allen's dogmatism: his urge to draw everything into one logical self-sustaining Grand Theory. For that gift, Allen was willing to forgive his master everything—or almost anything.

Perhaps, though, at the personal level, he liked what he saw rather less than he had done before. Curious evidence of this is the portrait of Spencer he drew in the wake of the visit, in his lively novel *Dumaresq's Daughter* (1891). Haviland Dumaresq has finished his life's work, the great Encyclopedic Philosophy, but he is lucky to sell a dozen sets of it a year. He is now seventy. (This age Spencer reached when the novel was being written.) Embittered by his lack of success, he lives in a rural cottage with his daughter, eking out an existence on "the merest scientific hackwork for London publishers—Universal Instructors, you know, and that sort of claptrap."[36] Dumaresq is, like Spencer, like Allen himself, a compulsive generalizer. "He saw nothing—not even the smallest small-talk—as isolated fact: every detail came to him as a peg on which to hang some abstract generalization": the first time we catch sight of him, at a tennis-party, he is discoursing learnedly on homophonic surnames. Both Spencer's inhuman detachment and blank disdain for art are pointed up and ridiculed: "the existing culinary utensil calls herself Maria," he says of his servant; and a water-color is for him "a piece of paper with the image or simulacrum of a common dwelling-house scrawled in colour upon it."

However, on an early page Dumaresq is allowed to tell the story of his early life, and he does so with dignity. It has been one of superhuman effort and privation, when for years he "lived like a dog in a kennel," at one point being rescued from actual starvation by a timely small inheritance, just as Spencer was. The old philosopher preserves a noble detachment. "We men are but parasites on the warped surface of a tiny satellite of a tenth-rate sun. . . . The book got done at last: that's the great thing."

The most interesting touch is the degree to which Allen fictionalizes Spencer's career as a way of analyzing his own temptations and, perhaps, mournfully anticipating his own old age. Dumaresq concedes his life has been nobly wasted. Philosophy has lured him on as gin lures drunkards, but what had it all been for? Now, at the end, he would advise the young differently. "Go the way of the world and do as the world does. Don't waste your life, as I've wasted mine. Work for the common, vulgar, low, personal aims—money, position, fame, power. Those alone are solid." After this outburst he is seen to swallow discreetly a small, silver-coated pellet. A later scene where, abandoning the principles of a lifetime, Dumaresq seeks to marry his beloved daughter Psyche off to a rich man come what may, offers an odd mixture of farce and pathos. In a narcotic haze, described with rhetorical flourishes worthy of De Quincey, he visualizes Psyche decked out in pearl and diamonds:

> Money, money, money, money: the dross he despised, the pleasure he looked down upon, the vulgar aims and ends that he himself had cast like dirt behind him—he dreamed them all for the daughter he loved, and was no longer ashamed: for Haviland Dumaresq the philosopher was dead within him now, and there remained for the moment but that shell or husk, Haviland Dumaresq the incipient opium-eater.

Here Allen cuts very close to the bone. Spencer's father, as he must have known, had died from an overdose of morphine and Spencer's invalidity after 1885 was almost certainly due to his having become a morphine addict in turn. Perhaps Allen saw evidence of that at Dorking. Spencer did not, of course, read popular fiction and there is no reason to believe he ever heard about *Dumaresq's Daughter*; still, the wonder is that Allen dared or wished to draw such a picture, knowing his friend's vanity and high sense of self-esteem. It is a peculiar illustration of the warring mixture of idealism and satire in his nature.

The decade ended for Allen with the most demanding excursion he ever undertook: a visit to Egypt in the company of Edward Clodd in the winter of 1889. The friends left London that November and traveled by train and boat to Alexandria, where they met Arnold, Clodd's son. After that, they followed the usual tourist round. They climbed to the top of the Great Pyramid and then took the train down to Luxor. There they hired a donkey and guide to explore the Valley of the Kings, and Clodd the financier noted the donkey cost eight piastres for the day, four times as much as the boy guide: the total amounted to two shillings. After a languid sail back down the Nile in a felucca, which offered endless hours of talk but little comfort, they were glad to see Sheppard's Hotel in Cairo. They were back in England by December 10 after five weeks in each other's company. Unfortunately Clodd was no Boswell. The diary he kept of this trip was scribbled in tiny memorandum books and half the entries are illegible, and where legible they record nothing substantial about Allen's talk, apart from mentioning that there was a great deal of it. Allen, unusually, wrote nothing about his Egyptian tour, only expressing the opinion that it was "a visit which he had no desire to repeat."[37]

So ended the 1880s. When the last decade of the century opened, Allen must have looked back with some satisfaction. He had drudged, yes, but he had drudged to no small effect. He had lived well, and the hardest days were behind him. At least some of the work he had to do now was more congenial than of old, and even in his own eyes was not entirely despicable. And far richer rewards lay ahead.

CHAPTER 5

THE STOCK IN TRADE: WRITING
SCIENCE

SCIENTIFIC POPULARIZATION IN
VICTORIAN ENGLAND

The miserly returns on his first two monographs had persuaded even Allen
that writing serious science for a living was impossible. But being thought a
"scientist" continued to be important to him. (Not that he ever used that
noun; he thought it a vulgar neologism.) Science, for Allen, was the supreme
product of the human intelligence. He believed that the three master discoveries of nineteenth-century science—that is to say, the atomic theory of
matter, Darwinian evolution, and the laws of thermodynamics—had utterly
transformed our understanding of reality. He expresses this creed best in the
wonderfully inclusive long essay "The Progress of Science, 1830–1880,"
which he wrote for the *Fortnightly* in 1887 to mark Victoria's Jubilee year.
This essay, a masterpiece of exposition, is a eulogy to the advancing spirit of
rationalism, a hymn to the underlying uniformity in nature, a paean to the
way naturalistic explanation accommodates all nature. Through his eyes,
we see the birth of the cosmos itself as the Victorians understood it, and then
the development of the solar system, as explained by the nebular hypothesis.
The earth forms, and he shows us Lyell's geology insisting that uniformitar-
ianism is the most economical theory, and fits the facts; we follow the gradual
increasing comprehension and delineation of the geological epochs and eras;
the successful grasping, against fevered opposition, of the principles of
organic evolution; the growth of paleontology and anthropology and comparative religion and what they have to tell us about human organic and
cultural evolution; advances in physics, chemistry, and technology generally:
it's all there, and it all describes a cosmos cut from one cloth:

> consisting everywhere of the same prime elements, drawn together everywhere
> by the same great forces, animated everywhere by the same constant and inde-
> structible energies, evolving everywhere along the same lines in accordance
> with the self-same underlying principles.[1]

The hero of this brilliant epitome is the scientific method itself—the self-correcting procedures of induction and hypothesis-formation which make all theories, and even laws, tentative and provisional. Scientific naturalism was Allen's religion. It gave him an esthetics, an ethics, a metaphysics, a social philosophy. Indeed, science, for Allen, exposed the very pith of the world so thoroughly, so lucidly, so beautifully, that he was sometimes incredulous that anyone could possibly need another creed. He called one of his books *Common Sense Science* and for him the phrase was an incantation to the god of rationality, readable forward and backward: science is organized common sense, and it is only common sense to be scientific. His entire career as a thinker and writer was built on that reversible proposition. He had no room for other gods and, naturally, his attitude to all revealed religions was hostile.

It is not surprising, then, that it was important to Allen's self-image to be thought a man of science, in the sense of one who did original work and offered it up to the communal judgment. He tried to maintain this role throughout his life, despite disdainful criticism, economic sacrifices, and great demands on his energy. His first two books were, as we have seen, contributions to perceptual psychology. At the outset of his career he was encouraged to think of himself as a scientist. When copies of his first semipopular collections of reprinted essays of evolutionary explication, *The Evolutionist at Large* and *Vignettes from Nature* (both 1881) were sent out to the famous, flattering testimonials came back. The aged Darwin wrote privately: "I quite envy you your power of writing—your words flow so easily, clearly, and pleasantly. Some of your statements seemed to me rather too bold; but I do not know that this much signifies in a work of the kind, and may perhaps be an advantage. Some of your views are quite new to me." T.H. Huxley spoke approvingly too: "I find much to admire in the way you conjoin precision with popularity—a very difficult art."[2]

But testimonials of this kind have to be understood for what they really signified in the subculture of Victorian scientific scholarship. The two just quoted come from routine letters thanking the author for presenting them with his books. Such presents were well understood to be a modest, coded way of soliciting a puff from a famous name. Huxley received hundreds of books from aspirants, and he usually dispatched a note of gruff praise when he could. Even the fact that Darwin, then near the end of his life, praised Allen's work does not mean a great deal, as he was invariably generous toward anyone who was following in his footsteps.

But when it came to the impersonal medium of the review, or a professional judgment by his peers, Allen's forays into experimental science were treated rather differently. His dealings with the journal *Nature* are illustrative. Founded in 1869, *Nature* was originally meant to present scientific research to a lay audience. By the 1880s, though, its audience had altered somewhat. By then, *Nature* was being read mostly by professional scientists, although it still dealt in general science and was perhaps most useful to scientists who wanted to keep in touch with what was going on in specialties other than their own. Perhaps because of that shift of emphasis, *Nature*'s reviewers were often hard on amateurs, and as far as it was concerned Allen decidedly belonged to that class. It reviewed many of his books and article collections, usually with a slight air of disdain. *Vignettes from Nature*, for instance, was criticized by W.B. Carpenter for speaking imprecisely about the size of extinct animals. Carpenter was a divine, known to his enemies as the silver-tongued Bishop of Ripon, and Allen fastened on that, by retorting "with all due deference to Dr Carpenter, for whose supreme authority on all matters of biological fact I have, of course, the profoundest respect," he was, in truth, writing for the popular reader. This heavy sarcasm drew down on his head a rebuke of truly episcopal proportions.[3] The exchange doubtless produced plenty of mirth in all quarters, but in the latter part of Allen's career, when he had become notorious, *Nature*'s tone toward him hardened. Allen's botany primer, *The Story of the Plants*, which he wrote for Newnes in 1895, was successful, being translated into Russian and Dutch and still in print in an expanded edition as late as 1926. But *Nature*'s editor allowed it to be reviewed under the sneering title "Parturiunt Montes" ("the mountains labored" [and brought forth a mouse]). The reviewer picked away ruthlessly at a number of small technical errors, and closed by saying that the more ignorant the reader, the more he was likely to find the book pleasant, but hardly profitable, reading. That review appeared only a few months after *The Woman Who Did*, and it would be naïve to think the two were not connected. *Nature* maintained that tone during his last years. The Victorian scientific establishment handled Allen as it had handled G.H. Lewes, a man with similar talents, before him. It knew how to put in their place those it regarded as amateurs and sciolists.

In his early days, though, Allen had the confidence to twice publish technical papers on botany in *Nature*. The results were not happy. One, in July/August 1882, was a series of four papers offering a new theory about how the colored petals of flowers evolved from stamens in a specific sequence of colors, from yellow through to blue. This passed muster. Darwin praised it to other people, and Allen even persuaded Macmillan's to bring it out as a monograph, *The Colours of Flowers*. In his next effort, which was four papers on "The Shapes of Leaves" in March 1883, he tried to show that leaves have taken on their specific shapes in response to, and in turn acted as an influence on, the micro-climates around the plants which bear them. But this thesis was cut up badly by professional botanists:

> It is no doubt pleasant, even fascinating, to sit down at one's desk and, having formulated a few fundamental assumptions, to spin out from these explanations of what we see in the world about us. But I think when done it should be understood that the result is merely a literary performance, and though, viewed in that aspect, one may admire the skill and neatness with which it is accomplished, I nevertheless venture to think that the whole proceeding is harmful.[4]

This rebuke was from Thistleton Dyer, a heavyweight of botany who became the Director of Kew Gardens, and despite its *de haut en bas* tone it is, unfortunately, true enough. What Dyer is defining here is deductive argumentation, a procedure Allen had acquired from Herbert Spencer and to whose limitations he was always curiously blind.

Writing "Real" Science

No other person, living or dead, did so much to form Allen's scientific naturalism as Spencer. As we have seen, Allen read him thoroughly in Jamaica and sought him out on his return to England. The acquaintance confirmed his opinion that, if Darwin has discovered evolution by natural selection, it was Spencer who had achieved even more by discovering cosmic Darwinism. Spencer had outstripped Darwin, and Aristotle and Newton and Galileo as well, by drawing the entire cosmos into one all-embracing, scientifically validated philosophical system, reaching "from nebula to man, from star to soul, from atom to society." This was his rational religion, and Herbert Spencer was its messiah.[5]

In this new religion the role of John the Baptist seemed to be vacant, so Allen took for his own. He promoted, and quoted, Herbert Spencer whenever he could right to the end of his life. If anything, his claims for him became ever more extravagant and rather less credible as time went on. In his first public reference to the philosopher in 1876, Spencer is already named as "the first in the history of our race to attempt the vast task of systematizing the whole circle of existences."[6] By 1887 we hear that not only Spencer's thought, but even his literary style, is nothing less than "the most perfect instrument for its particular purpose ever fashioned by the intellect of man."[7] Finally, in 1894, Allen is prepared to claim that no one else had correlated all the facts of the universe—all the facts that are known; indeed, by implication, all the facts that *can* be known—into a synthesis so magnificent, consistent and profound. Quite simply, Spencer "possessed the finest brain and the most marvelous intellect ever yet vouchsafed to human being."

This last remarkable assertion appears in a memoir which Allen wrote in 1894, "Personal Reminiscences." This is an odd but fascinating production. It is certainly no piece of hagiography. Allen was far from blind to the older man's faults, and here he relishes the chance to foreground them: the selfishness, the hypochondria, the deafness to all criticism. Indeed, he recycles some of the ripest anecdotes about Spencer and adds a couple of his own, rather more damaging than the commonly known ones. Then again, he gives a clear impression that he and Spencer were intimate over many years, and that Spencer regarded him as one of his two most important disciples in England. Such was Allen's perception of their acquaintance. But if we peer into Spencer's papers to try to fill out the picture of their relationship, the effect is disconcerting. It is as though we are looking over the shoulder of a man who is standing before a mirror, only to find that nothing of his shape is being reflected. In the two fat volumes of his autobiography Spencer makes only a single passing mention of Grant Allen.

Vanity and self-regarding egotism surely explains that. But to explain Allen's lifelong idolatry for the Spencerian system is more difficult. It is curiously difficult to put one's finger on what specific doctrines of Spencer's Allen found most valuable and fruitful. When speaking of Spencer's merits he tended, like the master himself, to speak in broad abstractions. What, in fact, *were* those staggering insights of which he thought so highly? Whatever possessed him to speak so absurdly of Spencer's "mighty generalizations— the Instability of the Homogeneous and the Multiplication of Effects— which will endure after Oxford and Cambridge are forgotten"?[8] Was it just bombast, a desire to shock or be mischievous, or was it sober conviction? It is one of those opaque regions of Allen's intellectual personality into which the biographer cannot penetrate far.

Could those new and brilliant truths have been the ones uncovered by Spencer's political theorizing? Surely not. Even for a man who called himself an Individualist Communist—splendid oxymoron—it is inconceivable that Allen, with his humanitarian ideals and simple niceness as a man, could ever have given any credence to Spencer's bleak libertarianism, which raised the most brutal form of economic *laisser-faire* to a cosmic principle. His hero was, after all, the man who taught that the national government should leave everything to be done, or not be done, by private initiative, save only defense and policing. Banks should not be regulated, for it is wrong to protect people against their imprudent habits. Doing so interferes with the evolutionary process which rightly brings "benefit to the sagacious and disaster to the stupid." The ultimate result of shielding people from their own folly is to fill the world with fools.[9] The Poor Laws and the Factory Acts; laws against the adulteration of food or those regulating medicines: all such laws should be abolished, for they hinder the process of deleting the "unfit." Naturally, Spencer opposed all public schooling. He held that education was for parents to supply; for, he argued, if the State were held responsible for providing the child with mental nutriment, then the State might be held responsible for giving needy children food, clothing, and shelter as well. (He thought this latter proposition too self-evidently stupid to merit further comment.) He declined to support the new Royal Society for the Prevention of Cruelty to Children on the grounds that it weakened parental authority. He opposed nearly all charity-begging, for instance should not be supported, for "it has called into existence warehouses for the sale and hire of impostors' dresses."

Several of these illustrations of Spencer's social philosophy have been drawn from *Social Statics* (1851), a book which Allen probably read at Oxford, if not earlier. One wonders what he made of passages like this, which display Spencer as an unremitting Social Darwinist before anyone had heard of Darwinism:

> The well-being of existing humanity and the unfolding of it into this ultimate perfection, are both secured by that same beneficent, though severe discipline, to which the animate creation at large is subject: a discipline which is pitiless in the working out of good: a felicity-producing law which never swerves for the avoidance of partial and temporary suffering. The poverty of the incapable, the distresses that come upon the imprudent, the starvation of the idle, and those shoulderings aside of the weak by the strong, which leave so many "in shallows and in miseries," are the decrees of a large, far-seeing benevolence.

Spencer goes on to complain that there are "many very amiable people" who "have not the nerve to look this matter fairly in the face." One wonders if Allen was prepared to do so. If he did, did he ever wonder what "unnatural" impulse had made him ignore these edicts in his own life? After all, Spencer refers explicitly to the way nature deals with tubercular people. "Consumptive patients, with lungs incompetent to perform the duties of lungs . . . are continually dying out, and leaving behind those fit for the climate, food, and habits to which they are born."[10] Why, then, did not Allen follow this clear mandate to "shoulder aside" (charming phrase!) his own sick wife? The question is of course rhetorical, and ridiculous. It is unimaginable that Allen could ever have found doctrines like these acceptable in real life, or that he could have based his own behavior on them.

In his memoir of Spencer, Allen concedes on an early page that he dissented from his hero on many subjects. But he gives the impression that it was an aberration of his old age that Spencer went "grievously wrong, more particularly in his social and political thinking."[11] Certainly toward the end Spencer did revise, and reverse, his views on the merits of universal suffrage, among other things. But *Social Statics* was not the product of Spencer's old age. He was barely thirty when he wrote it. Allen was not, of course, obliged to accept its sentiments, or any other particular component of the Spencerian system, although, logically, rejecting part of it was difficult because it was just that, a system. Its claim, as Allen insisted many times, was that, like the scientific naturalism supposedly underpinning it, it formed a seamless whole. Spencer's political economics was interknit with his psychology, his biology, and his sociology: each component meshed with, and was validated by, the rest.

Allen may have been able to ignore or sidestep Spencer's social science, but he had more trouble with his biology. Spencer claims to have raised his System on a foundation of indisputable scientific fact, and central to his biology, and his sociology and his psychology, was Lamarckian inheritance; that is to say, the inheritance of acquired characteristics, or, to employ the more descriptive term, use-inheritance. (Strictly speaking, use-inheritance is only one of several conceptualizations lumped together under the label of neo-Lamarckism.[12]) Most biological theorists active between the publication of the *Origin of Species* in 1859 and the end of the century assumed use-inheritance was a fact, including, as is well known, Darwin himself in his later years. Spencer, too, assumed that use-inheritance was a powerful factor in evolution, though not as powerful as natural selection.

It has been claimed more than once that Allen was no neo-Lamarckian, and that he disavowed use-inheritance because it approached too closely, for his taste, to teleological reasoning. But of course he was. He took it for granted that the children of acrobats are born with more supple limbs, and that the children of musicians or mountaineers inherit something of their parents' trained talents.[13] He thought it was inconceivable that the human nervous system could have evolved through natural selection alone. The structures of the human brain, especially the frontal lobes, must have undergone their lightning enlargement as a functional adaptation to a changed environment, as the humanoid ape emerged from the forest on to the grasslands of Africa. As he said, "to my humble intelligence the notion of accidental brains seems simply monstrous and incredible."[14]

A thorough cultural history of Victorian neo-Lamarckism is one of the most desirable of unwritten books, but it is plain enough that Allen had a strong emotional investment in it, like many other moralists, social theorists, teachers, and political philosophers. Use-inheritance had the useful property of being able to explain almost anything. It soothed the unease of those who supposed women were mentally inferior to men. Darwin himself speculated in the *Descent of Man* that the better women were educated, the more likely they were to pass on their superiority directly to their daughters; on the other hand, conservative men need not be alarmed, for he expected it to take generations to produce any distinct effect. Most of what use-inheritance was supposed to explain had a frighteningly moral tinge. As an anxiety-maker, it was without peer. How stimulating the thought that the best endeavors and acquired skills of our forebears, especially our parents, should descend to us! How frightening that our vices, indulged weaknesses, and bad habits should descend in turn to our children, even if in some masked or muted form! How heavy, then, the responsibilities weighing on those planning to become parents!

The neo-Lamarckians' position was maintained on grounds which were a mixture of *a priori* reasoning and anecdote. It was left to August Weismann (1834–1914), a German biologist at Freiburg, to apply a long-overdue empirical test. He asked not, "How does use-inheritance work?" but "Does use-inheritance actually happen?" After painstaking experiment, he established the principle of the "continuity of the germ-plasm." No injury to the body, no atrophy or hypertrophy, no acquired skills or cultural conditioning of any kind, is ever written back to the reproductive cells. Every generation starts afresh, neither stained nor blessed by the personal activities of its predecessors.

As use-inheritance became rather more problematic toward the end of the century, Allen, to his credit, never tried to duck the difficulties. He was fascinated by heredity on both the speculative and creative levels of his mind, and no other theme appears so often in his work. Literally dozens of his novels and stories turn on the consequences of inherited habits and (particularly) vices. It is not surprising, then, that he spent much time wrestling with the problem of trying to reconcile use-inheritance with Weismann's inviolate germ-plasm. The issue was critical because, as he put it, "if Weismann is right, we shall have to begin all over again; we shall have to reconstruct from its very basis the entire fabric of evolutionary psychology"—and by that he meant Spencerian psychology.[15] Use-inheritance via the physiological units is the pivot of the Spencerian explanation of human evolution, especially the evolution of the mental powers. It is absolutely central to the *Principles of Psychology*, for instance, first published in 1855, and to the *Sociology*. In the plan for the Synthetic Philosophy, use-inheritance is proposed as the source of much innate knowledge and the basis of certainty for the transcendental axioms. Without use-inheritance as an identifiable factor in evolution, Spencer's psychology, his sociology, his ethics, and his anthropology were all fatally compromised.

Allen was not prone to repeating himself, or even to recycling his subjects. It is noteworthy, then, that he made three attempts over seven years to clarify what had become, by 1890, the crucial issue in biological theory. In its most advanced form, his argument took the form of what he calls a "flank movement" against Weismann. That is to say, he wonders whether use-inheritance between generations is in fact the key issue.[16] He wonders whether inheritance is not actually a more specialized case of the mystery of assimilation. Isn't the conversion of food into tissue—that is, not-self into self—the real miracle? What is it that reads the blueprint and directs the conversion of nutrients into the precise form required for growth and repair? "If [the cellular blueprint] can rebuild the parent, why not also the offspring?"[17]

It was a good point, though critics noted that in "solving" the problem he was committing the fallacy of substituting one mystery for a larger one.[18] Still, if use-inheritance is the key issue, then he was eager to see the issue settled experimentally. "Can it be shown that in any case a capacity or habit acquired beyond a doubt during the life-time of the individual is transmissible to the off-spring? If that can be proved, Weismannism falls at once to the ground."[19] He did not add that, if it *cannot* be proved, Spencerism falls to the ground. He never saw the resolution, for the last gasp of use-inheritance, in the Soviet-style genetics of Lysenko, lay decades in the future. In one of his reviews Allen called for a David to tackle the formidable Goliath of Weismann. He thought the champion might come from psychology. "Psychology in the end will supply the smooth stones which may pierce the forehead of our German giant," he predicted hopefully.[20] By that late date, however, he could hardly have been expecting Herbert Spencer to wield the slingshot. Perhaps he had noticed that his hero was approaching the dangerous point where use-inheritance had to be true because he needed it to be true.

Just one year after Allen's death, the Mendelian factors of particulate inheritance were rediscovered after forty years of neglect, soon followed by the discovery of the sex chromosomes. Spencer's "physiological units" vanished into the limbo reserved for phrases naming things that don't exist, and his own reputation followed, sinking, as a reference book puts it, "to hitherto unfathomed depths."[21]

What else was there in Spencer to counter and overcome his unappealing and doctrinaire attitudes? There was, surely, the philosopher's methodology, which allowed Allen to believe that he too, lacking as he did both the time or resources for laboratory work, could nevertheless participate in science. Spencer never went near a laboratory—or into a monastery garden. It never seems to have occurred to him or his disciple that the secrets of heredity, for example, were unlikely to be uncovered by hiring assistants to pick through books and then spinning other men's observations into a mental cocoon. He was so wedded to *a priori* argument that he was incapable of reasoning in any other way. Francis Galton told an amusing story of the occasion when he happened to mention that the purpose of fingerprints is unknown. Spencer at once improvised an elaborate theory about protecting the sweat glands of the fingertips from abrasion, and reared up on this supposition "a wonderfully ingenious and complicated superstructure of imaginary results." Then Galton explained that the ducts of these glands open on the exposed crests of fingerprints, not in their valleys. The splendid edifice collapsed.[22] To be fair, Spencer recognized this trait in himself perfectly well, and he does repeat in his *Autobiography* T.H. Huxley's well-known epigram that Spencer's idea of a tragedy was a beautiful deduction slain by an ugly fact.

Allen himself smiled at dogged empiricism, which he thought was a typically bone-headed "English" (or originally Saxon) trait. He recognized that it was Darwin's patient methods of observation and fact-collection that had underlain his success, for Darwin knew his countrymen; knew exactly what was needed to touch "the slow and cautious elephantine intellect of the masses." No Englishman, Allen was sure, is ever satisfied with the elegantly abstract proof of Pythagoras' theorem. He isn't impressed or convinced by logical deductions. He needs to get out a few paper rectangles and shift them around to see the proof for himself. How different to the intuitive perceptions of the Celtic mind—like his own, for example![23]

But despite this bravado, after the criticisms in *Nature* Allen evaded any more professional disputes with botanists and others on their own ground. He made only one more adventurous foray into pure science—into theoretical physics, to be exact. In 1888 Longman's published a treatise, *Force and Energy*, which is unquestionably the oddest production of his career. This long-meditated work proposed a new theory of dynamics by redefining some of the fundamental concepts of physics. He uses "force," for instance, to mean "attractive power" and "energy" to mean "repulsive power." It need hardly be said that these are totally empty verbalisms—Allen does not use a single line of mathematics—and, for the rest, he either takes for granted, or ignores, the conceptualizations so arduously clarified and tied down into interlocking definitions by geniuses like Joule, Kelvin, and Clerk Maxwell.

Force and Energy was reviewed with baffled astonishment by several real physicists, including the kindly Oliver Lodge and the frighteningly polymathic Karl Pearson. Lodge decided sadly that the book contained nothing but the familiar and the erroneous. Pearson, a mathematician, statistician, and physicist at London University, could wield a ferocious pen, but this time was content to strike a note of seasonal good-will. "Mr Grant Allen may for his own personal convenience call the 'powers' to which he refers force and energy, just as he might have equally well christened them Jack and Gill. . . . We advise him to do penance at once by writing us a blood-curdling Christmas ghost story, and by promising to entertain no more heresies." With that sort of reception, it wasn't long before Allen heard from his publisher that the book was being converted into wallpaper.[24] Still, he remained proud of his theory, even claiming on his deathbed that recognition for it was the only memorial he wanted.

Force and Energy is a curious item in the literature of Victorian pathological science. Nothing exposes more tellingly Grant Allen's main intellectual weaknesses: too much reasoning *a priori*, a certain obstinate dogmatism, an independence of mind verging on pigheadedness, and a rage to systematize everything. It is a faintly alarming comment on human folly that if he had been a man of private means Allen might well have passed his life happily articulating a cosmic philosophical system in a series of books just like *Force and Energy*. He might have become, in fact, another Herbert Spencer.

POPULARIZERS VERSUS THE PROFESSIONALS

But there was never really any risk of that. For Allen it had to be the writing of popular science or nothing, for that was the only kind which paid. But not well. Except for textbooks, the rewards for any kind of nonfiction work—a nonspecialist biography, say, or a popular history—were, generally speaking, very modest indeed. Even Walter Besant, at the height of his career, was paid only £100 by Macmillan's for a biography of Captain Cook, of which more than half was consumed by expenses. Yet he claimed to have no hard feelings: "I do not grumble, because I was perfectly free to accept or refuse."[25]

This phlegmatic attitude was certainly tested if one's field happened to be science, for this was the most difficult to penetrate and the most poorly rewarded. In his writers' guide *The Pen and the Book* (1899) Besant deals with every kind of remunerative authorship, but he does not mention scientific writing at all. By that date the situation had become clearer and gloomier than it had been when Grant Allen was starting his career. Certainly the dice became more and more heavily loaded against the average scientific author right through the 1880s and 1890s. The market for their wares was always small. A recent estimate concludes that in the 1870s only about 5 percent of the articles in eight leading periodicals were on pure science. The proportion carried in popular weeklies like the *Illustrated London News* was no greater than 5 percent either, although applied science figured a little more.[26] The proportion may have grown a little over the next two decades, but not very much. Limited public interest meant that the specialized popular-science magazines found it hard to stay viable. Both the *Popular Science Review* and the *Quarterly Journal of Science* folded in the middle years of Allen's career, and even *Nature* was in deep financial trouble in the early 1880s.

Not only was the market small, but editors' standards were high. By the 1870s a group of eminent scientists who could write lucidly and stylishly about their work were well entrenched in the magazines. They were men of the stamp of Huxley, Carpenter, Mivart, Clifford, and Galton. All these men had an academic or industrial appointment, or private means. Their writing was a sideline, a means of self-expression, or a task they had imposed on themselves of educating the public. Editors could be selective when articles were coming in from men like Edwin Ray Lankester (b.1847). Lankester was an undergraduate contemporary of Allen's at Oxford, but their worlds soon moved far apart. Lankester had already secured the chair of zoology at University College, London by 1874, while Allen was still sweating it out in Jamaica.

When John Tyndall, the eminent physicist, delivered himself of a piece on "The Electric Light" for the *Fortnightly*, it is safe to suppose that he too did not lie in wait for the editorial cheque; similarly with Francis Galton on "Psychometric Facts" for the *Nineteenth Century* or T.H. Huxley in the same place on "Sensation and Sensiferous Organs." Allen never appeared even once in those pages. Probably he never tried, knowing full well that lesser popularizers were not required while august names like these were available. When James Knowles bought "science" for his *Nineteenth Century* he bought the very best communicators in the business.

"Many thanks for your abundantly sufficient cheque," T.H. Huxley once wrote to the editor of the *Fortnightly*. "Rather too much, I think, for an article which had been gutted by the newspapers."[27] What a bitter laugh that would have raised down in the regions where obscure men tried to write science for a living! Allen saw at first hand what miserable rewards were forthcoming from popular science in the career of his older friend R.A. Proctor (1837–1888). Like Allen, Proctor married while still a student. His writing career lasted about the same length of time as Allen's and he died at fifty-one, the same age as Allen. He never held any professional appointment. He was determined to force a living out of freelance science writing, apparently out of some mixture of idealism and stubbornness. He despised state-subsidized science, which he thought was a recipe for mediocrity, and claimed that research was best undertaken by men like himself, who could fund their serious work by popular writing. He thought it should be possible to earn between two and five thousand pounds a year by this means. This wildly improbable figure suggests what a martyr Proctor was to his own obstinacy. The reality was that in his early years he worked for five years straight without a single day's holiday, admitting, not very credibly, that he "would willingly have turned to stone-breaking or any other form of hard and honest, but unscientific, labour" if anything else had offered itself. He published fifty-seven books, innumerable technical papers and more than 160 semipopular articles, not just on astronomy but on topics such as "Mechanical Chess-players" and "Calculating Boys." He also edited his magazine *Knowledge*. Yet when Proctor died of fever in America in 1888 he left almost nothing for his wife and eight children. Eventually his wife was granted a Civil List pension. It was a scant £100 a year.

Allen must have noted the course of this career of almost frightening industry, shuddered, and determined that it would never happen to him. He probably had Proctor in mind when he commented that "a surprisingly small number of copies of a book—in the case of a serious or scientific work how surprisingly few would be almost incredible—suffices to bring it well within the reach of pretty nearly everybody who cares to read it."[28] Or perhaps he was thinking of the position he had been in himself a few years earlier. A rough calculation suggests that his first four volumes of popular science, comprising ninety-one essays, brought him about £125 in all. They were, of course, being reprinted; he had already received approximately £382 for their first appearance.[29] Still, a return of £500 or so spread over three years for an inordinate amount of work does illustrate graphically what the earning power of science writing was at this time. Allen needed a lot of more profitable work on top of that to keep afloat at all.

Allen's Qualities as a Scientific Journalist

One thing in Allen's favor as a popularizer and journalist-educator was that his favorite sciences were those most popular with readers. He was particularly adept at turning out the kind of product that Gissing defined rather more sympathetically than is his wont in *New Grub Street*. In describing Amy Reardon's intellectual growth after she has left her husband, he says that "she read a good deal of that kind of literature which may be defined as specialism popularized; writing which addresses itself to educated, but not strictly studious, persons, and which forms the reservoir of conversation for society above the sphere of turf and west-endism."[30]

Specialism popularized for educated but not studious persons: that was Allen's terrain. There were plenty of Amy Reardons, new readers for the New Journalism, especially in America, and it was to them that Allen's genius spoke most effectively. As a scientific popularizer, synthesizer, and middleman, Allen was without peer in his own day. Dozens, even hundreds, of examples attest to that. He had a genius for vividly concrete analogy. There is a splendid example, apparently thrown off just as effortlessly as any other, in "Big Animals." This article takes up the issue of how easy it is to make ludicrous mistakes about which plants and animals coexisted in prehistory and which were in fact separated by untold millions of years. Few readers enjoy being lectured, and especially not by a know-all of Allen's caliber. But Allen never lectures and never patronizes. He makes his point about errors in geological chronology in this fashion instead, and it is worth quoting at some length:

> Such a picture is really just as absurd, or, to speak more correctly, a thousand times absurder, than if one were to speak of those grand old times when Homer and Virgil smoked their pipes together in the Mermaid Tavern, while Shakespere and Moliere, crowned with summer roses, sipped their Falernian at their ease beneath the whispering palmwoods of the Nevsky Prospect, and discussed the details of the play they were to produce to-morrow in the crowded Colosseum, on the occasion of Napoleon's reception at Memphis by his victorious brother emperors, Rameses and Sardanapalus. This is not, as the inexperienced reader may at first sight imagine, a literal transcript from one of the glowing descriptions that crowd the beautiful pages of Ouida; it is a faint attempt to parallel in the brief moment of historical time the glaring anachronisms perpetually committed as regards the vast laps of geological chronology even by well-informed and intelligent people.
>
>   We must remember, then, that in dealing with geological time we are dealing with a positively awe-inspiring and unimaginable series of eons, each of which occupied its own enormous and incalculable epoch, and each of which saw the dawn, the rise, the culmination, and the downfall of innumerable types of plant

and animal. On the cosmic clock, by whose pendulum alone we can faintly measure the dim ages behind us, the brief lapse of historical time, from the earliest of Egyptian dynasties to the events narrated in this evening's *Pall Mall*, is less than a second, less than a unit, less than the smallest item by which we can possibly guide our blind calculations. To a geologist the temples of Karnak and the New Law Courts would be absolutely contemporaneous; he has no means by which he could discriminate in date between a scarabaeus of Thothmes, a denarius of Antonine, and a bronze farthing of her Most Gracious Majesty Queen Victoria. Competent authorities have shown good grounds for believing that the Glacial Epoch ended about 80,000 years ago; and everything that has happened since the Glacial Epoch is, from the geological point of view, described as "recent." A shell embedded in a clay cliff sixty or seventy thousand years ago, while short and swarthy Mongoloids still dwelt undisturbed in Britain, ages before the irruption of the "Ancient Britons" of our inadequate school-books, is, in the eyes of geologists generally, still regarded as purely modern.

But behind that indivisible moment of recent time, that eighty thousand years which coincides in part with the fraction of a single swing of the cosmical pendulum, there lie hours, and days, and weeks, and months, and years, and centuries, and ages of an infinite, an illimitable, an inconceivable past, whose vast divisions unfold themselves slowly, one behind the other, to our aching vision in the half-deciphered pages of the geological record. Before the Glacial Epoch there comes the Pliocene, immeasurably longer than the whole expanse of recent time; and before that again is the still longer Miocene, and then the Eocene, immeasurably longer than all the others put together. These three make up in their sum the Tertiary period, which entire period can hardly have occupied more time in its passage than a single division of the Secondary, such as the Cretaceous, or the Oolite, or the Triassic; and the Secondary period, once more, though itself of positively appalling duration, seems but a patch (to use an expressive modernism) upon the unthinkable and unrealizable vastness of the endless successive Primary eons.[31]

This is explication of the highest quality. No contemporary of Allen's could have fixed our attention so well on the immensities of geological time. T.H. Huxley's prose is a flexible instrument, and his lucidity and range of reference are very great; but he lacked Allen's lightness of touch and fantastical wit. His is always the prose of an elder statesman of science. H.G. Wells came closer, in passages of his science fiction, but he soon moved into social polemics. We may doubt whether any modern writer of popular science, not even the stylistically brilliant Richard Dawkins, could have come up with that opening extended analogy. It is a stroke of playful genius, absurd and charming ("while Shakespere and Moliere, crowned with summer roses, sipped their Falernian at their ease beneath the whispering palmwoods of the Nevsky Prospect"), and at the same time it drives home its educational point. Anyone who isn't sure whether pterodactyls were around to fly past the nose of a tyrannosaurus, or whether a stegosaurus trampled grass or some other herbage underfoot is likely to check a textbook when he remembers that image of Homer smoking his pipe at the Mermaid. This is an almost Metaphysical sensibility supremely in control of his material.

Although all his scientific journalism was produced against the clock, Allen maintained a remarkably high level of quality, not only in content but also in style. Reading though his colossal output of the 1880s we see a certain stiffness and verbosity giving way to that sparkle, charm and lightness of touch allied to an effortless range of reference and a copious vocabulary, which became his trademark. Allen was more than a master expositor. He had more to offer than clear expression. Scientific writing can be crystal clear yet dry and dull too. Allen's best prose is full of fanciful touches, even when applied to topics the reverse of frivolous. His most bread-and-butter productions show this; here is an example taken at random, on excavated ancient ceramics:

> That is the great merit of pottery, viewed as an historical document: it retains its shape and peculiarities unaltered through countless centuries, for the future edification of unborn antiquaries. *Litera scripta manet*, and so does baked pottery. The hand itself that formed that rude bowl has long since mouldered away, flesh and bone alike, into the soil around it; but the print of its fingers, indelibly fixed by fire into the hardened clay, remains for us still to tell the tale of that early triumph of nascent keramics.[32]

The thought here could be summarized in a sentence: Pottery is important to archaeologists because it resists decay. A critic might complain that the rest is padding, and the Latin tag sounds rather forced. But the three sentences are nicely balanced, and the last one, with its touch of alliteration, fits particularly neatly around the semicolon. And the slightly lapidary quality, the faint, appropriate hint of Thomas Browne's *Urne Buriall*, flatters the educated reader. Considering that he rarely revised, such sentences could not have been long deliberated. Their gracefulness is instinctive and the decorative effects are intrinsic; they are not "sugar-candy euphuism," as Le Gallienne once rudely defined Stevenson's prose.[33] Passages like this, and there is a wide choice of ones just as good, makes it a scandal that Allen's prose is never anthologized.

Allen, Wells and Science Fiction

It is rather disappointing to find that despite possessing, one would have thought, a blend of just the right kind of qualifications, Allen was no more than a minor pioneer in the genre of the scientific romance, as science fiction was then called. If we accept the familiar definition of this—the fictional projection and imaginative exploitation of a current scientific, or quasi-scientific notion—then very few of Allen's stories qualify. Certainly a good number of them, including some of the best, do turn on scientific issues (issues of heredity, atavism, and degeneration were his favorites), but they fail to extrapolate. In "Professor Milliter's Discovery," Cyril Milliter is both an anatomist and a preacher in a fundamentalist sect. (The model for Milliter must be, in part at least, Philip Gosse, who was still alive at the time, long since reduced to a semi-tragic figure after his attempt to marry Genesis and geology in the absurd *Omphalos*.) By accident Milliter discovers a bird-lizard in a layer of oolite.

He hides the discovery in fear and trembling, but when the truth comes out he finds to his surprise that neither his wife nor congregation are much concerned about the revelation. They have painlessly acquired and assimilated Darwinism, almost without knowing it. "He can hardly resist a quiet smile himself, nowadays, when he remembers how he once kept that harmless piece of pictured stone wrapt up carefully in a folded handkerchief," says the amused, patronizing narrative voice.[34] The story is constructed as a quaint piece of historical fiction, recording passions that have been sterilized twenty-six years after the *Origin*. Allen had no trouble publishing it in 1885.

But interestingly, when he reused his idea eight years later he struck problems. "The Missing Link" is a much sourer, more combative version. This time the hero is a stern and obdurate fundamentalist. Dr. Richard Hawkins is an amateur fossil-hunter, popular in his dreary Suffolk village because as an anti-Darwinian and professional man he is more than a match for the local atheist, a "blaspheming cobbler." One day Dr. Hawkins finds a fossil human finger with a Pliocene deposit on it; bones "ghastly in their reminiscence of the great anthropoids." Dr. Hawkins confides in the vicar, who warns him to be more flexible, but he is adamant:

> I won't play fast and loose with the plain words of the Book. If God made man in His own image, and breathed into his nostrils the breath of life on the Sixth Day of Creation, then I can understand all the rest: the Immortal Soul; Free Will; the Plan of Salvation; the difference that marks us off from the lower animals; the existence within us of a divinely-sent conscience. But if ever it can be shown conclusively, shown beyond the shadow of a doubt, we're descended from an ape, then I give up all. We can be nothing more than the beasts that perish.

Dr. Hawkins is nothing if not logical; having convinced himself with the fossil finger, he first turns atheist and then poisons himself. The vicar, however, is one of nature's survivors:

> The vicar knocked off his ash pensively, and perused his boots. Logically, he had nothing to answer to the doctor's argument; but practically, he knew in his own soul that if evolutionism were to prove man's animal origin beyond the shadow of a doubt tomorrow morning, he'd stick to the vicarage of Dimthorpe still, and debate as hotly as ever at the diocesan synod over apostolic succession and the eastward position.[35]

Probably this gibe at the trimming vicar was enough to doom the story all by itself. No editor would touch it. Even in the early 1890s some guardians of public opinion did not relish having the clash between science and religion spelt out quite as baldly as Allen does it here; it reminds us, too, that Allen's polemical style did grow rather more gratingly opinionated with the passage of time.

Apart from the special case of *The British Barbarians*, which is more of a politicoeconomic fable with ethnographical trimmings, a handful of stories do meet the definition of science fiction more exactly. The young H.G. Wells, whose career overlapped a little with Allen's, admitted he had learnt much from him: "I believe that this field of scientific romance with a philosophical element which I am trying to cultivate, belongs properly to you."[36] He was thinking of "Pausodyne," "The Child of the Phalanstery," *Dr. Palliser's Patient*, "The Dead Man Speaks" and a few others, which are still reprinted from time to time in historical anthologies of the genre.

As a novelist, scientific popularizer and social theorist, Wells was Allen's natural successor. He sent Allen a copy of *The Time Machine* in its book form when it was published in 1895. Of course Allen praised its "brilliant whimsicality" and originality. At the same time, there is something a little grudging about his determination not to be impressed by Wells' superb vision of future human degeneration.[37] But it is hard to blame Allen for this. For one thing, he knew Wells had written a merciless review of *The Woman Who Did* for the *Saturday Review* not long before. And for another, he would have had to be a saint not to have felt a stab of envy at Wells' triumphant debut. Many years later Wells recalled their meeting:

> In these days Hindhead was a lonely place in a great black, purple and golden wilderness of heath; there was an old inn called The Huts and a score of partly hidden houses. . . . We sat about in deck chairs through a long sunny summer afternoon under the pines in the garden on the edge of the Devil's Punchbowl. . . . Probably we talked a lot about writing and getting on in the world of books. I was a new and aggressive beginner in that world and I was being welcomed very generously.[38]

Wells was only twenty-nine, and his career was just starting. There is surely something a trifle melancholy about that sunny Sunday afternoon. Allen could hardly have failed to recognize that a brilliant new star was in the ascendant, working the same patch that he himself had worked as best he could, but with incomparably more energy and inventiveness. Over the last few years of Allen's life, the young Wells marched from triumph to triumph, demonstrating his ability to "domesticate" (as he called it) a scientific hypothesis in a fashion which Allen, even at his best, could never emulate.

Allen's home "The Nook," Dorking, Surrey. (The house still stands, derelict.) The family moved here in 1881 as Allen was struggling to establish himself as a novelist and journalist.

The drawing room of Allen's home "The Nook." This picture appeared in an auto-biographical article by Allen, serving the reading public's interest in the domestic details of writers' lives.

A cartoon illustrating Allen's assertion that it would be more profitable to buy a good broom and "annex a vacant crossing" than to take up a career in "literature." *Idler: An Illustrated Magazine*, September 2, 1892, 154–163. Illustration by George Hutchinson and Miss Fuller.

"FICTION."

"SCIENCE."

A cartoon illustrating Allen's point about the relative earnings of the novelist and the scientific writer. *Idler: An Illustrated Magazine*, September 2, 1892, 154–163. Illustration by George Hutchinson and Miss Fuller.

The King's House, Spanish Town, Jamaica (now destroyed). In 1873–1876, Allen taught at the short-lived Queen's College that was housed there. He disliked the experience and left Jamaica as soon as his post was abolished, determined to make a living as a freelance writer in England.

The rewards of authorship: Allen's final home, "The Croft," situated on several acres of land above the Devil's Punchbowl, Hindhead, Surrey. Allen designed most of the interior fittings himself, in the Arts and Crafts style, and some remnants of these still exist in the house. Reproduced courtesy of Haslemere Educational Museum.

CHAPTER 6

THE STOCK IN TRADE: LIGHT FICTION

"DECLINING" INTO FICTION

Grant Allen, author of more than thirty novels and much short fiction, was notorious for his derogatory opinion of that important part of his trade. He wrote fiction for money, he said, and nothing more. "I suppose no man ever took by choice to the pursuit of fiction," he wrote in the self-punishing tone, which, in one mood, was habitual with him:

> Fellows drift into it under stress of circumstances, because that is the particular ware most specially required by the market at the moment . . . the literary aspirations of an educated man generally lead quite elsewhere. It is only the stern laws of supply and demand that compel him in the end to turn aside from the Lord's work to serve tables for his daily sustenance.[1]

The Biblical allusion is only half joking. Allen came to believe about halfway through his career that he did have the Lord's work to do, figuratively speaking, and that most of his novel-writing was distracting him from it. He was wont to disparage all his "commercial" novels but one, *For Maimie's Sake*, which he thought superior to the rest.[2] It is not surprising that even his well-wishers took him at his word when he spoke of himself as *declining* into fiction "as many men drop into drink, or opium-eating."[3] That very proper man, Frederic Harrison, saw nothing improper in publicly brushing aside, on the sensitive occasion of Grant Allen's funeral, all the imaginative part of his friend's career. "Of his fiction I know nothing, nor need I speak. He himself treated it as a bye-play." Some of his hearers may have found that unnecessarily blunt, perhaps, but all of them must have heard Allen say the same thing at one time or another.[4]

It was almost inevitable that a restless, versatile writer of Allen's temperament, for whom money was very important, should have tried his hand at fiction sooner or later. Apart from school textbooks, no other product repaid the tradesman's labors like fiction, especially fiction which could be serialized. "The price it fetches is far in excess of that which is given for prose writing of any other kind, and is magnificent . . . other literary labour cuts a sorry figure is comparison," said Wilfred Meynell, in his beginners' guide.[5] In particular, the magazines' and newspapers' demand for light, bright short fiction and serial novels was insatiable. By the mid-90s, the yearly production of novels in Britain nearly exceeded that of all other types of books combined.[6] The supply rose to meet the demand throughout Allen's career, and though there were many casualties in that branch of the trade too, the ratio of failures to successes was lower than elsewhere. In the year of Allen's death Walter Besant estimated that there were thirteen hundred novelists active in Britain, of which about 60 were making £1,000 a year and another 150 a tolerable living: "the rest of the one thousand three hundred make little or nothing."[7] Allen was certainly one of the sixty, and had probably been in that select group for ten years or so. The production, first of short stories, then of novels and novellas, started to underpin his career quite early on, subsidizing all his other numerous activities and by itself earning him much of the income he thought was his due. But that did not stop him resenting it, or saying that he did.

It was the short story that started him on what he called, with typically protective self-disparagement, the "downward path" into fiction. In an attempt to make one of his early articles for Chatto's *Belgravia*, on Spiritualism, more palatable he cast it in the form of a narrative, "Our Scientific Observations on a Ghost." As a story it is crude enough. There is no plot; all that happens is that a ghost appears to a pair of medical students, and they apply a range of tests, with inconclusive results. But Allen was encouraged to try more, and he had placed a dozen stories in the *Belgravia* by January 1883, when James Payn took over the editorship of the *Cornhill* from Leslie Stephen, tasked with the job of reversing the magazine's slide into extinction.

Payn, a veteran in his fifties, was a light novelist in a sub-Dickensian style, and his intent was to make every issue of the *Cornhill* readable from cover to cover. He slashed the cover price and commissioned much shorter and lighter fiction. (The only fiction previously countenanced by the *Cornhill* had been serializations from the pens of Collins, Eliot, Gaskell, Hardy, and the like.) Grant Allen's articles on the evolution of feathers, or the influence of oolitic limestone on architectural styles, stylishly written and packed with information though they had been, were no longer required, and Payn wrote to tell him so. However, Payn's eye had been caught by "J. Arbuthnot Wilson's" fiction in the *Belgravia*, and he wrote via Chatto's to request more of it. Allen liked to tell how Payn's two letters had arrived together.[8] He set to and produced "The Backslider," a mordant tale of a young member of a fanatical religious sect who is sent out into the world as its emissary, but who apostatizes when exposed to Oxford and Herbert Spencer. He wrote eight more stories for the *Cornhill*, all of them more polished than his other work. The second one, "The Reverend John Creedy," about an African missionary who atavistically reverts to savagery, attracted much comment at the time. Each story probably earned Allen £30. Unlike Conan Doyle, who resented it, Allen cared not a jot that his stories for the *Cornhill* were anonymous. He pressed on with dozens of stories for *Belgravia*, *Longman's*, the *English Illustrated Magazine*, and (later) *Black & White*, the *Graphic* and others, collecting a first pick of the crop in 1884 under the title of *Strange Stories*. Five more collections followed and those left behind, forgotten in the magazines, were enough to fill several more volumes.

The most marketable short story in the late 1870s and 1880s, when Allen was producing most of his, was an unpretentious tale that would slip down easily, preferably leaving the sweet taste of an acceptable moral behind it. Far more readers were women than men; most of them belonged to the lower ranges of the middle class, and few wanted to have their wits challenged or their prejudices scrutinized. Judged collectively, Allen's short stories—he wrote at least 175, possibly 200 or even more—show that he could analyze the market and meet its needs, not engage in technical experiments. But he does merit a footnote in literary history for making very early contributions to the inter-racial tale and to science fiction, as well as to detective fiction and the horror story, or, more exactly, the tale of the bizarre.

Allen originally thought of calling his first collection of stories *Nightmares*. He did develop in time a certain gift for the tale of bizarre or supernatural events (e.g. "Wolverden Tower," "Pallinghurst Barrow," "Selwyn Utterton's Nemesis"), and a handful of these stories are still reprinted in genre anthologies. Unlike most Victorian ghost-story writers, Allen, the scientific rationalist, nearly always offers some sort of mundane explanation in the end. In "The Mysterious Occurrence in Piccadilly" he uses a simple but ingenious plot device to generate an inexplicable situation: an apparently simultaneously appearing double apparition. Allen was probably aware of the current labors of the Society for Psychical Research, which was investigating "crisis apparitions" for its first big book, *Phantasms of the Living*. Certainly Allen parodies rather well the frequently pompous style in which people contributed their host sightings to the Society. The founders of the Society suffered from the fatally ingenuous belief that "evidences" from upstanding people like judges, civil servants, and academics ought usually to be taken at face value. It was the first and last time Allen took any interest in the respectable side of Victorian Spiritualism, even as a joke. For the modern reader, the most supernatural detail of the plot is that it was possible, then, to post a letter in Oxford at 5pm and have it delivered anywhere in London the same evening.

Another vein Allen worked successfully was the study of sociopathic personalities, which is quite impressive in an age that was rather innocent about abnormal psychology. He made a full study of a psychopath in his novel *The Devil's Die*, with the character of Harry Chichele, a toxicologist, a brilliant, charming, but sadistic researcher. In the smaller compass of his stories, Allen offers criminal psychopaths ("The Curate of Churnside"); fanatics of religious fundamentalism ("Luigi and the Salvationist"); victims of atavistic regression and heredity ("Carvalho," "Harry's Inheritance"); superficially rational madmen ("Evelyn Moore's Poet"); and terrorists of the nihilistic persuasion ("The Dynamiter's Sweetheart" and "The Assassin's Knife"). As one might guess, they owed a certain amount to Browning's dramatic monologues. Allen said of "The Curate of Churnside" that it was "a psychical analysis of a temperament not uncommon among the cultured class of the Renaissance: the union of high intellectual and aesthetic culture with a total want of moral sensibility"—the same point Ruskin famously made about a Browning monologue.[9] Other stories show him capable of straightforwardly comic tales ("The Chinese Play at the Haymarket," "A Social Difficulty") and of man-of-the-world Somerset-Maughamish tale like "Major Kinfaun's Marriage," which cleverly inverts the convention of the gold-digging female. This is a stylish, urbane story, but the ending does not quite come off.

Allen claimed to have actually invented the anthropological romance, or what he called "the romance of the clash of races." Several of his originally most popular stories, like "Carvalho" and "The Beckoning Hand," deal with atavism and inter-racial sexual relations, although today they evoke little but embarrassment. Certainly these stories did pre-date the first huge success in the genre, Rider Haggard's *She* of 1886, as well as the later excursions by Kipling, Stevenson, Hall Caine, and others. Allen said later about this particular genre that he kept watch "with the interested eye of the dealer engaged in the trade, and therefore anxious to keep pace with every changing breath of popular favour."[10] He did keep pace with *The Great Taboo* (1890), a striking if bizarre story, which owes a good deal not only to Lang's theories about the origins of religion, superstitions, and taboos, but also to *The Golden Bough*: in fact, it is a fictionalization of Frazer's thesis. Allen is very good on the paranoid suspicion and ingrained system of taboos and rituals that govern life in tribal societies, but the novel is weakened by the thinly realized setting. Even Allen knew nothing of the actualities of Polynesian life, and it shows.

ALLEN'S NOVELS AFTER *PHILISTIA*

Philistia, which he had written so carefully and in which he had invested so many hopes, enjoyed only a modest success. It was not a triumphant start, and in a way its reception doomed Allen's career as a serious novelist at the outset. *Philistia* showed promise; it had serious flaws, but nothing that a committed artist could not have put right in his next attempt. Clearly Allen was constitutionally fitted to make a novelist of ideas. He had a satirical gift, an inexhaustible reservoir of odd facts, and a sportive way with complex notions. Something Peacockian, something in the manner of the early Aldous Huxley, might not have been beyond him. But unfortunately he was now on a treadmill and the economic wheel had to be kept turning. He did not have the leisure to reflect, learn, and do better. Nor, perhaps, did he have the inclination. One of his most admirable qualities was his capacity to shrug off crushed expectations and move on, but the other side of that virtue was a certain impatience and restlessness. He had tried his best; he had written a serious work on a serious theme, but the public would not bite. Very well, then: no time for casting more pearls. So for the rest of his life Allen fitted one, two or even more novels every year into his punishing schedule, very aware that only a regular output of semipopular fiction could underwrite his comfortable mode of living and other more congenial activities.

He wasted no time in moving on. By August of the same year, 1884, a new manuscript with the working title of *Art*, was in Chatto's hands. When they discussed terms, Chatto told Allen he would have liked to pay more than he had for *Philistia*, "but we regret to say that the small enquiry for that story as well as the very depressed state of the market for fiction in consequence of the over supply does not permit us doing so."[11] Nevertheless, he gave £300, an increase of £50, for all the rights: again, a remarkably high price.

The published title was *Babylon*, referring to the English and American artists' colony in Rome. It was an unexceptionable piece of social realism expressly for a female market. In *Babylon* there come together, eventually, two artistic geniuses—one a landscape painter, the other a sculptor—from very different humble backgrounds. Hiram Winthrop, a bashful lad and lover of nature, is raised on a hogs-and-corn farm in New York state, in a family of narrow-minded fundamentalists. Hiram is rescued from rural idiocy by Lothrop Audouin, a rich Boston intellectual, confirmed bachelor, and Transcendentalist who has more than a passing resemblance to the flaneur Rowland Mallet, in James's *Roderick Hudson* (1875).

Meanwhile on the other side of the Atlantic Colin Churchill is growing up in rural Dorset, modeling figures in clay from the river for his sweetheart Minna and astonishing the vicar with his innate grasp of plastic form. (He must be based on the sculptor John Gibson, most famous for his polychrome "Tinted Venus," who had died in Rome in 1866.) After some difficulties both Colin and Hiram are drawn to Rome and make names for themselves. There are various love interests too, including a sinister Italian model, Cecca, who tries to poison Minna. Allen "essayed domesticity," as he put it, in this novel; but, as a *künstlerroman*, especially as an account of the mysterious up-welling of innate artistic genius in totally unpropitious places, it is tolerably effective.

Domesticity in *Babylon* did not sell especially well either, but Allen soon had its successor, *In All Shades*, in manuscript. (He wrote it early in 1885, but it was delayed in print.) This time he suffered a distinct reverse. Chatto was lukewarm about it when he read it that May. We recall that this novel deals with the racism and arrogance of the West Indian planter class in a fairly uncompromising way. It was not likely to appeal to the conventional Chatto. He offered only £150 for the three-decker volume, and declined the serial altogether. However, Chatto was one of the very few publishers who dealt willingly with literary agents, and he did Allen a great service by introducing him to "a very highly valued friend," A.P. Watt (1834–1914), the agent whose career was just starting to blossom. Watt took Allen on at once, promising "I shall do my best to find you a constituency." He did just that, promptly disposing of the serial to *Chambers's Journal* in Edinburgh, an organ Allen knew little about, for a handsome two hundred guineas. Chatto paid another £75 for the book rights.[12] Thus started a profitable association for both men. Within a short time, under Watt's astute handling, Allen's short fiction and serializations started to be reprinted right across the English-speaking world. Later on, Watt issued a yearly volume of testimonial letters from satisfied authors, and Allen wrote one which must have gladdened Watt's heart. "Nothing could give me greater pleasure than to testify publicly to the great advantage I have derived from your management of my business," he wrote.[13] When Watt died in 1914, all those ten percent commissions had certainly added up. He left an estate ten times larger than Allen's fifteen years earlier, but Allen would never have grudged him a penny.

While negotiating over *In All Shades*, Allen pushed on with his next. Once again, he showed how adept he was at detecting a market trend and following it. This time he tried an out-and-out, full-blooded sensation novel, trading on the Fenian bomb outrages. The result, *For Maimie's Sake: A Tale of Love and Dynamite*, is a rather peculiar affair. Maimie Llewellyn is a dizzy, blonde, amoral child of nature very like the heroine of *Gentlemen Prefer Blondes* forty years later. She has been raised by her eccentric sea captain father, who is an admirer of Reason and Tom Paine and has instilled in her nothing but an artless egotism. Nevertheless, she is such a delightfully ingenuous, baby-faced *femme fatale* that every man and woman she meets is ravished. Marrying Chevenix, an explosives chemist, Maimie soon gets bored with him and accidentally on purpose shoots him. Her husband survives the wound, though assumed to be dead by everyone, and spends the rest of his life incognito while keeping a hidden watch over his wife and her lover—simply because to him she is still a lovable innocent who needs protection. The scenes where he devotedly observes her moods and habits through a pair of binoculars from his lodgings opposite stretch credulity far past breaking-point, but Allen must have felt such uxorious behavior was natural enough. There is also a subplot concerned with explosive cigars and Russian Nihilists, led by a ruthless woman with the soundly revolutionary name of Vera Trotsky—an odd coincidence, since Lev Bronstein only took that name from his jailer when he escaped to England in 1902.

Allen himself was very pleased with *Maimie*, which he described as a "wicked novel" written deliberately to appeal to the young female reader who liked to be shocked. He confessed to Chatto that he had been unable to sleep while writing the second half, being so caught up in the actions of "my marionettes."[14] The modern reader, however, is likely to close it with the wish to see, not a critic, but a psychoanalyst, getting to grips with the curious set of relationships it delineates.

For his part, Chatto was quite bowled over. "Allow me to congratulate you on the very powerful and startling story you have written in *For Maimie's Sake*," he wrote enthusiastically. "I found the interest so absorbing that after once committing to read the MS you so kindly sent I could not lay it aside until I finished every line of it. It is so entirely different from the ordinary serial and three volume story."[15] He judged it too racy for either the periodical or the library markets, and his opinion was reinforced when the printer who was setting it up protested that the language of one passage was "unnecessarily ardent."[16] Allen agreed that Maimie's morals might not do in a serial.

Another comment he made to his publisher about his heroine's morals ("they're really a thousand times better than those of many young women who do get the entrée of the best magazine society"[17]) is noteworthy for being the very first hint that Allen might hold, quite seriously, opinions about personal ethics, which were both radical and confrontational. Chatto might have protested, reasonably enough, that a heroine who shoots her husband down in cold blood, and yet prospers because she is so delightfully kittenish, hardly deserves a place on the moral podium high above her sisters'. But he held his peace. Others, later, would not be so forbearing.

POTBOILERS VERSUS "SERIOUS" FICTION

Allen's output of fiction was gathering speed now, and with a few exceptions it is neither necessary nor profitable to consider it in detail. For the rest of the decade he published, apart from the regular flow of short stories, one lengthy three-decker or novelette after another at intervals of four months or less. In his second and last full decade of activity he produced even more: another mass of short stories, twenty more novels including his two great popular successes, two children's stories and two more novelettes.

Enough survives of the correspondence between Allen and his agent, as well as with two of the shrewdest publishers then active in England, Andrew Chatto and John Lane, for us to see how matters were handled to secure the maximum financial benefit all round. Allen died before he could tap deeply into the lucrative American magazine market which, in the years from the First World War on into the Twenties, was willing to offer sums like the £3,000 *Harper's* gave for the serial rights to one of Arnold Bennett's minor works. Still, he was just in time to benefit from the scales of payment offered by the *Pocket Magazine, Forum, Cosmopolitan*, and their British imitators like the *Strand*. The letters from Andrew Chatto, in particular, which extend over many years, give much detail about the earnings that a moderately popular novelist like Grant Allen could achieve without having any very distinctive talent, always provided his production never flagged. All of Allen's versatility and productivity would not have counted for much if he had not essayed fiction: fiction alone propelled him into the upper reaches of middle-class prosperity.

Chatto took all eleven of Allen's longest novels of the 1880s and early 1890s and published them in the three-decker format. This in itself reveals something about his readership. By no means all, or even most, Victorian fiction appeared in this form. The three-decker was expensive and sold almost entirely to the circulating libraries, so repeated publication in that form was an accolade of a kind, for it meant one was meeting a particular market, and the most lucrative market at that. Chatto, sometimes working in conjunction with Watt, stuck to the same sequence of events. First came the serial publication. The periodicals and newspapers they used varied, depending on the best price Watt could secure. *Chambers's Journal*, the *People*, and the *Graphic* were the main ones, with, in later years, the provincial, U.S. and Australasian newspaper rights sold off separately. That was followed by a three-decker edition of a thousand sets or fewer, usually timed to appear in the last stages of the serial; that in turn was followed by the one-volume cheap "new edition." Allen had to wait, in the case of *Philistia*, for eleven years for the cheap edition, but soon it was following at ever closer intervals; within two or three years, and eventually, in the case of the popular *The Scallywag* (1893), in the same year. There was nothing surprising or distinctive in this pattern. It was simply a trend in the market, a response to changes in taste and changes in the economics of publishing and printing technology.

Chatto was not offered, or was not interested in taking, Allen's numerous shorter novels and popular novelettes, which Allen either marketed himself or (more likely) wrote under commission. They were undemanding romances and juvenile fictions which he could fling off virtually to order: novels and novellas like *Tom, Unlimited, Wednesday the Tenth, The Incidental Bishop, The White Man's Foot, An Army Doctor's Romance*, and so on. The first three of these were for the child or adolescent market. The last named was published in a series called The Breezy Library, described by the publisher as "an attempt to dissociate a shilling from a shocker, and to supply rather a series of 'Shilling Soothers.' "[18] Allen could turn out a good soother and reviewers often recommended him as good relaxing company in which to while away a railway journey. Titles such as *Dr Palliser's Patient* and *Blood Royal* met that prescription. *Recalled to Life* (1891) and some other shorter thrillers were put in the hands of J.W. Arrowsmith, a firm that, despite being based in Bristol had, in the mid-1880s, a surprising reputation for detecting potential best-sellers: the Grossmiths, Chesterton, Jerome, and Edgar Wallace all appeared under its imprint. The nadir of Allen's creative life was surely the three novelettes that he turned out for the Society for Promoting Christian Knowledge: *A Terrible Inheritance* (1887), *A Living Apparition* (1889) and *The Sole Trustee* (1890). These were diluted versions of the old-style penny bloods. The exact length of the tales was specified in the advertisements for this series, the Penny Library of Fiction: each one was guaranteed to contain thirty-two pages, neither more nor less. After a bit of practice, Allen was able to manufacture featherweight novelettes like these in a few hours, surely without engaging his higher mental processes at all. The last one, *The Sole Trustee*, appeared just as the Society for Promoting Christian Knowledge came under sustained fire from the Society of Authors for sweating its authors. It was revealed that they were paid between thirty shillings and £10 per novelette. Allen probably just shrugged his shoulders and got on with the job, but it speaks volumes for his circumstances that even at this point, near the end of his first decade of authorship, he felt he had to join the company of the nonentities—mostly hapless women—from whom the SPCK derived astonishing profits.

Chatto did take all his longer "blood and thunderers," however; those deliberately contrived thrillers where Allen shows his ability to devise and handle a fast-moving plot with plenty of highly colored incident. He wrote a string of these after *For Maimie's Sake*, and most of them are still capable of keeping the reader turning the pages today. The title of one, *This Mortal Coil* (1888), would do for them all, because they lack any vestige of internal structure and appear to have been constructed on the principle of supplying one remarkable scene after another until the third volume filled up. Once he had got to that point, Allen lost interest. At the close of *This Mortal Coil* the hero accidentally kills the villain as a train steams along the Riviera coast. Without further ado Allen makes the locomotive jump the track at a convenient point, plunging the carriages and the incriminating corpse into the depths of the Mediterranean, presumably because he lacked the space or need for any further complications.

Still, his best examples in this line do show an improvement in skill in the last years of the 1880s. One particular mark of success came with *The Tents of Shem* (1889), the fruit of Allen's winter in Algeria. It has a complicated and slightly more integrated plot than usual, turning on legal matters. For the first time, Watt managed to place the serial with the *Graphic*, which was quite a coup and definitely a mark of Allen's acceptability as a thoroughly saleable middlebrow novelist. Andrew Chatto wrote especially to congratulate him on it, as well as offering a further £120 for the volume rights. "The *Graphic* does not pay high prices—about £400 or £450 I imagine is their maximum for the serial use of a three volume novel, but I consider that there is a compensating value in the *prestige* gained by the publication of a novel in their columns and of this the management are aware and do not fail to avail themselves."[19] It's unlikely that Allen got quite as much as £450 this time from the *Graphic*, but he was moving towards a total return of about £600 for one of his three-deckers by the time he had reached mid-point in his career. The *Graphic* also took *The Scallywag* (1893), which received the best reviews of any of Allen's novels and, by the time Watt had sold off all the rights piecemeal, had certainly returned £700 or more. *The Scallywag* was filmed as late as 1921, with the contract calling for the author's name to follow the title in an easily readable typeface—an indication that Allen's name still had some drawing-power at that date. *Under Sealed Orders*, a tale of espionage and terrorism, did even better. Its British publication was in 1895, so it must have been one of the last in the long line of three-deckers. Andrew Chatto paid him a handsome £800 for all the rights.

Allen's most telling success in the popular fiction market was his entry for a competition run in 1891 by the magazine *Tit-Bits*, founded a decade earlier by George Newnes and the most successful of the penny weeklies. The prize was superb—a thousand pounds—and the incredible number of entries received (20,000 manuscripts) is evidence of the bottled-up literary aspirations of the age. Allen dashed off his entry in a month, in between a mass of other work. His rattling yarn, *What's Bred in the Bone*, won the prize, sold enormously, was translated into Danish and Icelandic, and was filmed in 1916. The pace never slackens for a minute: the heroine almost sits on top of the hero's large pet snake in a railway compartment within the first few pages and is entombed alive with both of them in a collapsed tunnel within the first ten. A murderous judge, multiple mistaken identities and scenes of barbaric tribal life and diamond smuggling in South Africa further decorate this extraordinary confection.[20]

What's Bred in the Bone does show Allen at the very top of his populist form. It is a tribute to the coldly analytical skill with which he could meet this particular level of literary taste. He panders shamelessly to female readers—the majority—by contrasting the "gross and clumsy male intellect" with the "unerring intuition" of his heroine, driving home the message with a cozy authorial aside as early as the third page: "That's one of the many glorious advantages of being born a woman. You don't need to learn in order to know. You know instinctively. And yet our girls want to go to Girton and train themselves up to be senior wranglers!"[21] Allen sometimes pained his friends and admirers by apparently admitting to a rather breathtaking hypocrisy, as when he was reported as saying that "for years I have been trying hard as a matter of business to imitate the tone of the people from whom I differ in every possible idea—religious, social, political, ethical, psychological, biological, philosophical, and literary."[22] Wanting to imitate the style, or tone, of popular novelists is not, of course, the same as wanting to imitate their sentiments. Nevertheless, as in the case of the example above from *What's Bred in the Bone*, Allen was careful to speak to the nascent feminism, and counterfeminism, of the 1880s. In these earlier novels he was adept at accommodating himself both to the conservatism of many of his readers and the radicalism of the few. It is a commonplace that the New Woman label of the 1890s actually encompassed a range of gender stereotypes, some of them mutually inconsistent, and Allen had no qualms about making studies of the most extreme types. For the conservatives, he offers the woman graduate who is a bag of nerves, reduced to a neurotic wreck by the pressures of higher education. Such a one is the young Blackbird in *Under Sealed Orders*. Weak and vacillating, she evades the dangers of maternity at least; for when her lover presses her to marry she applies her chemistry skills to distilling prussic acid from laurel leaves, and kills herself.

Blackbird is a barely disguised version of the young lesbian poet Amy Levy, who had attended Newnham but left in her second year. The ditties Allen puts into Blackbird's mouth are derived from Levy's collection of poems *A Minor Poet and Other Verse* (1884), many of which dwell morbidly on the dark beauty of self-annihilation. The Allens met Levy socially in 1889, in the last summer of her life, when she took a cottage in Dorking, and he wrote an obituary poem about her, "Amy Levy's Urn." (The publication history of *Under Sealed Orders* is tangled, but it was certainly written closer to the date of Levy's suicide, two or perhaps three years before it was published in 1894.) His version of Levy, "pallid little Amy Levy," he called her, neurotic, perversely sexed and unhinged by inappropriate education, made a convenient representation for his more conservative readers of what higher education could do to a young woman. An even more alarming case is that of Woodbine Weatherly, a feeble creature in *The Duchess of Powysland* (1892). For her, enrolment at Girton proves literally fatal when she dies in childbirth.

The narrator is quick to sheet home the cause of this hardly uncommon medical outcome. Forget puerperal fever or obstetric complications:

> The higher education of women, that fashionable Moloch and Juggernaut of our time, slays its annual holocaust so regularly nowadays that nobody is astonished when one more Girton girl, unequal to her self-imposed task of defying with impunity all the laws of nature, breaks down and dies in her first futile attempt to fulfill the natural functions of motherhood.[23]

These examples of authorial interjections, which could easily be multiplied, seem to confirm that Allen was ready to pander to his readers' prejudices, and he sometimes conceded things that convey that impression. "My line," he told an interviewer in 1893, "is to write what I think the public wish to buy, and not what I wish to say, or what I really think or feel; and to please the public, for a man of my temperament and opinion, is not so easy as an outsider might be inclined to imagine."[24] But, considered carefully, we see that he is not saying he had written things he did not believe; only that he had been obliged to refrain from writing about many things that he did believe. These opinions are a coarser and narrower version of his own actual opinions. For example, warnings, in fiction and elsewhere, about the fate awaiting the tertiary-educated woman were a commonplace of the time. George Gissing offered a similar and, if anything, even less sympathetic study of the force-fed woman student in his *In the Year of Jubilee*, a student whose last infirmity, after her mental collapse, is joining the Salvation Army.

In Allen's case, his interjections are not quite what they seem. It is important to place Allen's comments in the context of his no less vitriolic condemnation of the public-school curriculum for young men, which fed its victims into the universities. In the schools "there is," he complains, "no systematic teaching of knowledge at all; what replaces it is the teaching of the facts of language, and for the most part useless facts." They are "places for imparting a sham and imperfect knowledge about two extinct languages. . . . Besides, look at our results! The typical John Bull! pig-headed, ignorant, brutal. Are we really such immense successes ourselves that we must needs perpetuate the mould that warped us?"[25] So, since young women undergraduates were now being fed the same diet, it's not surprising that he detected, and portrayed, a Jane Bull type as well. He drew such a one in Ida Mansel, of *Dumaresq's Daughter*. Mrs. Mansel is an icily rational young matron who voices ferocious sentiments like "war's an outlet for our surplus population. It replaces the plagues of the Middle Ages. There are plenty more soldiers where those came from." Later we hear that "it vexed her righteous Girtonian soul" to "harp for ever on a single human life, when population tends always to increase in a geometrical ratio beyond the means of subsistence." Presumably Allen would have favored George Orwell's observation that there are some ideas so stupid that only an intellectual can be made to believe them.

Although even in Mrs. Mansel's case it is grudgingly conceded later that "even Girton had not wholly extinguished her feminine instincts,"[26] for some readers this was not enough: they wanted studies of healthy, cheerful, athletic, down-to-earth young women who have survived the university experience with their femininity intact, and Allen, attentive to all branches of his female readership, supplied these too once he perceived the demand. Examples are women like Ionè Dracopoli in *Under Sealed Orders* who rides across Morocco on horseback with only a male guide for company (although she has, in fact, attended a School of Art); or Iris Knyvett, late of Girton, in *The Tents of Shem*, who is neither a militaristic virago nor a sexless waif; or Lois Cayley, also of Girton, where she has taken Honors in mathematics and rowed for her college; or Miss Cayley, who travels the world on a shoestring budget, getting the better of many colorful characters en route; or Juliet Appleton, the typewriter girl of the novel of that title, who having lost her money, takes to a career, a flat of her own, and a bicycle in a mood of defiant recklessness. But in the end most are shown tamed by matrimony and maternity. None of Allen's heroines, save one, breaks the carapace of conventionality.

Towards the Polemical Novel

It would be idle to pretend that any of Allen's fiction mentioned so far rises above the level of a solid, journeyman's competency. Some of what he wrote shows signs of haste, which is not surprising in one who at one point published seven novels in two years: repetitiveness, space-filling conversations, implausible motivation and insipid heroines. Though he could fashion an eventful plot and write lively dialogue, Allen contributed nothing original to the art of fiction. He was well aware, of course, of what the French and Russian writers had been doing since the 1860s—Turgenev, Maupassant, the Goncourts, and their English disciples like Moore, Kipling, Stevenson, Conrad, James—but he took no creative interest in them; not even in Zola's experiments with "scientific" Naturalism, which one might think would have appealed to him. Of English novelists, he greatly admired Hardy and positively idolized Meredith, but his attitude was to praise and do otherwise.

Having no interest in innovative technique does not necessarily make for a poor novelist, though it may make for an unenterprising and dull one. But Allen's novels are rarely dull. Broadly speaking, they are an extension of his talk: an effortless, copious, allusive flow of talk from a seemingly bottomless reservoir. Everyone who knew him agreed that Allen's talk was something truly astonishing. "No pose-talk," insisted a friend, "but talk easily born of his knowledge and love of the subject that at the moment occupied him."[27] He created several characters who surely are, at least in part, self-caricatures in this respect—people like the camp music critic Florian Wood in *Linnet* (1898) whose conversation, or rather monologue, surges forward on a tidal wave of quotations and free association. Hugh Massinger, the villain of *This Mortal Coil*, has a similar line in cynical and fantastical talk; so does the sexually ambiguous romantic novelist Seeta Mayne in *The Devil's Die*. In life Allen practiced the art of conversation more successfully than do these characters of his—he was no Dr. Johnson, tossing and goring his opponents—but his written style, in his essays and the narrative parts of his fiction alike, is a more muted version of his characters': often, one can actually catch the rhythms of his speaking voice. What remaining value he has as a minor novelist is almost entirely due to his gifts as a brilliant journalist, social polemicist, and public instructor.

The most painful aspect of Allen's career as a novelist is that his reach always exceeded his grasp and made him bitter and impatient with his own success. Although he put aside—or said he had put aside—any higher ambitions for his novels than producing big-selling tales for the broadest possible audience, he never really gave up the idea that he should have been writing novels like *Philistia*—novels to lash the cruelties and fatuities of society; novels to promote its reform. His protestations that he literally could not afford to use the novel to say things he wanted to say, things overwhelmingly important to him, grew ever more vehement as time passed. Frustrated in that ambition until the last years of his career, he took refuge in self-deprecation as a protective pose. Nothing is more revealing, in this respect, than a letter he wrote to his friend George Croom Robertson, probably, but not certainly, in 1885. The context is that Robertson had encouraged him to try another serious, heart-felt novel in the wake of *Philistia*, and this had stirred ambitions he thought he had given up:

> I am so much exercised in mind about it, that I can't help writing you this long rigmarole (as if you were the editor of the *Family Herald*). . . . I ask myself, have I any right so to speculate—mainly for the gratification of one's own vanity—with time which is really by contract Nellie's and the boy's? Oughtn't I to be using it all to what I feel in my heart to be their best advantage? Ought I to go squandering it away on the remote chance of my own crude estimate of myself being the correct one? The more I rub against other men, the more do I feel that the opinion they form of me & of my work is very different from the opinion I was at first disposed to form myself.
>
> I can't tell you how much we both enjoyed your visit here. It was a real delight to us. I oughtn't to repay it by boring you with this letter.—Don't answer it.—I think after all I shall yield to vanity.[28]

The see-sawing emotions elsewhere in this long letter are remarkable. He is content, he says, to be "a good round hack," incapable of doing work "above mediocrity," but on the other hand ambition is by no means dead in him, and he closes on a note of defiance. His final determination to "yield to vanity," produced, after a long delay, the two novels bearing the "hill-top" label, *The British Barbarians* and *The Woman Who Did*. These two he marked out as types of those he would have written, if only he could have afforded to; the ones which he defined as truly his own "in thought, in spirit, in teaching."[29] "Teaching" is the operative word: he had no interest in the art novel, but he did value the semipopular novel as a educational tool. His opinion was that no one who had trenchant things to say about social questions, and Allen had a great deal to say, could afford to neglect the novel. But to use the novel for such a purpose was always controversial. It was held to be illegitimate and vulgar not only by art novelists like James but by proponents of the novel as romantic entertainment like Andrew Lang and the Henley circle. For Lang, who regarded the romances of Walter Scott and Rider Haggard as the touch-stones of genuine art, the idea of using fiction to persuade people to think and live differently was absurd. In his letters to Allen, and in reviews of his novels, Lang chaffed him mercilessly about his propagandist impulse. He refused to allow that the novel should be a campaigning weapon for reform, particularly sexual reform. Such cases should be made simply and directly; they "ought not to be mixed up with flirtations, love affairs, and fanciful episodes. Novels are not tracts, sermons or treatises." Zola's *Nana*, valuable though it is, should not be allowed to circulate in England among the readers of Miss Yonge.[30] So, when Allen sent him a review copy of *The Woman Who Did*, Lang's response was "many thanks I hope you have got it off your mind, now! Personally I prefer opinions in Treatises, not in novels, and I would hear you gladly on cuckoos, rather than on *cocks*."[31] The bawdy jest makes one blink in surprise. Presumably that was how they talked at Edward Clodd's hilarious weekend stag parties. It briefly flicks open a tiny window into the jovial and cynical smoking-room talk about Allen's doctrines, which must have lain just below the decorous surface of all public, and most of the private, debate. Yet the blunt speaking is appropriate enough. After ten years of light fiction Grant Allen, now a prosperous man of letters with money in the bank, was about to throw off the sheep-like mask of the inoffensive popular novelist to reveal the face of the polemical tiger behind.

CHAPTER 7

THE PROSPEROUS TRADESMAN
(1890–1895)

ALLEN AND THE AMERICAN PIRATES

Grant Allen in his prosperous years—in his last decade, that is to say; from 1890 onward—was a familiar figure in all the haunts of literary and scientific London: a neat, slightly built man in his forties, with a long, keen, bony, Scotch face, whitening sandy hair, a reddish-grey goatee beard and pale blue eyes. The gossiping journalist Douglas Sladen said that Allen reminded him of the gaunt, red-bearded figures one sees on French tapestries of the fifteenth century, as he had the same spare figure and the same habit of arching his back.[1] Another described him at this time as "all sugar, and seems to be a pleasant and gentle person; tall and thin, with plenty of grey or whitish hair and a pointed beard; light eyes, with a boyish look in them, a small and mincing mouth, and a nose that seems to have grown much longer than was at first intended, arched, thin, and pliant, giving him a somewhat foxy look. . . . He has a lot to say, and says it well; is more tolerant of contradiction than most . . . must have done a lot of various work in his time."[2] His manner was normally quiet, gentle, and confiding. Informal social occasions drew out the best in him, and then his conversation could be animated, energetic and, at times, acerbic and paradoxical. While he spoke, he constantly twirled the pocket lens which he kept in readiness for the examination of some flower or insect. Frank Harris noted his "air of clean alertness and vivacity," and thought that his constant walking exercise and moderate habits compensated for his physical ailments.[3] His tuberculosis continued to remain quiescent for long periods so long as he looked after himself, and fortunately he never suffered from hemorrhaging of the lung. His general health, though, was wretched. As early as 1883 William James had described him as "a poor long nosed sandy bearded consumptive looking fellow, but a charming talker."[4] His regular breakdowns, in the form of bronchitis and fever, continued to the end, and he had a cough which another acquaintance said sounded like a knock on Death's door. He also suffered from excruciating writer's cramp, which sometimes forced him to type one-handed.

In her biography of the publisher George Newnes (1911), Hulda Friedrichs gave a striking pen-picture of Allen as he entered his last decade. Allen was collecting his prize for *What's Bred in the Bone* from the offices of *Tit-Bits*, that popular organ of self-improvement for the lower middle classes:

> Brave, patient spirit! I see him now, sitting in the tiny waiting-room of the old *Pall Mall Gazette* in Northumberland Street, looking very frail and thin in his rough tweed clothes, and with the sad smile on his face; and I hear the pleasant, cultured voice that came rather as a surprise to those who saw him for the first time and noted that his bronzed face looked more like that of a farmer than a literary and scientific man. "Why not?" he said. "What is the matter with *Tit-Bits*, that I should be ashamed of having gained a prize in its literary competitions? I wish all the papers for which I have written pot-boilers were as interesting, and if some had paid me half as well I should not be where I am."[5]

"I should not be where I am." Where was he, in fact, in 1891, at the time of this word-picture? Somewhere not very attractive, it seems to tell us. We see a delicate, shy invalid ("frail and thin"), not very well off ("rough tweed clothes"), obliged to exile himself in the country (the "cultured voice"), and doomed to spend his time in outer offices waiting on the convenience of busy men more prosperous than he. It suggests someone who has been dragooned into an uncongenial occupation and who has been almost broken by it: a hero of adverse circumstances, to be sure, but still an object of pity.

Although this picture does reflect something of how Allen presented himself to the world, particularly in his depressed moods, it is misleading in many ways. For one thing, it seriously underplays the indisputably tough, shrewd, competitive, calculating elements in his nature. After all, he would hardly have been in the *Tit-Bits'* office waiting to collect his thousand-pound cheque if he had really been the broken reed we are shown here.

The truth is that by this date Allen was at the peak of his productivity, earning well and living well. After all, he published three other novels as well as the *Tit-Bits* winner in that very year, and yet he still had the time and the leisure to work on his translation of Catullus's *Attis*—not a critical edition, in fact, but a scholarly contribution to the poetic mythology surrounding ghost- and tree-worship. Allen found time for several such labors of love in his middle years, and they hardly suggest a man broken and exhausted by pen-slavery. He was able to do this, in part, because at long last he had begun to get some benefit from sales elsewhere in the world. Of these markets the American was the most important, though he gained very little personal profit until the last eight years of his career. Even more than most authors, he suffered from the piratical activities of American publishers. The United States did not sign the Berne Convention in September 1886, and no protection was available until the (limited) provisions of the American/British Copyright (Chace) Act of 1891. Any remuneration of British writers was left entirely to the benevolence of U.S. publishers who, not surprisingly, refused to pay much, if anything, for a British writer's copyright, which they in turn were unable to protect from their own predatory countrymen. The "first dozen" names in publishing had a gentleman's agreement—if that is the right phrase—that the original pirate should be left to enjoy his booty and not be pirated in turn, but needless to say the smaller fry took no notice of that.

Among the pirating periodicals, the *Eclectic Magazine* was one of the worst offenders. Each issue consisted of little but the best British writing of the day. Month after month, year after year, the *Eclectic* lived up to its name by calmly appropriating articles from the *Cornhill*, *Longman's*, and the *Belgravia* among many others, and reprinting them in its closely packed pages without paying their authors a cent. It lifted one of Allen's first articles, "The Origin of Flowers," in May 1878, and treated at least sixty more of them in the same fashion over the next two decades. *Littell's Living Age*, which eventually absorbed its rival *Eclectic*, was another offender. Sometimes, if he had known of it, Allen could have had the dubious pleasure of seeing the same pirated article of his printed in three different U.S. journals within a single month. As for his books of popular science, some were published by reputable firms like Appleton's and Funk & Wagnall's, both of whom paid small sums as conscience money. But rather more were reprinted by minor houses, which certainly paid him nothing at all. It was much the same story with his fiction.

Piracy, of course, ran both ways across the Atlantic, and American editors sometimes tried to muddle the issue by complaining in turn that their own articles were being pirated in Britain. The *Popular Science Monthly* protested in January 1888 that despite the "righteous indignation over the ways of American publishers" ten of its articles had been reprinted without any acknowledgment in the British *Health*. The editor said sanctimoniously that "American periodicals in good standing uniformly give full credit for articles." Perhaps that was broadly true; it was certainly true of the *Popular Science Monthly*. We note, however, the ambiguity of the editor's phrase "full credit." He does not go so far as to say that it paid the authors anything, or even acknowledged their existence. Indeed, it is surely suggestive that in the list of the ten articles complained of, an author's name is not given for any of them. The custom of anonymity, of course, which was fading by the late 1870s but far from extinct, made this easier.[6]

These depredations were particularly severe in Allen's case because he sold well in America. Popular science, and works appealing to the insatiable urge for self-improvement among the American middle classes, such as travel guides, found a ready audience. All of Allen's work of this nature was pirated, and all he had ever got, he complained in 1885, was a voluntary payment of $50 from one publisher and $100 from another. It was natural for him to feel the abuse the more because by the small geographical accident of being born on the wrong side of the St. Lawrence he could be pirated with impunity. If he had been an American citizen, even one living abroad, he would have been protected as Henry James was, to his great advantage. (Strictly speaking, Allen should have been protected from U.S. editions being circulated in Canada, but no one took much notice of that.) Small wonder that he reacted badly to a request from an American magazine for his autograph. "I can get no protection for the labour of my hands and brain in a great country for which I still feel a deep and enduring affection, in spite of its systematically robbing me of three-fourths of my paltry income. Under these circumstances I have to work far too hard for my living, and for those dependent upon me, to find time for writing my name over and over again on behalf of collectors of autographs. As a rule, I am glad enough to lay down the pen out of my aching fingers as soon as the day's work is fairly over." Another bitter comment in the same letter of protest hints at his state of mind at this point, in the mid-1880s, when he began to realize where his authorial future lay. "If people really cared about my work, they would buy my books; which they don't. For ten years I have been fighting a hard battle against poverty, in writing scientific works, and now I am just being compelled to retire from the hopeless contest and take to penny-a-lining for a livelihood at vulgar stories."[7] From 1891, though, a regular flow of dollar checks was crossing the Atlantic and adding its meed to Allen's bank account, where at last a good lump of capital was accumulating.

LIVING AT "MINDHEAD"

Another index of prosperity was that after twelve years at Dorking the Allens decided the town was becoming too suburbanized for their tastes. Allen's private index of where London ended was exactly at the point where the last gin-palace gave way to the swinging sign-board of the first country inn. By 1890, he decided that Croyden, Cheam, and even Epsom had surrendered to the "spider-like claws of that devouring national cancer."[8] Now the country started only at Leatherhead, and it would not be long before the straggling commuters' villas were rising there too. It was time to move on and out, deeper into south-west Surrey.

The choice of locale was not difficult. The high country around Grayshott, Haslemere, and Hindhead was useless for cultivation, the soil being half infertile clay and half a dry sandy loam covered in heather, gorse, and pinewoods. It seemed remote, and by road it was. The main Portsmouth to London highway was little more than a dusty track that was not sealed in Allen's lifetime. But it was only 80 km from London by rail and the service was excellent. Here for some years past had been forming the nucleus of an artists' and intellectuals' colony: Tennyson, George Eliot, G.H. Lewes, John Tyndall the physicist, Richard Le Gallienne, Conan Doyle, Bernard Shaw, Francis Galton, some of Bertrand Russell's family and many others. Not for nothing was the area known as "Mindhead." [9]

Attracted by both the climate and the scenery—promoters were extolling it as the English Switzerland—Allen bought a few acres and had a fine house, The Croft, built on a high saddle of land, a position which exposed it to the full force of the northerly winds, which he believed were good for his lungs. The site was on the very rim of a circular valley, called the Devil's Punchbowl, on one side, and overlooked the Golden Valley on the other. There were magnificent airy views from every room, with hardly a sign of human habitation anywhere, for the few farms were in the valleys and invisible, so that a vista of purple or golden heather and pinewoods stretched right to the horizon. The Allens moved there in the spring of 1893 after returning from their winter in the South. A letter to Clodd written in February 1893 suggests this visit included the great Italian cities, because he says that in early March he is to leave for Florence and then for Rome. "I am mugging up my Baedeker in anticipation, but I confess the vastness of all there is to see rather appalls me."[10]

The Croft was Allen's home for the six years remaining to him. They were good years. Here the family entertained, less pretentiously and more informally than custom required, but still in the effortless manner possible only for the moneyed classes with plenty of willing domestic labor to call on. Every summer weekend a lively company gathered on the lawn in deck-chairs: York Powell, Clodd, Swinburne, neighbors like Le Gallienne and the positivist and medievalist Rayner Storr. Netta Syrett, Allen's niece, then in her twenties, often stayed at The Croft and in her old age recalled that it was there that she first heard conversation practiced as an art; conversations that went on for hours at a time: at the lunch table, then outside for afternoon tea, and back in the house for dinner. She found some of Allen's themes disconcerting and the "frankness of his talk about sex" embarrassed her. "I think sex was something of an obsession with Grant," she said; but it did not prevent her from becoming a New Woman novelist herself, published by John Lane and promoted with his usual efficiency by her uncle.[11]

Allen was not averse to showing off his new house, and gossip columnists went into ecstasies over it: the good taste in evidence everywhere; the genial motto *Sibi et Amicis* over the entrance; the many signed first editions from famous authors on the shelves; the Hispano-Moorish tiles from Florence decorating the study; the heather running up to the edge of a garden full of rare plants; the general air of domestic comfort and honestly acquired affluence. Thus was the cult of the gentleman-author worshipped. Allen asserted (or so Morley Roberts said), that by now he could only write in a comfortable study, preferably one with rose-colored curtains. This observation earned a contemptuous snarl from Roberts' friend, the Spartan George Gissing, for whom the color of curtains, or the presence or absence of any window-dressing at all in his many scruffy abodes, was of little moment.[12]

His greatest pleasure was rambling or bicycling through the lanes around Hindhead and Grayshott. But when necessity called—and it often did—the Great Wen with its "tinsel Arcadias" was only ninety minutes away by train. The bracing moorland air made it possible for him to winter at home, and in these last years spring became the season for his travels. Now it was the art centers of Europe which held his interest, especially those of Italy; for Italian life, manners, and above all Italian art captivated him as never before.

WORKING FOR THE *STRAND* AND THE *WESTMINSTER GAZETTE*

Two new papers from the Newnes stable were launched early in the 1890s, and each offered Allen his last and most rewarding journalistic opportunities.

The *Strand* was an imitation of the smart American papers like *Harper's* and *Scribner's* and offered eyebrow-raising rates of pay to match. It was edited personally by George Newnes, then at the height of his proprietorial powers. The *Strand* specialized in light reading, and its formula called for lots of variety, plenty of bright fiction, and a picture on nearly every page. Allen contributed a story, "A Deadly Dilemma," to the first issue in January 1891 and he was rarely out of its pages in the later 1890s. Though his tales could not rival those of his friend Conan Doyle, who pocketed £620 for a single episode of *The Hound of the Baskervilles*, Allen showed his usual perspicacity in exploiting the latest trend. "The Great Ruby Robbery" (October 1892) is recognized as an early classic of the genre, and although the denouement relies on a trick—the investigating detective is the thief—it is carried off ingeniously. It has been reprinted several times in genre anthologies.

The other Newnes venture was a new evening paper, the Liberal *Westminster Gazette*, started in January 1893 with E.T. Cook as editor, and printed on pale green paper, which was supposed to be kinder on the eyes of tired, homeward-bound readers. It was one of those odd ideas that work wonders, and the *Westminster* soon proved that it had staying-power. It boasted from the outset a column from Allen, which would be "dealing with Popular Science and other matters." The emphasis, as it turned out, was very much on the other matters. Many of his fifty-six pieces, which appeared at intervals of about twice a week, are highly disputatious in tone and give, collectively, the fullest insight into Allen's social and political views. He collected twenty-five of them in a volume, *Post-Prandial Philosophy* (1894), and they do have an unbuttoned after-dinner air about them, though they also contain some of his best writing in a small compass. Some of them are "in their comparatively modest way, as complete and organic as sonnets," as Le Gallienne said.[13] Their relaxed tone is perhaps the result of Allen's not being obliged by this date to care very much about anyone's susceptibilities. Each one covered some broad topic with wit, grace, and economy of expression, and often with an intent so subversive as to make it a pellet of philosophical dynamite admirably contrived for the waistcoat pocket, as Le Gallienne also put it.[14] In one column he wrote dryly, "I get a great many letters in answer to these post-Prandials; and some of them, strange to say, are not wholly complimentary."[15] He vanished without notice from the *Westminster* in January 1895, but whether this was voluntary or because he had finally outstripped the editorial patience is unclear.

Allen's mature, broad political stance was formed from a baffling blend of ingredients. As we have seen, he repeatedly spoke of himself in his younger years as a Communist, which in practice meant an alignment with the would-be parliamentary socialists. By most measures he continued to be a man of the Left, a fairly extreme Radical. He joined the Fabians in 1891, although he never attended meetings and eventually allowed his subscription to lapse. In his *Post-Prandial* essays he writes against big landlordism, private ownership of raw materials, prostitution, working women, nationalism, militarism, vivisection, most aspects of imperialism and colonialism, the established Church, the

House of Lords, sexual double standards and the environmental degradation of cities. He was for fairly plain living and high thinking, little England and Home Rule, a country residence and early nights, the nationalization of land and primary industries, the right to roam across landed estates, early mating and divorce on demand, maternal women and large families encouraged by State-promoted initiatives. But as he got older he seems to have followed the familiar trajectory, drifting rightward into a kind of Liberal quietism. At one point he said "as socialistic as Marx, I am as individualist as Herbert Spencer. I will do better work for our common cause—so far as it *is* common—by holding aloof from all societies and saying my say in my own way. But I hope little. I am a gloomy pessimist."[16]

Whatever he meant exactly by calling himself an Individualist, it certainly did not preclude his having some savage fun with a prospectus from a League of that name, headed by the Earl of Wemyss, who is, Allen finds out, a land-holder of 62,000 acres. This Individualism was just a "fine old crusted Toryism"; a mere selfish grab for continued aristocratic privilege. Yet Allen's Individualism did include, apparently, elements of a libertarian, minimal-State philosophy. "We [individualists] do not believe that one man ought to pay for another man's books, or beer, or preaching, or amusement. We do not believe that the State . . . should take aught from any man for any purpose save for the most necessary public objects of defense against external or internal enemies."[17]

If that is taken literally as a denunciation of both free libraries and the welfare state, it is a position Herbert Spencer would have been glad to agree with. How Allen reconciled it with the need for state-funded awards for mothering duties—to cite his most definite proposal for state intervention—is anyone's guess. But it is always misleading and futile to try to lay a template of current sociopolitical alignments over those of a century ago. Probably we can say no more than that Grant Allen was an advanced Radical of that very familiar English stamp—the Radical with a powerfully puritan admixture, a man in the mould of Cobbett, Orwell, and D.H. Lawrence. Allen was never slow to take the moral high ground—quite literally so when he wrote some months after the Wilde trials:

> I am writing in my study on a heather-clad hill-top. When I raise my eye from my sheet of foolscap, it falls upon miles and miles of broad open moorland. My window looks out upon unsullied nature. Everything around is fresh and pure and wholesome. . . . Up here on the free hills, the sharp air blows in upon us, limpid and clear from a thousand leagues of open ocean; down there in the crowded town, it stagnates and ferments, polluted with the diseases and vices of centuries.

The geographical metaphor had both a personal and a cultural application. It referred to the location of the author's study at Hindhead, but it was also the coign of vantage from which to detect and denounce moral corruption: "below in the valley, as night draws on, a lurid glare reddens the north-eastern horizon. It marks the spot where the great wen of London heaves and festers."[18] This is a reminder, if one were needed, that Grant Allen was born when Queen Victoria had been on the throne for eleven years, and that he died before she left it; and that in his *personal* code of behavior and attitudes, as opposed to some of the theoretical positions he supported, he shows it. Despite his reputation, he was no libertine; nor was he especially broad-minded even by the standards of his day. Promoting a culture of pagan hedonism from the study chair was one thing; debauchery and degeneracy thrown in the public's face was another. He takes for granted the complicity of his reader in coming to judgment about what is "fresh" and "pure" and what the "vices of centuries" might be. It is an irritating occupational hazard of the controversialist that there is always someone still more radical who wants to co-opt you. Allen ignored an invitation to join in a debate with an even freer spirit, the homosexual activist George Ives, who thought that he was merely a disguised neo-puritan, for all his liberating talk.[19]

THE POLEMICAL NOVELIST EMERGES

By the mid-nineties, then, Grant Allen's career, his fame—or his notoriety—was reaching its apogee. He was forty-seven, prosperous and, on the surface at least, more or less resigned to the equivocal nature of his literary success. If he had sold out, at least he had done so for the top dollar. In 1895 he needed no consoling, however, for in that year he published two novels, which must have done a good deal for his self-respect. After years of cursing the power of the "British matron" to censor artistic expression, he stared down that formidable lady long enough to get into print his anti-marriage best-seller *The Woman Who Did*, followed in November of the same year by his no less outrageous *The British Barbarians*, a mordant satire on middle-class taboos. Within ten years these polemical novels would be scorned as hopelessly unrealistic and old fashioned, but they would never be entirely forgotten. Allen came more or less to accept that most of his work was for the day only, but he warmed himself with the thought that these two novels and some associated fiery articles would put a memorable stamp on his century. With them, he declared war on some aspects of the repressive literary and sexual mores of his time.

CHAPTER 8

DEALING WITH THE "DISSENTING GROCER"

CONFRONTING THE PHILISTINES

Rigid contracts are nowadays signed beforehand for the production of such and such piece of work. . . . Often enough, a clause is even inserted in the agreement that the work shall contain nothing that may not be read aloud in any family circle. Consider what, in the existing condition of English bourgeois opinion, that restriction means! It means that you are to follow in every particular the dissenting grocer's view of life: that you are carefully to avoid introducing anything which might, remotely or indirectly, lead man or woman to reflect about any problem whatsoever of earth or heaven, or morals, religion, cosmology, politics, philosophy, human life, or social relations.[1]

In Grant Allen's personal mythology the natural habitat of "dissenting grocers" is the land of Philistia. As early as 1827 Carlyle and others were using "Philistia" as a label for the most unenlightened or commonplace part of the British populace: "unenlightened" meaning, here, little more than holding views which the writer happened not to agree with. Matthew Arnold gave the term "Philistine" universal currency in *Culture and Anarchy* (1869), where it denotes a person deficient in liberal culture, "people who most give their lives and thoughts to becoming rich."

By the 1880s "Philistia" had become a convenient shorthand for the spiritual domain of the most boorish, censorious, narrow-minded sections of the population. After using it as the title of his first novel, Allen remained fond of it. Philistia, for him, was the home town not only of the dissenting grocer but of his spiritual spouse, Mrs. Grundy. She was the more formidable of the two, and what is she? Allen knows:

And who, after all, is this redoubtable Mrs. Grundy, who has such a good opinion of her own moral and critical character that she dares to set herself up, with inconceivable effrontery, as the censor of the highest of the highest and noblest minds in England? Why, just the average specimen of English middle-aged matronhood, with all its petty prejudices, all its selfish narrowness, all its hatred of right, all its persistent clinging to every expiring form of wrong or injustice. A pretty sort of censor! A pretty sort of sovereign! I know no spectacle more humiliating to British civilization than this spectacle of the average middle-aged married Englishwoman. . . . What a unit of the State is that English mother! Her very looks betray her for just exactly what she is, blandly inane and vacuously pig-headed.[2]

This is a fine example of the lambasting tone Allen had at his disposal— Stead called it admiringly "lordly scorn." But it must not blind us to the fact that nothing reads more queerly in Grant Allen's career than his attitude to censorship. His whole attitude to it appears, at first sight, to be so totally inconsistent. Why should a man whose professed ambition for each new work is "to go a step lower to catch the market" worry his head about constraints on his freedom of expression? What need for such a man to speak of "moral cancers"? How could he possibly see himself as a Samson, blinded and shorn by his enemies, forced to grind out cheap mental fodder for his Philistine captors?

The reason is that, intertwined and inseparable in Allen's mind, were two issues. First, there was censorship itself, particularly the tacit kind, which meant that editors and publishers would not accept work on morally adventurous subjects. Second, there was the socioeconomics of the writing trade to contend with. It rewarded writers far below their just entitlements (for reasons Allen believed he understood) and so, by keeping them poor, forced them to toe the line. In other words, censorship meant two things for Allen. Writers with socially reprehensible views could not afford to write the books they wanted to write; and if they did defy Mrs. Grundy and write them, it was hard to get them published, harder to get them circulated, and hardest of all to get published again afterwards. The ethics and the economics of censorship ran together. It was not that Allen had suffered from the attention of the "dissenting grocer" for the books he had written; it was his knowledge that he had other books within him that he saw no point in even trying to write that galled him.

The pusillanimity of publishers was a common target of writers' wrath in the 1880s. Since most publishers were in thrall economically to the circulating libraries that bought so many of their books, they in turn needed to force compliance from almost all their authors. George Moore waged a personal campaign against the libraries in 1884–1885. He launched an attack on "A New Censorship of Literature" in the *Pall Mall Gazette*, later developing his article as the famous pamphlet *Literature at Nurse*. Mudie's censorship, Moore opined, had managed to reduce the human figure in the novel from the full-blooded presentations offered by Fielding and Smollett in the novels of the previous century to the "pulseless, non-vertebrate jellyfish sort of thing which, securely packed in tin-covered boxes, is sent forth from the London depot and scattered through the drawing-rooms of the United Kingdom" in his own time.[3]

Allen doubtless agreed with every word of this—after all, he was obliged, during his lowest pot-boiling moments, to perpetrate numerous "nonvertebrate jellyfish" characters of his own—but, rather unusually, he did not inveigh much against the three-decker system, or the circulating libraries. His eye was on another target instead: the editors of periodicals and newspapers. Commonly these were even more stringent than either book publishers or the libraries. Usually a short story had to satisfy some very tight moral guidelines to be accepted. Allen took a small revenge by baiting these editors when he could. He once wrote to Clement Shorter, editor of the *Sketch*: "Herewith I enclose two out of five short stories as per your esteemed order. These stories are warranted to be free from any opinions whatsoever—political, religious, social, philosophical or literary. They would not raise a blush on the cheek of a babe unborn or shock the susceptibilities of a Cardinal Archbishop."[4] At another time he challenged an editor: "I enclose for your consideration a short story entitled 'A Study from the Life.' The Editor of the *Speaker* was afraid to publish it. Will you be, I wonder?"[5] The fact that the story has vanished gives a mute reply. Presumably it was added to the funeral pyre on which he said he was "in the habit of cremating all such stillborn children of my imagination."[6] Allen's metaphor is rather more lurid than was warranted in the circumstances. After all, the very book in which these remarks about "stillborn children" appear does in fact contain two stories that had been rejected by every editor who saw them. "The Sixth Commandment" and "The Missing Link" deal respectively with adultery sympathetically treated and the loss of religious faith under the impact of Darwinism. Yet Allen had not destroyed them and Chatto had published the collection without demur.

Even Allen did not claim that a magazine editor's declining a single short story was critical to a writer's financial well-being. He reserved his fullest resentment for another autocratic power they had: that of controlling the serialization of novels. As he explained in his long preface-manifesto to *The British Barbarians*, "the serial rights of a novel at the present day are three times as valuable, in money worth, as the final book rights. A man who elects to publish direct, instead of running his story through the columns of a newspaper, is forfeiting, in other words, three-quarters of his income."[7] This gave editors an economic stranglehold on authors (or so Allen claimed), and it was a situation he found infuriating.

Allen's case has two components: the financial and the ethical. Certainly the rewards from serialization did grow progressively more important as the 1880s wore on. Even at the start of the decade some novelists were already getting more from the syndicates that took serials for provincial newspapers than they could get from running their work as a serial through a single magazine. (Not that one mode excluded the other.)[8] In *New Grub Street* Jasper Milvain boasts that, given the chance, he could have quadrupled the £100 cash down that his timid friend Reardon has accepted for his latest novel. "I should have gone shrewdly to work with magazines and newspapers and foreign publishers, and—all sorts of people."[9] The hesitancy Gissing implies with his dash implies Milvain's inexperience, not authorial disbelief in what he is saying, although Gissing himself showed little talent for taking the advice. He sold all the rights to this very novel for £150 to one publisher, which proved atrocious terms indeed. Gissing, like George Moore, either would not or could not serialize, and accepted the consequences. But more perspicacious or more worldly authors took a different view. Henry James is a good instance. Serialization was certainly vitally important to James. When he arrived in London in 1876 he commented that it was "the deuce" to get any money out of the British magazines because "half the work is done by rich dilettanti gratis." Nor was the pay particularly good, compared to what the American "vulgar organs" offered. But James could never afford to ignore the periodicals of either country. Indeed, after a decade of hard labor he still felt obliged to shape *The Tragic Muse* specifically as a long serial.[10]

Allen, with the support of A.P. Watt, did very well out of his serials. It is true that some of his novels were never serialized: *For Maimie's Sake, Recalled to Life, A Splendid Sin, Linnet, Rosalba* and perhaps others.[11] In the case of the last three, he may have paid the price for his notoriety. In general, though, the surviving records pretty much substantiate his claim that refusing to bow the knee to Mrs. Grundy would have been an expensive matter of principle. For five of his long novels Chatto paid him £745 for the book rights. The serial rights, though, totaled £1,860, or two and a half times as much.[12]

So far we have spoken about the financial aspects of serialization, as they were the ones Allen always stressed himself. But he was really making an ethical point. He liked to quote from the Socialists' rhyme about freedom: "If you haven't got a dinner, why, you're free to go without." For a long time he was in no position to pay the cost of asserting his autonomy as a writer because the serial rights were important to him, although this did not prevent him railing against the editors' feebleness of spirit. For some reason he never tried Hardy's remedy of producing a self-censored version specifically for the serial market. One wonders why he did not explore this possibility. Perhaps this is a hint that this whole rather dreary matter of serialization, and monetary returns, and editors' and publishers' attitudes, was really a side-show. Such people were, after all, in business. They had their livings to earn, just as the writer-tradesman had his. As we saw earlier, Allen took a Manchester School line on literary economics. Publishers and authors, no less than the Mudies of the world of Victorian letters, had to meet the market in all its absurdities and prejudices or go under. He thought it was as pointless to complain about their stance as it would be to rail at the force of gravity.

No, the fact is that Allen's real argument was always with the reading public—or with that influential fraction of it that lived in the mental state of Philistia. Now, finally, he reached the point where he prepared deliberately to throw down the gauntlet at the foot of the "English matron," and he expected a battle royal. As far as can be ascertained, he started on this course right at the end of the 1880s, although his sexual radicalism had been formed much earlier, after his first wife's death. And, as he began to push against sexual and marital hypocrisies, so he became more vehement and incautious about his self-proclaimed role as a social prophet and truth teller.

He first tried the ground with *The British Barbarians*, a satirical fable, and sent it to Andrew Chatto for an opinion. It came back with a friendly but unambiguous warning that its appearance would destroy his career . . . or so Allen reported in a private letter six years later. He put it aside. But the pressure was clearly mounting. He was now on a collision course with the "dissenting grocers." Why? Because he had a message to convey, truths to tell, and he was being blocked. For the period between 1890 and 1894, Allen's growing irritation with his publishers and with public opinion is a study in the anatomy of frustration. It brought him into conflict with conservative literary elements who had a wit just as acid as his own, and were far more ruthless in deploying it.

THE WORM TURNS

Even as he started to plan a novel even more truth-telling than the abandoned *British Barbarians*, the first sign of the coming struggle was his launching a series of satirical assaults on the British literary marketplace, as he perceived it to exist in all its ignoble glory. As early as February 1889 he was complaining, "to have ethical theories superior to the morality of the grocer, the baker, and the Baptist minister; to have views of life more comprehensive than the views of blushing sixteen in the rectory drawing-room, is to write yourself anathema."[13] Two years later he was complaining how the novelist has to "fling his book point-blank at the head of Mr Mudie's erubescent young person. . . . Sentimentalism and romanticism are the breath of his nostrils. He moves ever in fetters, supplied him by girls from eighteen to thirty."[14] There is a distinctly self-pitying tone in this piece—that was one of Allen's weaknesses—and instantly he became the target for some ill-natured mirth. J.M. Barrie had a lot of fun with it in a squib in the *National Observer*. Here Allen stars as "The Man Who is Not Allowed." He has, the commentator tells us, "a great novel" in view, but the public's action "was so threatening that he had to desist. The public flung the great novel back in his face." Not that he had actually written it yet. "It was not precisely written, but he had quite made up his mind to write it"; it was, "if I may be allowed to use the expression, up his sleeve, but he dared not bring [it] down." Does Grant Allen complain out loud of his treatment? Not at all, concludes Barrie, sarcastically. "He is indeed one of those gentle spirits that dislike speaking of themselves. Yet what science, what literature, he could produce if only the public would allow him!"[15]

Allen was not dissuaded by assaults of this nature, although privately he hated this kind of public jousting, which he thought was one of the worst features of being a writer. While arming himself for this fight he published several more bitter stories and aggressive articles over the next few years, lamenting the plight of the idealistic, reformist writer in a rampantly commercial and puritanical age. It is interesting that these are roughly contemporary with some of Henry James's stories on the same theme, particularly "The Death of the Lion," which was the opening story in the first issue of John Lane's *Yellow Book* (April 1894). It tells of the hero Paraday's fatal encounters with mass culture. At the heart of the story is a sacred text, known to all to be in train, but never finished. This work, promoted as too wonderful ever to come to market, becomes the very basis of Paraday's celebrity. Could the germ of this story have been Allen's well-publicized but seemingly infinitely deferred manuscript?

Allen continued to pursue the attack. His "Letters in Philistia" (in the *Fortnightly* for June 1891) is a powerfully aggressive piece on censorship and middle-class morality, and would probably have been too strong meat for any editor except Frank Harris to serve up. Parnell's adultery was then very much in the news, as the uncrowned king of Ireland was being hounded to his death, and Allen's airy dismissal of it as a "breach of etiquette" equivalent to breaking one's breakfast egg at the wrong end was thought deplorable. W.T. Stead pooh-poohed the whole problem of censorship in England by claiming it didn't exist. "It is sheer nonsense to pretend that in England a man cannot say what he will. I may safely say without boasting that I have ventured to say and print in England that which no other journalist has said or printed, and yet here I am what I am." But the vaunted freedom an Englishman has "to say what he will" in England is not exactly a libertine's charter. It turns out to mean only "free and frank discussion"—as defined by Stead himself. The public will not tolerate "unclean speech": the products of Mr. Grant Allen's pen, for example.[16] This conflict did more damage to the wary and fragile relationship of the two men.

Then, in the summer of 1892, matters took another turn. By this time Allen had completed a draft of a new novel and again he sought an advance opinion on it. What happened is described in a letter, which he sent to the *Athenaeum* in July 1892—an odd choice in itself, since this journal was always one of his severest critics. In it he alludes to Barrie's attack more than a year earlier; it had obviously rankled. The *Athenaeum* printed the letter without comment under the title "The Worm Turns." Its tone is curious:

> For years those who know me well have said to me frequently, "Why do you never put anything of yourself into your novels?" But I knew my public too well; I gave it itself instead—which is what it wanted. Some months since, however, I was tempted by conscience to set to work at a more serious romance on a social theme that deeply interested me. I got absorbed in it; I was carried away by the subject; I wrote at white heat, in a glowing fever of moral enthusiasm. I put my soul into the thing. I put my religion into it. And I wrought long and hard at it, with graver and burnisher, till I believed for once I had made a work of art. It was a part—a small part, a first installment—of the authentic Message which, rightly or wrongly, I imagine the Power that inheres in the universe had implanted in me for transmission to humanity. When it was finished, I gave it to a publisher who is also a personal friend, and in whose judgment I have absolute confidence—he knows his public even better than

I do. After reading it, he implored me in the strongest terms not to publish. He said the book would ruin me. Nobody would afterwards take any other novel of mine. It would spoil my future. I am a very sane monomaniac. I yielded at once to his advice. I dare run no such risk. I shall destroy the manuscript.

I hope those who read this note, so wrung out of me, will pardon its egotism. However insignificant a man may seem to others, to himself the failure of his life-work must always be a tragedy.

But after this, nobody, I am sure, can ever laugh at me for saying free thought is gagged in England. GRANT ALLEN[17]

Could these be words from the same man who had said before, and would say again in similar words, that novels are "for the most part a futile and unprofitable form of literature"?[18] Andrew Lang wrote him a sympathetic note, saying he had had a similar experience and advising him, yet again, to save his social polemics for a "not-novel." The gesture was clumsy, but it sounds well-meaning.[19] Most of Allen's friends were nonplussed. Edward Clodd confided to his diary that he thought Allen's aggrieved tone was indefensible.

What had happened to make him write in such vatic terms, in words that, as he said, had been wrung out of him? We will examine some of the broader implications of this outburst in the next chapter, but there need have been no single incident to provoke it. More likely it was the culmination of mounting frustration, especially of having two serious novels rejected with the friendly warning that they could destroy him. He really believed that he was playing for high stakes; that his career might be terminated by publishers' bans on his work; even that he might be prosecuted. This may seem ridiculous, but it did not pay to be too insouciant. It was only three years since the quite respectable publisher Henry Vizetelly, though aged and ill, had gone to prison for publishing even expurgated translations of Zola and Maupassant. The laws relating to obscene publication were vague, unpredictable—and still dangerous.

Allen's threat to destroy his new work elicited protests from his friends. Nicholson, now Bodley's librarian, offered to house the offending document. Allen declined the offer. "Thanks for your flattering suggestion. I'll keep the MS during my lifetime, and ask my wife to pass it on to you after my departure from a planet which I shall have scanty cause to remember with gratitude."[20]

What was this incendiary book, which if published, would lead to ruin? Allen's private letters at the time, and another letter written after its publication, make it certain that it was a very early draft of *The Woman Who Did*. The long delay in publication, and the unfortunately phrased "The Worm Turns" letter, gave the forces of literary reaction an opportunity they could scarcely have dreamed of. An anonymous satire of 1892, *The Silver Domino*, usually ascribed to Marie Corelli and others, panned numerous reputations, and the lines on Allen, with their mocking references to divine inspiration, were clearly composed in the wake of the *Athenaeum* letter. They are vicious and clever:

> GRANT ALLEN hath a "heaven-sent" tale to tell,
> But much he fears its utterance would not "sell"
> Wherefore, to be quite certain of his cash,
> He writes (regardless of his "inspiration") trash;
> Practical ALLEN! Noble, manly heart!
> Wise huckster of small nothings in the mart, —
> To what a pitch of prudence dost thou reach
> To feel the "god," yet give thy thoughts no speech,
> All for the sake of vulgar pounds and pence!
> God bless thee, ALLEN, for thy common sense![21]

The Henley circle was soon barking at his heels as well. In August 1892 an anonymous column appeared, which surely sets a record for sheer spitefulness even for the *National Observer*, which was famed and feared for its hob-nailed critical assaults. This time it was either by Henley himself, or more likely, judging by the style, by his top attack dog, Charles Whibley. It too homed in on the *Athenaeum* letter. Quoting with relish some of its overheated phrases, it sneered: "Picture it! The author of *The Duchess of Powysland* [a pot-boiler] had 'put his soul' into this work. He had 'put his religion' into it. He had put as much as he could of the Power that inheres into it! But he 'was not allowed' (he never is) to publish it, and perhaps while we write it is being destroyed for ever and ever! You turn away in tears from this picture of noble struggle and heroic fall." The writer has an analogy for the position he saw Grant Allen as taking up. It was neither noble nor heroic:

> You make soap for so much a year; for so much a year less you could make pictures. You go on making soap, and complain that you are not rich enough to make pictures. Truly, a just and manly complaint. Yet are you better than he who, making soap, yet clamours for the credit for making pictures.

That was the main offence: a mere soap-maker having the effrontery to put himself forward as "a man of letters" when he "writes stuff which has no more concern with literature than his tailor's bills"! Still, there was one consolation. "Now that Grant Allen has put his 'soul' into a serious romance," the column concluded pitilessly, "and the serious romance is destroyed, it may be that were have heard the last of the soul of poor Mr Grant Allen. Yea, even of Mr Grant Allen: original, authentic, unique in human history: The Man That is Not Allowed, and tells the public all about it."[22]

Allen was cut to the quick by this savage abuse. Acting contrary to his own principles, he composed a reply, although it is uncertain whether Henley ever saw it. It is dated August 7, 1892, and has survived by chance only in a typewritten copy. It is a remarkable document, not only for its picture of the fierce literary cut-and-thrust of the day, but for its painfully raw revelations of how Allen regarded his own career by this date:

> I have just read with so much mental distress the article in your last number that I can't help writing and speaking to you about it. I know I am unwise: I know one oughtn't to wear one's heart upon one's sleeve; yet I can't resist it. . . . At a moment of profound depression, when life appears to me hardly endurable, your article comes as a further aggravation, and stabs me once more with a stab that I feel undeserved and cruel. My work and my personality may be worth as little as you think—and heaven knows I have had to do distasteful work enough in the hard fight for bread; but I think it is unmanly to strike a man through the tenderest and most sacred feelings as you or your critic have done with me; and I thank God I myself never struck anyone so, and never could strike them. I wrote a book which I profoundly believed to be a piece of work for the good of humanity. I may have greatly over-estimated my own powers; but still, I believed it so. It was to me something sacred. With a great sacrifice I decided at last to suppress it, for my wife's sake and my child's, and to go on writing Duchesses of Powysland. Now, however wrong I may be, I am still a man, with the usual claim to courtesy and consideration. One would have thought that the exact moment of what was obviously a great and bitter sorrow would not be chosen by any person as the moment for stinging a soul already despairing, and making a crisis of acute misery still acuter and bitterer. I sincerely trust that no critic will ever inflict upon you such misery as you have inflicted upon me; and as the object of the writer was evidently to give pain, it may be some consolation to him to know how thoroughly he has succeeded. I am a very earnest man, who takes life very earnestly; and I desire to do and say some good things in my generation. It is because I have some beliefs which seem to me important that I continue to say from time to time things that rouse this strange hostility in others. I believe I am almost cured now; but as long as I live I shall be proud to remember that I never used my pen to hurt another as you or your contributor have used yours to hurt and crush me at a moment of peculiar and profound bitterness.
>
> Yours very sincerely, Grant Allen. Writer's cramp compels type-writer.[23]

Henley never replied, either personally or in the *Observer*, but it's unlikely that if he did read it he would have been much impressed, and especially not by the rather too studied pathos of the writer's cramp.

We see that Allen professes in this letter to be staggered by Henley's animosity. It was true that Henley, who was just the same age as he, had given him work on *London* long before, and a bit later had taken a couple of his articles while editing *Cassell's Magazine of Art*. But could Allen really have been so surprised? How could he not have known that he stood for everything Henley hated?—and Henley, a bitter, clever man in constant pain from his tubercular leg, was a formidable hater. Allen's socialist politics, his "rosewater revolutionism," to use one of Henley's favorite phrases, were anathema to his belligerent conservatism. Allen's pacifism contrasted with the militarism promoted in the *Observer*, and with the far-right philosophy of its "Common Sense" platform, which called for a righteous, refining war against somebody—anybody, apparently—which would help separate "the slag from the metal."

The *Observer* stood for "art standards," but just being avant-garde and progressive did not admit one into Henley's magic circle. Henley was no aesthete art-for-art's-saker. Pater, James, and Wilde all incurred his displeasure at various times. His stance was much tougher than that; he liked manly writers, and wide popularity—of the kind enjoyed by Rider Haggard, Stevenson, Dickens, or Scott—was always very acceptable. But truckling to the mob-audience, and self-promotion, were despised. In particular, writers who gave the impression that making money was more important than their art were instantly blackballed. Henley, the cripple and survivor of agonizing surgery; the author of "Invictus" and the man for whom the phrase "stiff upper lip" might well have been invented, was not impressed by "shameless bleating," as he called it, about the pains of authorship.

The *Observer*'s rough handling seems to have exacerbated the tendency in Allen that we have noticed before and that now became a matter for public comment: a wobbling between extreme cynicism about his function and legitimacy as a writer and an angry frustration that he was blocked at every turn from using fiction to express the great truths he said were bottled up within him. Perhaps he feared that, as he put it, "the torpor of middle-age" was creeping over his conscience. Or perhaps it was more than that. Some of his language, public and private, in these years of the early nineties suggest some quite serious psychological upset. The sense of personal worthlessness supplanted so quickly and erratically by the conviction that one is being used by higher agencies, is very striking. The veering between gloom and exhilaration, between "profound depression, when life appears to me hardly endurable," and the "glowing fever of moral enthusiasm," to quote his own phrases, tempts a diagnosis of cyclothymia, or at least a sub-clinical mood disorder.

He worked his way through it, however, with personal therapy in the shape of several more short stories—more exactly, stories and fables—about the humiliations and temptations heaped on the writer in a commercial age. "The Pot-boiler" is obviously semi-autobiographical. Ernest Grey, an idealistic artist, is obliged to paint insipid pictures for cash; a bachelor friend flatters him, and "goaded [him] on into letting his wife and child starve for the benefit of humanity." However, when Grey's child nearly dies of scarlet fever, he recognizes this temptation as "a peculiarly seductive form of self-indulgence" and returns to his trade. "Still, it's a tragedy," concludes the narrator.[24] And in the next month (November 1892) the theme of the writer compromising himself through financial necessity pops up again in "Ivan Greet's Masterpiece." This story opens with a monologue by the fluent and versatile Charlie Powell, who is reveling in his new newspaper job, which pays "five guineas a column." As he has told the editor, who has warned him of the readers' susceptibilities:

> "Sir," said I, smacking his hand, "for five guineas a column I'd be tenderly respectful to King Ahab himself, if you cared to insist upon it. You may count on my writing whatever rubbish you desire for the nursery-mind."

Rubbish for the nursery-mind! This degree of cynicism is too much for the idealistic Ivan Greet. What a shame it is, he says, "because it'll take him still further away than ever from his work in life, which you and I know is science and philosophy," though he concedes that he himself is wasting his time on journalism too. He is very sorry to see the talented Charlie Powell going down the same path, and Charlie, suddenly sobered, agrees:

> "Ivan's right," he said slowly, nodding his head once or twice. "He's right, *as* usual. We're all of us wasting on weekly middles the talents God gave us for a higher purpose. We know it, every man Jack of us. But Heaven help us, I say, Ivan: for how can we help ourselves? We live by bread. We must eat bread first, or how can we write epics or philosophies afterwards?"[25]

The end of the story, though, seems to imply that that happy day may never arrive. Ivan leaves for a simple life in Jamaica, where he labors over an epic poem before dying of fever. His illiterate mistress devotes her life to earning the money to see it in print, but it is accidentally burnt long before she reaches her goal. The cynical reader may well think that Ivan should have arrived at some earlier accommodation with Philistia and the "nursery mind." That is what Allen did, after all, but it is hardly the moral he expects us to take away from his story.

Allen harped on the same theme more than once over the next year, most effectively in "How to Succeed in Literature." Montague Watts, novelist with a "cavity" in his lung, is "condemned to work like a galley-slave for most hours of every day at a thankless profession, and to receive in the end about half the reward that falls to the lot of an obscure country solicitor." He has solved the "mystery" of fiction, which is to subjugate himself to "the average level of sentiment and feeling in the mass of people." But then, in an evil hour, friends tempt him: "trust to your own genius," they tell him, and write a book from the heart. He falls for this, and writes a novel telling many truths, though "respect for the court made him also conceal and gloss over a great many." It fails dismally and editors refuse to take his work any longer, because the public now "are well aware that you hold Opinions." Watts, his wife and child begin quietly to starve. After failing to get a minor government post, he blows his brains out on the steps of 10 Downing Street. His wife is awarded a Civil List pension. Watts has made literature pay at last.[26]

The *Athenaeum* had been biding its time after publishing "The Worm Turns" letter. It sprang in March 1894, the final straw surely being the publication that month of Allen's most inflammatory and most-discussed of all his articles, "The New Hedonism." This also appeared in Frank Harris's *Fortnightly*. In it, and in public lectures which he gave based on it, Allen inveighs in the most forthright tones that he ever adopted against asceticism. He scorns the "most money-grubbing among us" for whom "love is a thing to be got over once for all in early life, and relegated thenceforth to the back parlour of existence in the most business-like way." And he follows this with a good deal more about the primary demands of self-development, including sexual liberation from puritanism, in the same acerbic vein. Allen probably took his title phrase from Wilde's *Picture of Dorian Gray*, where it appears twice as part of the Pateresque doctrine Lord Henry instills into the willing ear of his victim: "Be always searching for new sensations. Be afraid of nothing. . . . A new Hedonism—that is what our century wants." Despite this, the article is more of a reaction against the last phase of British Hellenism, as that movement declined into the Decadence of the mid-nineties, than an expression of it. Allen allows himself a passing mention of the Greeks' lack of shame about sex, but he devotes many more pages to biology: to proving that the New Hedonism is licensed by our new understanding of the evolutionary significance of sexual reproduction and sexual selection.

"The New Hedonism" caused quite a stir and was soon reprinted separately as a booklet. It had its supporters, though some of them wanted to know what lay behind its euphonious but rather vague phrasing. How *exactly* was, say, a well-disposed grocer, eager to reform himself, supposed to start living out in practice the antique Greek morality of "innocent love, innocent pleasure," which the article promotes?[27] Should he begin with naked gymnastics in his backyard?

"The New Hedonism" was, naturally, roundly condemned in all the expected quarters. There was quite enough in it to feed the wrath of the *Athenaeum*'s reviewer of Allen's collection of poems, *The Lower Slopes*. Referring darkly to Allen's oft-repeated inability to get published "a certain manuscript novel," the reviewer recommended, in effect, that he should put up or shut up:

> In the present condition of public taste it is possible for a man to publish in England, if not quite everything which it might be profitable for him to write, at all events very nearly everything; and Mr Allen has given us no reason to suppose that he is capable of writing a new masterpiece of narrative like the memoirs of Casanova. . . . He appears simply to be hovering feverishly round what is called forbidden fruit, for the sake of the phrase, but which is, after all, quite within easy, comfortable after-dinner reach of the average man. The relations of the sexes, on which Mr Allen conceives that he has something perilously new to say, have been the theme of literature since the beginning, and Mr Allen, with his tremors and his timidities and his juvenile consciousness of the delights of naughtiness, is merely bringing a somewhat misty vision to bear on the most hackneyed of all subjects.[28]

However offensive the language here, the reviewer had struck shrewdly at Allen's Achilles' heel, his much-cherished ability to spot and exploit new trends before anyone else. This time he was in danger of missing the boat. It is easy to forget just how quickly the limits of toleration in literature were being extended in the first half of the nineties. As early as 1883 Olive Schreiner, in *The Story of an African Farm*, had published an attack on marriage quite as vigorous as anything Allen had to say. During the years when Allen was working on and trying to publish *The Woman Who Did*, "Lucas Malet's" *The Wages of Sin* (1891) had appeared, and the journalist H.D. Traill, who liked to think he had his finger on the pulse of opinion, took it as conclusive evidence that Mrs. Grundy had abdicated her throne. As though taking him at his word, novelists pushed even harder at the limits. *Tess of the d'Urbervilles*, if it had had to be dismembered as a serial in the *Graphic*, escaped too much censure when it was reassembled as a novel in 1892. The negative reviews, though memorably and insultingly phrased in a few cases, were hardly representative of most readers' opinion of this masterpiece. It was followed by "Sarah Grand's" *The Heavenly Twins* (1893); "George Egerton's" *Keynotes and Discords* (1893, 1894); "Iota's" *A Yellow Aster* (1894); and Mona Caird's *The Daughters of Danaus* (1894). Very few of the reviewers of Moore's painfully grey *Esther Waters* (1894) struck a sour note. Zola himself, despite the Vizetelly prosecution, showed up in London in 1893 and was treated as a celebrity. Ibsen's three astonishing plays were seen in unlicensed London productions. Everyone concerned had survived these experiences without feeling the policeman's hand on their collars. Some had made money too, even if they had had to absorb a lot of abuse. Hardy's *Jude* appeared uncut late in 1895 and certainly touched the very edge of toleration. There was more severe condemnation, some of it very nasty, and its effect on Hardy himself is notorious. But neither Hardy nor his publisher incurred the displeasure of the law.

We see, then, that Allen's oft-repeated claim that "free thought is gagged in England" was starting to sound hollow. By the end of 1894, with so much having been promised, every month that passed with Allen giving "his thoughts no speech" (as *The Silver Domino* had jeered) increased the risk that his much-heralded, "heaven-sent" novel would be badly upstaged. It is easy to understand why, as the year advanced and publication was at last agreed for February 1895, Allen admitted to being in a "hot and excited" state. He really believed that this time he had a product that would make or break him. He had ground corn at the Philistines' mill for long enough. Now he had broken his shackles and braced himself between the pillars of the temple of Respectability. Was it all to end in a grand Samson-smash? "If it fails to boom, I go under for ever," he wrote dramatically to Clodd. "It is a serious crisis for me, and only a boom will pull me through."[29] The language here leaves it an open question whether Allen was speaking of his financial, or his psychological, stability. Perhaps it was both. But, at least in the short term, he need not have worried. The immediate impact and sales were tremendous. In the first weeks of that fiercely cold winter, herald of one of the most extraordinary years in the history of modern British literature, *The Woman Who Did* was flying out of the bookshops at the rate of five hundred copies a day.

CHAPTER 9

RETAILING *THE WOMAN WHO DID*

ALLEN, JOHN LANE AND W.T. STEAD

Whatever one's opinion of *The Woman Who Did*, one thing is indisputable: its appearance was a public relations and marketing triumph. Two sharp-witted men, the author and his publisher, collaborated over bringing it to market with a great flourish, and the results were all they hoped for.

Since the friend in the trade had implored him not to publish it, Allen's most difficult task was to find someone else to take the risk. As so often happens there was a man for the moment: John Lane. He sent Lane the manuscript in the autumn of 1893, and the readers' reports Lane secured before the year was out persuaded him to publish—eventually.

With his usual acumen Grant Allen had selected his new publisher wisely, though at first sight one might wonder about that. John Lane and Elkin Mathews (later the firm of The Bodley Head) had been in business together for four years, originally specializing in up-market editions of advanced literature. Lane himself, six years younger than Allen, a burly figure with a heavy walrus moustache, had a somewhat equivocal reputation. He was called "Petticoat Lane" behind his back for his attentions to his female authors, and there was a whiff of sharp practice about him. The firm's reputation was about to be made, however, with its Keynotes series of novels. The first appeared at the end of 1893, at about the time when the readers' reports on *The Woman Who Did* were coming to hand.

Though the Keynotes sold quite cheaply, they were got up in the best aesthetic style, some with cover designs by Aubrey Beardsley. Most of the Keynotes authors were near the beginning of their careers, many of them with various feminist and stylistic axes to grind: Ella D'Arcy, "George Egerton," "Victoria Crosse," M.P. Shiel, Arthur Machen. If there was a Keynotes profile, Grant Allen, a grey-beard novelist of forty-five, hardly fitted it. But all these negatives were outweighed by one fact. John Lane specialized in serious work. It was known that he never published "entertainers."[1] And that was exactly the spin that Allen, author of numerous entertainers, needed to have put on his reputation at this point in his career.

Two of Lane's readers for *The Woman Who Did* were Richard Le Gallienne and George Moore. Le Gallienne, Lane's trusted reader, and a good friend and neighbor of Allen's, claimed the book would be a sensation. George Moore, who was then working on his masterpiece of documentary realism, *Esther Waters*, was positive too, albeit in a more muted fashion. "There is absolutely no reason—no moral reason—why you should not publish it," he told Lane. "The book is as superficial in thought as it is in style. At the same time it cannot be denied that there is a certain amount of 'go' in the book and it was read with some interest. . . . I am inclined to think that it would be a success." Having delivered himself of this opinion, Moore was anxious to get paid for it. "You proposed to give me £2 for my opinion of this book. I have given it now send me the £2. Short accounts make long friends."[2] He knew Lane's habits of old.

Nevertheless, a whole year passed before Lane published *The Woman Who Did* as the eighth Keynotes volume in February 1895. Perhaps at the urging of his more cautious partner, Elkin Mathews, Lane took more advice, from the austere Catholic poet and essayist Alice Meynell. Her response is lost, but it was couched in terms that made Allen think she would only be satisfied "if Herminia got converted in the nick of time by Cardinal Manning, and spent the rest of her days in reconciling the Dean to the church of our fathers."

All this took time, and Allen was badgering Lane for a decision at the end of 1893 and into the new year. "When are you going to let me know about *The Woman Who Did*?" he asked. "I am alarmed at leaving her so long away from home among complete strangers." But Lane had a good deal on his plate over those winter months. He was working on plans for the new quarterly, the *Yellow Book*, and he was having problems with Oscar Wilde's new novel about Shakespeare. The Mathews partnership was dissolved in September 1894 and Lane probably decided to take the plunge after that, in time for the New Year season. When he eventually produced a contract the terms were not lavish. He offered a royalty of ninepence per copy sold, with £100 in advance, and half the sum received from American sales. (The agreement was for five years and therefore expired just a month before Allen's death. His widow inherited the copyright and promptly took it elsewhere, to Lane's fury.) Having extracted the contract Allen buckled down to making numerous small changes to satisfy George Moore's complaints about the style, and to supply some more credible touches to the characters' psychology.[3]

During the long delay the partners did bring out Allen's only collection of verse, *The Lower Slopes*, at the start of 1894. This stereotypical slim volume was got up in an art nouveau binding and announced as a limited edition of 600 copies. That kind of engineered "rarity" was one of Lane's marketing ploys. In fact, in this case he generated an even rarer rarity by surreptitiously releasing a few copies with a variant title page, one of which he offered to the author, who coldly declined it.[4]

Only seven of the poems had been printed before, and it is impossible to date the others. Efficient and well turned, like everything Allen wrote, some are ballades on topics of the day in the manner perfected by Andrew Lang; others are on philosophical issues, treated comically or seriously; yet others are rousing pieces of denunciation. A group of five seem to have some bearing on Allen's marriage to Caroline Bootheway. It was certainly not accidental that Allen put them into print in *The Lower Slopes* volume at that time, for he intended them to reflect and amplify the purpose of the forthcoming *The Woman Who Did*, as we shall see.

Once the novel was printing, Allen made sure that the pre-publication publicity campaign swung into action. He himself sent an advance proof copy to W.T. Stead, then at the height of his influence. Despite their previous jousting, Stead did Allen proud, making it the "Book of the Month" in his *Review of Reviews*. He was critical enough of the novel's message, as he thought that monogamy, far from wasting away, would become ever more rigorous as the sexes mingled in the workplace, engaging daily in "intercourse other than the ultimate." (Stead was speaking from rueful personal experience.) But he certainly took Allen seriously. For a full thirteen pages of extracts and commentary, interspersed with a scenic view of Perugia, he whetted the public appetite as only he knew how. The fact that this issue of the *Review*, let alone the novel itself, was prohibited in Ireland drove sales even higher, with Lane trumpeting the fact that eighteen or more "editions" (in fact impressions) were required in the first year alone. By good fortune, its publication was beautifully positioned. Several of the preceding Keynotes had sold well, and Lane's other venture, the quarterly *Yellow Book*, was now providing a regular dose of avant-garde sensation. Oscar Wilde was a Lane author at his zenith, and luckily his downfall occurred some months after *The Woman* was safely in print and selling hugely—about 25,000 copies immediately in Britain alone.

Despite his fear of prosecution, Allen did very well indeed out of *The Woman Who Did*. Thanks to Lane's marketing and Stead's advertising, not to mention his own wonderfully salacious title which instantly became a catchphrase used for years afterwards with a knowing smirk, it made him at least £1,000 at once. Naturally it was banned in Ireland, but translations soon appeared in Yiddish, Swedish, German, and (partly) in French. In America Roberts, Lane's co-publisher, sold another 10,000 copies in the first year. Numerous readers—mostly young women—wrote Allen fan letters, telling him how Herminia had given voice to their deepest thoughts ("except on *l'union libre*," one noted cautiously). "You have made one or two remarks that I myself have made in the same words during the last month or so. One is absolutely identical. You do not know me nor I, you—then why this mental sympathy or likeness?" She hoped to meet the author soon to explore this intriguing affinity.[5]

Quite fortuitously, the novel secured even more publicity from a brief but sensational court case later in 1895. A young woman, Edith Lanchester, the daughter of an architect and a women's rights activist, was briefly imprisoned in a private asylum for refusing to marry her lover, a workman. There was an immediate outcry and she was released after four days into suburban domesticity with her partner, but was never reconciled with her family. The resemblances between Edith Lanchester and Herminia Barton were quite accidental, but for Lane the affair was pure gold. Curiously, Allen had little sympathy with Lanchester's behavior. Could it have been because her union was across class lines, like Allen's own?[6]

The fame, or notoriety, of *The Woman Who Did* was not restricted to the London literary coteries. Allen became for a while the patron saint of every advanced cause in the country. Chris Healy, a bohemian Irish journalist based in Liverpool, belonged to a rumbustious club called The Drum, which he himself calls "the meeting-place of the chief cranks" of the city—Fabians, anarchists, actresses, Left-leaning business folk, would-be philosophers. He recalled how fully the younger denizens of The Drum, especially the women, welcomed Allen as "the prose laureate of the dumb giant Democracy, because he detested Respectability, Mrs. Grundy, and the Nonconformist conscience."[7] At the other end of the spectrum of propriety, the demure Flora Thompson, later famous as the author of the memoir *Lark Rise to Candleford* (1939–1945), recalled how everyone in her village, near Allen's house, read it and found it hard to believe that the quiet middle-aged gentleman with the field-glasses had written this shocking story. Some were quite disappointed that the fuss eventually died away leaving the author unscathed.[8]

HERMINIA BARTON: *GETTING* MARRIED AND *BEING* MARRIED

The Woman Who Did is only the length of a novella and the plot is simple enough. High-thinking, beautiful, Girton-educated Herminia Barton, aged twenty-two, is a teacher and lives alone in a Chelsea cottage. She despises the hypocrisies surrounding marriage, and has vowed never to marry. She has no objection, however, to *being* married, to living in what is a marital union in all but name. Indeed, she becomes a "wife" within the first six chapters. What she refuses is the act of *getting* married, with all the social endorsement it implies. Her objections to the marriage ceremony are a mixture of the practical and the ideological. As a matter of self-interest, she will not enter a binding contract for life, when she might "discover some other more fit to be loved by me." Then again, she knows what "vile slavery" marriage has sprung from, and on what "unseen horrors for my sister women it is reared and buttressed"; that is to say, on the foundations of prostitution.[9] Other women, like Mary Shelley and George Eliot, lived in free unions, but only because they had no choice. She will, rather, model herself on Shelley himself, who switched women when his heart told him to. She will act from the start out of pure principle, and will welcome social martyrdom because Shelley suffered it. For someone has to take a stand; someone "who would be free must himself strike the blow" (42).

Herminia is no hoyden, but she suffers from no shrinking modesty either. She wears "the face of a free woman," and how a free woman should react to an avowal of love from the man of her choice is made clear:

> "Not *will* be yours," Herminia corrected in that silvery voice of hers. *Am* yours already, Alan. I somehow feel as if I had always been yours. I am yours at this moment. You may do what you would with me'. (41)

In receipt of this dizzying offer is Alan Merrick, a barrister. Merrick is not without his flaws. He has not acted, according to the narrator, as an honorable man should act in his youth as soon as he feels the urge to find a partner. Such a man

> mates like the birds, because he can't help himself. A woman crosses his path who is to him indispensable, a part of himself, the needful complement of his own personality; and without heed or hesitation, he takes her to himself, lawfully or unlawfully, because he has need of her. That is how nature has made us; that is how every man worthy of the name of man has always felt, and thought, and acted. (37)

Alan Merrick has not done this: he has not mated like the birds, in the way that evolution has endorsed. He is not quite "one of the picked souls of humanity," because he is thirty and has been "prudential." We know what that means: Alan Merrick has allowed women of the lower orders to service his needs while making his mark in life. Still, he knows how to behave like a gentleman, and offers of their persons with no strings attached from well-born attractive young ladies are something he finds disconcerting:

> "Then, dearest," he cried tentatively, "how soon may we be married?"
> At sound of these unexpected words from such lips as his, a flush of shame and horror overspread Herminia's cheek. "Never!" she cried firmly, drawing away. "O Alan, what can you mean by it? Don't tell me, after all I've tried to make you feel and understand, you thought I could possibly consent to *marry* you?"
> The man gazed at her in surprise. Though he was prepared for much, he was scarcely prepared for such devotion to principle. "O Herminia," he cried, "you can't mean it. You can't have thought of what it entails. Surely, surely, you won't carry your ideas of freedom to such an extreme, such a dangerous conclusion?" (41)

The "flush of shame and horror" is striking, but, as with similar effects else-where in the novel, there is something a little calculated, even a little mere-tricious, about it. Like some of Wilde's epigrams which rely on inversions ("her hair turned quite gold from grief") it comes over as a little too studied to be natural. Still, it must have caused many a conventional soul to draw a sharp breath.

After failing repeatedly to overcome her principles, Merrick metaphorically shrugs his shoulders and, since the two are in love their union is soon consummated, though they continue to live apart to preserve that first fine careless rapture.

Herminia becomes pregnant almost at once. That is not surprising, because bearing a child is her next step of social defiance. In this respect *The Woman* does occupy a unique niche in the fictional debate over gender relationships. Illegitimate births are, of course, ten a penny in later Victorian fiction, but those heroines are seduced and abandoned, raped or simply ignorant victims. Allen was probably the first and perhaps the last British novelist to show an educated middle-class woman who, in cold blood, puts herself into the position of bearing a bastard out of pure principle, with the resolve of using the child as a blunt instrument against bourgeois sensibilities. Says Herminia:

> Brave women before me have tried for a while to act on their own responsibility, for the good of their sex; but never of their own free will from the beginning. . . . Here, of my own free will, I take my stand for the right, and refuse your sanctions! No woman that I know of has ever yet done that. Other women have fallen, as men choose to put it in their odious dialect: no other has voluntarily risen as I propose to do. (45–46)

Yet, for someone who has spent years brooding on the right form of union between men and women, Herminia displays a breathtaking naivety. The problem of the children resulting from this pursuit of nature, for instance, is airily waved aside. "Fools always put that question," says the narrator scornfully, "and think it is a crushing one." For any thinking person the solution is simple:

> They would be half hers, half his; the pleasant burden of their support, the joy of their education, would naturally fall upon both parents equally. But why discuss these matters like the squalid rich, who make their marriages a question of settlements and dowries and business arrangements? They two were friends and lovers; in love, such base doubts could never arise. (60)

As Stead commented dryly about this very passage, such crackpot idealism was precisely what had doomed "scores of unfortunate girls to be at this very moment in the lying-in wards of our workhouse infirmaries."[10] It is hard to credit that Herminia's idealism is not being satirically distanced here, but there is no evidence that it is.

Then there is the problem of her own maintenance. She insists on economic independence, of course; she will continue her school-teaching and, when driven from her post by the headmistress, she intends to "fall back upon literature." Clearly she has not read Grant Allen on the perils and pitfalls of freelance authorship.

Once he has got Herminia pregnant, however, the old Adam in Alan reasserts itself. Even the redoubtable Herminia quails before the force of biological determinism. She does so with the full support of the narrator. "It must be always so," we are lectured:

> She would be less a woman, and he less a man, were any other result possible. Deep down in the very roots of the idea of sex we come on that prime antithesis—the male, active and aggressive: the female, sedentary, passive, and receptive. (63–64)

So from there it is downhill all the way for Herminia, who surrenders all her autonomy with her virginity. She meekly resigns her job at his insistence; she lets Alan decide to take her abroad to avoid gossip; she lets him inscribe the hotel registers with the approved marital formula; she bows, in short, to all the usages of Philistia on the grounds of Alan's "masculine common-sense" and "greater worldly wisdom." Naturally, the reader wonders why Herminia was not vouchsafed a perception of these deep-rooted male virtues earlier on. It would have saved her a lot of pain.

As they wait for the birth in Perugia, Alan catches typhoid and dies. Now the reader catches sight of the puppeteer's strings. What we want to see—what we have been implicitly promised we *would* see—is how a rational free union might work out in the longer term. In particular, we want to see what happens when either Alan or Herminia feels impelled to take this specific, blunt advice which the authorial voice tells Alan he should be offering openly to the woman he loves:

> Give me what you can of your love and of yourself; but never strive for my sake to deny any love, to strangle any impulse that pants for breath within you. Give me what you can, while you can, without grudging. . . . Be mine as much as you will, as long as you will, to such extent as you will; but before all things be your own; embrace and follow every instinct of pure love that nature, our mother, has imparted within you. (112)

Not strangling impulses that pant for breath inside one; following every instinct of pure love wherever it leads: we seem to be moving into promising fictional territory, and we know Allen himself adhered to such principles—in theory. We want very much to see what free love might mean in the long term, in practice, in Victorian England. But that promise is withdrawn by a contrived blow of fate as soon as offered.

Called to his son's deathbed by telegram, Dr. Merrick arrives at Perugia just too late to see his son alive. The lack of a will permits the Merricks to cheat Herminia, and her own family abandons her. She bears her child and christens her Dolores. Virtually penniless, she returns to England. Now Herminia seems to have lost her taste for martyrdom. In order to put a London roof over her head she immediately sacrifices all her most cherished principles, and without too many qualms. She who disdained to pretend to be a wife does not scruple to pretend to be a widow. She has to work, of course, to support herself and her child. Fortunately she turns out to be a competent hack writer. Editors and journalists like to help her, being not too fond of respectability, but even there she is forced to compromise: "even the Bohemians refused to let their children ask after Miss Barton's baby" (95).

Thus she endures a life of semi-poverty into middle age, sacrificing everything for her daughter, Dolly, who is her last hope for carrying the torch onward. She turns down another suitor, a Fabian socialist, because he will not meet her requirement "to live with me on the terms on which I lived with Dolly's father" (110) and he, mindful of his reputation, marries someone else. Apart from this rather small gesture, Herminia takes no further interest in marital reform. Several feminists of the day like the redoubtable Millicent Fawcett, who probably never backed away from a difficulty in her life, demanded to know why the widowed Herminia is allowed to sink into such a slough of self-pity. What prevents her from joining some reform societies, involving herself in the causes of the day so dear to her heart, and pushing harder against life?

The worst aspect of Herminia's capitulation to middle-class morality is that she lies by omission to Dolly, by concealing the facts of her birth. Coupled with all that we have been asked to believe about Herminia's iron probity, this concealment is the most implausible element in the whole plot. Dolly, a conventional soul, not surprisingly hates her mother when she discovers the truth, for she rightly sees it as damaging her matrimonial prospects. By the end, Herminia Barton has proven such a nuisance all round that removing herself from the scene with prussic acid gives the unfortunate, and presumably undesired, impression that she is doing everyone a favor.

THE CRITICAL RECEPTION OF
THE WOMAN WHO DID

The Woman Who Did was widely reviewed. Richard Le Gallienne said admiringly, "here is a book that goes forth to certain death—gallantly, with its eyes open. There can be little doubt as to the nature of its reception. Every man's hand will be against it."[11] But that was not true, at least at first. The American reviews were, to be sure, almost uniformly hostile and uncomprehending. Harold Frederic in the *New York Times* thought it "lifeless to the point of tedium, and its characters, sinners and virtuous snobs alike, are all impossible puppets, who never convince, much less amuse, but simply bore one."[12] But some of the early British reviews were favorable and respectful. *The Westminster Review* called it "one of the most remarkable novels of the nineteenth century" and "the Evangel of Free Love."[13] The *Speaker* thought it a remarkable and powerful story. The *Pall Mall Gazette* judged Allen's sincerity to be undeniable, and Herminia's sentiments very noble and eloquent. It thought less of the style, however, judging that Allen's pot-boiling years had left "a thousand grooves and turns in his mind."[14] Other reviewers were not allowed even to explain properly what the novel was about. William Archer, the liberally inclined drama critic, wrote a thoughtful review for the *Daily Chronicle*, but discovered too late that even the phrase "free love" was on the newspaper's *index expurgatorius*, so the printed form of his review was badly mangled.[15]

Others, to be sure, exercised their wit on it, though usually in ways that surely intrigued rather than repelled many readers. *Punch* produced a cruelly funny parody, written by someone well acquainted with Allen's broader views and interests. "Perugino Allan" and "Pseudonymia Bampton" meet outdoors for an earnest discussion of marriage, seating themselves on "a carpet of sheep-sorrel, its orbicular perianth being slightly depressed by their healthy weight." Allen's proposal for early mating as a remedy for vice comes in for a particularly comical assault:

> Perugino sank back into the spongy turf, leaning his cheek against an upright spike of summer furze, of the genus *Ulex Europaeus*. "Some men," he began, "ignoble souls, 'look about' them before they marry. Such are calculating egoists. Pure souls, of finer paste, are, so to speak, born married. Others hesitate and delay. The difficulties of teething, a paltry desire to be weaned before the wedding, reluctance to being married in long clothes, the terrors of croup during the honeymoon—these and other excuses, thinly veiling hidden depths of depravity, are employed to defer the divine moment. I have known men to reach the preposterously ripe age of one-and-twenty unwedded, protesting that they dare not risk their prospects at the Bar. . . . Of course, it is not given to all to be born married. But this natal defect one can easily remedy. I knew a young fellow who did. The indispensable complement crossed his path before it was too late. He was still at his preparatory school; *he married the matron*."[16]

The "terrors of croup during the honeymoon" is a nice touch, but a *Punch* parody was, as always, too good-natured to put many readers off.

Among the more thoughtful reviewers the common response was puzzlement—even blank incomprehension. They found the peculiar ambiguity of its moral perplexing, especially given the humorless style. Some wondered whether Allen's gift for raillery had got the better of him. A few even speculated that *The Woman* had been written, not so much to denounce marriage, but to reinstate it with a muted "two cheers." They pointed to the dedication ("To My Dear Wife") as being a sly authorial judgment on Herminia's tirades. Indeed, just after Allen's death it was quite seriously proposed that the novel had been an elaborate spoof of a "New Woman" novel. The writer expected it to silence the marriage abolitionists for a century.[17]

This is nonsense, of course. But certainly it is hard to imagine why any woman would want to emulate the heroine's quest for social martyrdom. Stead had his tongue only half in his cheek when he spoke of the novel as "a Boomerang of a book," which ought to be pressed into the hands of every young lady to keep her on the path of virtue.[18] Certainly it is noticeable that *The Woman Who Did* was let off relatively lightly by the conservatives. They were aggrieved that Herminia Barton is allowed too many years to spread her poisonous doctrines, but at least she does die in the end with her theories exposed and her idealism shattered. Even Margaret Oliphant, Allen's most severe conservative critic, conceded that although Allen's pure "hill-top" was really nothing better than a moral dung-hill, it was, compared to Hardy's product, a sanitary and an odorless dung-hill.[19]

Severer condemnation came from the more liberal, or more consciously feminist, wing, who felt that Allen stood revealed as a turncoat or closet reactionary. Feminists, and male supporters of feminists, objected to the fate of the heroine because it seemed to confirm that the wages of sin is death just as severely as any Sunday-school tract. Such was the reaction of Millicent Fawcett, that pioneer of women's education, though no radical. "Mr Grant Allen has never given help by tongue or pen to any practical effort to improve the legal or social status of women. He is not a friend but an enemy."[20]

There was a personal animus at work here. Mrs. Fawcett's daughter Philippa had been a student at Newnham College and had earned the supreme accolade of being classed above the senior wrangler in the mathematics tripos in 1890. Naturally her mother cast a frosty eye over Herminia's airy dismissal of Girton as a useless place that had stunted her personal growth. ("I wouldn't stop at Girton," she says, "partly because I felt the life was one-sided—our girls thought and talked of nothing else on earth except Herodotus, trigonometry, and the higher culture.") Herminia's further supercilious remark that her own father, who had been a senior wrangler in his day, might be presumed to have "a certain moderate development of the logical faculties" (30) must have infuriated Fawcett even further, and she took a keen revenge.

Another notable review came from the pen of the young H.G. Wells, who tackled it for his first piece for the *Saturday Review*. Determined to prove himself in that abusive forum he did not spare the book, writing his review in what he defined himself as a "window smashing midnight-concertina-playing" style, even though he agreed with some at least of Allen's sentiments.[21] Figuratively dusting off his hands afterwards, he reported to a friend that he had "made Grant Allen howl in the *Saturday* over his blessed old *Woman Who Did*."[22] He has fun with the physical description of Herminia in her Aesthetic garb: "the reader must figure her sackful of lissome opulence and her dimpled, statuesque features for himself—the picture eludes us," he said. The novel is "strenuous without strength, florid without beauty, subtly meant and coarsely done," he concluded, though he too admitted to being puzzled. He could not quite put his finger on what it was that gave the novel a certain power. "Yet, withal, though it falls so short in execution and in art, there is something about it—that perfervid Keltic touch perhaps—that makes it readable. It warms one at times where better work might leave one cold. It may not merit praise, but it merits reading."[23] That was a common reaction, as it still is today.

SEXUAL RADICALISM IN *THE WOMAN WHO DID*

As must be clear by this point, it is hard to summarize *The Woman Who Did* without guying it. Once one has made the obvious points—that of all the productions of Grant Allen's pen, it is the only item that has indubitably survived its first century; that it was a huge bestseller so that even today it is remembered as the most typical, if not the most accomplished, of the New Woman fictions—once these points have been made, one starts to flounder. To apply to it the tools of literary criticism is to invite ridicule. Its characters, dialogue, and narrative style resist all attempts to reinstate it. Early admirers like Le Gallienne, who wanted to say for it all that they reasonably could, took the line that it is not a novel any more than *Rasselas* or *Paul and Virginia* or *The Coming Race* are novels: it is a fable, a morality tale, a pamphlet, a manifesto. But even manifestos must reckon with style and consistency of tone. As the sympathetic Clodd judged it, "there were passages in the book which furnished another illustration that the conviction of a mission is fatal to the play of humour";[24] or, to put the matter less charitably than Clodd cared to put it, *The Woman Who Did* does have its humorous side, but little of it, regrettably, is intentional.

Yet we have to reckon with the fact that, despite being a mass of contradictions, evasions, psychological absurdities and downright bad writing, *The Woman Who Did* has, in a way, fulfilled Allen's intention that it should be the acme and the justification of his career. As a cry of rage against the hypocrisies and stupid taboos of the time it is not ineffective, particularly because of the sense it gives of personal engagement; the quality that Wells caught in mentioning its "perfervid" tone. Even today it conveys a sense of febrile excitement which is far in excess of the needs of the rather silly plot and skimped motivation. Poor books, we may reflect, can be created with the same passion as great ones. As Wilde said, there is nothing so sincere as bad verse. And this is a quality worth exploring and understanding in biographical terms. *The Woman Who Did* emerged, like all books, from the antecedent experience of the author. For the biographer, the questions naturally arise: Why did Allen write it? And why did he write it when he did? Why did he himself think of it as a turning point in his career? And, finally, why was Allen—a perceptive man—so utterly bewildered, positively mystified, by the reactions he had from even his most sympathetic readers? There are answers to these questions, and they are biographical answers.

Our starting point must be this: *The Woman Who Did* was written in a spirit of deadly seriousness. Grant Allen had been preparing to write this book for the whole of his career. One accusation was that it had been rushed out to meet the market for New Woman fiction. Allen refuted that charge indignantly, and it is certainly false. On the contrary, as he said, it was long meditated and planned carefully over several years to bring some of his profoundest beliefs before the middle-brow public, using the only means of delivery it was capable of absorbing. It was written, he insisted, "with long and calm deliberation. I spent five years in maturing it, before I ever put pen to paper. I spent several months in writing the first outline. I spent two years in re-reading, polishing, correcting it, till every episode, every sentence, every image, every epithet had been considered and reconsidered eight or nine times over. Good or bad, it is my best possible work. There is not a word in it which I desire to change."[25]

As we have partly seen already, this timetable appears to be accurate. The reference in the *Athenaeum* letter of July 1892 to a book started "some months since" takes us back to the early months of that year. After he was advised to drop it for the sake of his reputation he must have continued to work on it right up to and during his stay at Perugia in the spring of 1893. It is true that we are left with an inconsistency here: the claim in the prefatory inscription that it was "written at Perugia Spring, 1893." But Allen could not have intended this to mean "conceived and wholly written": he contradicted this inference himself after publication.

The second point is that, despite the burning sincerity with which it was written, *The Woman Who Did* has a baffling, indeed paradoxical, relationship with Allen's pugnacious views on gender roles, marriage, and eugenics. These views he started to push forward in many articles from the end of the 1880s, once his financial position started to look secure and he felt able to begin his campaign against "the British matron" and her noxious influence on literary culture. It is illuminating, therefore, to study the emergence and evolution of Allen's views on these sexual questions.

The most succinct statement of them at their most mature may be found in a private letter to the Reverend Etheridge, the Rector of Haslemere, some eighteen months after *The Woman* was published. Etheridge had opposed Allen's nomination as the President of the Haslemere Microscope and Natural History Society on the grounds of his disgraceful opinions. Allen was elected anyway (but only just), and he then took the trouble to try to explain his beliefs to the hostile Rector:

> I regard our existing system of family and parental arrangements "as a whole," comprising these various elements—marriage, prostitution, seduction, abortion, infanticide, desertion, illegitimacy, divorce, and unnatural crimes. I also regard it as being responsible for much husband-murder, wife-murder, suicide, and misery; as well as for many terrible diseases and premature deaths, besides inducing (through the effects of prostitution) a great deal of hereditary consumption, cancer, and insanity. . . . [H]aving arrived at what I think solid conclusions as to the means by which prostitution, with its attendant diseases and evils, might be wholly avoided, and a perfectly pure system introduced, I cannot refrain from making my ideas public.[26]

What, then, was this "perfectly pure system," which might be introduced to rid society once and for all of its terrible evils? Naturally it did not spring into being fully formed. Exactly when Allen started to form his beliefs about sexual and marital morality must be conjectural, but there is little sign of them in anything he was writing in the late seventies or right to the end of the eighties. His explanation was that he needed to pander to the values of the marketplace earlier on, and that may be the answer. However, the matter is confused by the fact that Allen's sexual radicalism was a peculiarly patchy affair right through his life, and it was always underlain by conservative notions formed in his early manhood. His ideal wife and mother hardly differs from the angel in the house being promoted by John Ruskin back in

1865 when he was an adolescent. "The race that lets its women fall in their maternal functions will sink to the nethermost abyss of limbo," Allen pontificated in Ruskinian tones, "though all its girls rejoice in logarithms, smoke Russian cigarettes, and act Aeschylean tragedies in the most aesthetic and archaic chitons."[27] Such views, reinforced by his reading of Spencer's *Sociology*, formed early in Allen's life and he retained them to the end.

At some point, however—and it is hard to put an exact date on it—such mid-Victorian pieties started to be shot through with a darker vein of less avowable opinions. He hints at this for the first time, rather archly, in January 1889, in a column in the *Pall Mall Gazette* titled "A Biologist on the Woman Question." This casual piece, written in response to the emergent feminism of the 1880s then starting to gather momentum, and probably thrown off in half an hour, merely voices for most of its length the same views as summarized already. Women's biological destiny is to be "told off to bear the chief strain of reproduction, which in the human race is peculiarly long, severe, and exhausting." No plan of social reform can displace that inescapable reality. If you educate your women at the expense of their reserve fund of energy needed for maternity, you will find that "many of your seemingly healthy Girton and Newnham girls break down utterly." But there is a twist in the last paragraph, which seems, rather peculiarly, to shake itself free of the foregoing sentiments:

> If these ideas seem in any way conservative, I trust nobody will ever quote them as my "views" on the subject. . . . I am not such a fool as to say what I really think about such a subject as the relation of the sexes in this intolerant nineteenth century. If I did, my conclusions would certainly not be conservative; but I am wise enough, happily, to keep those to myself, locked up in the safe recesses of my inner consciousness.[28]

"Not such a fool as to say what I really think." But what *was* Allen really thinking, by this stage, about these delicate matters? The world was about to find out. The time of keeping things to himself, locked up in his inner consciousness, was coming to an end. Allen by this time had passed his fortieth year, and had taken to heart Clodd's astute advice to have five thousand pounds in the bank before he started to say things many of his readers would not want to read. He had reached this happy state, or something close to it, and was about to take the plunge into sexual polemics.

His preferred form, at first, was the article essay. He started with "Plain Words on the Woman Question" in October 1889 and continued seven months later with "The Girl of the Future." The latter piece so alarmed the editor of the *Universal Review*, Harry Quilter, that he added a nervous footnote dissociating himself or his magazine from it. There followed a long gap. Then two more articles, "A Glimpse into Utopia" and "The New Hedonism," followed in January and March of 1894. Allen published these two while *The Woman Who Did was* languishing in Lane's office waiting for a final agreement to be struck, and they might be considered semi-promotional pieces. All of them were much excoriated, and much discussed, especially the last. In them, Allen offered opinions about sexual, marital, and parental roles, which are a truly extraordinary blend of the narrowly orthodox and the wildly radical. They earned him a formidable reputation in the popular mind as an agitator and atheist. Conan Doyle tells a story about a couple who came to call on the Allens for the first time. As they waited on the doorstep Allen, inside, heard the wife say: "Remember, John, if he openly blasphemes, I leave the room."[29]

The first element of Allen's proposal was to encourage early mating—free unions—between young men and women at about the age of twenty. If love failed, either partner ought to look elsewhere, pursuing "the divine impulse of the moment, which is the voice of Nature within us."[30] Defying his critics who, not surprisingly, called this liberality by a grosser name, Allen looked them in the eye and insisted it was he, not they, who belonged to the "social purity" school. He said so without any conscious sense of paradox, because his aim was to balance out the degree of sexual freedom enjoyed by both sexes, and the "social purity" he had in mind was the abolition of prostitution, which he thought would follow hard upon it.

There is no mystery about the origin of this line of argument. Allen took it over wholesale, right down to some of the phrasing, from Shelley; specifically, from the short essay on free love attached to *Queen Mab*, published in 1813 when Shelley was twenty, and dedicated, as Allen dedicated his own book, to his wife. (Harriet Westbrook Shelley, however, was to be abandoned soon afterwards as Shelley followed his own "divine impulse of the moment.") Pre-marital chastity for either sex is, says Shelley, "a monkish and evangelical superstition." The young should pair off, but only as long as love lasts: "any law which should bind them to cohabitation for one moment after the decay of their affection, would be a most intolerable tyranny." The marriage ceremony itself is that tyranny in action.

Shelley expected to see prostitution vanish in the wake of marriage. Prostitution may well be called the "legitimate offspring" of marriage, because it services the needs of young men who are "excluded by the fanatical idea of chastity from the society of modest and accomplished women." If these ladies were accessible, it would be superfluous. Like Allen, Shelley has no effective answer about what to do when children arrived to force responsibility on lovers. But, unlike Allen, he carried this reckless indifference into his personal life, at least in the case of the children of his first marriage.[31]

Just as he makes Herminia Barton do over the dinner table in the Milan hotel, to the scandal of the diners, Allen himself promoted Shelley as a martyr. He tries to persuade us that the poet was "vilified and calumniated by wretched penny-a-liners, or (worse insult still) apologized for, with half-hearted shrugs, by lukewarm advocates. The purest in life, and the most unselfish in purpose of all mankind, he was persecuted alive with the utmost rancor of hate."[32] No matter that Shelley, in brute actuality, hardly lived up to even the most quixotic redefinition of "purity" in his private life. His extramarital excursions were conducted on no very elevated plane. As in the matter of his cavalier treatment of his creditors, he followed the aristocratic norms of his day. In every possible way, Grant Allen's personal code of conduct—fastidious, punctilious, honorable almost to excess—was the exact opposite of all this. Why he should have wanted to base part of his views on gender relations on those of an eccentric adolescent genius who never even began to live up to his own principles can only be put down to native perversity or, to some extent, a lack of information.[33]

Naturally Allen agreed with Shelley's brief remarks on prostitution in *Queen Mab*, but he pursued them much further. He abominated the time-honored view of prostitution, particularly powerful in Victorian sexual ideology, that it was not just a necessary evil but actually advantageous to society. It drained off male lust and deflected the attempts of rakes on the virtue of respectable women, married and unmarried. It stabilized family life and provided a safety-valve for ill-sorted couples in an age of limited divorce. In the case of the prudent paterfamilias who wanted to husband his domestic resources, it could serve as a kind of extra-mural contraceptive. And finally, one presumes, it had the unspoken benefit of taking the pressure off wives to meet sexual demands that no angel in the house could contemplate satisfying or, in the eyes of most men, should be asked to satisfy. The root idea that prostitution is the guard of public decency is as old as Augustine and Aquinas. Aquinas compared the whore to the cesspool in a palace: unpleasant, but necessary.[34] Early Protestantism tacitly admitted their Catholic predecessors' point by tipping the solution upside down: let boys and girls marry the instant they feel the sexual impulse, Luther recommended, and vice will disappear.

In the High Victorian era, rampant prostitution permitted, in fact encouraged, "prudent" marriages for men; that is to say, a marriage delayed until a man's career was settled. Before they reached that prudential age most men were not celibate, nor, of course, did they have recourse to women of their own class. They went to prostitutes. There were plenty of manuals and doctors to frighten them about the consequences of celibacy—genital disease, spermatorrhoea, chlorosis, hysteria, enfeeblement, morbidity. Some men, indeed, with sex available at a price to suit every purse, saw no reason ever to marry: Why keep a cow when you can buy a bottle of milk, as Samuel Butler, that confirmed bachelor, put it. (Naturally, this whole pseudo-medical discourse spoke to men; genteel unmarried women were deemed to need no sexual expression at all.) "The greater number of men," argued Allen, "are introduced to the sexual life through prostitution alone; they bringing at last to marriage and the production of future generations only the leavings and relics of an effete constitution."[35] The last phrase probably refers to that medical nightmare of the age, inheritable syphilis. At any rate, he thought free unions for the young would solve that problem and others.[36]

The perception that, because of the fashion for marital prudence among the greatly expanded middle classes, prostitution had grown to astonishing proportions was no special insight of Allen's. In Grant Allen's young manhood, the definitive, if ambiguously phrased, statement of this position—the prostitute as a necessary martyr to social virtue—was put by W.E.H. Lecky in his *History of European Morals*:

> Herself the supreme type of vice, she is ultimately the most efficient guardian of virtue. But for her, the unchallenged purity of countless happy homes would be polluted, and not a few who, in the pride of their untempted chastity, think of her with an indignant shudder, would have known the agony of remorse and of despair. On that one degraded and ignoble form are concentrated the passions that might have filled the world with shame. She remains, while creeds and civilizations rise and fall, the eternal priestess of humanity, blasted for the sins of the people.[37]

Allen obviously knew this purple passage, for he virtually paraphrases it in his poem "Sunday Night at Mabille," probably written when Lecky's *History* appeared in 1869. The Bal Mabille was a notorious Parisian dance hall of the Second Empire, where the dancers sported a characteristic lace bonnet with silk bow. It was a haunt of Lecky's "priestesses of humanity," and Allen draws a similar, if more challenging, conclusion to the historian:

> You tell me we must shut our eyes to all
> That turns this gaudy Mabille to a hell,
> If we would keep our wives and daughters pure . . .
> One question that I scarcely dare to breathe: —
> If woman's virtue cost so much to keep,
> Good friend, is woman's virtue worth the price?[38]

The answer, of course, is No: at least as far as the conventional meaning of "virtue" goes. For, whether it was dressed up in the blunt language of the man of the world or in Lecky's poetic prose, it was the hypocrisy that Allen found nauseating. His "decent" society was, to use his own simile, like a medieval castle reared on its foul dungeon vaults: vaults wherein helpless, lower-class women were daily sacrificed on the altar of prudent bachelordom. It was no less revolting to the Evangelical conscience, and this led to a strange alliance between extreme sexual radicals, like Allen and Havelock Ellis, and nonconformist puritans like Stead. But the latter were certainly not willing to pursue Allen's logic to the next stage: that if young couples could pair off and part without social odium whenever they wished, what need then for prostitution? It would vanish. Curiously, for a socialist, Allen rather discounted the powerful economic motive for sex work: the fact that it paid so much better, and was no more unhealthy, than being, say, a sweated seamstress in an attic sewing boys' knickerbocker suits complete for sixpence, or becoming a factory hand for five shillings a week.

Prostitution and the Biographical Context

Returning to *The Woman Who Did*—and considering it now as a social polemic—it is astonishing how little of all this finds its way between its covers.

All the expectations of the knowledgeable reader were frustrated a century ago, and that is still the main reaction of readers today. Anyone who followed Grant Allen's work and read the magazines must have been aware of his views, and some did express their bewilderment at the way these convictions are skirted or shirked. They complained that his heroine barely follows the precepts of his essays at all, and that his Woman Who Did is less notable for what she did that what she did *not* do. Even Richard Le Gallienne was disappointed that Allen's characters "don't submit themselves to the really significant tests. To have an illegitimate baby abroad is easily done, and any unmarried mother can pass as 'respectable' by describing herself as a widow."[39] Le Gallienne recognized that the union of Herminia Barton and Alan Merrick is in all but name a high-minded monogamic marriage while it lasts, and that Herminia Barton's rebellion amounts to two things only: a determination to flout the bourgeois marital code, and bearing a child in secret. If one were affluent, as these characters are, money could conceal both transgressions. Indeed, we see it starting to do so once the couple choose to leave England.

To summarize, then, the most remarkable feature of *The Woman Who Did* is *not* its fidelity to its author's deepest beliefs about love, marriage, and the family, but the way it simplifies, sanitizes and evades all the most important aspects of them. It is, as W.T. Stead shrewdly put it, "milk and water compared with his esoteric doctrine";[40] so much so that as a dramatization of Allen's well-publicized and incendiary views, the novel might almost have been the product of someone else's pen altogether. Although the novel has attracted more attention than all the rest of Allen's work put together, this intriguing fact and its meaning has been almost totally ignored.

Our starting point must be the blurred focus of the novel; its muddled intent: the way it seems to want to be about one thing while actually being about another. Most people who have heard of *The Woman Who Did* at all suppose that what the heroine "did" was to espouse and practice free love between equals. They assume that the issue at stake is the one Shelley described so memorably in "Epipsychidion": that monogamy is stifling and unhealthy; that love, unlike gold and clay, can be infinitely divided without loss; that, in short, it is inhuman to expect that anybody will or should, for a whole lifetime, with "one chained friend, perhaps a jealous foe/The dreariest and the longest journey go." They assume, in fact, that the novel is a tract in favor of free love. This has caused some extreme misrepresentations. One recent historian described the novel as being about a woman who "abandoned marriage and satisfied her sexual needs as she wished to so as to prevent racial degeneration which was following on personal frustration and genetic mismating," which makes her sound like a cross between Messalina and Francis Galton.[41] In fact, of course, Herminia does not "abandon" marriage and we certainly do not see her satisfying her sexual needs "as she wished" for an instant, either before her quasi-marriage or after her partner's death. We see her practicing only the strictest monogamy and, as a widow, an equally strict celibacy.

The Woman Who Did's driving force, which is moral indignation, comes from one source only: the issue of prostitution, considered in its widest aspect. But this is not an emphasis that would strike the average reader. Herminia Barton is not, of course, a prostitute nor ever at risk of becoming one. She is the daughter of a Dean, and apart from her heterodox views on the marriage ceremony, she behaves like one throughout. No prostitute is a character in the novel; no scene of vice is shown; no transgressive sexuality, apart from the lack of a wedding, figures in any way at all. The reader is obliged to read between the lines in order to appreciate the actual situation. Allen was promoting free unions and other even more radical social rearrangements, *not* because of their intrinsic merits, or because they would in themselves increase the sum of human happiness, but primarily because they would eliminate the market for bought sex. Few contemporary readers or reviewers had the external knowledge or the patience to work this out, and it has barely been mentioned since.

However, Allen's correspondence and public utterances on his creation make it quite clear that this was his intention. For example, when he sent an advance copy of the proofs to Stead he said that he was used to criticism from "the wretched creatures who spend their lives in lounging about the Empire or the Alhambra"—very probably an allusion to G.A. Sala, the journalist whose dissolute habits were familiar enough and who died, broke, that December. But he hoped Stead would try to be objective. "We two alone have realized the horror of prostitution in England; let us try to see eye to eye with one another."[42] Stead was still associated in the public mind with "The Maiden Tribute of Modern Babylon," his notorious exposure of child prostitution in the *Pall Mall Gazette* nine years earlier. And though he and Allen really had little in common, Allen wanted him for an ally on this subject. As things turned out, Allen found Stead's reaction almost incomprehensible. He was quite bewildered by Stead's "boomerang" jibe. He was afraid Stead, despite his campaigns, was himself becoming a bulwark of prostitution. The last is a curious charge. Stead had hardly mentioned the subject. Why, then, does Allen press so hard on it? The same note of puzzled frustration sounds in a letter he sent to the *Westminster Gazette*, objecting to the comments of its reviewer. "Against [prostitution] I have endeavoured to wage war to the utmost. The moral of my book is, we must put down this hateful slavery of women. . . . I thought I had put this contention in the plainest possible language; but so far, strange to say, not one of my critics seems to have grasped it."[43]

But why should they have grasped it? Pronouncing against marriage out of solidarity with her fallen sisterhood is only a very small part of Herminia Barton's rhetoric, and after the first pages it vanishes altogether. It drives no part of the plot at all. Nevertheless, Allen found it incredible that few of his readers seemed to understand that he had written the novel to promote a remedy for prostitution and all the evils stemming from it. Indeed, at times he seems to have been not quite sane on the subject, particularly when he came to believe, quite sincerely, that he had a quasi-divine mission to expunge it from society. For we need to add to the picture the extraordinary emotional state he was in when he started to work seriously on the novel early in 1892. He wrote in the letter to the *Athenaeum*, we recall, that he composed the first draft in a white heat of enthusiasm to bring his "authentic Message" to humanity.[44] Such a tone of messianic fervor is not what anyone, at any time, would have associated with the urbane, atheistic, self-deprecating and market-conscious Allen. Certainly he was not given to moral hand-wringing; yet here, and only here, his habitual light, skeptical tone had deserted him totally. We get a sense of unleashed repression, of feelings submerged for years because he could not write of them for fear of damaging his career, and of a bursting out at last in public indignation. It is natural, therefore, to look more closely at his personal relationships, and in particular his first marriage, contracted with such serious consequences more than twenty years before. Vexingly obscure though the circumstances are, it is possible to piece together something of the story from the few clues and suggestive silences that remain.

Little enough can be discovered about Caroline Bootheway, and nothing of a personal nature. But the dry public records do show that she was of impeccably working-class stock. At the census of 1851, when she was five, her family was living in Quorndon (now Quorn), a village of some 1,600 people where the main activity was framework knitting. Her father was a porter or pub landlord, although on the Allens' marriage certificate his rank is downgraded to "Labourer": perhaps the youthful Allen, that self-proclaimed Communist, encouraged this as a defiant gesture![45]

Since nothing is known of Caroline Bootheway between 1851 and 1868, we can only guess that she moved from Leicestershire to London to work as a domestic servant or nursemaid. Very probably they met, somehow, in Brompton during Allen's first summer vacation. Not yet rechristened South Kensington, the suburb of Brompton in the late 1860s was a slightly *louche* quarter. Ten years later the area had started to move up-market and was being pummeled in *Punch* as "passionate Brompton," home to young aesthetic married couples wondering earnestly if they can live up to their new blue-and-white teapot. (Du Maurier's famous cartoon appeared in 1880.) It is in the Brompton of this era that H.G. Wells houses young George Ponderevo, fresh to London, in a thinly disguised autobiographical passage in *Tono-Bungay*:

> My apprehension of spaces and places was reinforced by a quickened apprehension of persons. A constant stream of people passed by me, eyes met and challenged mine and passed—more and more I wanted them to stay—if I went eastward towards Piccadilly, women who seemed then to my boyish inexperience softly splendid and alluring, murmured to me as they passed. Extraordinarily life unveiled. . . .[46]

It is easy to imagine the immensity, the temptations, the huge exciting indifference, of high-Victorian London rushing to Allen's head as it did to the young Wells later. His background may have been cosmopolitan, but he had known nothing so far except a provincial life well cushioned by money: Kingston at first; then New Haven, Dieppe, Birmingham, Oxford. This was his first summer off the leash—and perhaps some of those devil-may-care Merton attitudes had rubbed off on him after all. We do not need to envision him hanging around the Argyll Rooms or the Blue Posts in the Haymarket. That would have hardly have been his style. But it was virtually certain that he would run, somehow, into a pathetic and pretty young woman who either literally or metaphorically was on the streets. Again, *Philistia* provides a clue, this time in the form of the solitary musings of Ernest Le Breton's brother, the lustful and unscrupulous Herbert:

> A man must have some outlet for the natural and instinctive emotions of our common humanity; and if a monastic Oxford community imposes celibacy upon one with mediaeval absurdity—why, Selah Briggs is, for the time being, the only possible sort of outlet. One needn't marry her in the end; but for the moment it is certainly very excellent fooling. . . . The idea flitted across my mind vaguely—"Why not send her for a year or two to be polished up at Paris or somewhere, and really marry her afterwards for good and always?" But on second thoughts, it won't hold water. . . . It would be awfully awkward if any Oxford people were to catch me here walking with her on the cliff over yonder—some sniggering fellow of Jesus or Worcester, for example.[47]

Unlike his caddish Herbert, or Wells, Allen was not cut out for sexual adventures, or "outlets." What would have been in less refined hands "very excellent fooling" soon became legal wedlock. After the ceremony, the young couple continued to live in a back street quite close to the developing South Kensington Museum complex, where Allen scraped a living as a private tutor. They were living very privately or even secretively, because late in the following year Allen told Nicholson in Oxford that "since you have tracked the lion to his den, you may as well address here for the future."[48] Was he still anxious not to be spotted with his unavowable wife and her "doubtful aspirates" by "some sniggering fellow of Jesus or Worcester"?

Thirty years later, when Edward Clodd came to compose his *Memoir*, the problem of how to handle this marriage must have loomed large. There were the feelings of Allen's wife and son to consider. He asked at least two of Allen's oldest friends, Andrew Lang and York Powell, by then a Professor of History at Oxford, for information about what they knew, and probably for advice on how to handle it.

Andrew Lang had not known Allen when he married. They did not meet until the *Daily News* days. But he knew the earlier story in outline. "In circumstances very trying he displayed noble attributes of character which I can only hint at. Indeed, Mr Allen behaved, if I may say so, more thoroughly in the spirit of the Gospel than any man I have ever met, though his intellect rejected so much that religion believes."[49] The "spirit of the Gospel" raises echoes of a certain behest about sexual sin and not casting the first stone. But he wasn't talking: "A great ox hath trodden on my tongue," he told Clodd.

He added, mysteriously, "probably without knowing it you give the story of that first marriage away. Every Oxford man will see the point." Lang was given to writing with irritating allusiveness. However, the "point" that an "Oxford man" (in particular) will get can only be one about an illicit, or socially dubious, cross-class entanglement.

Such relationships between literary or artistic men of the student class and working-class young women, sometimes more or less respectable, sometimes definitely not, were of course a cliché of the times. In literature and art the theme had been, and would continue to be, a favorite, in all of its many possible permutations. Pygmalion and Galatea, and King Cophetua and the Beggar Maid, were two of the most popular myths of Victorianism, treated by Burne-Jones, Watts, Tennyson, Gérôme, du Maurier, Hardy, and many others. And literature reflected life: there is Ernest Dowson's idealized relationship with Adelaide Foltinowicz, the daughter of a Soho restaurateur, and above all George Gissing and his tortured affair with the prostitute and alcoholic Nell Harrison in the late 1870s. In the case of the more scrupulous men these relationships did sometimes end in marriage. But the outcome was not necessarily as catastrophic as it was in Gissing's own case, nor as miserable as in his creation Alfred Yule's. Lang was surely hinting at a marriage of this kind.

If Lang refused to be drawn, York Powell was more forthcoming. He was an urbane man of liberal views, who had been one of the few Establishment figures publicly to support Oscar Wilde a few years earlier. "You must not leave out the earlier marriage," he told Clodd warmly. "It is not fair to GA. It is a high credit to him. He was a martyr for a year and he never let the poor girl see that he was suffering for her. He made the end of her life happy and peaceful by his self-sacrifice and if Xtianity were true which it isn't GA would be safe for a good place in heaven."[50]

Clodd accepted some of this advice and rejected the rest when he worded this section of his *Memoir*. On the negative side, he deprived Caroline Bootheway Allen of her very name and said nothing at all about her background or her situation when the couple met. We are told only that Allen had given "hostages to fortune" by marrying so young, and that he had done so "with more chivalry than prudence."[51] The second phrase can only mean that this was far from being a marriage between social equals. We learn that Caroline Allen became ill soon after the marriage, with a "paralysis," and was an invalid until her death. Eager to dispose of the marriage as quickly as possible, Clodd implies that it lasted only two years. In fact it was three and a half.

On the positive side, though, Clodd solicited from Powell, and printed, the only glimpse we have of the young couple:

> I remember being presented to his first wife—a gentle, quiet, soft-speaking woman, in poor health even then in the early days of their wedded life—and noticing the tenderness and care with which he anticipated her wishes, and spared her all fatigue or trouble, while it was delightful to see how she appreciated in her silent, grateful way his affectionate attention and guardianship.[52]

So far, so bland; even York Powell was too reticent to want to go further. It was left to Clodd to print the most meaningful revelation of all. He had in his possession a single, telling clue which reveals more of the relationship than anything else. It was the MS of a poem entitled "La Dame aux Camélias (To Alexandre Dumas, fils)." This Allen had omitted from his sole volume of poetry, *The Lower Slopes*. Although this collection was published as late as 1894 when Allen was forty-six, most of the poems in it had been written years before. It is to this early period of his life that "La Dame aux Camélias" must belong. Clodd had recovered it from Franklin Richards, Allen's brother-in-law and intimate friend. And now he not only printed it in full in the *Memoir*, but added the revealing comment that it was "one more personal than those published," thereby confirming that the basic situation is factual.[53]

"La Dame aux Camélias" is a poem of sentimental recollection. It tells how the narrator has a valuable keepsake, which he keeps constantly by him; it is a "dog's-eared, thumb-marked" copy of Dumas' novel. This had been his young wife's favorite reading and, when newly married, he and "Maimie" had often sat over it together, on a bank above "the tumbling Rhone." This itself is suggestive, as the novel in the 1860s was regarded as a typical piece of French lubriciousness which even a married Englishwoman could hardly show an interest in without attracting comment. Reading it aloud with her husband was practically an erotic act:

> And later when my Maimie's cheek was pale,
>   And weak her failing voice and low her breath,
> And in her bloodless hands we read the tale
>   Of slowly creeping death,
>
> Yet she would often raise her heavy head
>   To fix upon my face a tearful glance,
> And whisper, "Read me from the book we read
>   Long, long ago, in France."

The connection between this fond recollection and Dumas' story of the prostitute Marguerite Gautier, who is redeemed by her passionate love, is made explicit. Dumas' novel, and Verdi's opera, had made the consumptive courtesan, with her discreetly blood-spotted handkerchief, into the most romantic of figures. The novel appeared the year Allen was born. Alphonsine Plessis, Dumas' mistress and the model for the heroine, was one of the most celebrated courtesans of her day, and she died of tuberculosis at twenty-three. This was Caroline's age at marriage. In the novel Marguerite's true love, Armand, is younger than she, and she tries to give him up to avoid conflict with his father and damaging his career. The relevance to Allen's situation is obvious.

To put the question bluntly, then: Was Caroline Bootheway a prostitute, whom Allen had rescued from the streets and married out of some amalgam of romantic love, chivalry, pity, and political idealism? We recall that the cult of the rescued magdalen became popular in his adolescent years. Apart from all the novels dealing with the theme, there were the pictures so dear to the Victorian heart, lithographs of which were to be seen in many a home right up to the end of the century: Watts' *Found Drowned*; Millais' *Virtue and Vice* and *The Order of Release*; Rossetti's *Found*; Holman Hunt's *The Awakening Conscience*; George Harcourt's dramatic *Forgiven*. The gentle, retiring, humble prostitute did, occasionally, in real life match the "tart with a heart" literary stereotype. According to the expert, Dr. Acton, a certain number of these women "are notable for the intensity of love with which they will cling. . . . The sick man is safe in their hands, and the fool's money also."[54] Was Caroline a member of this branch of the trade, and did Allen later on idealize her death as a sacrifice, and she herself as the victim of the hypocritical social machinery that immolated her and women like her to protect her respectable sisters' virtue? One of the poems published in *The Lower Slopes*, "Forget-Me-Not," provides a hint that this was indeed Allen's attitude. At first sight this could be taken for a mere sentimental exercise:

> Her soft white hand lay tremulous, clasped in his;
>   Her soft grey eye with pearly dew was wet:
> He said, "Though all things else, yet never this
>   Will I forget."
>
> He went his way, and seeking his own rest
>   Forgot love's little tender, stifled sigh,
> Forgot the upheaval of that throbbing breast
>   Once clasped so nigh.
>
> And bending o'er an unmarked, uncared grave,
>   Too late for any penance save regret,
> He said, "The single sin God ne'er forgave
>   Is, to forget."

But its placement within *The Lower Slopes* is significant. It is the fourth of a group of five poems, which are expressly and overtly about prostitution. For example, the first poem of the group was obviously inspired by George Herbert's "The Collar." The stern voice of Duty orders its "servant," the poet himself, to rise and sing against the "blight of a terrible wrong." The poet says he is unfit; he wants to sing only of love. But he is ordered: "I bid thee arise with a sword in thy hand for a pen" and the poem ends submissively "Master, I hear and obey."[55] These poems were the ones that Allen pressed on Stead when the volume was published in 1894. He particularly urged Stead to read the first three of the group. "If you read those three, I don't care about the rest of them. There are two men in England really in earnest about the horrible slavery of prostitution. You are one, and I am the other. Don't condemn without reading. Read those three and then read 'Sunday Night at Mabille'."[56]

We notice that in recommending four of the five poems, the one that he omitted was "Forget-Me-Not." It is easy to see why. Whereas the other poems have an indignant tone that is effective but impersonal, this one is tenderly personal. Its sense of guilt, even of self-contempt, is palpable. It is surely autobiographical. While we do not know when it was written, it is easy to suppose that Allen felt compelled to requite his neglect, his "single sin" that God—the God he did not believe in—would never forgive. The silent reproach of that "unmarked, uncared grave" in the Cheltenham cemetery surely colored all the rest of his life. Caroline Bootheway was the original woman who did, in the sense that what she did was to inspire Allen's book. It is permissible, perhaps, to indulge in a little further speculation about the psychic mechanisms involved here. After all, if Caroline had been a victim of other men's monstrous "prudential" arrangements, she had not been the only one. There was her husband too. He had wrecked, or damaged, his own promising academic career by rescuing her. Hadn't he also been a victim, indirectly, of men's cautious and hypocritical sexual lives? Was resentment, perhaps, an additional ingredient in his recipe for the salvation of society: early mating and reproducing? Did he feel that those prudent young men— they and their chaste women, preserved like wax fruit under a glass dome— deserved to be "punished" by an early pairing-off and a quick buckling-down to their parental responsibilities? Even more speculatively, one might wonder whether Allen saw a personal analogy between his own condition in life, the way he earned his bread, and that of his long-dead wife's. At one point, in speaking of the forces compelling the author to meet the needs of the marketplace, he has an oddly telling comment:

> If you don't supply what the public wants, somebody else will step in and oust you; and the somebody else will survive in the struggle for life, while you go to the wall or into the workhouse. That is the gospel according to Darwin and Malthus applied to art. "*Saltavit et placuit*" is all the epitaph you can ever hope for; and not to please is simply fatal.[57]

Allen took his Latin epitaph for the writer-tradesman—"he danced and gave pleasure"—from a Roman gravestone of a 12-year-old boy from the North, found on the Riviera. It is likely that he was aware of the sexual innuendo, and that he expected his readers to pick it up as well. Perhaps his antipathy toward prostitution, no less than his sympathy for its workers, stemmed partially from his recognition that one can be obliged to service a market in ways other than, but analogous to, the sexual.

We see now where *The Woman Who Did* fails, and, to some degree, why. Its moving force is moral outrage, but the reason for it is never properly articulated because Allen lacked the ability to find an adequate objective correlative. We may speculate that, at one level, he wanted to create a heroine rather like Hardy's Tess Durbeyfield. He admired *Tess of the d'Urbervilles* enormously, and he read it just as he was working out his own conception of a heroine who is more sinned against than sinning. Probably he too wanted a pathetic heroine who could be offered up on the sacrificial slab of male hypocrisy; one who remains a "pure woman" even at the gallows' foot.

But if that was his intention, he miscalculated badly. Allen, unlike Hardy, was a polemicist with a case to make, and he had to have a clever and educated woman to act as a mouthpiece. This fatally divided conception means that what he produced was a self-pitying, posturing ideologue whom, even at best, it is impossible to regard as being more than a misguided idealist.

Furthermore, Allen was probably constitutionally incapable of devising any plot, or any character, which would have truly dramatized his views. He is a good example of a type—the armchair sexual radical—which flourished briefly in the particular conditions of the 1890s. He started by claiming more than the codes of the day would allow, but within a few years they were permitting more freedom than he was able to take. We recall the *Athenaeum*'s comment about Allen's "tremors and his timidities and his juvenile consciousness of the delights of naughtiness."[58] This is a rude observation which needs qualifying in all kinds of ways, but there is some truth in it. His long campaign against the censors and his blustering that he was "condemned to provide milk for babes" while wishing to "purvey strong meat for men"[59] always sounded a little factitious. It is surely significant that Allen was reduced to public silence by *Jude the Obscure*. Although he thought it was Hardy's best work and that the characters of the two women had been wonderfully drawn, he must have found such a scene such as the one where Jude chases Arabella, with a warm egg between her breasts, up the stairs to her bedroom, stronger meat than anything he ever wanted to purvey. What we are left with is that "perfervid" enthusiasm, which lingers long after the cardboard characters and implausible motives are forgotten.

CHAPTER 10

LAST ORDERS (1896–1899)

THE ANTHROPOLOGICAL FANTASY: *THE BRITISH BARBARIANS*

The last four years of Grant Allen's life brought him into smoother waters. He lived better than he ever had before, more at ease and with more opportunities to work as and when he wished. His health seems to have stabilized as he passed through his forties. He had several thousand pounds in the bank and investments in land and companies, and the expensive question of launching his son on a suitable career was settled, temporarily, when Jerrard was placed in his cousin's publishing house. "Don't take to literature if you've capital enough in hand to buy a good broom, and energy enough to annex a vacant crossing," we recall Allen had advised the neophytes. But it had been years now since he had needed to think of requisitioning that broom for himself. In George Gissing's *Diary* there is a lively pen-portrait of Allen in the splendid summer of 1895, when he was basking in the success of *The Woman Who Did*. Gissing met Allen at one of Clodd's Whitsun weekends at Aldeburgh. The creator of Rhoda Nunn in *The Odd Women* had no reason to think he would have anything in common with the supposed apostle of pagan free love, and he had already confided to his diary his opinion of his fiction: "Got from lib. Grant Allen's *This Mortal Coil*. The time I waste reading trash such as this." Yet he found himself liking Allen very much. His charm, his unaffected, naïve manner, won him over. Signally lacking much of either commodity himself, he confided to his diary his envy at Allen's dual marital and financial success:

> Grant Allen I liked much better than I had expected. He is white-haired; and all but white-bearded (a little sandy remaining) though only 47. Very talkative, and, with me, confidential about his private life. Says his wife suits him admirably, and shares all his views of sexual matters. Showed me a letter just received from her, beginning "My darling Daddy." . . . His special study is anthropology. Thinks there never was a man Jesus: his whole story a slowly perfected mythus. Has rather high-pitched and sing-song voice, to me pleasant.[1]

In letters describing the same occasion he added these impressions: "a simple genial fellow, absorbed in scientific studies—caring not a rap for the kind of work by which he lives. . . . Not a trace of pretence about Allen. He dresses roughly, talks with enthusiasm of his own matters, is devoted to a country life—says that he was never out of doors in London after 11 at night. His memory is astounding. . . . Has known everybody worth knowing, & seems in some marvelous way to combine infinite leisure with remarkable productiveness."[2] And again: "I went with a prejudice against Allen, but, as so often happens, got to like him very much. He is quite a simple & genial fellow; crammed with multifarious knowledge; enthusiastic in scientific pursuits. With fiction & that kind of thing he ought never to have meddled; it is the merest pot-boiling. He reads nothing whatever but works of scientific interest." And finally: "Personally he is a good cordial fellow, & delightful in talk so long as he can keep off fiction—when he becomes acrid and unjust. An amazing store of knowledge! And does his work with incredible ease."[3]

Some of the buoyancy that Gissing recorded wore off as the year closed. Allen feared that he might emerge from his *annus mirabilis* with his forehead fatally stamped as a novelist with opinions, like his character Montague Watts, and might possibly share his fate. The Wilde trials of April–May 1895 could hardly have eased his mind. John Lane was running scared for a while—Wilde instantly vanished from his list and he sacked Beardsley—but it did not prevent him from issuing Allen's *The British Barbarians* late in the year. Allen dusted off this manuscript, which he had kept in his drawer for six years, and added a lengthy, defiant preface-manifesto in which he promised, as we saw earlier, to stick the "hill-top" label on all his serious fiction in future, as a guarantee of its probity.

This short novel—really a satirical fable with minor science-fiction elements—marks a return to the anthropological novels and stories that had been written in the late 1870s and 1880s, but has an entirely different and more sophisticated perspective. *The British Barbarians* uses the device of a mysterious stranger, Bertram Ingledew, an anthropologist on a field trip from a future century, who turns up one Sunday in a Home Counties village and proceeds to analyze their customs and taboos just as though its stuffy residents belong to a savage tribe—which, from his perspective, they do. He succeeds in converting Frida Monteith, the wife of a boorish businessman, to his point of view. They run away together and enjoy a few idyllic days on the breezy uplands. They are hunted down by Monteith, who, much too barbarously monogamous to permit the theft of his marital property, promptly shoots Ingledew dead. His body evaporates into the ether, leaving only a pleasant smell behind. The novel ends with Frida's apparently planning to drown herself and her children in order to join him.

A fable like this suited Allen's talents rather well, by precluding the sentimentality and repetition that clogs so much of his other fiction. It also allows him to indulge unimpeded his acid wit. His mouthpiece, Ingledew, a Candide-like figure as well as a scientist, is perfect for the calm delivery of innocently outrageous notions. We expect a man from a utopian future to find the peculiar taboos of the nineteenth century morally repellent—mourning clothes, "No Trespassing" signs, marital proprietorship and many others—but we expect him to remain fairly detached from them. He is, after all, a visiting scientist gathering data. Allen's self-consciously guileless, mock-ingenuous tone can be irritating in the other novels, but here it is appropriate enough. *The British Barbarians*, as well as being amusing and sharp, is Allen's most formally satisfying novel. But the reviews were terrible. H.G. Wells, despite his recent friendly meeting with Allen, did not spare the novel: it was "redolent of bad taste and bad English, destitute alike of dramatic incident and character analysis." He joined the queue of people advising Allen that if he wanted to say "a good many things that require saying . . . let him call his sermon a sermon and be content." It was curious advice from a writer who would himself go on to use the novel as a polemical tool to an unprecedented degree.[4]

But whether editors really shunned Allen's work after his scandalous books and notorious views had become widely dispersed is not easy to say. Allen himself seemed unsure about the overall effect of what he had done. There was a brief period, he told friends, when he felt he "stood idle in the marketplace, because no one dared hire him," but he also told Herbert Spencer at the beginning of 1897 that any fall in demand, for his fiction anyway, was due simply to his being "crushed out" by younger men.[5]

The periodicals editors, those most sensitive barometers of public opinion, showed no very overt reaction. His stories continued to appear much as before. George Newnes, who was strong on bright wholesomeness in fiction, continued to take all of his episodic crime stories for the *Strand* after 1895, although he risked nothing as they were all entirely innocuous. Allen did not, however, contribute any more single stories to the *Strand*. Excluding the three episodic crime series, Allen wrote six novels after 1895: *A Splendid Sin, Tom, Unlimited, The Type-writer Girl, Linnet, The Incidental Bishop, and Rosalba*. Not one was issued either by Chatto & Windus or John Lane. Two of them were published by his nephew's house, Grant Richards, and the rest by minor publishers like C. Arthur Pearson, whose more usual fare was titles like *Fun on the Billiard Table*. Furthermore, two of them appeared under the same innocuous female pseudonym.

Not one of them was serialized either. Was the failure to serialize a free choice? That is hard to believe. In the manifesto preceding *The British Barbarians* Allen had promised that he was going to sacrifice three-quarters of his income "for the sake of uttering the truth that is in me, boldly and openly, to a perverse generation."[6] But that was intended to apply only to novels carrying the "hill-top" label. So many of his earlier books had been serialized that we must assume Allen would have serialized most of the rest if he could have found any takers. So he had paid an economic cost. However, the financial damage, if any, must surely have been cancelled out by the success of his episodic stories for the *Strand* and his new venture, the guide-books to European art centers published by his nephew Grant Richards.

In any case he was no longer quite as much in thrall to the marketplace. Whether Allen found more fame than notoriety from his "hill-top" fiction is a moot point. What is certain is that he found affluence. His two best-selling novels alone must have brought him several thousand pounds. He now had money to invest, and where else to invest it but in the book trade? He had already invested £200 in George Newnes Ltd., when it became a joint stock company in 1891. Now, when his nephew Grant Richards, at the age of only twenty-four, wanted to start his own publishing house, Allen capitalized the company to the extent of £750 for its opening in 1897. No doubt he would have invested even more himself, had he not lent John Lane, who was suffering cashflow problems, much of what he had earned from *The Woman Who Did*.

Allen's Other Anthropological Work

The most remarkable way in which Allen reshaped his career after 1895 was that he finished so abruptly with sexual controversy. He wrote no more confrontational essays like "The New Hedonism" and when he lost, or surrendered, his platform at the *Westminster Gazette* he did not find a replacement. Perhaps he feared the backlash from the Wilde prosecution, as Clodd hints; perhaps he felt he had been outpaced by events and did not want his "purity" fiction linked to other people's "erotomaniac literature";[7] perhaps he believed he had now done all that he could do to requite his first wife's memory. Or perhaps concern for his second wife's feelings was a factor. He said something of this to George Bedborough, who wanted him to be president of the Free Press Defense Committee after he, Bedborough, had been prosecuted for selling Havelock Ellis's *Sexual Inversion*:

> I will be frank. I married legally, young, a wife with whom I have lived and still live, after twenty-four years, in unusually close harmony. Although from one point of view [she] is a tower of strength to me, but from another I cannot help regretting that my writings have been held by many as a slight upon her, and that she herself has had to bear the imputation that they are so. Hence I do not desire to take any more prominent position than is necessary in this matter.[8]

Or was this just a convincing excuse? He could not have had much personal interest in bailing out an equivocal character like Bedborough. Possibly what the reply really hints is that Allen had simply grown tired of being, in his own eyes, so hopelessly misunderstood. For the promise he had made that his most serious work would henceforth carry the "hill-top" label was never fulfilled. It turns out, however, that it was not entirely for want of trying. He did complete a third "hill-top" novel, titled *The Finger Post*, which presumably he wrote in the closing months of 1895. Whether he submitted it to Lane and had it declined is unknown. But he did, yet again, ask Andrew Chatto for a candid opinion on it. And, as usual, he got one:

> I am constrained to say that I am unable to agree with the teaching of the story either as regards its pervading pessimistic view of life or of its contention that marriage is a curse, and that prostitution is a necessary concomitant evil with

marriage. . . . I hope in spite of what I have now ventured to tell you of my views, that I may be privileged to make an offer for any other novel you may write of a less controversial nature and more on the lines of say *The Tents of Shem* and *At Market Value*, which are stories I think that have certainly added to the brightness and happiness of life.[9]

How perfectly these remarks of Chatto's delineate the long relationship between Allen and his main publisher! Andrew Chatto was a humane and civil man, prompt and punctilious in his dealings with his authors. But he was a firm and unsentimental businessman, as he had to be, and his business was to know what would sell and to make money out of it. As is obvious here, the two men had so little common ground other than a desire to see each other prosper. The clash of values, their mutually incomprehensible assumptions about what literature is for and, in particular, the quite unconscious cruelty of that last sentence, must have had Allen tearing his hair out and, one assumes, tossing *The Finger Post* manuscript into the fire, because none of his last novels answers to Chatto's description of it.[10] Further, it may have caused a permanent rupture in relations between the two. No more of Allen's work went to Chatto, not even his pot-boilers, and it seems that personal relations between them nearly ceased too.[11]

But Allen's innate optimism and creative resilience saw him through this time, just as we have seen them doing earlier. He remained as productive as ever. Some of his last novels do exploit the new freedoms, probably to the limit that he was constitutionally capable of. All are pot-boilers. *A Splendid Sin* (1896) is a light-hearted social comedy. An upright young Englishman, Hubert Egremont, a physiologist who researches into heredity, fears he cannot marry his aristocratic Italian fiancée Fide because he has discovered he is the son of a dissolute English colonel. All comes right when Hubert's mother reveals he is really the bastard son of an American poet and a hero of Italian nationalism, news which is received with surprising equanimity all round. Attitudes were shifting, and no one was more acute than Allen at spotting this. He attempted to exploit the emerging market for white-blouse fiction with *The Type-writer Girl* (1897). Using first-person narrative, this follows the fortunes of feisty young Juliet Appleton, American-born Girton graduate, who suddenly needs to earn her living as a secretary. Like Allen's detective-women, Appleton is very much Allen's revisionist model of educated femininity—cheerful, managing, and independent; not at all like the educationally force-fed neurotics who had figured earlier, or that self-destructive ideologue Herminia Barton. This novel starts in Allen's brightest, most sprightly manner as his heroine tries out a sleazy lawyer's office and an anarchist colony in Horsham, suffering sexual harassment in both. It could have been an effective piece of social realism like Wells' *Ann Veronica* of a few years later. As it is, it subsides into little more than a romantic romp.

His mainstay in these years was his work for the profitable *Strand*, whose circulation was going from strength to strength in the last years of the century, due in no small part to his friend Conan Doyle's Sherlock Holmes stories, which had started to appear there in July 1891. Allen and others modified Doyle's formula slightly by introducing a thin narrative thread connecting all the semi-detachable episodes. He tried his hand at this new genre in mid-1896, with twelve related "adventures" starring a confidence trickster Colonel Clay. They are distinctly lightweight, but the plotting is ingenious and only occasionally tumbles over into the frankly incredible. Immediately afterward, although he was not quite the first with the idea, he developed a new twist: a female detective as heroine.[12] The *Strand* took two more series in this vein, running them from March 1898 to February 1900. They were published as *Miss Cayley's Adventures* and *Hilda Wade*.

Allen did more than episodic fiction for the highly-paying *Strand*. Two final series of his natural-history articles, *Glimpses of Nature* (1897–1898) and *In Nature's Workshop* (1899) appeared there as well, both consisting of lengthy, closely written pieces illustrated with fine drawings by a technical artist. In all, he made sixty-six contributions to the *Strand* in eight years, and in some issues he had fiction and popular science running simultaneously. The stories, in particular, were very lucrative. For *An African Millionaire* he got £5 per thousand words, a high return when each episode ran to about 6,000 words. These adventures were so popular that Newnes paid him £1,000 down for the serial rights to *Miss Cayley*. (The *Strand* could well afford them, however. Soon after Allen's death, its readership in the English-speaking world was said to be three million a month.) Then there were the carefully reserved residual rights, all sold off piecemeal by the industrious Watt: for *An African Millionaire* alone, £200 for the U.S. book rights; forty guineas for the French translation rights; £80 for the German rights with illustrations. . . . This was the living that Allen had looked forward to, back in the hard days of the late 1870s: the annual income of a very successful solicitor or doctor. You could call a doctor a tradesman, or an author a professional man, whichever you liked; it all came down, in the end, to the size and frequency of those checks coming through the letter-box for services rendered.

Allen may have finished with popular sex controversy, but when he allowed more of his energies to flow into other interests, especially art history and religious anthropology, he was still not afraid of airing heterodox opinions. In 1897 Richards published as one of the first ventures of the company *The Evolution of the Idea of God. An Inquiry into the Origins of Religions* (1897). This was a long labor of love for which Allen had been collecting the materials for his entire career and had then written slowly over ten years amid all his other work. *The Evolution* is an exercise in the anthropology of religion. (Allen took no interest in the ethical codes of religion, which he assumed are entirely detachable from, and do not illuminate, the origins of religious belief.) In it he tries to answer three questions. What is the origin of polytheism? What is the origin of monotheism? And, finally, what is the origin of Christianity? He traces the religious impulse back to corpse-worship, or rather the worship of the deified memories of the dead. More specifically, he thought he could offer a connecting link between Spencer's account of the origin of religion and the one proposed in James Frazer's *The Golden Bough*. Spencer thought that the religious impulse had originated in a fear of the spirits of dead people, perhaps because they seem to visit the living in dreams. The erection of tumuli or standing stones, or the planting of sacred trees, were originally an attempt to keep ghosts in their place, while the ancestors themselves were deified and had to be placated with offerings and sacrifices. Eventually this differentiated into polytheism and finally into monotheism.

Frazer, Max Müller, and others, including Andrew Lang, did not believe animism could be reduced to ancestor worship in this fashion. In *The Golden Bough* (1890; 1906–1915), Frazer presented animism as the first, primeval expression of humanity's religious belief: that is to say, the attribution of conscious life to the most impressive objects of the landscape. The sun, great rocks, rivers, and trees were thought to be the abode or the embodiment of potent spirits.

Allen proposed a theory that effectively was a blend of the two. He accepted Spencer's view that all gods were originally ghosts, but he proposed that sacred trees and standing stones planted on the tumuli or barrows of the deified ancestor gradually acquired the sanctity of the people buried below, and came to be worshipped independently after ancestor-worship was superseded and forgotten. In *The Evolution* he describes many traditions from different cultures where tree-gods, or bleeding or speaking trees, were originally associated with burial mounds. The legend of the Christian crucifixion grew out of such a tradition, he thought. He took it for granted that the origins of Christianity are almost entirely a mixture of mythical elements and pious invention.

Allen argued further that this primary stage of religious belief was bound up with the origins of agriculture, and could therefore explain the fertility rituals described so dramatically by Frazer. Why were ghosts ever connected to vegetation-growth? Because, in the hunter-gatherer stage of human culture, the disturbed soil piled over a grave was especially fertile. The corpse below added nutrients; so did the blood, milk, and oil poured out as propitiatory offerings. The natural vegetation on the mound therefore grew miraculously lush and green. Later, seeds were deliberately sown as part of the burial ritual; their vigorous sprouting encouraged further experiments, and so began the deliberate cultivation of the soil. The human sacrifice of temporary vegetation gods, "green men" killed and scattered in the fields to ensure fertility, arose from the same cause. It was not just a matter of propitiating the gods.

Allen presented this thesis with his usual vigor and clarity and, as usual, he was optimistic about its reception. "When it comes out," he said, "the rock of animism is going to be ground to powder."[13] But the standing of *The Evolution* was irretrievably damaged at the start, when it was reviewed scathingly in the *Athenaeum* by an authority on folklore, and rather more politely but just as devastatingly by Andrew Lang. As a Christian, Lang deplored this kind of anthropological reductionism, but he kept that animus well in the background in his review. He concentrated on the evidential difficulties instead.[14] He detected a problem in the logical sequence of Allen's theory. The most ancient burial sites, with their decorations and careful arrangement, suggested a loving care on the part of primitive men toward their dead: how, then, did this come to be transformed into the fear of corpses and their spirits, as Allen's theory required? "I am making sumptuous hay of you . . . I have you on toast," he had told Allen in his jaunty, needling way, during an earlier exchange about sacred stones, and so it proved again.[15] To Allen's chagrin, the early sales of *The Evolution* were thin—about 750 copies in three weeks, and a mere handful thereafter. Even committed freethinkers were not very interested in the subtle theoretical distinctions he makes; for them, Frazer and Lang had said it all already. Perhaps it would have sold more if Allen had ignored Spencer's cautious advice to introduce the central phrase into its title, and had called it, *tout court, The Evolution of God*. Certainly its aggressively skeptical style suited the next generation better. An abridgement in 1903 sold very well. Despite G.K. Chesterton's quip that he would rather read about God's idea of Grant Allen than the other way round, it was still going strong in "The Thinker's Library" series in the 1940s, by which time eighty thousand copies had sold, making it easily the most successful of all of Allen's nonfiction books.

Allen's most characteristic books of these last years are the travel guides which he tackled strictly as a moneymaking venture for his nephew's firm. He financed his springtime visits to Europe with these guidebooks, devoting each one to an art capital. He gave his guides a distinctive quality by being sublimely indifferent to the practical questions of where the visitor might lodge or eat or shop. (He resolved the first of these requirements for himself by always putting up at the most luxurious hotel available.) Brisk, hectoring, and self-opinionated, they are formidable in their focus on high culture, relentlessly educational, and enviable in their certainty of taste. Allen's last effort in this direction was *The European Tour. A Handbook for Americans and Colonists* (1899). He aimed this at the North American college student market, and perhaps of all of Allen's books it gives the very best sense of what a superlative instructor he was. As always, it exudes self-confidence. Art, and history discovered through art, is the only motive he recognizes for going to Europe at all. And Europe hardly includes Britain, for Allen asserted that, apart from the London art galleries and a few country towns, there is no reason for anyone from the new world to linger there. Odd advice from one who had so eagerly transplanted himself decades earlier! For three hundred pages the pace never slackens for an instant. Go here, go there, it commands, with different typefaces to tell the eager youth what to see and, indeed, what to think about what they had seen. "This lightning Baedeker—this Bovrilised Murray," said the *Academy*'s bemused reviewer.[16] These guides were immensely popular, particularly in the United States, where they appeared for years afterwards in multiple editions, and they are still readily obtainable, and useful, today. Grant Richards heard that half the English and American visitors to the Louvre and the Uffizi could be seen clutching the little books in their floppy green jackets. Unfortunately this popularity was not actually reflected in sales. Richards put it down to the lending habit: people will not buy a guidebook if they can borrow a copy.

The last of Allen's enthusiasms was to cultivate his love for all things Italian, and especially Italian religious painting. He wrote numerous essays in his last years on art history, and some of his articles on that subject were collected after his death as *Evolution in Italian Art* (1907). It was his last play for Spencerian evolutionism. What he does here is trace the "evolution" of the narrow subjects of Christian art—the annunciation, the Madonna and child, and so on—in the hands of successive painters and schools. He classifies them and constructs an evolutionary tree, as he might do for a species. But constructing a typology of art is only metaphorically a study in evolution; paintings are not really subject to variation and selection. Nor is the evolutionary biologist much concerned with the individual organism; whereas we want to know very much why this painter's Saint Sebastian is more worth looking at than that one. As a critic, Allen had far more ability as a classifier and typologist than as an evaluator. His critical judgments on particular works of art are never more than rudimentary noises of approval: a fresco is "distinctly alive"; a Sposalizio is "exquisite" and "the longer we look at it [a Fra Angelico], the more we love it"; Botticelli's *Primavera* is an "exquisitely spiritual and delicate work . . . one of those profound pictures which must be visited again and again," and so on. He is best, as usual, at exposition: identifying the figures, describing their attendant symbolism, comparing and contrasting and grouping. When he attempts to explain what is actually happening in a picture, his interpretations are sometimes rather too simple, for he had little understanding of the subtle symbolism of Renaissance painting, particularly secular painting. For example, he interpreted the *Primavera* on no fewer than three occasions as a simple allegory of the spring months. We cannot expect Allen to have grasped the arcane neo-Platonic symbolism of the picture, for that would be recovered only by scholars of the next century. But it is curious that he did not realize that the right-hand figures do not only represent the months of March, April, and May, as he claimed, but obviously picture the rape of Chloris by Zephyr. Since Ovid tells the story in the *Fasti*, it was an odd omission for a classical scholar.

THE LAST SCENE

It was during a stay in Venice in the early spring of 1899 that Allen was attacked with symptoms which were at first diagnosed as malarial. He tried the remedy of staying for some time with Herbert Spencer—now aged seventy-nine—at Brighton, but it did no good. After he returned home, he was pursued by anxious letters from the philosopher, who was just as assiduous in pursuing health cures for others as for himself. This time the advice was to chew one's food more. He could not accept his friend's ignorance of "the importance of reducing food to small fragments. That you, a scientific man, should not recognize this is to me astonishing."[17]

But there was much more wrong with Grant Allen than his habits of mastication. By mid-summer he was too weak to hold a pen and had to dictate everything. His last months were blighted by agonizing pain, relieved in the end only by constant morphine injections. Despite this, he seemed to think right to the end that his complaint was malarial fever. As mortal illness took him in its grip and as the moorland visible in both directions from his bedroom windows changed from green to gold, he had also to watch all his dearest values being trampled in the mire on the international political stage. For the public talk, in that last summer, was of nothing but the struggle with the Boers. On October 10 President Kruger issued an ultimatum to the British; it was rejected and war was declared. The Boers quickly took the initiative, laying siege to Mafeking, Kimberley, and Ladysmith, but by that time Grant Allen was dead. The end came on Wednesday October 25. Winifred Storr, the teenaged daughter of some family friends who lived nearby, wrote in her diary: "Exquisite but sad day Dear Grant Allen Died at 11.50 this morning. . . . Oh! poor darling little Mrs. Allen! It is too terrible for her. Left almost alone in the world! He passed away after very great suffering last night, it is better as it is for his sake. Poor man!"[18] A postmortem examination was conducted the following day and revealed a malady that was judged to have been incurable: probably it was liver or pancreatic cancer.

Arthur Conan Doyle, also a Hindhead neighbor, was at the death-bed. By the time he wrote down his recollections years afterward Doyle had become a convinced spiritualist, and his account has all the bluff, mildly sanctimonious cheerfulness of the true believer:

> I well remember that death-bed of Grant Allen's. He was an agnostic of a type which came very near atheism, though in his private life an amiable and benevolent man. Believing what he did, the approach of death must have offered rather a bleak prospect, and as he had paroxysms of extreme pain the poor fellow seemed very miserable. . . . I can see him now, his knees drawn up to ease internal pain, and his long thin nose and reddish-grey goatee protruding over the sheet, while he croaked out: "Byzantine art, my dear Doyle, was of three periods, the middle one roughly coinciding with the actual fall of the Roman Empire. The characteristics of the first period—" and so on, until he would give a cry, clasp his hands across his stomach, and wait till the pain passed before resuming his lecture. His dear little wife nursed him devotedly, and mitigated the gloom of those moments which can be made the very happiest in life if one understands what lies before one.[19]

Allen was in fact unafraid of death, though not, of course, because he had any belief in spiritualism. Rather, Allen had lived close enough to death's embrace for most of his life, and an incident from his childhood in Canada, where he nearly drowned after falling through the ice, persuaded him that "the actual dying itself, as dying, is quite painless . . . death itself, it seems to me, need have absolutely no terrors for a sensible person."[20]

This cool, dry rationalism sufficed him to the end. Typically, one last matter which agitated him was meeting a professional obligation. The *Strand* had been running his serial *Hilda Wade*, and the final two episodes were yet to be produced. Doyle, one of the kindest of men, either wrote them both or finished them off. The last episode appeared the following February, and was titled "The Episode of the Dead Man Who Spoke."

But for Grant Allen dead men never spoke. He expected from death nothing but personal extinction. Conan Doyle was quite wrong. Allen was definitely no type of agnostic at all, and he once took pains to correct a newspaper story that he was. The agnostic takes his stand on the position that he cannot know what lies beyond the phenomenal world. Allen's position was simpler: There is nothing to be known. His uncompromising opposition to all supernaturalism is well captured in a letter he wrote to a clergyman at Hindhead, who had written declining to know him socially because of his immoral and atheistic views. "No man is bound to know another," replied Allen, in a dignified response, "or to give any reason why he does not know him." He enlarged on his position:

> To me, the first religious duty of man consists in the obligation to form a distinct conception for himself of the universe in which he lives. . . . Many years of study, historical, anthropological, scientific, and philosophical, have convinced me that the system of the universe which you accept as true is baseless and untenable.[21]

Allen's own conception of the universe was an austere one. It was the very epitome of nineteenth-century materialism. Science reveals many wonders and esthetic delights, but of purposiveness it reveals nothing at all—because there is none. There is no spiritual dimension to existence which is beyond the province of science. No mystical insights, no privileged revelations into the nature of reality, are genuinely available and anything offered as such is at best fancy or wishful thinking; at worst, it is hallucination, delusion or a fraud. There is only one kind of knowledge, and one means of acquiring it; and the boundaries of the various sciences are synthetic, for all real knowledge forms a seamless whole. The laws of physics fully explain the behavior of the universe, past, present and to come. Darwinian evolution—itself reducible, ultimately, to biochemistry and thence to physics—explains the organic world, and it has no destination. The mind *is* the electrochemical activity of the brain, an "incidental phosphorescence, so to say, that regularly accompanies physical processes," in the formulation of the psychologist James Ward.[22]

As for other existential dilemmas, such as the meaning and purpose of life, or how a person ought to live with the knowledge that death is inevitable, Allen thought these were spurious problems worth very little of a sensible man's attention. The cosmic pessimism of the *fin-de-siècle* attracted him no more than the optimistic pleasures of supernaturalism. Near the end of his life he showed some interest in Catholic doctrines. One of his last and best-turned stories, "Luigi and the Salvationist," pits the faith of an Italian peasant against an English Salvation Army zealot who is trying to convert him, to the considerable advantage of the former:

> "We are born: well and good; they baptise us instantly: and thereby we obtain baptismal regeneration. We grow up: we are catechised: we make our first communion. We become men and women: we consult our parish priest: we confess at least three times a year: we communicate at Easter: if we do anything

wrong, we seek penance and absolution. By-and-bye we grow old: we feel death draw near: we send for our good father: we receive the viaticum: we obtain extreme unction: and we depart, forgiven. To make all sure, our children and friends after our demise see that masses are said for the repose of our souls." He expanded his palms. "What would you have?" he asked rhetorically. "We do all that the Church demands. We fulfil every obligation. We leave no command unobeyed. Where is the need for this strange thing called *conversion*?"[23]

None of this had any personal reference, of course. Like many atheists Allen was intrigued by the internal coherence of Catholic dogma and the way it handles human frailty more realistically than the reformed churches—but that was all. His interest in religious belief was exclusively psychological and esthetic. Chesterton said that T.H. Huxley was always talking about the religion he did not have, but Allen seemed to find all metaphysical questions fairly pointless.

On Friday, October 27, the body was taken in a coffin of papier-mâché covered with white cloth to the Brookwood Crematorium, Woking. The only ceremony was a moving, simple, and short memorial address by Frederic Harrison. It would, Harrison said rightly, be "an outrage on the life and last wishes of Grant Allen that any theological hopes or invocations should be uttered over his helpless body now resting in the sublime stillness of death." Accordingly none was offered.[24] His ashes were scattered in the garden of The Croft.

Soon afterward, his will was published in the *Daily Chronicle*. His estate was valued at £6,455.3*s*.3*d*. His wife was the sole legatee.[25] In the same issue of the paper a cheese monger was reported as having left £275,810. Grant Allen, tradesman-writer, would have appreciated the conjunction.

GRANT ALLEN'S REMAINS

Back in Canada, Joseph Allen, by now a widower, survived the death of his son by one year, dying at the age of eighty-six. Alwington, which he had finally inherited, was demolished in 1959 and a plaque on a traffic island is all that marks the site. On Wolfe Island, Ardath House, Allen's childhood home, was already derelict by the turn of the century. In 1902 a historian touring the property had pointed out to him by a local guide the very bedroom where, according to tradition, Grant Allen had been born. However, the fact that the same historian referred to Allen's nineteen published books says little for his credibility.[26] Nothing but some foundations and walling remain today.

Allen's wife and son, aided by Grant Richards and other friends, continued to publish his literary remains and float new editions of his work whenever they could. Richards republished *The Woman Who Did* in 1906 in a cheap one-shilling edition with a big print run of 20,000 copies, especially for the station bookstall market. There was a brief scare when one of the railway companies refused to sell it, causing Richards to plead in vain that its theme was far too old-fashioned to give offence. Yet it must have sold tolerably well, for he followed it in 1908 with another edition at the rock-bottom price of sixpence. York Powell put another book together over Allen's name by extracting forty-four of the short essays on local history and topography that Allen had done for the two *Gazettes* at the very start of his career. All these enterprises were, as Richards put it, more a question of familial piety than commerce.

Jerrard Allen was twenty-one when his father died. Soon after the turn of the century he moved into the theatrical world, becoming an impresario and agent, and here he enjoyed a somewhat checkered career. In June 1912 he was telling his friend Theodore Dreiser in America that "I am running a thundering good show on the halls—*The Bachelor Girls*—: I wish you could see it for it's good. Just five good smart girls in gorgeous frocks—none of that damned nonsense about intellect in it but it's a big show and I know you'd like it." The following year he made a lot of money in a Tango tea-dance venture, but his partner cheated him and he reported ruefully, "I don't mean that I have just lost a lot: I've lost *everything*."[27] He spent much time and energy, in the years before the outbreak of the First World War, in trying to get back to the New World, which his father had been equally anxious to leave. The one wish of his life, he said, was to set foot in New York. During the war he managed it, leaving behind a financial shambles, which his cousin "Grantie" Richards had to clear up. Clearly Jerrard Allen was in some ways his father's son. He inherited his optimism, energy, and readiness to seize the next trend. But he also seems to have had a insouciant nature verging on recklessness, very different to his diligent and punctilious father. He was still alive in 1937, aged fifty-nine, but after that the last traces of the family vanish from sight.

Nellie Allen survived her husband by nearly forty years. She continued as a sleeping partner in Grant Richards' company and presumably drew some of the profits. Edward Clodd and other legal friends helped her invest her legacy and royalties in a trust fund, which kept her comfortably for the rest of her life. She took frequent rest cures in genteel hotels and nursing homes and traveled a good deal with her relatives. By the tenth year of her widowhood her nephew noticed that she seemed to find life rather boring; it had surely never been that during her husband's lifetime. She died in 1936 at the age of eighty-three.

Of Grant Allen's two main homes, The Nook still stands today, abandoned and derelict in a secluded hollow of the grounds of a hospital. At Hindhead the intellectuals' colony dispersed in the early years of the century and the houses of its more prosperous members became hotels or offices, or were pulled down. But the Croft avoided that fate and still stands off the Tilford Road as a private house, though its grounds are a little depleted and it is now surrounded by dense woodland blocking those expansive views of heather, heath and pine that gave Allen so much pleasure a century ago. But it still has the fine rolling lawn on which, in those almost unimaginably peaceful summer afternoons just before the splendors and horrors of the twentieth century started to unfold themselves, the Allens played host to their circle of wits and Grant shocked his young niece with his frank talk and daring speculations.

CONCLUSION

"WE OF THE PROLETARIATE . . ."

ALLEN'S CAREER: AN EVALUATION

"All the goodness, the humour, the tenderness, the imagination, the intellect, the brilliance, the love and laughter that were Grant Allen are now a little dust."[1] With these sad words Richard Le Gallienne, the most steadfast of his disciples, wrote *finis* to his friend's vivid existence. To die in one's years of productive maturity is always a cruel fate, but it was especially so for Grant Allen. He died just when the Western world was on the threshold of fascinating novelties. His reaction to the Great War and Russian revolution, to Modernism generally, to Postimpressionism, to Surrealism, to Freud and to early twentieth-century technology, especially the new technologies of entertainment, would have been very well worth having. It is curious to consider that, had he lived to no very exceptional age, we might have had his response to reading *Ulysses*. And what would he have made of post-Mendelian genetics, or the new physics? At the time of his death, his cosmic progressivism, qualified though it always was, was starting to look quaint. Einstein's paper on special relativity would be published in a few years' time, and by then Max Planck had already devised the foundations of quantum mechanics, despite once admitting that he found his own conclusions almost too peculiar to be credible. Such men had started to put the mystery back into science. The mathematical physics of the twentieth century would prove far more challenging to the imagination than Allen's cut-and-dried atomic materialism. But his attitudes were far from ossified as he entered his fifth decade, and he would surely have come to terms with the transformations and dislocations of the Edwardian years. It is only the fact that he died in his prime that fixes him so irrevocably as a Victorian. If he had lived as long as Thomas Hardy or H.G. Wells and had lasted to the end of the Twenties, he would be remembered more as an interestingly transitional figure.

It was not to be, however, and Allen's many friends and admirers recorded their sense of loss and tried to sum up his truncated career. There were many obituaries, and they paint a consistent picture, especially of his personal qualities.[2] Everyone spoke of him as a loveable, kindly, delightful, and honorable man. His moral courage, his transparent sincerity, his eager and generous enthusiasms, had impressed most people who had known him personally. The journalist Chris Healy spoke up for "the priceless gift of his sympathy" toward junior struggling journalists, and the Chatto correspondence shows how often he put new work before his own publishers.[3] William Sharp ("Fiona Macleod"), for whom Allen had been the best champion of Celtic literature, told a friend how much he felt the loss. "I loved the man—and admired the brilliant writer and catholic critic and eager student. He was of a most winsome nature. The world seems shrunken a bit more."[4] George Gissing wrote from Paris, "I liked him; indeed, I liked him very much. I found his talk delightful, & was always sorry that I could not have more of it; there was a great charm for me in his honest, gentle personality—thoroughly honest and gentle, spite of his occasional scoffing at himself or at others."[5] All agreed as to this sweetness of character. More than one person spoke of him as simply the most interesting man they had ever met, and perhaps that is the memorial Allen would have liked best himself.

They spoke up for his professionalism too. His old sparring-partner Andrew Lang, said that he had differed from him on almost every issue; nevertheless, "those who knew him as a man, and a friend, will never forget his unusual genius for kindness, gentleness, and dignity of character; for common-sense, too, in practical affairs."[6] He had no secretary; he handled himself all business that was not in Watt's hands, and his attention to detail and deadlines made him popular with editors. If you want something done, give it to a busy person, runs the maxim. And Allen, who liked to call himself as "the busiest man in England" illustrates its truth.[7] Not for him the endless deferrals, vague excuses and spent-up advances supposedly typical of authors. Once he had promised, he delivered—always. He had a will of iron, forged by years of toil in one of the most insecure and uninsurable of professions.

Certainly the persona he presented in his writings had some obvious failings. Even well-disposed contemporaries mentioned the occasionally irritating and aggressive tone of his writing. To that we can add a tendency to self-pity and petulance; we notice, too, that he can veer between an unconvincing humbleness of manner when he is on weak ground and a grating cocksureness when he feels confident. He was far from lacking a sense of humor, but it took on a biting, carping tone when his gift for satire got out of control, and even in his milder moments his love of paradox and flippancy and the throwaway remark did not always do him justice. His sense of humor failed him altogether over matters which he took seriously. And there were many of those, for he thought of himself as a man who wanted very much "to do and say some good things in my generation."[8] Sometimes his earnestness tipped over into a brittle obduracy and crankiness, which made him a natural victim of the ill-disposed. As his friend York Powell said, "he is such a good fellow and so earnest, and so deaf to the comic side of things that he has always an open place to be attacked in—and it hurts him."[9] Allen was too thin-skinned to be the thorough iconoclast he would have liked to be.

United as they were about his personal qualities, Allen's friends could not agree whether his career was a failure or a success, either in others' eyes or his own. Most thought he had put a brave face on things. For W.T. Stead he was a man who knew he had failed, and his life was therefore pathetic.[10] Andrew Lang offered this: "he was patient with a life in which his true genius was thwarted by circumstance: in which he succeeded where he had little or no wish to succeed, working at popular tasks, *invita Minerva*."[11] The *Academy* said that "he wrote seventy-two books, and in a sense regretted them all."[12] Even Le Gallienne concluded that he had been forced to prostitute his great gifts, which he thought was one of the saddest things he knew of in recent literary history.[13] The anonymous obituary in the *Athenaeum* concluded that he was a man of indomitable industry who never found his true vocation.[14] Grant Richards wrote complaining about the phrasing of this, but the *Athenaeum* refused to give ground. A man who complained so much about his need to write fiction for money cannot be said to have died fulfilled, it insisted.[15]

The editor Clement Shorter was the only one to dissent radically from all this. He warned against taking Allen's own moody comments too seriously, for temperamentally he was given to exaggeration. "I do not for a moment believe," said Shorter, "that Allen, had he in early years come into a fortune, would have concentrated himself upon science in the way that Huxley did; or that if he had done so his life would have been as happy as it undoubtedly was."[16]

Such claims—on either side—are easy to make and impossible to disprove. They lead nowhere. It is more fruitful to consider what remains of Allen's reputation after a century and what his well-documented life tells us about the freelance writer's lot. Edward Clodd ended his *Memoir* with a good question. "Naturalist, anthropologist, physicist, historian, poet, novelist, essayist, critic—what place is to be assigned to this versatile, well-equipped worker? Time . . . will alone determine what, if any, of Allen's writings will survive."[17] So what, in fact, has time determined? What, out of that great outpouring from Allen's pen, has survived as a living cultural force?

Little enough. Grant Allen's talents and position were correctly judged by those of his contemporaries who were not blinded by prejudice against his sexual polemics. While he lived, he was known as a lively, efficient, variously talented author-journalist who could be relied on to amuse, instruct, challenge and, occasionally, outrage. He was a man of his day. As a scientific worker, the reputation he wanted for himself, Allen was no deep thinker nor, except in a few technical areas of botany, an original thinker. This also was perceived at the time. "He was not a profound scientific man in any direction," said the anonymous obituarist in the *Daily News*. "The Darwinian St. Paul, somebody dubbed him and certainly his power of expounding and popularizing Darwin's teaching to those could not for themselves take it at first hand was very remarkable."[18] As we have seen, his most characteristic "scientific" productions are his hundreds of short essays on topics of natural history, especially botany. Here Allen was working the same vein as Charles Kingsley,

Richard Jefferies and W.H. Hudson. The "nature essay"—armchair botany, entomology and ornithology—was very much a nineteenth-century genre. Its popularity started to wane after Allen's death, though it lingered long enough for Evelyn Waugh to parody it in the form of the weekly essay by "William Boot, Countryman." Boot's "Lush Places" is found in the *Daily Beast* squeezed between a recipe for Waffle Scramble and the Bed-time Pets column, and it has a distinctly antiquarian flavor—just like Boot himself. That is why Waugh treats it with his most benign and tender humor. Most of Allen's vast output in this genre was ephemeral and soon it was forgotten. By its very nature most of Allen's work could not last: it was quotidian, responsive to passing interests, essentially disposable. His fate was that of all successful cultural middlemen. First they help to shape a climate of opinion; then they are then absorbed by it; finally their role is elided or denigrated.

What claim can be made for Allen's residual value as a minor novelist? His skills and limitations as a novelist are rather similar to Aldous Huxley's two generations later. Huxley said once that some writers are not really congenital novelists, but are clever enough to be able to mimic a novelist's behavior convincingly. That, surely, was Allen's gift. It is certainly true that for him, as for Huxley, the novel was more of a convenience than a compulsion. The most memorable parts of his novels are embedded essays and his characters are alive only insofar as they are ideas on legs. As an anonymous reviewer of *The Scallywag* said, "if a novel of Mr Grant Allen's were to survive for a century or two, though it would reveal no essential facts of life and society in our time, it would not be valueless, for a certain superficial tone and accent of the educated middle classes would be nowhere better reflected."[19] That is well said; for, like Huxley's early satirical novels, the best half-dozen of Allen's do embody and exploit many of the aspirations and phobias, fantasies, and silences of his day. His fiction taps especially into socio-biological anxieties: racial degeneration; transgressive and dissident female sexuality; atavism and primitive reversion; miscegenation; the rampant sexuality and fertility of the inferior stocks; the increasing androgyny of the young and the enfeeblement of sexual desire; and above all the dire effects of inheritance, especially inherited disease and criminality. It could be said that all of Allen's fiction is essentially a set of footnotes to Darwinism. Nothing that he wrote in fiction will ever detain the literary critic for long, but he was adept at bridging the two cultures and for that reason a part of his work will probably survive as a quarry for the social and cultural historian.

Life at the Better End of Grub Street

We of the proletariate cannot be pickers and choosers . . . the poor man (and the mass of littérateurs have always been poor, from the days of Grub Street onward) must take the first work that turns up to his hand.[20]

We of the proletariate? Grant Allen as a poor man? As a wage slave? We raise a quizzical eyebrow. "Has he *starved*?" George Gissing liked to inquire when he suspected a writer of not having paid his dues. Allen had never starved. He had settled at the better end of Grub Street in his first days and despite his own forebodings had stayed there.

Consider, by way of contrast, the early years of the writer-journalist Arthur Machen, who was also briefly a Keynotes author with John Lane. Born in 1863, Machen was fifteen years younger than Grant Allen, but Machen started his career much earlier and in that sense the two men were roughly contemporaries. In 1884, while Allen was being paid a surprisingly high price for his first novel, Machen was living in Holland Park in an unheated room so small that he kept his few books on the rungs of a stepladder outside his door. His food was dry bread and green tea. For weeks on end he spoke to no one apart from the brief exchanges of street and shop. Starting in 1881, Machen wrote eighteen books, including a translation of Casanova in twelve volumes. He had a brief success with *The Great God Pan*, but the total of his literary earnings over forty-two years was £635, or about £15 a year. "I believe that business men, engaged in manufacture, always 'write off' a considerable sum for legitimate wear and tear and depreciation of plant. What about the wear and tear of mind and heart and that T,e,a,r which is pronounced in another manner?" asked Machen, rhetorically, in his old age. Only newspaper journalism kept him from the workhouse.[21]

By comparison with a story like that, Grant Allen did very well indeed. Arthur Machen might have been thinking of him when he contemplated those writing men who were plugged into the network of privilege; the men who belonged to the world of quiet words in the right ear; the "others," Machen calls them. Allen's first decade was hard indeed, but a helping hand was there when he needed it. In the context of a career such as Machen's, is it not the merest posing to speak of yourself as a "proletarian" when you winter on the Riviera each year and are enjoying so many other fringe benefits of the trade? Those benefits were not despicable, after all; some of them were vividly described by Anthony Trollope:

> There is perhaps no career in life so charming as that of a successful man of letters. . . . The clergyman, the lawyer, the doctor, the member of Parliament, the clerk in a public office, the tradesman, and even his assistant in the shop, must dress in accordance with certain fixed laws; but the author need sacrifice to no grace, hardly even to Propriety. He is subject to no bonds such as those which bind other men. Who else is free from all shackle as to hours? The judge must sit at ten, and the attorney-general, who is making his £20,000 a year, must be there with his bag. . . . During all that Sunday which he maintains should be a day of rest, the active clergyman toils like a galley-slave. The actor, when eight o'clock comes, is bound to his footlights. The Civil Service clerk must sit there from ten till four,—unless his office be fashionable, when twelve to six is just as heavy on him. The author may do his work at five in the morning when he is fresh from his bed, or at three in the morning before he goes there.[22]

When Trollope's confessional account appeared in 1883 it described a level of success Allen could only dream of. Yet eventually he had come to enjoy in full measure all these perquisites—the "incidental consolations," he called them. We have documented how quite sudden socioeconomic changes within the world of letters threw up new opportunities, and how quickly new men bounded forward to seize them. A journalist, Raymond Blathwayt, a contemporary and friend of Allen's, records in his autobiography the moment when he leapt from obscurity to fame in a single week. Having lost his job as an East-end curate—allegedly because he could not recite in order the Ten Plagues of Egypt—the young Blathwayt was nearly reduced to penury. Then inspiration struck. He would seek out famous men and persuade them to do "interviews," a mode of publicity then barely heard of in Britain. The rewards were exhilarating. Even after thirty years, Blathwayt could scarcely believe his luck. He was well aware of the uniqueness of that point in the history of journalism:

> On one Monday I was practically starving; on the following Monday the cheques had begun that delightful flow which they have never altogether ceased ever since. It was as though I had gone into an oil district and at once started a "gusher" . . . never again, I suppose, certainly not within the working life of the young people of the present day, will such a golden era, journalistically speaking, present itself as presented itself to me.[23]

In a quieter and slower-maturing way, this was the pattern of Allen's success too. His prosperity stemmed from a happy conjunction of the man, milieu, and moment. It was made possible through an interaction between his particular abilities and his fortuitous arrival at just the time when his kind of talent could find its reward; the moment which the publishing historian Simon Eliot has called that "fleeting golden age for the facile writer of easily-read prose."[24]

And the socio-technological milieu he inhabited was one where every change in the production and consumption of text played into his hands. There was the expanding, eager readership created by Forster's Education Act; the rise of the new (mass) journalism, itself made feasible by the rotary press and the linotype typesetter; the lucrative provincial syndication markets; the new American copyright provisions; the emergence of middlemen with useful skills for hire that most authors did not have and did not want. Such a career as Allen's would have been impossible a few decades earlier, and a few decades later it would necessarily have taken a different course and had a different shape, though it might have been rewarded even better than it was.

Not that it was ill-rewarded. Allen was by no means an average literary jack-of-all-trades, but it is still surprising to discover just how well a hardworking but still fairly minor professional writer could live in this period. He benefited from the low cost of living, particularly the cheap cost of labor. A point of comparison is that Grant Richards, no exploitative skinflint, was paying his live-in cook £35 *a year* a decade after his uncle's death. Thirty years earlier, then, Grant Allen had only to write three *Cornhill* articles to pay for a service like this, and toward the end of his career he was getting more than twice that cook's annual wages for just *one* monthly episode of a lightweight serial in the *Strand*.

Nor was it only a matter of income. Let us not underrate those nonfinancial "consolations" to which most professional men could not aspire, let alone the proletarians. Many must have sighed as Andrew Chatto did when the Allens invited him on a spring holiday abroad, an offer he had half promised to accept: "Ah yes, when we felt young and hopeful. . . . It was a very pleasant daydream to think so while it lasted, but we are awakening now to the reality that it is impossible for one to leave the business."[25] Not for most of *them* four months on the Riviera each year. Even in his darkest days Allen never knew real privation. He worked hard, but he knew no "shackle as to hours" for most of his career. He had plenty of Trollope's "amenities of society," or at least the limited society he wanted. For the kind who eyed him askance he cared nothing anyway.

Yet, as we have seen repeatedly, his attitude to his own material success was paradoxical. He insisted it was important to him, yet it seemed not to satisfy him. Authorship, he complained, is

> the worst market into which a man can take his brains. Mr Besant makes much of the fact that a certain number of authors make incomes of over £1000 a year. But the same number of painters, barristers, doctors, make £20,000 a year. For the most part even tolerably successful authors only just pull through somehow. Thy can't make fortunes; they seldom even leave their wives and children properly provided for. I don't complain of all this; I don't see how it can be prevented; the profession is overcrowded, and the competition keen; but as you ask me what I think of it compared with other professions I should say distinctly it's an excellent one to keep out of.[26]

He knew how hard he worked, and he was not content to be a thousand-a-year man. Few writers felt the tension between Art and Mammon so acutely as Allen. He could not escape from the literary life, but he thought hard about why there is such a gulf between the incomes of authors and those others who live on their wits: "painters, barristers, doctors." Why are the rewards for the first so scanty? Are writers intrinsically so much less valuable to society? He returned repeatedly to this question, twice devoting strong and penetrating essays to it. The first, written when his fortunes were at low ebb, is the more bitter, more self-questioning and self-punishing. The second, when he was emerging from the ruck and could see a clearer path ahead, is more analytical, witty and dispassionate.

What *is* the social utility of the writer, not only in the existing world but in the fairer world that socialism might one day usher in? As early as May 1883, when he was struggling hard to find a footing, he meditated this theme in a *Cornhill* article, "A Scribbler's Apology," which right from the self-denigrating title is the most ruthless piece of self-examination he ever made in public. Doubtless it was inspired by the appearance of Anthony Trollope's *Autobiography*. Trollope had drawn a notorious comparison between the novelist's trade and the shoemaker's. His claim was that his own honest labors were just as socially meritorious as the shoemaker's. Allen inclined to the opposite view. Watching a shoemaker at work from his study window as he sits plying his own trade of scribbler, he envies that tradesman his useful day's production, compared to his own dubious role in the national economy. What has he done himself to come to table in response to "the clanging dinner-bell of collective humanity?" How has his day been spent? Dismally: "I have contributed a column of political abuse to my daily paper, and I have written half an unfavorable review, for a weekly journal, of a foolish and vulgar sensational novel." Can such work be defended, especially by a man who counts himself a Communist? And, in particular, what can be said for the mere "tootler"—one like Grant Allen, for instance? One answer is that the tootler fills a want. But that is unsatisfying. What troubles Allen most is the suspicion that he is a parasite of the ruling class. Few people produce the really useful goods of the world, like "bread, meat, clothing, science and poetry." Far more workers are expending their labor uselessly on "mother-of-pearl card-cases, malachite boxes, ivory-handled brushes, crests and monograms, or papier-mâché monstrosities." Is not the tootler similarly employed? Still, there is a hierarchy of uselessness. People, after all, must be amused; and a skilled hand can inform while entertaining. At the very best, then, the tootler may be doing little good, but he should see to it that he does no harm.[27]

Rather a dusty answer, to be sure. Though he was about to leave the *Cornhill*, Leslie Stephen was so concerned about the self-destructive mood of this manuscript that he wrote Allen a supportive letter, explaining how he had resolved the same dilemma for himself:

> I have often thought over your problem and have answered it pretty much to my own satisfaction. I cannot think any man blameworthy for making his living in any honest way: & I think journalism indifferent honest if does not lie or pander to clearly evil tastes. . . . I don't flatter myself that it matters two straws to the world whether I write or dig in my garden; but it makes a difference to my own little world, where I can really produce some effect.[28]

One wonders how Stephen's well-meant advice, the advice of a veteran of fifty, was received by the younger man. Allen might well have reflected that Stephen's quietism was a pretty self-indulgent philosophy. It was based foursquare on a private income and an assured place among the English intellectual aristocracy. Allen would have despised the opinion that it didn't matter "two straws" to the world whether he wrote or dug his garden. He expected his writing—the kind of writing he wanted to do—to matter a great deal. But he could not have thought, by the end, that too much of it really had mattered.

Six years later Allen returned more specifically to the money question in one of his most brilliant essays, "The Trade of Author." Based on his first full decade of dearly won experience, it is witty, bitter, and shrewd. As we have seen, Allen had an almost neurotic concern for his own earning power, and his opening question goes, as usual, straight to the financial heart. "How does it arrive that the wage of the average author, usually a person of some little education and some modest intelligence, falls so infinitely below the average wage of the other learned professions?" A barrister, whose special skills are known to few, can mark his brief at a hundred guineas, and get it. Doctors charge twenty-five shillings a minute for chatting to you. Even an unknown water-colorist can ask thirty pounds for a small square of painted paper. Only in authorship does breadth of reputation bring no commensurate reward. How very odd it is, then, muses Allen, that when admirer comes to seek out a writer "known to half the world in a dozen countries" his hero is likely to be discovered living in a suburban cottage, subsisting on a twentieth of the income gained by any other professional man known to no one outside the little circle of his clients. How can this be?[29]

The answer, Allen argued, lay in the peculiar disadvantages under which authors labor. The worst, he thought, is the effect of the Competition of the Dead. In law or medicine or accountancy or any other service trade, you, the client, must resort to those who are active now, inferior though they may be to their dead predecessors. But the consumer of literature is under no such handicap. The illustrious dead are just as accessible as the living, and require no payment. Thus is driven down the living writer's price. "Who will care to buy a new book by a rising author," asks Allen, "when he can get the pick of Thackeray, and Dickens, and Carlyle, and Macaulay any day for a shilling?" Eager though he was to embrace fresh young talent, he had little faith in its ability to draw money out of pockets. Writing as he was in 1889, he probably had in mind the plunging prices of publishers' reprint series. The head-to-head competition between Routledge and Cassell had recently seen a huge range of classic authors become available for three pence each. There the price bottomed out: the great writers had become accessible for the cost of three cheap newspapers.

Between them, therefore, these two articles suggest why Allen was not being fatuous when he defined himself as a proletarian. He felt he shared the vulnerability of all sweated out-workers to fluctuations in demand, the insolence of employers, sickness or other ill-fortune. In fact their plight was worse than average, for freelance author-journalists like Allen participated in the most primitive economic transaction between capital and labor that it is possible to imagine. Until the Society of Authors was formed in 1883/1884 the freelance was alone as few workers are alone, his alienation total, his wage-slavery manifest. Even Walter Besant, who was sometimes criticized for his rosy view of the rewards of authorship, had to admit, "no worker in the world, not even the needlewoman, is more helpless, more ignorant, more cruelly sweated than the author."[30] Each day the freelance wrote with only his native wit to guide him. The conventions discouraged personal approaches. The contributor was expected to mail his work in with just a name and address written discreetly in the corner—Allen's own MSS show he followed this convention. Then the editor either took it (at *his* price) or rejected it. Rarely was there room for negotiation. Sometimes there was no human interchange at all for years on end, and even multiple acceptances did not necessarily create any reservoir of good-will or obligation. Under such a regimen Allen passed all his career. Toward the close of *The Woman Who Did* we hear that the worst aspect of the aging Herminia Barton's career as a literary journeywoman is having her work "publicly criticized as though it afforded some adequate reflection of the mind that produced it, instead of being merely an index of taste in the minds of those for whose use it was intended."[31] This bitter observation—obviously a cry from the author-narrator's heart—was intended to be a self-defensive stroke. The truth, however, was that it is the very fact that Allen was an "index of taste," echoing and defining the preoccupations of the day that gives him his best chance of survival. In another mood he seemed to accept this fate for himself, as when he closed his introduction to *The British Barbarians* by asserting that the ideas in that book are guaranteed "by that spirit of the age, of which each of us is but an automatic mouthpiece."[32]

Allen was indeed a mouthpiece for the Zeitgeist. His interests were so various, his grasp on his own time and its fleeting concerns and tastes so perceptive and lucid, that he will surely continue to command a small audience in each generation. Despite his repeated gloomy appraisals of his situation, he actually handled his own plight rather well. His energy protected him from the worst consequences, for he could always make some time for his own interests. Other writers would have been destroyed or swallowed up by the killing workload he suffered for years, but he was, in his versatility and flexibility and restless pursuit of the new, not merely the first among equals but unique. A man who could translate Catullus' *Attis* and publish it with a useful exposition and essays on tree-worship in the middle of all his other labors must have been a man of overflowing mental vigor. And the work is of surprisingly high quality. He wrote quickly, and had to write too much, but he had no reason to despise his own powers. He was rarely prolix, hardly ever repeated himself, and, rather like George Orwell, was good at finding a fresh and vivid way of phrasing near-truisms. His best work has a verve, a lightness of touch, a self-delighting play of fancy and information, which quite belies the circumstances under which most of it was produced. All this added up to a lot more than "tootles on the penny-trumpet." Anyone who does more than dip into his work—into his nonfiction especially—will be struck by how well, in the end, Grant Allen succeeded in having his cake, and eating it.

Abbreviations in the Notes

ALS   Autograph letter signed.

Blathwayt   Raymond Blathwayt, "Mr Grant Allen at Home," *Interviews. With Portraits, and a Preface by Grant Allen. A.W. Hall*, 1893, 68–75.

Bodleian   Papers held in the Bodleian Library, University of Oxford.

Clodd   Edward Clodd, *Grant Allen: A Memoir . . . With a Bibliography*. Grant Richards, 1900.

CW   Letterbooks, 1883– (Outgoing Correspondence). Chatto & Windus Archives, University of Reading Library, UK.

GA   Grant Allen.

GRA   Grant Richards Archives, 1897–1948. *Archives of British Publishers on Microfilm*. Cambridge: Chadwyck-Healey, 1979. (71 reels.)

Leeds   Papers held in the Brotherton Collection, Brotherton Library, University of Leeds, United Kingdom.

NGS   George Gissing, *New Grub Street*, ed. Bernard Bergonzi. Harmondsworth: Penguin, 1968.

PAP   Grant Allen, *"Physiological Aesthetics and Philistia," My First Book. With an Introduction by Jerome K. Jerome*. Chatto & Windus, 1894.

PSU   Grant Allen Literary Manuscripts and Correspondence 1872–1937. Rare Books and Manuscripts, the Pennsylvania State University Special Collections Library.

TLS   Typescript letter signed.

WAC   Letters from GA to John Lane. The William Andrews Clark Memorial Library, UCLA.

Watt   Letterbooks, 1884–1891 of A.P. Watt & Co Ltd. The Berg Collection, New York Public Library.

NOTES

INTRODUCTION

1. Richard D. Altick, "The Sociology of Authorship: The Social Origins, Education, and Occupations of 1,100 British Writers, 1800–1935," *Bulletin of the New York Public Library*, 66 (June 1962), 403.
2. *NGS*, 38–39.
3. Frederic Harrison, *Grant Allen, 1848–1899; An Address Delivered at Woking on October 27, 1899*, privately printed [the Chiswick Press], 1899, 8.
4. A selection by GA is in Alberto Manguel, ed., *By the Light of the Glow-worm Lamp. Three Centuries of Reflections on Nature*, Plenum, 1998. This gives the title "Prophetic Autumn" to a passage from *Moorland Idylls* (1896), which is merged without explanation with an article "Our Winged House-fellows," which first appeared in the *English Illustrated Magazine* in 1894.
5. "Mr Grant Allen," *Daily News*, October 26, 1899, 6, unsigned.
6. Andrew Lang, "At the Sign of the Ship," *Longman's Magazine*, 34 (December 1899), 183–192.
7. Frank Harris, *Contemporary Portraits. Fourth Series*, Grant Richards, 1924, pp. 94–95.
8. [Douglas Sladen], "The Diner Out: Gossip About Authors," *The Queen: The Lady's Newspaper and Court Chronicle* (March 16, 1895), 450.
9. Harris, *Contemporary Portraits*, 94.
10. Richard Le Gallienne, "Grant Allen," in *Attitudes and Avowals with some Retrospective Reviews*, John Lane, 1910, 204–205.
11. TLS, GA to Clodd, "Feb. 18" ["1893" added in another hand], Leeds.
12. Clement Shorter, "The Late Grant Allen," *The Critic* [New York], 36 (January 1900), 41.
13. GA, "The Burden of the Specialist," *Westminster Gazette*, 3 (February 27, 1894), 1.
14. GA as Teacher: Anecdotes from Clodd, 108, and Elizabeth O'Connor, *I Myself*, G.P. Putnam's Sons, 1914, 240.
15. ALS, Nellie Allen to Clodd, "April 9" [1900], Leeds.
16. Letter to Clodd, June 7, 1900, *Collected Letters of George Gissing*, ed. Paul F. Mattheisen, Arthur C. Young, and Pierre Coustillas, Ohio University Press, 1990–1998, VIII, 58.
17. "The Biography of a Rebel," *Review of Reviews*, 22 (July 1900), 92; unsigned (probably W.T. Stead).
18. "[Review of] *Grant Allen* by Edward Clodd," *Academy*, 58 (January/June 1900), 547; unsigned.
19. "Grant Allen," *Gentleman's Magazine*, 74 (1905), 134–149.
20. "Grant Allen, Naturalist and Novelist," *Moderns and Near-Moderns: Essays on Henry James, Stockton, Shaw, and Others*, Grafton, 1928. Chislett's account of

GA's books contains so many errors that one wonders how many of them he had actually read.

21. Critical discussions of GA's work over the last 30 years have been almost entirely about *The Woman Who Did* and its context: Elaine Showalter, *A Literature of Their Own*, Princeton University Press, 1977; Lloyd Fernando, *New Women in the Late Victorian Novel*, Penn State University Press, 1977; Gail Cunningham, *The New Woman and the Victorian Novel*, Macmillan, 1978; Patricia Stubbs, *Women and Fiction: Feminism and the Novel 1880–1920*, Harvester, 1979; Elaine Showalter, *Sexual Anarchy*, Viking, 1990; Ann Ardis, *New Women, New Novels: Feminism and Early Modernism*, Rutgers University Press, 1992; Victor Luftig, *Seeing Together: Friendship between the Sexes in English Writing, from Mill to Woolf*, Stanford University Press, 1993; Lucy Bland, *Banishing the Beast: English Feminism and Sexual Morality 1885–1914*, Harmondsworth: Penguin, 1995; Sally Ledger, *The New Woman: Fiction and Feminism at the fin de siècle*, Manchester University Press, 1997; Arlene Young, *Culture, Class, and Gender in the Victorian Novel: Gentlemen, Gents, and Working Women*, Macmillan/St Martin's Press, 1999; and Ann Heilmann, *New Woman Fiction: Women Writing First–Wave Feminism*, Macmillan/St Martin's Press, 2000. Four studies have dealt with other aspects of GA: Gerald Levin, "Grant Allen's Scientific and Aesthetic Philosophy," *Victorians Institute Journal*, 12 (1984), 77–89; Christopher Keep, "The Cultural Work of the Type-writer Girl," *Victorian Studies*, 40 (Spring 1997), 401–426; and Barbara Arnett Melchiori, *Terrorism in the Late Victorian Novel*, Croom Helm, 1985; and *Grant Allen: The Downward Path Which Leads to Fiction*, Rome: Bulzoni Editore, 2000.

22. Regarding biographical information, the only published material that substantially supplements Clodd is to be found in the following: Blathwayt, *Interviews*, 68–75; "JSC" [James Sutherland Cotton], "Allen, Grant," *Dictionary of National Biography*, 22 (Supplement), 36–38; Andrew Lang, "Mr Grant Allen. In Memoriam," *Daily News*, October 28, 1899, 7; Richard Le Gallienne, "Grant Allen," *Fortnightly Review*, 66 (December 1899), 1005–1025, reprinted as *Grant Allen*, Tucker [1900] and again in his *Attitudes and Avowals* (1910); and Frank Harris, *Contemporary Portraits. Fourth Series*, Grant Richards, 1924. Allen's nephew Grant Richards provides more information in the following: "Mr Grant Allen and His Work," *Novel Review*, 1 (June 1892), 261–268; *Memories of a Misspent Youth 1872–1896*, Heinemann, 1932; and *Author Hunting By an Old Literary Sportsman: Memories of Years Spent Mainly in Publishing, 1897–1925*, Hamish Hamilton, 1934. There are a few extra details about Allen's ancestry in George Herbert Clarke, "Grant Allen," *Queen's Quarterly*, 45 (1938), 487–496.

23. "The Trade of Author," *Fortnightly Review*, 51/45 (February 1889), 264. The article is unsigned and unattributed in the *Wellesley Index to Victorian Periodicals 1824–1900*, ed. Walter E. Houghton, II, 259, item 2795. But it is certainly by GA as it rehearses many of his favorite themes and some of the same phrases appear in his novel *Dumaresq's Daughter* (1891), which was being written contemporaneously.

24. Walter Besant, *The Pen and the Book*, Thomas Burleigh, 1899, 134.

25. Regarding GA and his publishers and agent, see the following. For John Lane see J.W. Lambert and Michael Ratcliffe, *The Bodley Head 1887–1987*, The Bodley Head, 1987; Wendell V. Harris, "John Lane's 'Keynotes' Series and

the Fiction of the 1890's," *PMLA*, 83 (October 1968), 1407–1413; J. Lewis May, *John Lane and the Nineties*, The Bodley Head, 1936; Katherine Lyon Mix, *A Study in Yellow: The Yellow Book and Its Contributors*, Constable/University of Kansas Press, 1960; James G. Nelson, *The Early Nineties: A View from the Bodley Head*, Harvard University Press, 1971; Margaret D. Stetz and Mark Samuels Lasner, *England in the 1890s: Literary Publishing at the Bodley Head*, Georgetown University Press, 1990; Margaret Diane Stetz, "Sex, Lies, and Printed Cloth: Bookselling at the Bodley Head in the Eighteen-Nineties," *Victorian Studies*, 35:1 (Autumn 1991), 76–86. There is also one file about Lane/GA business in CW.

For GA and Grant Richards, see GRA; the microfilmed papers therein that relate to GA, his family, and his circle are indexed in Alison Ingram, *The Archives of Grant Richards, 1897–1948*, Cambridge: Chadwyck-Healey, 1981.

For GA and Andrew Chatto, see correspondence in CW; this is mostly letter-books of copies of outgoing correspondence business from 1878. A few letters from GA are tipped into the letter-books, but most of the incoming correspondence is lost.

For GA and A.P. Watt, see Watt. This comprises an incomplete run of the firm's letter-books over the relevant years. There are copies of Watt's letters to GA over the period 1883–1891. GA's incoming letters have not survived. Some other records of the firm of A.P. Watt relevant to GA's affairs (letters, contracts, notes, etc.) are held in the Manuscripts Department of the Wilson Library, University of North Carolina at Chapel Hill, Records #11036.

26. Most discussions of scientific popularization by nonprofessionals have focused on the high Victorian period: the heyday of "natural history." For the last quarter of the century and after, there is Peter Broks, "Science, Media and Culture: British Magazines, 1890–1914," *Public Understanding of Science*, 2 (1993), 123–139. Part of Bernard Lightman, "'The Voices of Nature': Popularizing Victorian Science," in *Victorian Science in Context*, ed. Bernard Lightman, University of Chicago Press, 1997 provides a useful overview.

27. The "bookmen's" background and their cultural context is discussed by John Gross in his invaluable *The Rise and Fall of the Man of Letters: Aspects of English Literary Life Since 1800*, Harmondsworth: Pelican, 1973, 149ff.

28. ALS to Hubert Bland, "Aug. 9," Bodleian Library, Oxford. MS.Eng. lett.e.120, fols. 30–31. Allen did join the Fabians in 1891 but took no active part in the society. See Norman and Jeanne MacKenzie, *The First Fabians*, Weidenfeld and Nicolson, 1977, 148. He joined the Society of Authors in 1889 but played no significant role in it and is not mentioned in the history of the Society, Victor Bonham-Carter's *Authors by Profession* (1978).

29. The comparison with Baring-Gould was drawn in several obituaries. One said GA shared with Baring-Gould "the distinction of being the most prolific English author of the latter half of this century." "Grant Allen, Author, Dead," *New York Times*, October 26, 1899, 7, col. 2; unsigned.

CHAPTER 1   CANADA AND OXFORD (1848–1873)

1. GA, "Among the Thousand Islands," *Belgravia: A London Magazine*, 36 (October 1878), 414; signed J. Arbuthnot Wilson.

2. "Grant Allen" was the name he consistently used as a writer and in private life in all but the most formal documents. At various times Allen used one of four

noms-de-plume: "J. Arbuthnot Wilson," "Cecil Power," "Olive Pratt Rayner," and "Martin Leach Warborough." However, none of these pseudonyms was anything more than a very temporary, quickly surrendered, expedient. He made no real attempt to conceal his identity from his public.

3. GA, "Among the Thousand Islands," 415. This describes Kingston as it appeared to Allen on his visit to his hometown *en route* from Jamaica to England in 1876, although some of the personal details in the article are fictive.

4. GA, "Among the 'Thousand Islands,'" *Longman's Magazine*, 10 (May 1887), 61. This was a second article with the same title.

5. A.R. Wallace describes his meeting with the senior Allens at Washington and Kingston in *My Life: A Record of Events and Opinions*, Chapman & Hall, 1905, II, 187.

6. ALS, J.A. Allen to Charles Darwin, July 29, 1878, item 11633 of the Darwin Correspondence Project, Cambridge University Library.

7. Information about the Grant family and Joseph Allen's social position is derived from Allan J. Anderson, *The Anglican Churches of Kingston*, Kingston, Ontario, 1963, 67–68. Margaret Angus, "Alwington House," *Historic Kingston*, 40 (1992), 21–32 traces the history of the Grant/Allen home in very useful detail.

8. Clodd gives this as his age when the family started their tour. But in Grant Richards's interview of Allen, "Mr Grant Allen and His Work," *Novel Review*, 1 (June 1892), his age at the start of the tour is given as ten, and it is said that he spent two years at Dieppe. This is unlikely to be correct. Richards' interview contains other factual errors.

9. GA recalled his time at Yale in a letter reprinted in the *Pall Mall Gazette*, 46 (August 1, 1887), 6–7.

10. Clodd refers to the Dieppe school by this name. It was almost certainly the ancient foundation renamed in 1914 the Collège Jehan Ango. The handsome building still exists on the Quai as an infant school. See Simona Pakenham, *Sixty Miles from England. The English at Dieppe 1814–1914*, Macmillan, 1967.

11. Information from the school archives, King Edward's School, Birmingham. The Allen family was then living at Frontenac Villa, Beaufort Road, Edgbaston. The name (that of the Allens' home county in Ontario) suggests this was the home of Grant's relatives.

12. The paucity of science scholarships at Oxford is discussed in *The History of the University of Oxford. VII: Nineteenth-Century Oxford*, Part 2, ed. M.G. Brock and M.C. Curthoys, Oxford: Clarendon Press, 2000, 12.

13. George Saintsbury, "Oxford Sixty Years Since," *A Second Scrap Book*, Macmillan, 1923. Saintsbury's reminiscences are summarized in Dorothy Richardson Jones, *"King of Critics": George Saintsbury, 1845–1933, Critic, Journalist, Historian, Professor*, University of Michigan Press, 1992.

14. Quoted in [Louise Creighton], *Life and Letters of Mandell Creighton*, Longman's, Green, 1904, I, 17.

15. Joseph Allen's employment at Queen's University is described in D.D. Calvin, *Queen's University at Kingston: The First Century of a Scottish-Canadian Foundation 1841–1941*, Kingston, Ontario: The Trustees of the University, 1941, 184.

16. GA, "The Positive Aspect of Communism," *Oxford University Magazine and Review*, 2 (December 1869), 97–109.

17. Allen/Bootheway marriage: GRO Entry of Marriage dated September 30, 1868. Nothing is known of his family's reaction to the marriage.

18. ALS, Richard Pope to Clodd, undated, bound in Clodd's copy of his *Memoir*, Leeds.

19. Clodd, 17.

20. Quotations from two ALS to Edward Williams Byron Nicholson, Bodleian Library, Oxford, MS.Top.Oxon.d.120, fols. 68, 70. The first was written after Christmas Day, 1869, and the second on New Year's Day, 1870.

21. Quoted in Walter Leuba, *George Saintsbury*, Twayne, 1967, 18.

22. J.G. Swift MacNeill, *What I Have Seen and Heard*, Boston: Little, Brown, 1925, 91.

23. GA, "Modern College Education: Does It Educate in the Broadest and Most Liberal Sense of the Term?" *Cosmopolitan*, 23 (October 1897), 613, 615. *Cosmopolitan* was one of the new smart American glossy magazines, and Allen chooses his tone accordingly; but he repeated such ideas elsewhere.

24. *PAP*, 43.

25. GA, *Philistia*, new ed., Chatto & Windus, 1895, 167.

26. Frank Harris, in *Frank Harris: His Life and Adventures. An Autobiography with an Introduction by Grant Richards*. Richards, 1947 reminisces as follows: "[a friend] came to me with the news that Grant Allen, the writer, had thrown up his post as Professor of Literature at Brighton College. 'Why should you not apply for it; it's about two hundred pounds a year'" (154). Harris then explains how he was soon appointed by "Dr Bigge," the headmaster (actually the Rev. Charles Bigg). The truth is that Harris went to Brighton as a French teacher, and not until 1875. This was four years after Allen had left his post as a Classics teacher, and he was never, of course, "Professor of Literature" there.

27. Collected in a group of MS poems titled "Poems/by Grant Allen," Bodleian Library, Oxford, MS.Eng.poet.c.14, fol. 8.

28. GA, *Philistia*, 164.

29. Clodd, 162.

CHAPTER 2   JAMAICA (1873–1876)

1. Allen recorded his first impressions of Kingston in the *St James's Gazette*, 1 (October 23, 1880), 12–13, and in an unpublished and undated article "Jamaican Reminiscences," PSU.

2. [Charles J.G. Rampini], *Letters from Jamaica. "The Land of Streams and Woods,"* Edinburgh: Edmonston & Douglas, 1873, 19.

3. Anthony Trollope, *The West Indies and the Spanish Main*, 4th ed.; rpt. Dawsons, 1968, 14.

4. Sir Sibbald David Scott, *To Jamaica and Back*, Chapman & Hall, 1876, 76.

5. There are some further details about the political context of the foundation of the College in Lloyd Braithwaite, "The Development of Higher Education in the British West Indies," *Social and Economic Studies* [West Indies], 7:1 (March 1958), 1–64, but little about GA's tenure there.

6. An autobiographical detail in the story "Ivan Greet's Masterpiece," *Ivan Greet's Masterpiece Etc*, Chatto & Windus, 1893, 32.

7. Trollope, *The West Indies*, 19.

8. ALS, July 5, 1873, PSU. There are contemporary photographs of King's House and a reproduction of a painting of the Great Hall in Clinton V. Black,

Spanish Town: The Old Capital, Spanish Town: The Parish Council of St Catherine, 1960.

9. *Gall's Packet Newsletter* [Kingston], December 11, 1873, 3.

10. *Colonial Standard and Jamaica Despatch* [Kingston], March 24, 1874, 2.

11. *The Gleaner and De Cordova's Advertising Sheet* [Kingston], May 27, 1874, 4.

12. Edward Clodd prints the full text of the rhyming letter in *Memories*, 2nd ed., Chapman & Hall, 1916, 25–26.

13. Allen's ALS to Herbert Spencer, February 9, 1875 mentions that Nellie Allen was in England with her parents. University of London Library, MS791, fol. 104. A poem "To F.L.R. On Leaving Jamaica" dated July 1876 mentions his wife's absence at that date, PSU.

14. Edward Clodd recorded the gossip of a Kingston journalist in his diary entry for February 24, 1905, while visiting Jamaica, but only part of the entry is decipherable. MS Clodd Diary, Leeds.

15. Scott, *To Jamaica and Back*, 246. Scott lunched with the Allens during his travels and provides the only known pen-picture of them "at home" there.

16. *The Morning Journal* [Kingston], July 3, 1875, 1.

17. A.C. Sinclair and Laurence R. Fyfe, *The Handbook of Jamaica for 1883: Comprising Historical, Statistical and General Information Concerning the Island*, London/Jamaica: Edward Stanford/Government Printing Establishment, 1883, 329.

18. Clodd, *Memories*, 22.

19. GA, "The Great Tropical Fallacy," *Belgravia*, 35 (June 1878), 413–425. This is one of several pieces about life in Jamaica that Allen wrote for the *Belgravia* soon after his return to England.

20. GA, "Among the Blue Mountains," *Belgravia*, 39 (July–October 1879), 355, 357.

21. GA, "The Epicure in Jamaica," *Belgravia*, 44 (May 1881), 285–299; signed J. Arbuthnot Wilson.

22. GA, "The Great Tropical Fallacy," 423; "Tropical Education," *Longman's Magazine*, 14 (September 1889), 489.

23. GA's opinions on Jamaican education and race relations are quoted from Allen's letters home in Clodd, 41, 43, 40.

24. [W.G. Palgrave], "Jamaica," *Quarterly Review*, 139 (July 1875), 72.

25. GA, *In All Shades*, Rand, McNally (1888), 73.

26. GA, "Down the Rapids," *Belgravia: A London Magazine*, 37 (January 1879), 288–296; Signed J. Arbuthnot Wilson.

27. GA, "The Human Face Divine," *New Quarterly Magazine*, 2 n.s. (July 1879), 167, 180. Unsigned and authorship not quite certain, but GA expressed notions similar to these elsewhere.

28. *Letters from Jamaica*, 81.

29. *Letters from Jamaica*, 16.

30. Lord Oliver, *Jamaica, the Blessed Isle*, Faber, 1936, 206.

31. GA, "Tropical Education," *Longman's Magazine*, 14 (September 1889), 478–489.

32. GA, "Ivan Greet's Masterpiece," *Ivan Greet's Masterpiece Etc*, Chatto & Windus, 1893, 23. First published in the *Graphic*, November 28, 1892.

33. GA uses these examples in his "Excursus II: On the Origin of Tree-Worship" in his translation and edition of *The Attis of Caius Valerius Catullus*, David Nutt, 1892, 60–61.

34. An account of this episode appeared in the *Colonial Standard and Jamaica Despatch* [Kingston], March 28, 1874, 2.

35. Offprints of this paper, "Force and Energy," *Canadian Monthly and National Review*, 10 (July 1876), 20–31 may be what Clodd, 44, refers to as "a treatise . . . first printed for private circulation in 1876." In 1888 GA expanded it into a book with the same title.

36. GA, "To Herbert Spencer," reprinted in *The Lower Slopes: Reminiscences of Excursions Round the Base of Helicon, Undertaken for the Most Part in Early Manhood*, Elkin Mathews & John Lane, 1894.

37. GA printed Spencer's response to his poem and details of their first meeting in "Personal Reminiscences of Herbert Spencer," *Forum*, 35 (April 1904), 610–628, a memoir written in 1894.

CHAPTER 3   SETTING OUT THE STALL (1876–1880)

1. *PAP*, 44; a claim repeated in Clodd, 58.

2. GA, "The Trade of Author," *Fortnightly Review*, 51/45 (February 1889), 267–268; unsigned.

3. The preceding quotations are taken from GA, *Physiological Aesthetics*, Henry S. King, 1877, from 261ff.

4. *PAP*, 46.

5. Late Victorian incomes: 30s a week (£78 p.a.) was the stereotypical income of a skilled workman in the 1870s and still taken to be "a general average" in 1901. The Realist novelist Arthur Morrison showed in detail how, "assuming that his wife is not a fool," a family man with three children could enjoy a "fairly comfortable standard of living" on this. See his "Family Budgets. 1. A Workman's Budget," *Cornhill Magazine*, 10 (April 1901), 446–456. Miranda Hill, in "Life on Thirty Shillings a Week," The *Nineteenth Century*, 23 (March 1888), 458–463 drew up a similar (real-life) budget. For many workers, of course—especially women—30s a week was an impossible dream. Many families existed on a man's wages of a pound a week, and Maud Pember Reeves showed how it was done in *Round About a Pound a Week* as late as 1913. Both Reardon and Biffen are shown sustaining life as single men on 12s and 6p a week in *New Grub Street*.

6. GA, "My Lares and Penates," *American Magazine*, 6 (October 1887), 721. Sir William Wilson Hunter's *Imperial Gazetteer of India* was published by Trübner in 1881 in nine volumes. In his Preface, Hunter thanks Allen for his help; they remained on good terms because he was one of Allen's informants for *The Colour-Sense*. J.S. Cotton of the *Academy*, who much later would write the entry on Allen in the *DNB*, worked on the same project. GA called Hunter a "literary whitewasher" in an undated letter to A.R. Wallace, partially quoted in the latter's *My Life: A Record of Events and Opinions*, Chapman & Hall, 1905, II, 263.

7. So described by Richard Le Gallienne, quoted in Roger Lancelyn Green, *Andrew Lang*, Bodley Head, 1962, 31.

8. Saintsbury's amusements are described in Dorothy Richardson Jones, *"King of Critics": George Saintsbury, 1845–1933, Critic, Journalist, Historian, Professor*, University of Michigan Press, 1992, 17.

9. Letter to Longman, quoted in Clodd, 203.

10. Andrew Lang, "Grant Allen," *Argosy*, 71 (August 1900), 412; emphases added. He describes Allen's scientific interests as "stinks" in an undated letter to Clodd [dated "1900" in another hand]. Clodd silently omitted this comment when he printed the letter, Leeds.

11. These are the figures quoted in Roger Lancelyn Green, *Andrew Lang: A Critical Biography*, Leicester: Edmund Ward, 1946, x.

12. Lang's destructive review of *The Evolution of the Idea of God* appeared in the *Contemporary Review*, 72 (December 1897), 768–781.

13. Andrew Lang, "Mr Grant Allen. In Memoriam," *Daily News*, October 28, 1899, 7. Lang was right in his identification, but a letter to Nellie Allen at the time (probably 1888) suggests he misrepresents slightly what happened. "I owe you an apology for inadvertently suggesting that I fancied Mr Massinger a caricature of me. Alas—I never had that hero's beauty, bravery, and luck at roulette: and I really never dreamed of anything but the most vacant chaff . . . I hope Mr Allen is convinced that nothing would ever cause me to suspect, or expect, anything but the greatest kindness from him, even if it comes to pitching sacred stones at each other." ALS undated, Poetry/Rare Books Collection, State University of New York at Buffalo Library.

14. GA, "The 'Diversions of Priestley,'" *London*, 4 (November 2, 1878), 422–423; (November 9, 1878), 447–448; (November 16, 1878), 471–472; unsigned.

15. "[Review of *The Colour-Sense*]," *London: The Conservative Weekly Journal*, 5 (March 1, 1879), 176–177; unsigned.

16. GA, "The Philosophy of Drawing-Rooms," *Cornhill Magazine*, 41 (March 1880), 312–326; GA, "Cimabue and Coal-scuttles," *Cornhill Magazine*, 42 (July 1880), 61–76; GA, "Decorative Decorations," *Cornhill Magazine*, 42 (November 1880), 590–600; Alison Adburgham, *Shops and Shopping 1800–1914*, 2nd ed., Barrie & Jenkins, 1981.

17. GA's income was in the top 1% judging from the income tables in Harold Perkin, *The Rise of Professional Society: England Since 1880*, Routledge, 1989, 29–30. An article by G.S. Layard, "How to Live on £700 a Year," *Nineteenth Century*, 23 (February 1888), 239–244 describes such a lifestyle.

18. Clodd, 85.

19. *NGS*, 230.

20. GA, "*Some New Books*," *Fortnightly Review*, 32 (July 1879), 154.

21. *PAP*, 47.

22. GA, *Philistia*, new ed., Chatto & Windus, 1895, 270–271.

23. ALS, Charles Darwin to G.J. Romanes, July 23, 1879, item 12168 of the Cambridge University Library's Darwin Correspondence Project.

24. John Pemble gives a good picture of the consumption resorts in late Victorian times in *The Mediterranean Passion: Victorians and Edwardians in the South*, Oxford University Press, 1987, and there are more details of the English colonies in Patrick Howarth, *When the Riviera was Ours*, Century, 1977.

25. GA, "Wintering in Hyères," *Belgravia: A London Magazine*, 41 (May 1880), 46; signed "J. Arbuthnot Wilson."

26. Allen speculated that the interglacial age might be coming to an end, in "Glacial Epochs," *St James's Gazette*, 2 (22 January 1881), 12–13; unsigned.

27. GA, "Monaco and Monte Carlo," *Belgravia*, 43 (January 1881), 324; signed "J. Arbuthnot Wilson."

28. ALS, GA to George Croom Robertson, "Feb 23" [1885?], University College Library, University of London, MS Add.88/12.
29. *PAP*, 52.
30. "X", "*New Grub Street*" [letter], *Author*, 2 (August 1, 1891), 92.
31. GA, "The Trade of Author," 263.
32. GA, "My Lares and Penates," 725.
33. Walter Besant, *The Pen and the Book*, Thomas Burleigh, 1899, 30.
34. Authorship as an occupation, ca. 1880: census figures quoted by Richard D. Altick, "The Sociology of Authorship: The Social Origins, Education, and Occupations of 1,100 British Writers, 1800–1935," *Bulletin of the New York Public Library*, 66 (June 1962), 400. Altick warns against taking them entirely at face value, for reasons that we need not pursue here. Perkin, *The Rise of Professional Society*, 80, gives slightly lower figures for the category "authors, journalists," but these include male workers only. The other estimate is Walter Besant's, as quoted in Richard D. Altick, "Publishing," in *A Companion to Victorian Literature and Culture*, ed. Herbert F. Tucker, Oxford: Blackwell, 1999, 297.
35. Quoted in James Hepburn, *The Author's Empty Purse and the Rise of the Literary Agent*, Oxford University Press, 1968, 15.
36. For Henry James's earnings over the period of GA's career see Michael Anesko, *"Friction with the Market": Henry James and the Profession of Authorship*, Oxford University Press, 1986. Anesko's meticulous work allows this figure to be derived from his Table 1 (176) for the period 1877–1899, converted at the rate of $4.85 to the pound sterling.
37. Saintsbury's earnings as reviewer are detailed in John Gross, *The Rise and Fall of the Man of Letters: Aspects of English Literary Life Since 1800*, Harmondsworth: Pelican, 1973, 158.
38. J.W. Saunders, *The Profession of English Letters*. Routledge/University of Toronto Press, 1964, 175. For a broader sampling of Victorian authors of note who were insulated in one way or another from the market forces see Valentine Cunningham's witty "Unto Him (or Her) That Hath': How Victorian Writers Made Ends Meet," *Times Literary Supplement*, September 11, 1998, 12–13.
39. The quotations from Conrad are all drawn from Peter D. McDonald, *British Literary Culture and Publishing Practice 1880–1914*, Cambridge: Cambridge University Press, 1997, 22, 24, 26.
40. George Saintsbury, quoted in Jones, *"King of Critics,"* 98.
41. *NGS*, 347.
42. "Does Writing Pay? The Confessions of an Author," *Belgravia* (January 1881), 283, 284, 296; unsigned.
43. Margaret Beetham, "Towards a Theory of the Periodical as a Publishing Genre," *Investigating Victorian Journalism*, ed. Laurel Brake et al., Macmillan, 1990, 19–32.
44. This and the other epithets are drawn from Kelly J. Mays, "The Disease of Reading and Victorian Periodicals," in *Literature in the Marketplace: Nineteenth-Century British Publishing and Reading Practices*, ed. John O. Jordan and Robert L. Patten, Cambridge University Press, 1995, 176.
45. A. St John Adcock, "The Literary Life," *Modern Grub Street and Other Essays*, Herbert & Daniel, [1913], 12.
46. *NGS*, 454.

47. Besant, *The Pen and the Book*, 9.
48. "The Trade of Author," 266.
49. *The Pen, as a Means of Earning a Livelihood, by an Associate of the Institute of Journalists*, John Heywood, 1894, 7.
50. [Arnold Bennett], *The Truth about an Author*, Constable, 1903, 61–62.
51. Adcock, "The Literary Life," 21.
52. John Oldcastle [i.e. Wilfred Meynell], *Journals and Journalism: With a Guide for Literary Beginners*, Field and Tuer, 1880, 41–42.
53. Besant, *The Pen and the Book*, 135, 230.
54. Walter Besant, "Literature as a Career," *The Forum*, 13 (August 1892), 702–703.
55. Besant, "Literature as a Career," 701–702.
56. GA, "Depression," *Westminster Gazette*, 5 (January 19, 1895), 1–2.

CHAPTER 4   "A PEDLAR CRYING STUFF": SELLING THE WARES (1880–1889)

1. GA, "Geology and History," *Fraser's Magazine for Town and Country*, 21 (June 1880), 780.
2. GA, "Annals of Churnside. I.—King's Peddington," *Pall Mall Gazette*, 33 (January 31, 1881), 10–11; unsigned.
3. GA, "Springtide, North and South," *Pall Mall Gazette*, 5 (April 1883), 4; unsigned. This article inspired a poem from the Laureate, Alfred Austin. See *The Autobiography of Alfred Austin Poet Laureate 1835–1910*, 2 vols., Macmillan, 1911, II, 184.
4. So GA claimed in Richards, "Mr Grant Allen and His Work," *Novel Review*, 1 (June 1892), 264. Actually there were at least three signed turnovers before Allen's piece appeared on September 25, 1883. (One of these used a pen name.) Allen's cowriter of turnovers for the *Pall Mall*, Aaron Watson, recalls Allen's labors in *A Newspaper Man's Memories*, Hutchinson [1925].
5. See GA's letter "A Doubtful British Mollusc," *Nature*, 22 (September 9, 1880), 435.
6. GA, "The Philosophy of a Visiting Card," *Cornhill Magazine*, 46 (September 1882), 273–290; unsigned.
7. GA, "A Scribbler's Apology," *Cornhill Magazine*, 47 (May 1883), 542; unsigned.
8. *The Autobiography of Arthur Machen*, Richards, 1951, 236.
9. Information on payscales from John Dawson, *Practical Journalism, How to Enter Thereon and Succeed. A Manual for Beginners and Amateurs*, L. Upcott Gill, 1885, 113. Another source quotes sixpence a line for the *Pall Mall*, which amounts to about the same for middles of the length that Allen contributed.
10. GA, "*Rural America*," *St James's Gazette*, 1 (October 1, 1880), 12–13; unsigned.
11. GA, "Among the Thousand Islands," *Belgravia: A London Magazine*, 36 (October 1878), 415; signed J. Arbuthnot Wilson.
12. GA, "A Scribbler's Apology," 540.
13. GA, "*An American Farm*," *St James's Gazette*, 1 (October 4, 1880), 12–13; unsigned.

14. GA's loathing of London is illustrated by quotations drawn from his "Preface," Science in *Arcady*, Lawrence & Bullen, 1892, ix; and his article "Beautiful London," *Fortnightly Review*, 60 (July 1893), 44, 50.

15. ALS, GA to Croom Robertson, October 9, 1881, University College Library, University of London, MS.Add.88/12. Robertson (1842–1892) was the editor of *Mind* and Grote Professor of Mind and Logic at University College London.

16. Letters passing between Darwin, Romanes, Croom Robertson, and Allen on this matter are items 12168, 13600, 13627, 13633, 13638, 13644, and 13736 of the Cambridge University Library's Darwin Correspondence Project.

17. Quoted in Grant Richards, "Mr Grant Allen and His Work," *Novel Review*, 1 (June 1892), 265.

18. This is claimed by Kiernan Ryan in "Citizens of Centuries to Come: The Ruling-class Rebel in Socialist Fiction," *The Rise of Socialist Fiction 1880–1914*, ed. H. Gustav Klaus, Brighton: Harvester, 1987. Ryan's essay is valuable in setting *Philistia* into the early context of the subgenre to which it belongs.

19. ALS, Chatto to GA, November 5, 1883, CW.

20. Clodd, 122–123.

21. ALS, Chatto to GA, October 29, 1883, CW.

22. ALS, GA to Croom Robertson, "Feb 23" [1885?], University College Library, University of London, MS.Add.88/12.

23. The following quotations are from *Philistia*, new ed., Chatto & Windus, 1895, 2–115.

24. Frank Harris's editorial policy: Grant Richards, "A Note on Frank Harris," *Frank Harris: His Life and Adventures. An Autobiography with an Introduction by Grant Richards*, Richards, 1947, x. Richards implies that Allen was a victim of this behavior while Harris was editor of the *Fortnightly*. But Harris did not take this post until 1886, two years after *Philistia* appeared. Harris was formerly a newspaper editor, like the editor in the novel, and may have behaved in such a fashion in that capacity, although Allen himself could not have been a victim.

25. ALS, GA to George Croom Robertson, "Feb 23," University College Library, University of London, MS.Add.88/12.

26. The work appeared as *The Tidal Thames. With Twenty Full-page Photogravure Plates Printed on India Paper, and Other Illustrations, After Original Drawings, by W.L. Wyllie, and Descriptive Letterpress by G. Allen*, Cassell [1892].

27. GA, "Untrodden Provence," *St James's Gazette*, 1 (November 30, 1880), 13; unsigned.

28. GA, "Cap d'Antibes," *Longman's Magazine*, 15 (March 1890), 505–514.

29. Alice Bird's reminiscences in a letter of January 12, 1900, quoted in Clodd, 108, 110.

30. Quoted in Doris Langley Moore, *E. Nesbit: A Biography Revised with New Material*, Ernest Benn, 1967, 156–157.

31. ALS, Chatto to GA, September 14, 1886, CW.

32. MS Clodd Diary, entry for Tuesday January 26, 1886, Leeds.

33. Clodd, 105.

34. ALS, Lang to GA, "Jun 29" [1888], Poetry/Rare Books Collection, State University of New York at Buffalo Library.

35. Herbert Spencer, *Autobiography*, Williams & Norgate, 1904, II, 412.

36. These quotations are from *Dumaresq's Daughter*, new ed., Chatto & Windus, 1893, 9–92.

37. Clodd, 140. The MS Clodd Diary, 1889, covers the Egyptian tour. Leeds holds a partial typewritten transcript of the diary prepared by Clodd's son, which covers the full period of his acquaintance with Allen until the latter's death, but it is highly selective and unreliable. Many of the MS entries are illegible.

Chapter 5   The Stock in Trade: Writing Science

1. GA, "The Progress of Science from 1836 to 1886," *Fortnightly Review*, 47 (June 1887), 883.

2. The flattering testimonials are quoted in Clodd, 111–112.

3. The GA/Carpenter exchange over *Vignettes from Nature* is in *Nature*, 25 (March 16, 1882), 459 and 25 (March 23, 1882), 480–481. The unsigned review "Parturiunt Montes" is in *Nature*, 52 (August 15, 1895), 364–365. The description of *Moorland Idylls* as "science diluted with sentiment" comes from the unsigned review in *Nature*, 52 (March 26, 1896), 486. The accusation of plagiarism is in "Our Bookshelf," *Nature*, 59 (January 19, 1899), 268; signed "L.C.M."

4. W.T. Thistleton Dyer, "Deductive Biology," *Nature*, 27 (April 12, 1883), 554.

5. The intellectual relations between GA and Spencer from GA's perspective are best described in his "Spencer and Darwin" [an article review of *Pioneers of Evolution* by Edward Clodd], *Fortnightly Review*, 67 (February 1897), 251–262.

6. GA, "Force and Energy," *Canadian Monthly and National Review*, 10 (July 1876), 29.

7. GA made this claim about Spencer in his contribution to "*Fine Passages in Verse and Prose*; Selected by Living Men of Letters," *Fortnightly Review*, 48/42 n.s. (August 1887), 300.

8. The quoted judgments about Spencer are taken from GA, "Personal Reminiscences of Herbert Spencer," *Forum*, 35 (April 1904), 610, 628. How the *Forum* came by the article is unclear, but no U.K. publication is known.

9. Herbert Spencer, *Autobiography*, Williams & Norgate, II, 4–5. Spencer's essay advocating leaving banks unregulated appeared in the *Westminster Review* in 1857.

10. The quotations from Spencer that follow are all drawn from *Social Statics; or, the Conditions Essential to Human Happiness Specified, and the First of Them Developed*; Williams & Norgate, 1868 (a reprint of the American ed. and identical to the first British ed. of 1851), 257, 353–4, 414.

11. GA, "Personal Reminiscences," 611.

12. Peter J. Bowler, *The Eclipse of Darwinism: Anti-Darwinian Evolution Theories in the Decades around 1900*. Johns Hopkins University Press, 1983 covers the biological aspects of the theory very thoroughly. A.R. Wallace, for instance, set his face against use-inheritance but was credulous about accepting

examples of prenatal influence, including an absurd case where a pregnant woman nursed a gamekeeper after his arm was amputated, only to produce a baby with a stump for an arm: Wallace found this very convincing indeed.

13. Children of acrobats: this and similar examples are mentioned quite uncritically in GA, "Second Nature," *Common Sense Science*, Boston: D. Lothrop, 1886.

14. GA, "The Genesis of Genius," *Atlantic Monthly*, 47 (March 1881), 377.

15. GA reviewed Weismann's *Essays upon Heredity and Kindred Biological Problems in the Academy*, 37 (February 1, 1890), 84.

16. GA, "The Mystery of Birth," *Fortnightly Review*, 64/58 n.s. (July 1895), 113–120. This is a reworking of a simpler version published under the same title four years earlier in the *New Review*, 4 (June 1891), 531–539, and an even earlier version, "A Living Mystery," *Popular Science Monthly*, 33 (October 1888), 730–739.

17. GA, "The Mystery of Birth," 118–120.

18. This charge was made in "Mr Grant Allen's Views," *Natural Science: A Monthly Review of Scientific Progress*, 7 (September 1895), 160; unsigned.

19. GA, "Our Scientific Causerie: The New Theory of Heredity," *Review of Reviews*, 1 (June 1890), 538.

20. GA's review of Weismann's *Essays upon Heredity*, *Academy*, 37 (February 1, 1890), 84.

21. The phrase "unfathomed depths" is Michael Ruse's. See his article "Herbert Spencer," *The Oxford Companion to Philosophy*, ed. Ted Honderich, Oxford University Press, 1995.

22. Galton's anecdote about fingerprints is quoted in David Duncan, *Life and Letters of Herbert Spencer*, Methuen, 1908, 502.

23. GA, *Charles Darwin*, Longmans, Green, 1885, 62.

24. O[liver] J. Lodge, "Mr Grant Allen's Notions about Force and Energy," *Nature*, 39 (January 24, 1889), 291. Among other howlers, Lodge noted that Allen seems to suppose that a cannon ball fired horizontally employs its energy in counteracting the force of gravity. He seems unaware that it will reach the ground as the same moment as another ball dropped vertically from the same height. Karl Pearson reviewed the book in *Academy*, 34 (December 29, 1888), 421–422. The news that *Force and Energy* was being "converted into wallpaper" is mentioned in a dictated LS from GA to Edward Clodd, "March 17th" [1889], Leeds.

25. Walter Besant, *The Pen and the Book*, Thomas Burleigh, 1899, 171. Besant's comments about treatises are in Ch. IV, *passim*.

26. The statistics about scientific articles carried by periodicals are derived from A.J. Meadows, "Access to the Results of Scientific Research: Developments in Victorian Britain," in *Development of Science Publishing in Europe*, ed. A.J. Meadows, Amsterdam: Elsevier, 1980, 54. Stead's comments about scientific journalism are quoted in "Introduction" to *Index to the Periodical Literature of the World. (Covering the Year 1892)*, *Review of Reviews*, 1893, 2.

27. Meadows, "Access to the Results," 57, quoting from a letter of 1874.

28. GA, "The Trade of Author," *Fortnightly Review*, 51/45 (February 1889), 264; unsigned.

29. These calculations ignore tiny sums in royalties paid in later years, totalling a few pounds. Chatto sent him a cheque for current sales on his first two books as late as 1897: it was for 12s 2d. The returns from the periodical publications are estimates. I have assumed the *St James's Gazette* paid 3 guineas an

essay; the *Pall Mall* £4 each; and that the long essays in *Flowers and Their Pedigrees* earned 12 guineas each. The total sum quoted probably errs on the generous side.

30. *NGS*, 397.
31. GA, "Big Animals," *Eclectic Magazine of Foreign Literature, Science, and Art*, 41 (June 1885), 778–786; unsigned. Reprinted from *Cornhill Magazine*, 4 (April 1885), 405–419.
32. GA, "The First Potter," *Longman's Magazine*, 6 (July 1885), 265.
33. Richard Le Gallienne's phrase "sugar-candy euphuism": "Grant Allen," *Attitudes and Avowals with Some Retrospective Reviews*, John Lane, 1910, 181.
34. GA, *The Beckoning Hand and Other Stories*, Chatto & Windus, 1887, 277. The story first appeared in *Belgravia*, 56 (April 1885), 172–195.
35. GA, "The Missing Link," in *Ivan Greet's Masterpiece, Etc*, Chatto & Windus, 1893, 179.
36. Letter from Wells to GA [late summer 1895?], *The Correspondence of H.G. Wells*, ed. David C. Smith, Pickering & Chatto, 1998, I, 245–246.
37. TLS to Wells, "June 11. 95" added by hand, H.G. Wells collection, University of Illinois Library, Chicago, A78.
38. H.G. Wells, *An Experiment in Autobiography: Discoveries and Conclusions of a Very Ordinary Brain (Since 1866)*, Gollancz, 1934, II, 551–552.

CHAPTER 6   THE STOCK IN TRADE: LIGHT FICTION

1. GA, "The Trade of Author," *Fortnightly Review*, 51/45 (February 1889), 268.
2. Richard Le Gallienne, "Grant Allen," *Attitudes and Avowals with Some Retrospective Reviews*, John Lane, 1910, 197.
3. *PAP*, 43.
4. Frederic Harrison, *Grant Allen, 1848–1899; an Address Delivered at Woking on October 27, 1899*, privately printed [at the Chiswick Press], 1899, 8. Allen's widow would not have liked hearing that, however. She told Clodd that her husband "really had a much higher idea of his novels than many people had, and used to say how much thought and work he had put into his later ones. He believed this would be recognized some day." ALS, "April 9th" [1900] to Edward Clodd, Clodd Correspondence, Leeds.
5. John Oldcastle [i.e. Wilfred Meynell], *Journals and Journalism: With a Guide for Literary Beginners*, Field & Tuer, 1880.
6. *The Pall Mall Gazette* reported that 1,315 novels were published in Britain in 1894. The next largest category was educational works, mostly textbooks (615). None of the other identified categories amounted to more than a few hundred each. Simon Eliot's Fig.26 shows that 31% of published titles were fiction over the period 1890–1899, while the next three named categories did not exceed 12% each. See *Some Patterns and Trends in British Publishing 1800–1919*, The Bibliographical Society, 1994, 14.
7. Walter Besant, *The Pen and the Book*, Thomas Burleigh, 1899, 137, 143.
8. Anecdote in *PAP*, 49.
9. GA, "Introduction," *Strange Stories*, Chatto & Windus (1884).
10. GA, "The Romance of the Clash of Races," *Westminster Gazette*, 1 (March 15, 1893), 4; reprinted in *Post-Prandial Philosophy*, Chatto & Windus, 1894, 75.
11. ALS, Chatto to GA, August 14, 1884, CW.

12. ALS, Watt to GA, May 19 and July 15, 1885, Letterbook vol. IX. "I think you will be satisfied with this transaction," Watt wrote modestly. He was right.

13. Quoted in "From Grant Allen Esq. Author of *Philistia, In All Shades*, etc etc," in *Collection of Letters Addressed to A.P. Watt by Various Writers*, The Literary Agency, 1893, 1–2.

14. Blathwayt, 72–73. GA's reference to "My marionettes": ALS to Chatto, October 9, 1885, CW.

15. ALS, Chatto to GA, October 5, 1885, CW.

16. ALS, Chatto to GA, November 2, 1885, CW. Chatto did not insist on a deletion, however.

17. ALS, GA to Chatto, October 9, 1885, CW.

18. Flyleaf matter to *An Army Doctor's Romance*, Raphael Tuck, 1893.

19. ALS, Chatto to GA, February 28, 1888, CW.

20. A spin-off competition launched another literary career, as it was won by Arnold Bennett. See "Twenty Guinea Condensation Prize," *Tit-Bits*, 21 (December 19, 1891), 192. More than one of Bennett's biographers calls this a parody but what it does is retell Allen's plot in a mildly satirical way.

21. Quotations from GA, *What's Bred in the Bone*, Newnes [n.d.], 4.

22. Quoted in "Obituary. Mr Grant Allen," *Daily News*, October 26, 1899, 6; unsigned.

23. GA, *The Duchess of Powysland*, new ed., Chatto & Windus, 1894, 134.

24. Blathwayt, 72–73.

25. GA, "Science in Education," *Westminster Gazette*, 1 (February 11, 1893), 4; reprinted in *Post-Prandial Philosophy*, Chatto & Windus, 1894, 25–26.

26. Quotations from GA, *Dumaresq's Daughter*, new ed., Chatto & Windus, 1893, 184, 188, 194.

27. Le Gallienne, "Grant Allen," 210.

28. ALS to George Croom Robertson, "Feb 23.," University College London Library, MS.Add.88/12. Clodd dates the letter to 1885, which is probably correct. It is true that in it Allen refers to "novels" written since *Philistia*, whereas only one other had been published by 1885. However, the Chatto archives make it clear that he already had both his third and fourth novels in manuscript by late 1885.

29. GA, "Introduction," *The British Barbarians*, John Lane/G.P. Putnam's Sons, 1895, xi.

30. Lang is quoted in "Mr Grant Allen: His Work and His Critics," *Review of Reviews*, 6 (September 1892), 266; unsigned; probably W.T. Stead.

31. ALS, "Feb 11" [1895?], Rare Books Collection, State University of New York at Buffalo Library; emphasis in the original. The reference is almost certainly to *The Woman Who Did*, as Lane was sending out review copies early in that month of 1895. The mention of the "cuckoo" is metonymic for GA's articles on natural history, and another letter discusses the habits of the bird. Apart from the obvious bawdy joke, Lang may also be punning on "cock," meaning of a heap of dung or straw.

CHAPTER 7   THE PROSPEROUS TRADESMAN
(1890–1895)

1. Douglas Sladen, *Twenty Years of My Life*, Constable, 1915, 258.

2. Henry W. Nevinson, *Changes and Chances*, Nisbet, 1923, 85.

3. Frank Harris, "Grant Allen," in *Contemporary Portraits. Fourth Series*, Grant Richards, 1924, 94.

4. Letter to Alice Howe Gibbens James, January 18, 1883. *Correspondence of William James*, ed. Ignas K. Skrupskelis and Elizabeth M. Berkley, University Press of Virginia, 1997, 5, 397.

5. Hulda Friedrichs, *The Life of Sir George Newnes, Bart*, Hodder & Stoughton, 1911, 91–92. Even Allen would have jibbed at entering the preceding competition for the best short story. The prize for that was a house, which had to be named "Tit-Bits Villa."

6. "English Literary Piracy," *Popular Science Monthly*, 32 (January 1888), 424; unsigned. The *Popular Science Monthly* was very quick off the mark in pirating GA. It appropriated one of his first pieces for the *Cornhill*, "Aesthetic Analysis of an Obelisk," for its monthly supplement, 7–12 (1878), 152–159 and 47 more articles thereafter.

7. "The Woes of an English Author. A Pathetic Letter from Grant Allen," *Pall Mall Gazette*, 46 (August 1, 1887), 6–7. No explanation is offered as to why the letter was being reprinted two years after its appearance in the United States.

8. GA, "To Dorking by Coach," *The Magazine of Art*, 10 (July 1887), 284–285.

9. For more information on the Allen circle at Hindhead, see Derek Hudson, "English Switzerland in Surrey," *Country Life* (May 10, 1973), 1310–1311; and W.R. Trotter, *The Hilltop Writers: A Victorian Colony among the Surrey Hills, Lewes*: The Book Guild, 1996, although the account of GA's time there has minor errors.

10. Clodd, 148.

11. Netta Syrett, *The Sheltering Tree: An Autobiography*, Geoffrey Bles, 1939, 46–47.

12. Morley Roberts, *The Private Life of Henry Maitland. A Portrait of George Gissing*, ed. Morchard Bishop, Richards, 1958, 90. The article that Roberts remembered Gissing alluding to with "angry amusement" was perhaps "My Lares and Penates," although that referred to the Dorking house.

13. Richard Le Gallienne, "Grant Allen" in *Attitudes and Avowals with Some Retrospective Reviews*, John Lane, 1910, 179.

14. Richard Le Gallienne, "[Review of] *Post-Prandial Philosophy*," in *Retrospective Reviews: A Literary Log*, II (1893–1895), John Lane, 1896, 93.

15. GA, "A Point of Criticism," *Westminster Gazette*, 3 (January 30, 1894), 1–2; reprinted in *Post-Prandial Philosophy*, Chatto & Windus, 1894, 207–208.

16. ALS to Hubert Bland, "Aug. 9," Bodleian Library, Oxford, MS.Eng. lett.e.120, fols. 30–31.

17. GA, "Individualism and Socialism," *Contemporary Review*, 55 (May 1889), 730–741.

18. GA, "Introduction" to *The British Barbarians*, John Lane/G.P. Putnam's Sons, 1895, xvii–xviii.

19. George Ives was a young member of the Wilde circle. Wilde, with surprising caution, recommended him not to demand so insistently why homosexuals were not catered for in GA's New Hedonism, but, daring all, he did so anyway: "Mr Grant Allen, after having so courageously unfurled the flag of love and liberty, sheathed his strong sword and hauled down that flag when called upon to defend it." ("The New Hedonism Controversy," *Humanitarian*, 5 [October 1894], 294.) W.T. Stead, commenting on this, wondered

mischievously whether "any periodical in the English language will deliberately make its pages the arena for discussing the ethics of unnatural vice." ("In Praise of Two Crimes," *Review of Reviews*, 10 [October 1894], 356.) Either GA made no reply or the *Humanitarian* refused to print it. The episode is mentioned in Richard Ellmann, *Oscar Wilde*, Hamish Hamilton, 1987, 404.

CHAPTER 8   DEALING WITH THE "DISSENTING GROCER"

1. GA, "Letters in Philistia: A Bourgeois Literature," *Fortnightly Review*, 55 (June 1891), 953.
2. GA, "Fiction and Mrs. Grundy," *The Novel Review*, 2 (July 1892), 294–315.
3. George Moore, "A New Censorship of Literature," *Pall Mall Gazette*, 40 (December 10, 1884), 1–2. The article generated some correspondence, but few were very sympathetic to Moore's position. A common response was that Mudie was a businessman not a promoter of the arts, and his customers' desires were paramount.
4. ALS, GA to Clement Shorter, undated, Shorter Correspondence, Leeds. The stories were presumably some of those that appeared in the *Illustrated London News* or the *Sketch*.
5. ALS recipient unknown, "Nov 29th," Bodleian Library, MS.Autogr.b.9, no. 275.
6. GA, "Preface," *Ivan Greet's Masterpiece, Etc*, Chatto & Windus, 1893.
7. GA, "Introduction," *The British Barbarians*, John Lane/G.P. Putnam's Sons, 1895, x.
8. The question of syndication and its effect on authors' incomes is thoroughly discussed in Graham Law, *Serializing Fiction in the Victorian Press*, Palgrave, 2000.
9. *NGS*, 19.
10. Quoted in Michael Anesko, *"Friction with the Market": Henry James and the Profession of Authorship*, Oxford University Press, 1986, 38.
11. It may be that some other novels were first serialized in newspapers, where they are effectively untraceable. None of Allen's surviving private papers or his publishers' and agents' records gives any more information.
12. This calculation is based on figures drawn from Watt, CW, and papers in the Manuscripts Department of the Wilson Library, University of North Carolina at Chapel Hill, Records #11036. Details are as follows. *In All Shades*: serial rights (*Chambers's Journal*) £210 (plus another £100 due to breach of contract); volume rights £75. *This Mortal Coil*: serial rights (*Chambers's Journal*) £300; Australian serial rights £70; volume rights £100. *Dumaresq's Daughter*: serial rights (*Chambers's Journal*) £300; U.S. rights £40; volume rights £180. *The Duchess of Powysland*: serial rights (*People*) £300; U.S. rights £50; volume rights £190. *The Scallywag*: serial rights (*Graphic*) £400; Australian serial rights £50; U.S. rights £40; Italian rights £2; volume rights £200. The sums quoted are gross amounts from which Watt's commission and other expenses were deducted. Of the rest of GA's long novels, the price he obtained for the serializations, at home and/or overseas, for three (*The Devil's Die*, *The Tents of Shem*, and *At Market Value*) is not known. For

three more, Chatto bought the entire copyright—*Philistia* (£250); *Babylon* (£300); and *Under Sealed Orders* (£800)—and arranged serialization himself.

13. GA, "The Trade of Author," *Fortnightly Review*, 51/45 (February 1889), 273; unsigned.

14. GA, "A Literary Causerie," *The Speaker: A Review of Politics, Letters, Science and the Arts*, 2 (November 1, 1890), 495–496.

15. [J.M. Barrie], "The Conspiracy against Mr Grant Allen," *National Observer*, 1 (November 22, 1890), 12–13. Presumably it was "A Literary Causerie," published at the beginning of the month, which triggered this squib.

16. [W.T. Stead], "Philistia and Mr Grant Allen: A Word of Expostulation," *Review of Reviews*, 3 (June 1891), 585.

17. GA, "The Worm Turns," *Athenaeum* (July 30, 1892), 160. It is certain that the work in question was an early draft of *The Woman Who Did*: see later.

18. GA, "Falling in Love," *Falling in Love, with Other Essays on More Exact Branches of Science*, D. Appleton, 1890, 13–14.

19. Lang's sympathetic note to GA: ALS, "Aug 8" [1892], Poetry/Rare Books Collection, State University of New York at Buffalo Library.

20. Quoted by Clodd, 154. He does not date it, and the letter is lost, but it must belong to 1892 because an unpublished ALS to a Mr Turner, to which the date "Tuesday Aug 2nd /92" has been added, probably by Nicholson, alludes to it. In this letter GA thanks Turner for his advice about the disposition of a manuscript and continues: "one of them [i.e., another letter, the one Clodd quotes] came from the Bodleian librarian at Oxford, asking me to deposit the MS in the library under a promise of secresy [*sic*] during my life time. I don't think I will quite accept this offer. I'll keep the MS while I live, and then leave it to my wife to dispose of in some way afterwards," Bodleian Library, Oxford, MS.Eng.lett.d.298, fol. 23.

21. *The Silver Domino; or Side Whispers, Social and Literary*, 16th ed., Lamley, 1894, 342–343; first pub. 1892. Usually attributed to Marie Corelli, George Eric Mackay, and Henry Labouchere.

22. "'The Man that Was Not Allowed,'" *National Observer: A Record and Review*, 8 (August 6, 1892), 291; unsigned. There is an excellent summary of the strident opinions of the *Observer* circle in Peter D. McDonald, *British Literary Culture and Publishing Practice 1880–1914*, Cambridge University Press, 1997, from which some of the following details have been drawn.

23. TLS [copy?], August 7, 1892, in GRA, Reel 50: Correspondence: "Allen."

24. GA, "The Pot-boiler," *Longman's Magazine*, 20 (October 1892), 591–602.

25. GA, "Ivan Greet's Masterpiece," *Ivan Greet's Masterpiece, Etc*, Chatto & Windus, 1893, 3–4, 6–7; first published in the *Graphic: An Illustrated Weekly Newspaper*, 46 (Christmas Number [November 28] 1892), 11–13.

26. GA, "How to Succeed in Literature," *The Speaker: A Review of Politics, Letters, Science and the Arts*, 8 (September 9, 1893), 271–272.

27. GA, "The New Hedonism," *Fortnightly Review*, 61 (March 1894), 390. The quotation from *The Picture of Dorian Grey* is from Ch. 2. One example of a sympathetic but puzzled response was T.G. Bonney's: reviewing it in the *Humanitarian: A Monthly Review of Sociological Science*, 5 (July 1894), 106–113, he challenged GA to define his program for individual redemption more closely.

28. "[Review of *The Lower Slopes*]," *Athenaeum* (March 24, 1894), 368; unsigned.

29. Quoted in Clodd, 165–166.

CHAPTER 9   RETAILING THE WOMAN WHO DID

1. Peter D. McDonald, *British Literary Culture and Publishing Practice 1880–1914*, Cambridge University Press, 1997, has an excellent discussion of Lane's policy and practices (77–78).

2. The readers' reports, one (2pp.) by Richard Le Gallienne dated "October 1893," and another (8pp.) by George Moore dated "4 November" [1893] are in a private collection. I am grateful to the owner for making them available.

3. Dictated LS to John Lane, "Jan 14th" and "Nov 19th" [1894], WAC.

4. Lane's engineered rarities are discussed in Margaret D. Stetz and Mark Samuels Lasner, *England in the 1890s: Literary Publishing at the Bodley Head*, Georgetown University Press, 1990, 46; and Margaret Diane Stetz, "Sex, Lies, and Printed Cloth: Bookselling at the Bodley Head in the Eighteen-Nineties," *Victorian Studies*, 35:1 (Autumn 1991), 74. GA's response to Lane's offer was dismissive. "Many thanks for your offer of copies with the old title page: but no thank you, I would prefer the new one. To tell you the truth, being an author, I prefer that my friends should have the title of the books in the way I intended it than have a mere rarity." Dictated LS to John Lane, "Jan 23rd" [1894], WAC.

   The University of Liverpool Library holds an apparently unique copy of *The Lower Slopes* dated 1893, which must be one of these "rarities."

5. ALS, Cicely McDonald to GA, April 8, 1895, PSU.

6. The Lanchester affair: discussed, e.g., in David Rubinstein, *Before the Suffragettes: Women's Emancipation in the 1890s*, Harvester, 1986, 58–63; Karen Hunt, *Equivocal Feminists: The Social Democratic Federation and the Woman Question 1884–1911*, Cambridge University Press, 1996, 94–106. For GA's reaction, see MS Clodd Diary, entry for March 22, 1896: "Talk fell on the Lanchester case: Allen quite surprised me by his hesitation to approve in the concrete what he preaches in the abstract," Leeds. Lanchester received scant sympathy from the SDF or its mouthpiece *Justice*, as Hunt shows.

7. Chris Healy, *The Confessions of a Journalist*, Chatto & Windus, 1904, 31.

8. I am grateful to John Owen Smith for these details of Flora Thompson's reminiscences.

9. GA, *The Woman Who Did*, Introduced by Sarah Wintle, Oxford University Press, 1995, 43–44. Further page references are in the text.

10. [W.T. Stead], "The Book of the Month," 185.

11. Richard Le Gallienne, *Retrospective Reviews: A Literary Log. Vol II (1893–1895)*, John Lane, 1896, 225.

12. Harold Frederic, "*The Woman Who Did*," *New York Times* (February 17, 1895), 8.

13. D.F. Hannigan, "Sex in Fiction," *Westminster Review*, 143 (1895), 619.

14. "An Unemancipated Novelist," *Pall Mall Gazette* (February 20, 1895), 4; unsigned; the author may have been H.G. Wells, writing a second review.

15. ALS, Archer to GA, February 14, 1895, PSU.

16. "The Woman Who Wouldn't Do (She-Note Series)," *Punch, or the London Charivari*, 108 (March 30, 1895), 153; unsigned.

17. *The Woman Who Did* was proposed as an elaborate spoof in Lafcadio Hearn, "Grant Allen," *Victorian Philosophy*, Tokyo: Hokuseido Press, 1930, 85–97. This is the text of a lecture given in 1900, probably after Clodd's *Memoir* appeared. Millicent Fawcett, "*The Woman Who Did*," *Contemporary Review*,

67 (1895), 626, mentions that even in 1895 this was a speculation among her friends.

18. [W.T. Stead], "The Book of the Month," 178. Stead also called it "a handy drawing-room tract for the extermination of certain heresies popular among advanced young persons."

19. [Margaret Oliphant], "The Anti-marriage League," *Blackwood's Magazine*, 159 (January 1896), 142.

20. Fawcett, "*The Woman Who Did*," 630.

21. Wells described the tone of his review in these terms in a half-apologetic letter after GA had praised *The Time Machine*. See *The Correspondence of H.G. Wells*, ed. David C. Smith, Pickering & Chatto, 1998, I, 245–246. Smith dates the letter provisionally to the late summer of 1895, just before Wells and GA met for the first time, as described years later in Wells' *Experiment in Autobiography*. If that is correct, then Wells' even more swingeing review of *The British Barbarians in the Saturday Review*, 80 (December 14, 1895), 785–786 appeared after their meeting.

22. Letter, Wells to A.T. Simmons, ca. March 1895, *Correspondence of H.G. Wells*, I, 235.

23. [H.G. Wells], "[Review of *The Woman Who Did*]," *Saturday Review of Politics, Literature, Science and Art*, 79 (March 9, 1895), 319–320; unsigned.

24. Clodd, 155.

25. GA, *Saturday Review of Politics, Literature, Science and Art*, 79 (March 16, 1895), 351. This letter to the editor was a protest against a sneer to this effect by H.G. Wells in his review.

26. Letter of July 4, 1896, quoted in Clodd, 169–170. GA was president for three years up to his death. The Society dealt with broader social and scientific issues than its name suggests, and many of the intellectuals resident in the area were members.

27. GA, "The Girl of the Future," *Universal Review*, 7 (May 1890), 52.

28. GA, "A Biologist on the Woman Question," *Pall Mall Gazette*, 49 (January 11, 1889), 1–2.

29. GA's other main polemical articles appeared as follows: "Plain Words on the Woman Question" appeared in the *Fortnightly Review*, 46 (October 1889), 448–458; "A Glimpse into Utopia" in the *Westminster Gazette*, 3 (January 9, 1894), 1–2; "The New Hedonism" in the *Fortnightly Review*, 61 (March 1894), 377–392. Conan Doyle's anecdote is in his *Memories and Adventures*, 2nd ed., Murray, 1930, 305.

30. GA, "The Girl of the Future," 55.

31. Shelley's notes to *Queen Mab*: Cited from *The Complete Works of Percy Bysshe Shelley*, ed. Roger Ingpen and Walter E. Peck, Ernest Benn/Gordian, 1965, 1, 141–142.

32. GA, "The Role of Prophet," in *Post-Prandial Philosophy*, Chatto & Windus, 1894, 61–62; originally published in the *Westminster Gazette*, 1 (March 8, 1893), 1–2.

33. While wintering on the Riviera, GA ordered a copy of the first substantial biography of Shelley, Edward Dowden's *The Life of Percy Bysshe Shelley* (1886). It is not a question of whether Dowden is reliable but whether GA ignores and distorts Dowden's picture for his own ends, which he certainly does. Dowden quotes from the brief of Shelley's own counsel: "Mr Shelley marries

twice before he is twenty-five! He is no sooner liberated from the despotic chains, which he speaks of with so much horror and contempt, than he forges a new set, and becomes again a willing victim of this horrid despotism!" Dowden quotes also Shelley's own notes for the court, in which he asserted, "he had [now] in his practice accommodated himself to the feelings of the community" (Dowden, *Life*, Routledge & Kegan Paul, 1951, 343, 348). If it be objected that Shelley may have been modifying his views under duress here, it should be noted that Dowden also quotes Shelley's later opinion that *Queen Mab* was "villainous trash," and describes how Shelley tried to suppress a pirated edition. GA (and his mouthpiece) ignores all this. No doubt GA was also reacting against Arnold's notorious review essay on Dowden's biography ("What a set! What a world! is the exclamation that breaks from us as we come to an end of this history of 'the occurrences of Shelley's private life,'" etc.), which appeared in the *Nineteenth Century* for January 1888. Perhaps it is just as well that GA did not live to see the retrieval by Hotson in 1930 of Shelley's letters to his wife at the time of their separation.

34. All these threads are traced admirably by Keith Thomas in "The Double Standard," *Journal of the History of Ideas*, 20 (April 1959), 195–216.

35. GA, "About the New Hedonism," *Humanitarian: A Monthly Review of Sociological Science*, 5 (September 1894), 184–185.

36. Inheritable syphilis was by no means all a folk panic. GA presumably felt unable to discuss the horrors of syphilis in detail but, as Ibsen's *Ghosts* (1881) and Sarah Grand's *The Heavenly Twins* (1893) had shown, the knowledge that it could be transmitted to the next generation stands behind many such vague warnings. Elaine Showalter reminds us that in this period 1,500 infants a year were dying from congenital venereal diseases. (*A Literature of Their Own*, Princeton University Press, 1977, 188.) See also her "Syphilis, Sexuality, and the Fiction of the *Fin de Siècle*," in *Reading* Fin de Siècle *Fictions*, ed. Lyn Pykett, Longman, 1996, 166–183.

37. William Edward Hartpole Lecky, *History of European Morals from Augustus to Charlemagne*, 13th impression, Longman's, Green, 1899, II, 283 [first ed. 1869].

38. GA, "Sunday Night at Mabille," *The Lower Slopes: Reminiscences of Excursions Round the Base of Helicon, Undertaken for the Most Part in Early Manhood*, Elkin Mathews & John Lane, 1894.

39. Le Gallienne, *Retrospective Reviews*, 227.

40. W.T. Stead, "The Death of Grant Allen," *Review of Reviews*, 20 (November 1899), 447. Stead was almost alone, then or later, in noticing this publicly.

41. Susan Budd, *Varieties of Unbelief: Atheists and Agnostics in English Society 1850–1960*, Heinemann, 1977, 163.

42. TLS, GA to Stead [undated; 1895], Allen/Stead Correspondence, Churchill Archives Centre, Churchill College, Cambridge, fol. 5. By his reference to "wretched creatures," GA might have meant Sala; Edmund Yates, late editor of the society sheet *The World*, who had once written under the name of *Le Flâneur*; or Henry Labouchere, or, conceivably, all three.

43. GA, "*The Woman Who Did* [letter to the editor]," *Westminster Gazette*, 5 (February 23, 1895), 2.

44. GA, "The Worm Turns," *Athenaeum* (July 30, 1892), 160.

45. The extreme rarity of the name Botheway/Bootheway, which is virtually exclusive to a small area of the Midlands, made it possible to obtain these details from the directories, parish records, and Leicestershire census records held at the County Archives Centre at Wigston, Leics.

46. H.G. Wells, *Tono-Bungay*, Book 2, Chapter 1; first published 1908.

47. GA, *Philistia*, new ed., Chatto & Windus, 1895, 113–115.

48. ALS to E.W.B. Nicholson, Bodleian Library, Oxford, MS.Top.Oxon.d.120, fol. 65. The letter is undated, but is one of several about the business of the *Oxford University Magazine and Review* (1869–1870), which the two friends jointly edited. GA was then living in rooms at 9 South Street, off Thurloe Square.

49. Andrew Lang, "At The Sign of the Ship," *Longman's Magazine*, 34 (December 1899), 183–192.

50. Information on GA's first marriage supplied by Lang and Powell: contained in ALS dated "1900" in another hand and "1 Jan 1900" respectively, bound in Clodd's own copy of his *Memoir*, Leeds.

51. Clodd, 17.

52. Clodd, 26.

53. Clodd, 152. There is a copy of this poem in GA's handwriting in PSU.

54. Acton is quoted by Eric Trudgill, *Madonnas and Magdalens: The Origins and Development of Victorian Sexual Attitudes*, Heinemann, 1976, 291, who discusses the rise and fall of this cult in detail.

55. "In the Night Watches," *The Lower Slopes*.

56. Clodd, 151.

57. GA, "The Trade of Author," *Fortnightly Review*, 51/45 (February 1889), 269; unsigned.

58. "[Review of *The Lower Slopes*]," *Athenaeum* (March 24, 1894), 368.

59. "Introduction," *The British Barbarians*, John Lane/G.P. Putnam's Sons, 1895, xi.

CHAPTER 10   LAST ORDERS (1896–1899)

1. Diary entries of June 3, 1893 and June 6, 1895. *London and the Life of Literature in Late Victorian England: The Diary of George Gissing, Novelist*, ed. Pierre Coustillas, Hassocks: Harvester, 1978, 306, 375.

2. Letter to Algernon Gissing, June 9, 1895. *Collected Letters of George Gissing*, ed. Paul F. Mattheisen, Arthur C. Young, and Pierre Coustillas, Ohio University Press, 1990–1998, V, 347.

3. Letters to Henry Hick, June 16, 1895 and Morley Roberts, June 29, 1895. *Collected Letters of George Gissing*, V, 349–350, 354.

4. H.G. Wells, "[Review of *The British Barbarians*]," *Saturday Review*, 80 (December 14, 1895), 785.

5. Richard Le Gallienne, "Grant Allen," *Attitudes and Avowals With Some Retrospective Reviews*, John Lane, 1910, 208; Clodd, 175.

6. "Introduction," *The British Barbarians*, John Lane/G.P. Putnam's Sons, 1895, xi.

7. "Erotomaniac literature" is James Ashcroft Noble's phrase, from his "The Fiction of Sexuality," *Contemporary Review*, 67 (April 1895), 490–498. Noble was a kindly, struggling journalist and a good friend of the Allens; some attractive letters he wrote to them survive. His career is outlined in Cross,

The Common Writer, Cambridge University Press, 1985, 228. GA is not mentioned as one of the erotomaniacs in Noble's article.

8. Dictated LS to George Bedborough, in Nellie Allen's hand, May 12, 1899, PSU. For the Bedborough affair and the Free Press Defense Committee, set up after two tons of literature were seized from his rooms, and some mention of GA's part in it, see Samuel Hynes, *The Edwardian Turn of Mind*, Princeton University Press/Oxford University Press, 1968 and A. Calder-Marshall, *Lewd, Blasphemous and Obscene*, Hutchinson, 1972.

9. ALS, Chatto to GA, February 25, 1896, CW.

10. Two letters from H.G. Wells to GA in 1896 allude to a further hilltop novel. In one, Wells says he is looking forward to "that third novel of yours—of the Hill Top strain," and the other (undated) says "I'm very sorry to hear the third novel [illegible word]." See *The Correspondence of H.G. Wells*, ed. David C. Smith, Pickering & Chatto, 1998, I, 264, 274–275.

11. Two years later, Chatto closed a strictly business letter with a rather plaintive invitation to a lunchtime "symposium" he was arranging at his office "on the impact of the ether as the mechanical cause of gravity" (Chatto liked to dabble in speculative science). ALS, October 13, 1898, CW.

12. Female detectives figured in at least two novels as early as the 1860s. GA may have known Catherine Pirkis's *The Experiences of Loveday Brook, Lady Detective*, which first appeared in six short stories in the *Ludgate Monthly*, February–July 1893. George R. Sims's *Dorcas Dene, Detective: Her Adventures* was published in 1897. See http://www.chriswillis.freeserve.co.uk/loveday.htm. A general overview of this subgenre is Patricia Craig and Mary Cadogan, *The Lady Investigates: Women Detectives and Spies in Fiction*, Gollancz, 1981.

13. Quoted in Clodd, 174.

14. Andrew Lang, "The Evolution of the Idea of God," *Contemporary Review*, 72 (December 1897), 768–781. The anonymous *Athenaeum* review (November 20, 1897, pp. 700–701) was by Joseph Jacobs.

15. ALS to GA, undated [probably 1890], Poetry/Rare Books Collection, State University of New York at Buffalo Library.

16. *Academy*, 57 (October 14, 1899), 429; unsigned.

17. David Duncan, *Life and Letters of Herbert Spencer*, Methuen, 1908, 415.

18. Winifred Storr MS diary, Haslemere Museum, The Rayner Storrs of Haslemere were on intimate terms with the Allens, and the young Winifred Storr (b.1885) records a constant coming and going between the two houses on social engagements.

19. A. Conan Doyle, *Memories and Adventures*, 2nd ed., Murray, 1930, 304.

20. Clodd, 192–193.

21. Clodd, 167–168.

22. Ward is quoted in Frank Miller Turner, *Between Science and Religion: The Reaction to Scientific Naturalism in Late Victorian England*, Yale University Press, 1974, 16.

23. GA, "Luigi and the Salvationist," *Pall Mall Magazine* (December 19, 1899), 489–501.

24. "Obituary. Mr Grant Allen," *Daily News* (October 26, 1899), 6; unsigned.

25. The two wills are mentioned in Reginald Pound, *The Strand Magazine 1891–1950*, Heinemann, 1966, 68. According to his will (GRO), the gross value of GA's estate was £6455.3s.3d and the net value of his personal estate £3500.19s.0d.

26. Quoted in Wallace G. Breck, "The Le Moynes: Longueuil, Kingston and Wolfe Island," *Historic Kingston*, 37 (1989), 40.
27. Quoted from ALS, June 23, 1912 and January 1, 1913, Dreiser/Jerrard Grant Allen Correspondence, Annenberg Rare Book and Manuscript Library, University of Pennsylvania, MS Coll. 30, folder 80.

CONCLUSION

1. Richard Le Gallienne, "Grant Allen," *Attitudes and Avowals with Some Retrospective Reviews*, John Lane, 1910, 210.
2. Apart from those quoted in the text, other substantial obituaries were: William L. Alden, "London Literary Letter," *New York Times—Saturday Review*, November 25, 1899, 790, col. 2; Henry Rushton Fairclough, "Grant Allen's Personality," *Montreal Life*, November 17, 1890, 12–13. (Fairclough was a brother-in-law.)

    There were unsigned obituaries in *Literature*, October 25, 1899, 423; *Times*, October 26, 1899, col. 2; *Fortnightly Review*, 66 (December 1899), 1005; *Literary Digest*, 19 (November 18, 1899); *Writer*, 12:11 (November 1899); *Bookman*, 10:4 (December 1899); *Daily News*, October 26, 1899, 6; *Nature*, 61 (November 2, 1899). See also "Books and Literary Topics. Grant Allen's Death and Things Said about Him," *New York Times*, July 7, 1900, 455, col. 1.
3. Chris Healy, *The Confessions of a Journalist*, Chatto & Windus, 1904, 217.
4. Elizabeth A. Sharp, *William Sharp (Fiona Macleod): A Memoir*, Heinemann, 1912, II, 151.
5. Letter to Edward Clodd, November 7, 1899, *Collected Letters of George Gissing*, ed. Paul F. Mattheisen, Arthur C. Young, and Pierre Coustillas, Ohio University Press, 1990–1998, VII, 397.
6. Andrew Lang, "Grant Allen," *Argosy*, 71 (August 1900), 415.
7. A self-description in a letter to William Sharp. Sharp, *Memoir*, II, 18.
8. Letter to W.E. Henley, GRA, Reel 50: Correspondence: "Allen."
9. Oliver Elton, *Frederick York Powell: A Life and a Selection from His Letters and Occasional Writings*, 2 vols., Oxford: Clarendon Press, 1906, I, 187.
10. [W.T. Stead], "The Biography of a Rebel" [review of Clodd's *Memoir*], *Review of Reviews*, 22 (July 1900), 92.
11. Andrew Lang, "Mr Grant Allen. In Memoriam," *Daily News*, October 28, 1899, 7.
12. "The Writer's Trade," *Academy*, 59 (July 7, 1900), 15–16; unsigned.
13. Richard Le Gallienne, "Grant Allen," in *Attitudes and Avowals with Some Retrospective Reviews*, John Lane, 1910, 204.
14. "Mr Grant Allen," *Athenaeum* (October 28, 1894), 589; unsigned.
15. Grant Richards, "Mr Grant Allen," *Athenaeum* (November 4, 1894), 621.
16. Clement Shorter, "The Late Grant Allen," *Critic* [New York], 36 (January 1900), 40.
17. Clodd, 207–208.
18. "Obituary. Mr Grant Allen," *Daily News*, October 26, 1899, 6; unsigned.
19. "[Review of] *The Scallywag*," *Bookman*, 5 (October 1893), 26–27; unsigned.
20. GA, "A Scribbler's Apology," *Cornhill Magazine*, 47 (May 1883), 543.
21. Arthur Machen, *The Autobiography of Arthur Machen, with an Introduction by Morchard Bishop*, Richards, 1951, 187–188.

22. Anthony Trollope, *An Autobiography*, Williams & Norgate, 1946, 189–190; first published in 1883.

23. Raymond Blathwayt, *Through Life and Round the World: Being the Story of My Life*, E.P. Dutton [n.d.; 1917?], 154, 157.

24. Simon Eliot, *Some Patterns and Trends in British Publishing 1800–1919*, The Bibliographical Society, 1994, 14.

25. ALS, Chatto to GA, February 22, 1892, CW.

26. Grant Richards, "Mr Grant Allen and His Work," *Novel Review*, 1 (June 1892), 266.

27. GA, "A Scribbler's Apology," *Cornhill Magazine*, 47 (May 1883), 538–550; unsigned.

28. ALS, Leslie Stephen to GA, September 10, 1882, PSU.

29. GA, "The Trade of Author," *Fortnightly Review*, 51/45 (February 1889), 261–274; unsigned.

30. Walter Besant, "Literature as a Career," *Forum*, 13 (August 1892), 696.

31. GA, *The Woman Who Did*. Introduced by Sarah Wintle, Oxford University Press, 1995, 101.

32. "Introduction," *The British Barbarians*, John Lane/G.P. Putnam's Sons, 1895, xxiii.

BIBLIOGRAPHY

Note: Place of publication is London and/or New York, unless stated otherwise, and is not given for the publications of university presses.

WORKS BY GRANT ALLEN

Grant Allen (GA) was too prolific a writer for everything from his pen to be listed here. An annotated bibliography of all his identifiable published work and related material is maintained at http://ehlt.flinders.edu.au/english/GA/GAHome.htm. This site lists all his journalism, never-reprinted articles and stories, translations and reprints in microfiche and digital form, contemporary reviews, and provides an annotated listing of all the extant primary documents bearing on GA and his circle.

GA's voluminous output for the daily and weekly papers—particularly for the *Daily News* in the late 1870s and the *Pall Mall Gazette* and the *St James's Gazette* in the early 1880s—was for the most part anonymous. The bibliography is conservative, including unsigned contributions only where the attribution is certain, either because there are internal autobiographical references or because the article treats subjects that GA took up again elsewhere. This has meant passing over numerous short essays and (especially) reviews that, on stylistic grounds, are probably GA's work. For example, it is certain that he contributed articles on natural history, as well as leaders and reviews, to the *Daily News*, but none is traceable now. The *Academy* had some reviews signed, so GA's contributions to that weekly give some small notion of the extent and variety of his reviewing work, nearly all of which was anonymous.

The following is a chronological checklist by category of GA's books.

(a) Novels and Novellas

Philistia. By Cecil Power. 3 vols. Chatto & Windus, 1884.
Babylon. By Cecil Power. 3 vols. Chatto & Windus, 1885.
For Maimie's Sake. A Tale of Love and Dynamite. Chatto & Windus, 1886.
In All Shades. A Novel. 3 vols. Chatto & Windus, 1886.
Kalee's Shrine. [With May Cotes]. Bristol/London: J.W. Arrowsmith/Simkin, Marshall, 1886.
A Terrible Inheritance. Society for Promoting Christian Knowledge, [1887].
The Devil's Die. A Novel. 3 vols. Chatto & Windus, 1888.
This Mortal Coil. A Novel. 3 vols. Chatto & Windus, 1888.
The White Man's Foot. Hatchards, 1888.
Dr. Palliser's Patient. Samuel Mullen, 1889.
The Jaws of Death. A Novel. Simpkin, Marshall, [1889].
A Living Apparition. Society for Promoting Christian Knowledge/E. & J.B. Young, 1889.
The Tents of Shem. A Novel. 3 vols. Chatto & Windus, 1889.

The Great Taboo. Chatto & Windus, 1890.

The Sole Trustee. Society for Promoting Christian Knowledge, [1890].

Wednesday the Tenth. A Tale of the South Pacific. D. Lothrop, 1890.

The Duchess of Powysland. United States Book company, [1891].

Dumaresq's Daughter. A Novel. 3 vols. Chatto & Windus, 1891.

Recalled to Life. Bristol/London: J.W. Arrowsmith/Simkin, Marshall, Hamilton, Kent & Co., [1891].

What's Bred in the Bone. £1000 prize novel. "Tit-Bits" Offices, 1891.

Blood Royal. Cassell, [1892].

An Army Doctor's Romance. Raphael Tuck, [1893].

Michael's Crag. Leadenhall, 1893

The Scallywag. 3 vols. Chatto & Windus, 1893.

At Market Value. A Novel. 2 vols. Chatto & Windus, 1894.

Under Sealed Orders. A Novel. Peter Fenelon Collier, 1894.

The British Barbarians. A Hill-top Novel. John Lane, 1895.

The Woman Who Did. London/Boston, MA: John Lane/Roberts, 1895.

A Splendid Sin. F.V. White, 1896.

An African Millionaire: Episodes in the Life of the Illustrious Colonel Clay. Grant Richards, 1897.

Tom, Unlimited: A Story for Children. By Martin Leach Warborough. Grant Richards, 1897.

The Type-writer Girl. By Olive Pratt Rayner. C. Arthur Pearson, 1897.

The Incidental Bishop. A Novel. C. Arthur Pearson, 1898.

Linnet. A Romance. Grant Richards, 1898.

Miss Cayley's Adventures. Grant Richards, 1899.

Rosalba: The Story of Her Development: With Other Episodes of the European Movement, More Especially as They Affected the Monti Berici near Vicenza. By Olive Pratt Rayner. C. Arthur Pearson, 1899.

Hilda Wade. Grant Richards, 1900.

(b) Short Story Collections

Strange Stories. Chatto & Windus, 1884.

The Beckoning Hand, and Other Stories. Chatto & Windus, 1887.

Ivan Greet's Masterpiece etc. Chatto & Windus, 1893.

The Desire of the Eyes and Other Stories. Digby, Long, 1895.

A Bride from the Desert. R.F. Fenno, [ca. 1896].

Twelve Tales with a Headpiece, a Tailpiece, and an Intermezzo: being select stories by Grant Allen. Chosen and Arranged by the Author. Grant Richards, 1899.

The Backslider. Lewis, Scribner, 1901.

Sir Theodore's Guest and Other Stories. Bristol/London: J.W. Arrowsmith/Simpkin, Marshall, Hamilton, Kent, 1902.

(c) Poetry

The Lower Slopes: Reminiscences of Excursions round the Base of Helicon, Undertaken for the Most Part in Early Manhood. Elkin Mathews & John Lane, 1894.

Magdalen Tower. [Pamphlet, n.p.], [1894?].

The Return of Aphrodite. [Pamphlet, n.p.], [1894?].

The Bold Buccaneer. By the Late Grant Allen. Stop-The-War Committee. No. 8. [n.d.].

(d) Scientific Works

Physiological Aesthetics. Henry S. King, 1877.
The Colour-sense: Its Origin and Development. An Essay in Comparative Psychology. Trübner, 1879.
The Evolutionist at Large. Chatto & Windus, 1881.
Vignettes from Nature. Chatto & Windus, 1881.
Colin Clout's Calendar. The Record of a Summer, April–October. Chatto & Windus, 1882.
The Colours of Flowers, as Illustrated in the British Flora. Macmillan, 1882.
Flowers and Their Pedigrees. Longmans, Green, 1883.
Nature Studies. By Grant Allen, Andrew Wilson, Thomas Foster, Edward Clodd, and Richard A. Proctor. Wyman, [1883].
Common Sense Science. D. Lothrop, [1886].
Force and Energy. A Theory of Dynamics. Longmans, Green, 1888.
Falling in Love, with Other Essays on More Exact Branches of Science. Smith, Elder, 1889.
Science in Arcady. Lawrence & Bullen, 1892.
The Story of the Plants. With Illustrations. George Newnes, 1895.
Moorland Idylls. Chatto & Windus, 1896.
The Evolution of the Idea of God. An Inquiry into the Origins of Religions. Grant Richards, 1897.
Flashlights on Nature. Doubleday & McClure, 1898.
In Nature's Workshop. George Newnes, 1900.

(e) Essays, Belles-Lettres, Criticism

The Tidal Thames. With Twenty Full-page Photogravure Plates Printed on India Paper, and Other Illustrations, After Original Drawings, by W. L. Wyllie, and Descriptive Letterpress by G. Allen. Cassell, [1892].
Post-prandial Philosophy. Chatto & Windus, 1894.
Evolution in Italian Art. Grant Richards, 1907.
The Hand of God and Other Posthumous Essays Together with Some Reprinted Papers. Watts, 1909.

(f) Biography

Biographies of Working Men. Society for Promoting Christian Knowledge/Young, 1884.
Charles Darwin. Longmans, Green, 1885.
In Memoriam: George Paul Macdonell. Percy Lund, 1895.

(g) History

Anglo-Saxon Britain. Society for Promoting Christian Knowledge, [1881].
County and Town in England together with Some Annals of Churnside. With an Introduction by Frederick York Powell, Regius Professor of Modern History, Oxford University. Grant Richards, 1901.

(h) Travel Guides

Cities of Belgium. Grant Richards, 1897.
Florence. Grant Richards, 1897.

Paris. Grant Richards, 1897.

Venice. Grant Richards, 1898.

The European Tour. A Handbook for Americans and Colonists. Grant Richards, 1899.

Cities of Northern Italy. By Grant Allen and George C. Williamson. 2 vols. Boston, MA: LC Page, 1906.

(i) Translations and Editions

The Miscellaneous and Posthumous Works of Henry Thomas Buckle. A New and Abridged Edition Edited by Grant Allen. 2 vols. Longmans, Green, 1885.

C. Valeri Catulli Attin annotavit, illustravit, anglicè reddidit Carolus Grant Allen, B.A. Coll Merton. Apud Oxon. Olim Portionista. The Attis of Caius Valerius Catullus. Translated into English Verse, with Dissertations on the Myth of Attis, on the Origin of Tree-Worship, and on the Galliambic Metre. By Grant Allen, B.A., Formerly Postmaster of Merton College, Oxford. Londini MDCCCXCII. Apud Davidem Nutt in Via Dicta Strand/London: David Nutt, 1892.

The Natural History of Selborne by Gilbert White. Edited with Notes by Grant Allen. John Lane The Bodley Head, [1899].

PRIMARY SOURCES

The correspondence, manuscripts, and archival records of GA and his circle are held by libraries and other institutions in the United Kingdom, Canada, and the United States. The largest single holding of GA materials is in Rare Books and Manuscripts, Special Collections Library, University Libraries, Pennsylvania State University. The Register of the Grant Allen Literary Manuscripts and Correspondence 1872–1937 (Accession no. 1989-0059R) is available online at http://www.libraries.psu.edu/speccolls/FindingAids/grantallen.html.

The following is a list of all other institutions known to hold documents relating to GA and his circle.

Aberystwyth. National Library of Wales. GA letter.

Austin. Harry Ransom Humanities Research Center, University of Texas. GA MSS stories and letters.

Bath. Reference Library. GA letter.

Berkeley. University of California Library. GA letters.

Birmingham. King Edward's School Archives. GA school records.

Birmingham. Reference Library. GA letters.

Birmingham. University of Birmingham Library. GA letter.

Brighton. Brighton College Archives. GA records as schoolmaster.

Bristol. Record Office. GA letter.

Bolton. Central Library. GA letter.

Buffalo. State University of New York Library. Andrew Lang/GA letters.

Cambridge. Churchill Archives Centre, Churchill College. GA/W.T. Stead letters.

Cambridge. Darwin Correspondence Project, University Library. Editions of GA/Darwin letters and Darwin circle letters relating to GA's affairs.

Cambridge. University Library. GA/Benjamin Kidd letters.

Chapel Hill. Wilson Library, University of North Carolina. A.P. Watt & Co. letters and contracts with GA.

Chicago. H.G. Wells collection, University of Illinois Library. GA/Wells letters.

Cleveland. Dittrick Medical History Center, Case Western Reserve University. Letters to GA from Wallace, Galton, and A.B.O. Wilberforce; GA/Darwin letters.

Dorchester. Dorset County Museum. GA/Thomas Hardy letters.

Edinburgh. National Library of Scotland. GA letters.

Georgetown. Georgetown University Library. GA/Jerrard Grant Allen/Grant Richards letters.

Haslemere. Museum. Winifred Storr MS diary, 1898–9.

Kingston, Ontario. Public Library. 124 condolence letters to Nellie Allen, 1899–1900.

Leeds. Brotherton Collection, Brotherton Library, University of Leeds. GA/Clodd letters; other letters to/from people in GA's circle; Clodd MS diary; J.A. Allen's "notes" to Clodd; Clodd's annotated copy of his *Memoir*.

Liverpool. Hornby Library, Liverpool City Libraries. GA letters.

London. British Library, Department of Manuscripts. GA letters.

London. Family Records Centre. Birth, marriage, and death certificates.

London. Royal Institution Library. GA letters.

London. University College Library. GA/Croom Robertson letters.

London. University of London Library, Senate House. GA/Spencer letters.

Los Angeles. The William Andrews Clark Memorial Library, University of California. GA/Lane letters.

Lyme Regis. Museum. Material relating to the Jerrard family.

New Haven. Beineke Rare Book and Manuscript Library, Yale University. GA/Gosse/Clodd/Barrie letters.

New York. The Berg Collection, New York Public Library. Letterbooks of correspondence with GA from A.P. Watt & Co. in vols. VII (July 1883–July 1884); IX (July 1884–April 1885); X (January–July 1886); XIII (June–November 1887); XV (April–October 1888); XVI (October 1888–January 1889); XVIII (May–August 1889); XIX (August–November 1889); XXV (March–June 1891).

New York. The Morgan Library. GA/James Payn letters.

Oxford. Bodleian Library. GA MSS of poems; GA/E.W.B. Nicholson letters.

Philadelphia. University of Philadelphia Library. Jerrard Allen/Theodore Dreiser letters.

[Private Collector]. MS of *The Woman Who Did* and readers' reports obtained by John Lane.

Reading. University of Reading Library. Chatto & Windus archives.

Toronto. Thomas Fisher Rare Book Library, University of Toronto. Holograph draft of *The Tents of Shem* and GA letters.

Wigston. Leicestershire Records Office. Census records of the Bootheway family and commercial directories.

SECONDARY SOURCES

Minor biographical and critical summaries in reference works and anonymous contemporary short reviews are omitted.

(a) Bibliographical and Biographical

Alden, William L. "London Literary Letter," *New York Times Saturday Review*, October 14, 1899, 700, col. 1.

Alden, William L. "London Literary Letter," *New York Times Saturday Review*, November, 25 1899, 790, col. 2.

"Allen, Grant." In John Sutherland, ed. *Stanford Companion to Victorian Fiction*. Stanford University Press, 1989.

Angus, Margaret. "Alwington House," *Historic Kingston*, 40 (1992).

Asimov, Isaac. "Grant Allen 1849–1899 [*sic*]." In Isaac Asimov, Martin H. Greenberg, and Charles G. Waugh, eds. *Isaac Asimov Presents the Best Science Fiction of the 19th Century*. Knightsbridge, 1991.

Barzun, Jacques Martin and Wendell Hertig Taylor. *A Catalog of Crime*. Harper and Row, 1971.

Benstock, B. and Thomas F. Staley, eds. *Dictionary of Literary Biography*, 70: *British Mystery Writers 1860–1919*. Gale, 1988.

Blackburn Harte, W. "Some Canadian Writers of To-day," *The New England Magazine*, 9:1 (September 1890), 26, 33–34.

Blathwayt, Raymond. "Mr Grant Allen at Home." *Interviews. With Portraits, and a Preface by Grant Allen*. A.W. Hall, 1893.

Bleiler, Everett F. *The Guide to Supernatural Fiction*. Kent State University Press, 1983.

Bleiler, Everett F. "(Charles) Grant (Blairfindie) Allen." In John M. Reilly, ed. *Twentieth Century Crime and Mystery Writers*, 2nd edn. St. James Press, ca. 1985.

Bleiler, Everett F. *Science-Fiction: The Early Years*. Kent State University Press, 1990.

"Books and Literary Topics. Grant Allen's Death and Things Said about Him," *New York Times*, July 7, 1900, 455, col. 1.

"Books and Literary Topics. Grant Allen's Story Finished by Conan Doyle," *New York Times*, March 17, 1900, 170, col. 1.

"Charles Grant Allen." In Charles Dudley Warner et al., eds. *Library of the World's Best Literature*. 30 vols. R.S. Peale & J.A. Hill, 1902.

"(Charles) Grant (Blairfindie) Allen." In Jacques Martin Barzun and Wendell Hertig Taylor. *A Catalog of Crime*. Harper and Row, 1971.

"(Charles) Grant (Blairfindie) Allen." In Chris Steinbrunner and Otto Penzler, eds. *The Encyclopaedia of Mystery and Detection*. McGraw-Hill, 1976.

Clarke, George Herbert. "Grant Allen," *Queen's Quarterly*, 45 (1938), 487–496.

Clodd, Edward. [Obituary of GA], *Daily Chronicle*, October 26, 1899, 3.

Clodd, Edward. *Grant Allen. A Memoir . . . with a Bibliography*. Grant Richards, 1900.

Clodd, Edward. *Memories . . . with Portraits*. 2nd edn. Chapman & Hall, 1916.

Clodd, Edward. "Grant Allen 1848–1899," *Fortnightly Review*, 106 (July 1916), 124–135.

C[otton], J[ames] S[utherland]. "Allen, Grant." In *Dictionary of National Biography*, 22 (suppl.), 36–38.

[?Cotton, James Sutherland]. "*Grant Allen* by Edward Clodd [review]," *Academy*, 58 (January/June 1900), 547.

"Death of Grant Allen," *New York Daily Tribune*, October 26, 1899, 9, col. 5.

"Death of Grant Allen," *Bookman*, 10 (December 1899), 4.

"Death of Mr Grant Allen," *Times*, October 26, 1899, col. 2.

Doyle, Arthur Conan. *Memories and Adventures*. 2nd ed. John Murray, 1930.

Fairclough, Henry Rushton. "Grant Allen's Personality," *Montreal Life*, November 17, 1890, 12–13.

Fairclough, Henry Rushton. *Warming Both Hands: The Autobiography of Henry Rushton Fairclough Including His Experiences under the American Red Cross in Switzerland and Montenegro*. Stanford University Press and Oxford University Press, 1941.

Fernald, F.A., comp. *Index to the* Popular Science Monthly *from 1872–1892 Including Volumes I to XL and the Twenty-one Numbers of the Supplement*. D. Appleton, 1893.

Foster, Joseph. *Alumni Oxonienses . . .* 4 vols. Oxford: Parker, 1888.

"Funeral of Mr Grant Allen," *Daily News*, October 28, 1899, 7.

[Grant Allen obituary], *Nature*, 61 (November 2, 1899), 13.

"Grant Allen [obituary]," *Fortnightly Review*, 66 (December 1899), 1005.

"*Grant Allen: A Memoir*, by Edward Clodd [review]," *Saturday Review*, July 7, 1900, 21.

"Grant Allen, Author, Dead," *New York Times*, October 26, 1899, 7, col. 2.

"*Grant Allen* by Edward Clodd [review]," *Athenaeum*, 16 June 1900, 749.

"Grant Allen, i.e. Charles Grant Blairfindie Allen 1848–99." In Joanne Shattock, ed. *The Cambridge Bibliography of English Literature*, vol. IV. Cambridge University Press, 1999.

"Grant Allen: References from Writers," *New York Daily Tribune*, June 24, 1900 (suppl.), 12, col. 2.

Grant Richards Archives, 1897–1948. *Archives of British Publishers on Microfilm*. Cambridge: Chadwyck-Healey, 1979.

Harris, Frank. "Grant Allen." *Contemporary Portraits: Fourth Series*. Grant Richards, 1924.

Harris-Fain, D., ed. *Dictionary of Literary Biography, 178:British Fantasy and Science-Fiction Writers before World War 1*. Gale, 1997.

Hubin, Allen H. *Crime Fiction: A Comprehensive Bibliography*. Garland, 1984.

Hudson, Derek. "English Switzerland in Surrey," *Country Life*, May 10, 1973, 1310–1311.

Ingram, Alison. *The Archives of Grant Richards, 1897–1948*. Cambridge: Chadwyck-Healey, 1981.

James, William. *Correspondence*, Vols. 1 and 5, edited by Ignas K. Skrupskelis and Elizabeth M. Berkley. University Press of Virginia, 1997.

Lang, Andrew. "Mr Grant Allen. In Memoriam," *Daily News*, October 28, 1899, 7.

Lang, Andrew. "At the Sign of the Ship," *Longman's Magazine*, 34 (December 1899), 183–192.

Lang, Andrew. "Grant Allen," *Argosy*, 71 (August 1900), 410–415.

Le Gallienne, Richard. "Grant Allen," *Fortnightly Review*, 66 (December 1899), 1005–1025.

Morton, Peter. *Grant Allen (1848–1899): A Bibliography*. Victorian Fiction Research Guide no. 31. Brisbane: Victorian Fiction Research Unit, University of Queensland, 2002.

"Mr Grant Allen [obituary]," *Academy*, 57 (October 28, 1899), 489.

"Mr Grant Allen [obituary]," *Athenaeum*, October 28, 1899, 589.

"Mr Grant Allen at Dinner," *Speaker*, May 16, 1891, 577–578.

"Mr Lang's Tribute," *New York Daily Tribune*, November 18, 1899, 10, col. 3.

New, W.H., ed. *Dictionary of Literary Biography, 92: Canadian Writers 1890–1920*. Gale, 1990.

"Obituary. Mr Grant Allen," *Daily News*, October 26, 1899, 6.

"Portrait of Grant Allen," *Canadian Magazine*, 17 (May 1901), 16.

Reilly, John M., ed. *Twentieth Century Crime and Mystery Writers*, 2nd edn. St. James Press, ca. 1985.

Review of Reviews. *The Annual Index of Periodicals and Photographs for 1890*. Review of Reviews, 1891.

Review of Reviews. *Index to the Periodical Literature of the World (Covering the Year 1891)*. Review of Reviews, 1892.

Review of Reviews. *Index to the Periodical Literature of the World (Covering the Year 1892)*. Review of Reviews, 1893.

Richards, Grant. "Mr Grant Allen and His Work," *Novel Review*, 1 (June 1892), 261–268.

Richards, Grant. "Mr Grant Allen," *Athenaeum*, November 4, 1899, 621.

Richards, Grant. *Memories of a Misspent Youth 1872–1896.* Heinemann, 1932.

Richards, Grant. *Author Hunting by an Old Literary Sportsman: Memories of Years Spent Mainly in Publishing, 1897–1925.* Hamish Hamilton, 1934.

Rothenstein, William. *English Portraits: A Series of Lithographed Drawings.* Grant Richards, 1898.

Rozendal, Phyllis. "Grant Allen." In B. Benstock and Thomas F. Staley, eds. *Dictionary of Literary Biography,* 70: *British Mystery Writers 1860–1919.* Gale, 1988.

Ruddick, Nicholas. "Grant Allen." In D. Harris-Fain, ed. *Dictionary of Literary Biography, 178: British Fantasy and Science-Fiction Writers before World War 1.* Gale, 1997.

Shattock, Joanne, ed. *The Cambridge Bibliography of English Literature,* Vol. IV. Cambridge University Press, 1999.

[Stead, W.T.] "The Death of Grant Allen," *Review of Reviews,* 20 (November 1899), 447.

[Stead, W.T.] "The Biography of a Rebel [review of Clodd's *Memoir*]," *Review of Reviews,* 22 (July 1900), 92.

Steinbrunner, Chris and Otto Penzler, eds. *The Encyclopaedia of Mystery and Detection.* McGraw-Hill, 1976.

Stephensen-Payne, Phil and Virgil Utter. *Grant Allen: Hill-Top Philosopher. A Working Bibliography.* Galactic Central Bibliographies for the Avid Reader Vol. 52. Leeds: Galactic Central Publications, 1999.

St. Pierre, Paul Matthew. "Grant Allen." In W.H. New, ed. *Dictionary of Literary Biography, 92: Canadian Writers 1890–1920.* Gale, 1990.

Sullivan, Alvin, ed. *British Literary Magazines, Vol. 3: The Victorian and Edwardian Age, 1837–1913.* Greenwood, 1984.

Sutherland, John, ed. *Stanford Companion to Victorian Fiction.* Stanford University Press, 1989.

Temple Bar. *The One Hundredth Volume of The Temple Bar Magazine. Being an Alphabetical List of the Titles of All Articles Appearing in the Previous Ninety-Nine Volumes.* Bentley, 1894.

Trotter, W.R. *The Hilltop Writers: A Victorian Colony among the Surrey Hills.* Lewes: Book Guild, 1996.

Warner, Charles Dudley et al., eds. *Library of the World's Best Literature.* 30 vols. R.S. Peale & J.A. Hill, 1902.

Waterloo Directory of English Newspapers and Periodicals 1800–1900. Series 1 of 5. 10 vols. Waterloo: North Waterloo Academic Press, 1997.

Wolff, Robert Lee. *Nineteenth-Century Fiction. A Bibliographical Catalogue Based on the Collection Formed by Robert Lee Wolff.* 5 vols. Garland, 1981–86, I, item [129].

"World Biographies: Grant Allen," *Literary World,* 10:10 (May 10, 1879).

(b) Historical and Critical

Adburgham, Alison. *Shops and Shopping 1800–1914: Where, and in What Manner the Well-Dressed Englishwoman Bought Her Clothes.* 2nd edn. Barrie & Jenkins, 1981.

Adcock, A. St. John. "The Literary Life." *Modern Grub Street and Other Essays.* Herbert & Daniel, [1913].

Addleshaw, Percy. "*The Woman Who Did* [review]," *Academy,* 47 (March 2, 1895), 186–187.

Addleshaw, Percy. "*The Woman Who Did* [letter in reply to GA's comments on review]," *Academy,* 47 (March 16, 1895), 351.

Alden, William L. "*The Woman Who Did* [review]," *Idler*, 7 (February–July 1895), 565–567.

Altick, Richard D. "The Sociology of Authorship: The Social Origins, Education, and Occupations of 1,100 British Writers, 1800–1935," *Bulletin of the New York Public Library*, 66 (June 1962), 389–404.

Altick, Richard D. *The English Common Reader: A Social History of the Mass Reading Public, 1800–1900.* 2nd edn. Ohio State University Press, 1998.

Altick, Richard D. "Publishing." In Herbert F. Tucker, ed. *A Companion to Victorian Literature and Culture.* Oxford: Blackwell, 1999.

Anderson, Allan J. *The Anglican Churches of Kingston.* Kingston, Ontario: n.p., 1963.

Anderson, Patricia. "Free Love and Free Thought: *The Adult, 1897–1899*," *Studies in Newspaper and Periodical History* (1993), 179–181.

Andrews, E.F. "Grant Allen on the Woman Question [letter]," *Popular Science Monthly*, 36 (February 1890), 552–553.

Anesko, Michael. *"Friction with the Market": Henry James and the Profession of Authorship.* Oxford University Press, 1986.

Ardis, Ann. *New Women, New Novels: Feminism and Early Modernism.* Rutgers University Press, 1992.

Armstrong, Tim. "Supple Minds and Automatic Hands: Secretarial Agency in Early Twentieth-Century Literature," *Forum for Modern Language Studies*, 37 (2001), 155–168.

Austin, Alfred. *The Autobiography of Alfred Austin Poet Laureate 1835–1910.* 2 vols. Macmillan, 1911.

Banks, J.A. and Olive Banks. *Feminism and Family Planning in Victorian England.* Liverpool University Press, 1964.

[Barrie, J.M.] "The Conspiracy against Mr Grant Allen," *National Observer*, 1 (November 22, 1890), 12–13.

Beckman, Linda Hunt. *Amy Levy: Her Life and Letters.* Ohio University Press, 2000.

Beetham, Margaret. "Towards a Theory of the Periodical as a Publishing Genre." In Laurel Brake et al., eds. *Investigating Victorian Journalism.* Macmillan, 1990.

Bennett, Arnold. "Twenty Guinea Condensation Prize," *Tit-Bits*, 21 (December 19, 1891), 192.

[Bennett, Arnold]. *The Truth about an Author.* Constable, 1903.

Besant, Walter. "Literature as a Career," *Forum*, 13 (August 1892), 693–708.

Birdwood, George. "Does India Pay?" *St James's Gazette*, 1 (October 21, 1880), 5.

Black, Clinton V. *Spanish Town: The Old Capital.* Spanish Town: Parish Council of St. Catherine, 1960.

Bland, Lucy. *Banishing the Beast: English Feminism and Sexual Morality 1885–1914.* Penguin, 1995.

Blathwayt, Raymond. *Through Life and round the World: Being the Story of My Life.* Dutton, [ca. 1917].

Blavatsky, H.P. "Mr Grant Allen's Ideal of Womanhood," *Lucifer*, 6 (July 1890), 353.

Bonney, T.G. "The New Hedonism," *Humanitarian: A Monthly Review of Sociological Science*, 5 (July 1894), 106–113.

Bower, F.O. "Mr Grant Allen's Article on 'The Shapes of Leaves,'" *Nature*, 27 (April 12, 1883), 552.

Bowler, Peter J. *The Eclipse of Darwinism: Anti-Darwinian Evolution Theories in the Decades around 1900.* Johns Hopkins University Press, 1983.

Bowyer, E.M.N. [Reply to GA's article "An English Wife"], *North American Review*, 161 (December 1895), 759–760.

Braithwaite, Lloyd. "The Development of Higher Education in the British West Indies," *Social and Economic Studies* [West Indies], 7:1 (March 1958), 1–64.

Brake, Laurel et al., eds. *Investigating Victorian Journalism.* Macmillan, 1990.

Breck, Wallace G. "The Le Moynes: Longueuil, Kingston and Wolfe Island," *Historic Kingston*, 37 (1989), 40.

Britten, James. "Grant Allen on Human Sacrifice among the Abruzzi Peasantry," *Month*, 92 (October 1898), 390.

Brock, M.G. and M.C. Curthoys, eds. *The History of the University of Oxford, Vol. VII: Nineteenth-Century Oxford, Part 2.* Oxford: Clarendon Press, 2000.

Broks, Peter. "Science, Media and Culture: British Magazines, 1890–1914," *Public Understanding of Science*, 2 (1993), 123–139.

Brown, J.H. Balfour. *Recollections Literary and Political.* Constable, 1917.

Budd, S.C. "The Woman Who Did the Right Thing," *Belgravia*, 91 (1896), 337.

Budd, Susan. *Varieties of Unbelief: Atheists and Agnostics in English Society 1850–1960.* Heinemann, 1977.

Bury, Blaze de. "Grant Allen." *Les Romanciers anglais contemporains*, Paris: Perrin, 1900.

Calder-Marshall, A. *Lewd, Blasphemous and Obscene.* Hutchinson, 1972.

Calvin, D.D. *Queen's University at Kingston: The First Century of a Scottish-Canadian Foundation 1841–1941.* Kingston, Ontario: The Trustees of the University, 1941.

Cameron, Mrs. Lovett [Caroline Emily]. *The Man Who Didn't; or The Triumph of a Snipe Pie. Dedicated to Married Men.* F.V. White, 1895.

Caracciolo, Peter L. "The Buddha under the Golden Bough: Central African Sculpture, Grant Allen, Edward Clodd and *Heart of Darkness*," *L'Epoque-Conradienne* (1990), 87–103.

Carpenter, William B. "*Vignettes from Nature*," *Nature*, 25 (March 9 and 23, 1882), 435–436 and 480–481.

Chislett, William. "Grant Allen, Naturalist and Novelist." *Moderns and Near-Moderns: Essays on Henry James, Stockton, Shaw, and Others.* Grafton, 1928.

Cleve, Lucas [i.e. Adeline Georgina Isabella Kingscote]. *The Woman Who Wouldn't.* Simpkin, Marshall, 1895.

Clodd, Edward. "*The Evolution of the Idea of God* [review]," *Folk-Lore*, 11 (1897), 63–64.

Clodd, Edward. "Introduction." In GA, *In Nature's Workshop.* George Newnes, 1900.

Cobbett, Ethel. "Woman and Natural Selection," *Humanitarian: A Monthly Review of Sociological Science*, 4 (April 1894), 315–319.

"Constant Reader." "Grant Allen's Writing," *Literary Review*, February 10, 1923, 451.

[Corelli, Marie, George Eric Mackay, and Henry Labouchere]. *The Silver Domino; or Side Whispers, Social and Literary.* 16th edn. Lamley, 1894 (first published 1892).

Cotes, Alison. "Gissing, Grant Allen and 'Free Union,'" *The Gissing Newsletter*, 19:4 (October 1983), 1–18.

Cowie, David. "The Evolutionist at Large: Grant Allen, Scientific Naturalism and Victorian Culture." Ph.D. thesis, University of Kent at Canterbury, April 2000.

Coyne, W.P. "Mr Grant Allen and the New Hedonism," *Month*, 81 (June 1894), 468.

Craig, Patricia and Mary Cadogan. *The Lady Investigates: Women Detectives and Spies in Fiction.* Gollancz, 1981.

[Creighton, Louise]. *Life and Letters of Mandell Creighton.* 2 vols. Longmans, Green, 1904.

Cross, Nigel. *The Common Writer: Life in Nineteenth Century Grub Street.* Cambridge University Press, 1985.

Cross(e), Victoria [i.e. Annie Sophie "Vivian" Corey Griffin]. *The Woman Who Didn't.* John Lane, 1895; *The Woman Who Did Not.* Roberts, 1895.

Cunningham, A.V. "The New Woman Fiction of the 1890s," *Victorian Studies*, 18 (December 1973), 177–186.

Cunningham, Gail. *The New Woman and the Victorian Novel.* Macmillan, 1978.

Cunningham, Valentine. "Darke Conceits: The Professions of Criticism." In Jeremy Treglown and Bridget Bennett, eds. *Grub Street and the Ivory Tower: Literary Journalism and Literary Scholarship from Fielding to the Internet.* Oxford: Clarendon Press, 1998.

Cunningham, Valentine. " 'Unto Him (or Her) That Hath': How Victorian Writers Made Ends Meet," Times Literary *Supplement*, September 11, 1998, 12–13.

David, Deidre, ed. *The Cambridge Companion to the Victorian Novel.* Cambridge University Press, 2001.

Dawson, John. *Practical Journalism, How to Enter Thereon and Succeed. A Manual for Beginners and Amateurs.* L. Upcott Gill, 1885.

Dellamora, Richard, ed. *Victorian Sexual Dissidence.* University of Chicago Press, 1999.

[Discussion of GA's "Sacred Stones"], *Contemporary Review*, 57 (March 1890), 353–365.

Dixon, Ella Hepworth. *"As I Knew Them": Sketches of People I Have Met on the Way.* Hutchinson, 1930.

"Does Writing Pay? The Confessions of an Author," *Belgravia*, 47 (January 1881), 283–296.

Dorson, Richard M. *The British Folklorists: A History.* Routledge & Kegan Paul, 1968.

Dowden, Edward. *The Life of Percy Bysshe Shelley.* 2 vols. Kegan Paul, 1886.

Draper, Harry Napier. "Fact and Fiction," *Nature*, 38 (July 5, 1888), 221.

Duncan, David. *Life and Letters of Herbert Spencer.* Williams & Norgate, 1911.

Dyer, W.T. Thistleton. "Deductive Biology," *Nature*, 27 (April 12, 1883), 554–555.

Edwards, P.D. *Dickens's "Young Men": George Augustus Sala, Edmund Yates and the World of Victorian Journalism.* Aldershot: Ashgate, 1997.

Eliot, Simon. *Some Patterns and Trends in British Publishing 1800–1919.* Bibliographical Society, 1994.

Eliot, Simon. "The Business of Victorian Publishing." In Deidre David, ed. *The Cambridge Companion to the Victorian Novel.* Cambridge University Press, 2001.

[Ellis, Havelock]. "The Changing Status of Women," *Westminster Review*, 128 (October 1887), 826.

Ellmann, Richard. *Oscar Wilde.* Hamish Hamilton, 1987.

Elton, Oliver. *Frederick York Powell: A Life and a Selection from His Letters and Occasional Writings.* 2 vols. Oxford: Clarendon Press, 1906.

"English Literary Piracy," *Popular Science Monthly*, 32 (January 1888), 424.

Fawcett, Millicent G. *"The Woman Who Did," Contemporary Review*, 67 (1895), 625–631.

Fernando, Lloyd. *"New Women" in the Late Victorian Novel.* Penn State University Press, 1977.

Fichman, Martin. "Biology and Politics: Defining the Boundaries." In Bernard Lightman, ed. *Victorian Science in Context.* University of Chicago Press, 1997.

Frederic, Harold. *"The Woman Who Did* [review]," *New York Times*, February 17, 1895, 8.

Friedrichs, Hulda. *The Life of Sir George Newnes, Bart.* Hodder & Stoughton, 1911.

Gagnier, Regenia. "Production, Reproduction, and Pleasure in Victorian Aesthetics and Economics." In Richard Dellamora, ed. *Victorian Sexual Dissidence.* University of Chicago Press, 1999.

Gardiner, Juliet, ed. *The New Woman.* Collins & Brown, 1993.

Gerard, J. "The Theorist at Large," *Month,* 64 (November 1888), 346.

Gilder, Jeannette. "According to Grant Allen," *The Critic,* 26 (April 1895), 292.

Gissing, George. *New Grub Street,* edited by Bernard Bergonzi. Harmondsworth: Penguin, 1968.

Gissing, George. *London and the Life of Literature in Late Victorian England: The Diary of George Gissing, Novelist,* edited by Pierre Coustillas. Hassocks: Harvester, 1978.

Gissing, George. *Collected Letters of George Gissing,* edited by Paul F. Mattheisen, Arthur C. Young, and Pierre Coustillas. Ohio University Press, 1990–1998.

Gosse, Edmund. "Literature as a Trade," *Author,* 1 (November 15, 1890), 179–180.

"Grant Allen on England's Military Preparation," *New York Daily Tribune,* February 24, 1900, 10, col. 1.

"Grant Allen's Assault upon Marriage," *Literary Digest,* 10 (April 27, 1895), 8.

Green, Roger Lancelyn. *Andrew Lang.* Bodley Head, 1962.

Greenwood, Frederick. "Philosophy in the Market-place: Grant Allen and the New Hedonism," *Contemporary Review,* 65 (May 1894), 635–648.

Gross, John. *The Rise and Fall of the Man of Letters: Aspects of English Literary Life Since 1800.* Harmondsworth: Pelican, 1973.

Hannigan, D.F. "Sex in Fiction," *Westminster Review,* 143 (1895), 616–625.

Harman, Lillian. "Cast off the Shell!" *The Adult: The Journal of Sex,* 1 (January 1898), 149–150.

Harris, Frank. *Frank Harris: His Life and Adventures. An Autobiography with an Introduction by Grant Richards.* Richards Press, 1947.

Harris, Wendell V. "John Lane's 'Keynotes' Series and the Fiction of the 1890's," *PMLA,* 83 (October 1968), 1407–1413.

Harrison, Frederic. "The Emancipation of Women," *Fortnightly Review,* 50 (October 1891), 445.

Harrison, Frederic. *Grant Allen, 1848–1899; An Address Delivered at Woking on October 27, 1899.* Privately printed [Chiswick Press], 1899.

Healy, Chris. *The Confessions of a Journalist.* Chatto & Windus, 1904.

Hearn, Lafcadio. "Grant Allen," *Victorian Philosophy.* Tokyo: Hokuseido Press, 1930.

Heilmann, Ann. *New Woman Fiction: Women Writing First-Wave Feminism.* Macmillan/St. Martin's Press, 2000.

Hepburn, James. *The Author's Empty Purse and the Rise of the Literary Agent.* Oxford University Press, 1968.

Hill, Miranda. "Life on Thirty Shillings a Week," *Nineteenth Century,* 23 (March 1888), 458–463.

"'Hill-top' Novels and the Morality of Art," *Spectator,* November 23, 1895, 722–724.

Hogarth, Janet E. "Literary Degenerates," *Fortnightly Review,* 57 (April 1895), 586–592.

Honderich, Ted, ed. *The Oxford Companion to Philosophy.* Oxford University Press, 1995.

Howarth, Patrick. *When the Riviera Was Ours.* Century, 1977.

"How Novelists Write for the Press. Facsimiles of the MSS of William Black, Walter Besant, Bret Harte, and Grant Allen [opening of 'Jerry Stokes']," *Strand*, 1 (March 1891), 295–298.

Hudry-Menes, J. "L'Individualisme féminin dans la littérature," *La Société Nouvelle* (May 1896), 658–678.

Hughes, David Y. "H.G. Wells and the Charge of Plagiarism," *Nineteenth-Century Fiction*, 21 (June 1966), 85–90.

Hughes, David Y. "A Queer Notion of Grant Allen's," *Science-Fiction Studies*, 25 (July 1998), 271.

Hunt, Karen. *Equivocal Feminists: The Social Democratic Federation and the Woman Question 1884–1911*. Cambridge University Press, 1996.

Hunter, William Wilson. *Imperial Gazetteer of India*. 9 vols. Trübner, 1881.

Hynes, Samuel. *The Edwardian Turn of Mind*. Princeton University Press/Oxford University Press, 1968.

Iverach, J. "Immortality and Resurrection—Reply to Grant Allen," *Thinker*, 7 (March 1895), 227.

Ives, George. "The New Hedonism Controversy," *Humanitarian*, 5 (October 1894), 292–297.

James, William. "Grant Allen's Physiological Aesthetics," *Nation: A Weekly Journal Devoted to Politics, Literature, Science, and Art*, 25 (1877), 185.

Jones, Dorothy Richardson. *"King of Critics": George Saintsbury, 1845–1933, Critic, Journalist, Historian, Professor*. University of Michigan Press, 1992.

Jordan, John O. and Robert L. Patten, eds. *Literature in the Marketplace: Nineteenth-Century British Publishing and Reading Practices*. Cambridge University Press, 1995.

Keating, Peter. *The Haunted Study: A Social History of the English Novel 1875–1914*. FontanaPress, 1991.

Keep, Christopher. "The Cultural Work of the Type-writer Girl," *Victorian Studies*, 40 (Spring 1997), 401–426.

Kennelly, Louise. "*The Woman Who Did. Edited by Sarah Wintle* [review]," *English Literature in Transition*, 39:1 (1996), 139.

Kent, Susan Kingsley. *Sex and Suffrage in Britain, 1860–1914*. Princeton University Press, 1987.

Kevles, Daniel J. *In the Name of Eugenics: Genetics and the Uses of Human Heredity*. 2nd edn. Harvard University Press, 1995.

Klaus, H. Gustav, ed. *The Rise of Socialist Fiction 1880–1914*. Brighton: Harvester, 1987.

Lambert, J.W. and Ratcliffe, Michael. *The Bodley Head 1887–1987*. Bodley Head, 1987.

Lang, Andrew. "*The Evolution of the Idea of God* [review]," *Contemporary Review*, 72 (December 1897), 768–781.

Lang, Andrew. "Was Jehovah a Fetish Stone?" *Contemporary Review* (March 1890), 353–365.

Law, Graham. *Serializing Fiction in the Victorian Press*. Palgrave, 2000.

Layard, G.S. "How to Live on £700 a Year," *Nineteenth Century*, 23 (February 1888), 239–244.

L.C.M. "Our Bookshelf [review of GA, *Flashlights on Nature*]," *Nature*, 59 (January 19, 1899), 268.

Lecky, William Edward Hartpole. *History of European Morals from Augustus to Charlemagne*. 13th impression. 2 vols. Longmans, Green, 1899 (first published 1869).

Ledger, Sally. *The New Woman: Fiction and Feminism at the* fin de siècle. Manchester University Press, 1997.

Le Gallienne, Richard. *Retrospective Reviews: A Literary Log. Vol II (1893–1895).* John Lane, 1896.

Le Gallienne, Richard. *The Romantic '90s.* Putnam, 1951 (first published 1926).

Le Gallienne, Richard. *Attitudes and Avowals with Some Retrospective Reviews.* John Lane, 1910.

Leuba, Walter. *George Saintsbury.* Twayne, 1967.

Levin, Gerald. "Alfred Russel Wallace and Grant Allen: Five Letters in the Robert N. Stecher Collection 1877–1899," *Bulletin of the Cleveland Medical Library,* 26 (Spring/Summer) 1980, 17–39.

Levin, Gerald. "Grant Allen's Scientific and Aesthetic Philosophy," *Victorians Institute Journal,* 12 (1984), 77–89.

Lightman, Bernard. " 'The Voices of Nature': Popularizing Victorian Science." In Bernard Lightman, ed. *Victorian Science in Context.* University of Chicago Press, 1997.

"Literature as a Profession: A Fragment of an Autobiography by a Successful Author," *Eclectic Magazine,* 32 (December 1880), 699.

Lodge, O[liver] J. "Mr Grant Allen's Notions about Force and Energy," *Nature,* 39 (January 24, 1889), 289–292.

Lorimer, Douglas A. *Colour, Class and the Victorians: English Attitudes to the Negro in the Mid-nineteenth Century.* Leicester University Press/Holmes & Meier, 1978.

Luftig, Victor. *Seeing Together: Friendship Between the Sexes in English Writing, from Mill to Woolf.* Stanford University Press, 1993.

M.A.B. "Normal or Abnormal," *The Englishwoman's Review of Social and Industrial Questions,* 20 (December 14, 1889), 533–538.

Machen, Arthur. *The Autobiography of Arthur Machen. With an Introduction by Morchard Bishop.* Richards Press, 1951.

MacKenzie, Norman and Jeanne MacKenzie. *The First Fabians.* Weidenfeld & Nicolson, 1977.

MacNeill, J.G. Swift. *What I Have Seen and Heard.* Boston, MA: Little, Brown, 1925.

Macpherson, Margaret M. "Grant Allen's Verses," *Academy,* 82 (April 13, 1912), 477.

"The Man That Was Not Allowed," *National Observer: A Record and Review,* 8 (August 6, 1892), 291.

Manguel, Alberto, ed. *By the Light of the Glow-worm Lamp. Three Centuries of Reflections on Nature.* Plenum, 1998.

Marchant, James. *Alfred Russel Wallace: Letters and Reminiscences.* 2 vols. Cassell, 1916.

May, J. Lewis. *John Lane and the Nineties.* John Lane, 1936.

Mays, Kelly J. "The Disease of Reading and Victorian Periodicals." In John O. Jordan and Robert L. Patten, eds. *Literature in the Marketplace: Nineteenth-Century British Publishing and Reading Practices.* Cambridge University Press, 1995.

McDonald, Peter D. *British Literary Culture and Publishing Practice 1880–1914.* Cambridge University Press, 1997.

McLaren, Angus. *Birth Control in Nineteenth-Century England.* Croom Helm, 1978.

McLeod, Roy M. "Evolutionism, Internationalism and Commercial Enterprise in Science: The International Scientific Series 1871–1910." In A.J. Meadows, ed. *Development of Science Publishing in Europe.* Elsevier, 1980.

Meadows, A.J. "Access to the Results of Scientific Research: Developments in Victorian Britain." In A.J. Meadows, ed. *Development of Science Publishing in Europe.* Elsevier, 1980.

Melchiori, Barbara Arnett. *Terrorism in the Late Victorian Novel.* Croom Helm, 1985.

Melchiori, Barbara Arnett. *Grant Allen: The Downward Path Which Leads to Fiction*. Rome: Bulzoni Editore, 2000.

Miller, George Noyes. *The Strike of a Sex*. W.H. Reynolds, 1891.

Mivart, St. George. "The Degradation of Women," *Humanitarian*, 9 (October 1896), 250–257.

Mivart, St. George. "It is Degradation (A Brief Re-statement)," *Humanitarian*, 9 (December 1896), 417–419.

Mix, Katherine Lyon. *A Study in Yellow: The Yellow Book and Its Contributors*. Constable/University of Kansas Press, 1960.

Monroe, H. [Reply to GA's "Novels without a Purpose"], *North American Review*, 163 (August 1896), 504–505.

Moore, Doris Langley. *E. Nesbit: A Biography Revised with New Material*. Ernest Benn, 1967.

Moore, George. "A New Censorship of Literature," *Pall Mall Gazette*, 40 (December 10, 1884), 1–2.

"*Moorland Idylls* [review]," *Nature*, 52 (March 26, 1896), 486.

Morris, William. *Collected Letters*, edited by Norman Kelvin. Princeton University Press, 1996.

Morrison, Arthur. "Family Budgets. 1. A Workman's Budget," *Cornhill Magazine*, 10 (April 1901), 446–456.

Morton, Peter. *The Vital Science: Biology and the Literary Imagination*, 1860–1900. Allen & Unwin, 1984.

Morton, Peter. "Grant Allen: A Centenary Reassessment," *English Literature in Transition 1880–1920*, 44:4 (2001), 404–440.

"Mr. Grant Allen's Theogonies," *Bookman*, 7 (March–August 1898), 82.

"Mr Grant Allen's Views," *Natural Science: A Monthly Review of Scientific Progress*, 7 (September 1895), 159–160.

Mullen, D. "*The British Barbarians* [review]," *Science Fiction Studies*, 2:2 (July 1975).

Nelson, James G. *The Early Nineties: A View from the Bodley Head*. Harvard University Press, 1971.

Nevinson, Henry W. *Changes and Chances*. Nisbet, 1923.

Nicholl, E.M. "A Plea for the English Wife," *North American Review*, 161 (December 1895), 759–760.

Nield, Keith. *Prostitution in the Victorian Age: Debates on the Issue from 19th Century Critical Journals*. Gregg, 1973.

Noble, James Ashcroft. "The Fiction of Sexuality," *Contemporary Review*, 67 (April 1895), 490–498.

O'Connor, [Elizabeth]. *I Myself*. Putnam's Sons, 1914.

Oldcastle, John [i.e. Wilfred Meynell]. *Journals and Journalism: With a Guide for Literary Beginners*. Field & Tuer, 1880.

O'Lear, C.M. "A New Theory of Aesthetics [review of GA, *Physiological Aesthetics*]," *Catholic World*, 36 (1882/1883), 471.

[Oliphant, Margaret], "The Anti-marriage League," *Blackwood's*, 159 (January 1896), 135–149.

Oliver, Lord. *Jamaica, the Blessed Isle*. Faber, 1936.

Pakenham, Simona. *Sixty Miles from England. The English at Dieppe 1814–1914*. Macmillan, 1967.

" 'Parturiunt Montes' [review of GA, *The Story of the Plants*]," *Nature*, 52 (August 15, 1895), 364–365.

Paston, George [i.e. Emily Morse Symonds]. *A Writer of Books*. Chicago: Academy Chicago Publishers, 1999 (first published 1898).

Payne, William Morton. "*An African Millionaire* [review]," *Dial*, 23 (December 16, 1897), 391.

Pearson, Karl. "*Force and Energy: A Theory of Dynamics* [review]," *Academy*, 34 (December 29, 1888), 421–422.

Pember Reeves, Maud. *Round about a Pound a Week*. Bell, 1913.

Pemble, John. *The Mediterranean Passion: Victorians and Edwardians in the South*. Oxford University Press, 1987. *The Pen, as a Means of Earning a Livelihood, by an Associate of the Institute of Journalists*. John Heywood, 1894.

Perkin, Harold. *The Rise of Professional Society: England Since 1880*. Routledge, 1989. "The Philistine." "The New Fiction: A Protest against Sex Mania. Fifth Article: Recapitulation," *Westminster Gazette*, 5 (March 5, 1895), 1–2.

Pound, Reginald. *The Strand Magazine 1891–1950*. Heinemann, 1966.

"Proctor, Richard Anthony." In *Dictionary of National Biography*, 46, 419–420.

Pullar, Phillipa. *Frank Harris*. Hamish Hamilton, 1975.

Pykett, Lyn, ed. *Reading* Fin de Siècle *Fictions*. Longman, 1996.

[Rampini, Charles J.G.] *Letters from Jamaica. "The Land of Streams and Woods."* Edinburgh: Edmonston and Douglas, 1873.

[Ranyard, Arthur Cowper]. "The Late R. A. Proctor," *Knowledge*, 4 (November 1, 1886), 25.

Robb, George. "The Way of All Flesh: Degeneration, Eugenics, and the Gospel of Free Love," *Journal of the History of Sexuality*, 6:4 (1996), 589–603.

Roberts, Morley. *The Private Life of Henry Maitland. A Portrait of George Gissing*, edited by Morchard Bishop. Richards Press, 1958.

Rollins, A.W. "Ad Absurdum [review article of *The Woman Who Did*]," *The Critic* [London], 27 (September 28, 1895), 193–194.

Romanes, George J. "*Physiological Aesthetics* [review]," *Nature*, 16 (June 7, 1877), 98–100.

Romanes, George J. "*Colin Clout's Calendar* [review]," *Nature*, 28 (June 28, 1883), 194–195.

Romanes, George J. "*Charles Darwin* [review]," *Nature*, 33 (December 17, 1885), 147–148.

Rubinstein, David. *Before the Suffragettes: Women's Emancipation in the 1890s*. Harvester, 1986.

Ruse, Michael. "Herbert Spencer." In Ted Honderich, ed. *The Oxford Companion to Philosophy*. Oxford University Press, 1995.

Ryan, Kiernan. "Citizens of Centuries to Come: The Ruling-Class Rebel in Socialist Fiction." In H. Gustav Klaus, ed. *The Rise of Socialist Fiction 1880–1914*. Brighton: Harvester, 1987.

"Sabine's Reminiscences," *New York Daily Tribune*, November 25, 1899, 8, col. 6.

Saintsbury George. "Oxford Sixty Years Since," *A Second Scrap Book*. Macmillan, 1923.

Saunders, J.W. *The Profession of English Letters*. Routledge & Kegan Paul/University of Toronto Press, 1964.

Scott, JW. Robertson. *Story of the Pall Mall Gazette: Of Its First Editor Frederick Greenwood and of Its Founder George Murray Smith*. Westport: Greenwood, 1971 [1950].

Scott, Sir Sibbald David. *To Jamaica and Back*. Chapman & Hall, 1876.

Sharp, Elizabeth A. *William Sharp (Fiona Macleod): A Memoir*. 2 vols. Heinemann, 1912.

Shelley, Percy Bysshe. *The Complete Works*, edited by Roger Ingpen and Walter E. Peck. Ernest Benn/Gordian Press, 1965.

Shorter, Clement K. "The Late Grant Allen," *Bookman* [London], December 1899, 76–78; *The Critic* [New York], 36 (January 1900), 38–43.

Showalter, Elaine. *A Literature of Their Own.* Princeton University Press, 1977.

Showalter, Elaine. *Sexual Anarchy: Gender and Culture at the* Fin de Siècle. Viking Penguin, 1990.

Showalter, Elaine. "*The Woman Who Did* [letter]," *Times Literary Supplement,* August 27, 1993, 17.

Showalter, Elaine. "Syphilis, Sexuality, and the Fiction of the Fin de Siècle." In Lyn Pykett, ed. *Reading* Fin de Siècle *Fictions.* Longman, 1996.

Sinclair, A.C. and Laurence R. Fyfe. *The Handbook of Jamaica for 1883: Comprising Historical Statistical and General Information Concerning the Island.* London/Kingston: Edward Stanford/Government Printing Establishment, 1883.

[Sladen, Douglas]. "The Diner Out." "Gossip about Authors," *The Queen: The Lady's Newspaper and Court Chronicle* (March 16, 1895), 450.

[Sladen, Douglas]. "The Diner Out." "Gossip about Authors," *The Queen: The Lady's Newspaper and Court Chronicle* (March 23, 1895), 494.

Sladen, Douglas. *Twenty Years of My Life.* Constable, 1915.

Soloway, Richard Allen. *Birth Control and the Population Question in England, 1877–1930.* University of North Carolina Press, 1982.

Spencer, Herbert. *Social Statics; or, the Conditions Essential to Human Happiness Specified, and the First of the Them Developed.* Williams & Norgate, 1868 (first published 1851).

Spencer, Herbert. *Autobiography.* 2 vols. Williams & Norgate, 1904.

Starr, Frederick. "Mr Grant Allen as an Anthropologist: *Evolution of the Idea of God* [review]," *Dial,* 24 (January 16, 1898), 45–46.

[Stead, W.T.] "A False Prophet of Coming Ill. Mr Grant Allen's Vision of the Future," *Review of Reviews,* 1 (May 1890), 511.

[Stead, W.T.] "There is no Religion but Democracy, and Mr Grant Allen Is Its Prophet," *Review of Reviews,* 3 (May 1891), 462.

[Stead, W.T.] "Philistia and Mr Grant Allen: A Word of Expostulation," *Review of Reviews,* 3 (June 1891), 585.

[Stead, W.T.] "Mr Grant Allen: His Work and His Critics," *Review of Reviews,* 6 (September 1892), 266.

[Stead, W.T.] "The Book of the Month: *The Woman Who Did* by Grant Allen," *Review of Reviews,* 11 (February 1895), 177–190.

Stead, W.T. "The Book-stall Censorship," *Westminster Gazette,* 5 (March 2, 1895), 1–2.

[Stead, W.T.] "The Book of the Month. How God Revealed Himself to Man [review of GA, *Evolution of the Idea of God*]," *Review of Reviews,* 16 (November 1898), 519–525.

[Stead, W.T.] "In Praise of Two Crimes," *Review of Reviews,* 10 (October 1894), 356.

Stetz, Margaret Diane. "Sex, Lies, and Printed Cloth: Bookselling at the Bodley Head in the Eighteen-Nineties," *Victorian Studies,* 35:1 (Autumn 1991), 76–86.

Stetz, Margaret D. and Mark Samuels Lasner. *England in the 1890s: Literary Publishing at the Bodley Head.* Georgetown University Press, 1990.

Stevenson, Lionel. *The Ordeal of George Meredith.* Peter Owen, 1954.

Strahan, S.A.K. "Woman and Natural Selection," *Humanitarian: A Monthly Review of Sociological Science,* 4 (March/May 1894), 186–194 and 396–398.

Stubbs, Patricia. *Women and Fiction: Feminism and the Novel 1880–1920.* Sussex: Harvester, 1979.

Stuewe, Paul. "Britishers at Home and Overseas: Imperial and Colonial Identity in the Work of Grant Allen, Robert Barr and Sir Gilbert Parker." Ph.D. thesis, University of Waterloo, December 2000.

Stutfield, Hugh. "Tommyrotics," *Blackwood's Magazine*, 157 (June 1895), 837–851.

Stutfield, H.E.M. "The Psychology of Feminism," *Blackwood's Magazine* (January 1897), 104–117.

Sully, J.T. "Grant Allen's *Physiological Aesthetics* [review]," *Mind*, 2 (July 1877), 387–392.

Sutherland, J.A. *Victorian Novelists and Publishers*. Athlone Press, 1976.

Syrett, Netta. *The Sheltering Tree: An Autobiography*. Geoffrey Bles, 1939.

Thomas, Keith. "The Double Standard," *Journal of the History of Ideas*, 20 (April 1959), 195–216.

Tompkins, Herbert W. "Grant Allen," *Gentleman's Magazine*, 74 (1905), 134–149.

Tooley, Sarah A. "Heredity and Pre-natal Influences: An Interview with Dr Alfred Russel Wallace," *Humanitarian*, 4 (February 1894), 87.

Traill, H[enry] D[uff]. *The Barbarous Britishers: A Tip-top Novel*. John Lane, [1896].

Treglown, Jeremy and Bridget Bennett. *Grub Street and the Ivory Tower: Literary Journalism and Literary Scholarship from Fielding to the Internet*. Oxford: Clarendon Press, 1998.

Trollope, Anthony. *An Autobiography*. Williams & Norgate, 1946 (first published 1883).

Trollope, Anthony. *The West Indies and the Spanish Main*. 4th edn. Dawsons, 1968 (first published 1859).

Trotter, David. *The English Novel in History 1895–1920*. Routledge, 1993.

Trudgill, Eric. *Madonnas and Magdalens: The Origins and Development of Victorian Sexual Attitudes*. Heinemann, 1976.

Tucker, Herbert F. *A Companion to Victorian Literature and Culture*. Oxford: Blackwell, 1999.

Turner, Frank Miller. *Between Science and Religion: The Reaction to Scientific Naturalism in Late Victorian England*. Yale University Press, 1974.

Tyrell, R.Y. [Review of GA's *Attis* by Catullus], *Classical Review*, 7 (1893), 44.

Ussher, R. *Neo-Malthusianism: An Enquiry into That System with Regard to Its Economy and Morality*. Gibbings, 1898.

Utter, R.P. and B.B. Needham. *Pamela's Daughters*. Russell & Russell, 1972 (first published 1927).

Vedder, Catherine Mary. "New Woman, Old Science: Readings in Late Victorian Fiction," *Dissertation Abstracts*, 54 (1993), 537–538a.

Wallace, Alfred Russel. "Colour in Nature [review essay of *The Colour-sense*]," *Nature*, 19 (April 3, 1879), 501–505.

Wallace, Alfred Russel. "*Vignettes from Nature* [review]," *Nature*, 25 (February 23, 1882), 381–382.

Wallace, Alfred Russel. "Human Selection," *Fortnightly Review*, 48 (September 1890), 325–337.

Wallace, Alfred Russel. "Human Progress: Past and Future," *Arena*, 5 (January 1892), 143–159.

Wallace, Alfred Russel. *My Life: A Record of Events and Opinions*. 2 vols. Chapman & Hall, 1905.

Ward, L.F. [Reply to GA's "Woman's Intuition"], *The Forum*, 9 (June 1890), 401–408.

Watson, Aaron. *A Newspaper Man's Memories.* Hutchinson, [1925].

Watt, A.P. *Collection of Letters Addressed to A.P. Watt by Various Writers.* Literary Agency, 1893.

[?Wells, H.G.] "An Unemancipated Novelist," *Pall Mall Gazette*, February 20, 1895, 4.

[Wells, H.G.] "*The Woman Who Did* [review]," *Saturday Review of Politics, Literature, Science and Art*, 79 (March 9, 1895), 319–320.

[Wells, H.G.] "*The British Barbarians* [review]," *Saturday Review*, 80 (December 14, 1895), 785.

Wells, H.G. *Tono-Bungay.* Macmillan, 1908.

Wells, H.G. *An Experiment in Autobiography: Discoveries and Conclusions of a Very Ordinary Brain (Since 1866).* 2 vols. Gollancz, 1934.

Wells, H.G. *The Correspondence of H. G. Wells*, edited by David C. Smith. 4 vols. Pickering & Chatto, 1998.

Wilde, Oscar. *Letters*, edited by R. Hart-Davis. Hart-Davis, 1962.

Wintle, Sarah. "Introduction." In *The Woman Who Did*. Oxford University Press, 1995.

"The Woman Who Wouldn't Do (She-Note Series)," *Punch, or the London Charivari*, 108 (March 30, 1895), 153.

"A Woman's View of Grant Allen's Free-Love Novel," *Literary Digest*, 11 (June 15, 1895), 7.

"Writers and Their Work, No. 50," *Pearson's Weekly*, 104 (August 20, 1892).

"The Writer's Trade," *Academy*, 59 (July 7, 1900), 15–16.

"X." "*New Grub Street*" [letter], *The Author*, 2 (August 1, 1891), 92.

Young, Arlene. *Culture, Class and Gender in the Victorian Novel: Gentlemen, Gents, and Working Women.* Macmillan/St. Martin's Press, 1999.

Zirkle, Conway. *Evolution, Marxian Biology and the Social Scene.* University of Pennsylvania Press, 1959.

INDEX